# The Next Victim

## K. J. Kirk

K. J. Kirk

ISBN:9781520192499

## DEDICATION

To Philip, for his constant support and belief in me.

To Katie, for her encouragement.

To Clare, for listening.

To Jock, for finding the file.

## Note from the Author:

The method of contraception mentioned in this book is UNRELIABLE
I made it up.

Please do NOT use it.

It will NOT prevent pregnancy.

It will NOT prevent you from getting or passing on sexually transmitted
diseases and I think the vinegar might *really*, **really** sting…

# CONTENTS

# CHAPTER ONE

WHITECHAPEL, LONDON 1888

There was no moon tonight and back alleys were never lit. Polly groped for the rusted railing she knew was somewhere in front of her. She found the cold spears of metal and grasped them with both hands.

It was August, but they had called this the year without a summer. Needles of rain stung her face and ran in rivulets down her neck as a shiver skittered down the length of her spine.

She could hear water splashing on to the mud-caked cobblestones and icy water seeped into her shabby old boots.

'Come on *girly*. What you waiting for?' a voice behind her growled.

Meekly, Polly gathered her skirt and petticoat up to her waist, looping the bundled fabric over each of her forearms.

She assumed her client would find his own way to what he wanted, instead, she had to show him the goods. She still had a lot to learn about being a whore.

She grasped the railing again, bending over to bare her naked buttocks to this stranger. Humiliation made nausea cramp her gut and she braced herself for the pain.

Last night she had lost her nerve. This time, she must go through with it. As if to remind her of her predicament, hunger pecked ferociously at her stomach.

She had drunk as much water as she could to quell the sick feeling that had been with her all day, but it gave little relief from the burning acid that gnawed at her insides.

Polly knew every inch of Whitechapel but had not worked Brady Street before. It had been a mistake. She had taken this punter because he seemed the least intimidating of the bunch in *The Roebuck* that evening, but this side of the manor attracted men who were passing through the city. They were often sailors and transient workers who had no fear of any consequences for their actions.

This man had turned out to be an awful specimen. Polly was overwhelmed by the stench of fish, sweat and tobacco amongst several other noxious odours that made her stomach heave.

She cursed the fact that he was sober. Hadn't the girls told her to make sure he was drunk? Hadn't they said he would give her less trouble if he was drunk? In her nervousness, she had forgotten all their advice when she made the bargain with him. She was amazed how men like him could drink draft after draft of the strongest ale without any sign of drunkenness. The only effect of the booze was to make them want a woman.

Her mother and Auntie May used to tell her that a good girl who kept her knees together would never get into what they euphemistically referred to as "trouble".
They knew nothing of the real world, Polly thought. Here she was, proof that you could be a very bad girl and still keep your knees together.

Thinking about her family and former home made a lump rise in her throat, but she saw no point in giving in to self-pity. She had brought about her own misery and that was that.

Her client gave a grunt as he found what he wanted. As far as he was concerned, she was an object to be used for his pleasure. He had bought her like a shiny little trinket to which he had taken a fancy. They had made a bargain and so she bore it silently, enduring the endless minutes of him plundering her most intimate places.

Polly was young and pretty, so she could ask a punter for sixpence. Living on the streets, she knew her looks would not last long. Soon it would be three pence, then two, then one. Once you sank into this pit of misery, it sucked you in deeper and deeper until death was the only way out.

Apart from his roughness and gut wrenching odour, this one seemed harmless, though she was well aware that she took a risk when she led a client into a dark alley. Survivors in this life had to develop sharp instincts for danger. Vile diseases or a brawny hand around the throat were commonplace ways for a working girl to die.

Her shoulders were hunched in misery. He was either oblivious to the effect he was having on her or he did not care. Either way, there was no reason why he should, so she steeled herself against the pain and remained silent. She preferred not to make a sound. That way, she was not emotionally involved in the act. It was business.

If she complained and made a fuss, it would only prolong her ordeal and he might not be able to satisfy himself. If that happened, he could take his frustration out on her and refuse to pay.

A whimper escaped her throat as he suddenly grabbed the back of her neck and forced her head down. Her cheek hit the railing and she stifled a gasp.

She had been warned not to expect any consideration from a punter, but this one was pulling her around like a life-sized rag doll, at times lifting her off her feet.

The collision between her cheek and the railing would leave a bruise. Still, she preferred that to having his booze rotted breath in her face. Nor could he kiss her if he took his pleasure from behind. She shuddered at the thought. *Kissing,* for heaven's sake. As if this dirty little act in a filthy back alley had anything to do with love and affection. No kissing was a firm rule.

She felt a rough, leathery hand plunge into the front of her bodice. He cupped her breast and moved his other hand across her belly. This seemed to give him additional pleasure, but Polly was shaken by a shudder of revulsion.

His hands were calloused and they scratched her tender skin. Her ordeal seemed endless. She wanted to struggle free and run away, but she was desperate, destitute and saw no other choice.

She wondered if he was a sailor off one of the hundreds of big ships that came into the new Royal Albert Dock. She had been told that sailors were good for business. They spent months at sea without sight of a woman and their first thought on hitting dry land with their wages was to buy as many whores as they could find. They flocked to Whitechapel like starlings. If this one was a sailor, she would think twice next time before agreeing a bargain.

She held on to the railing tightly and clenched her teeth so hard she thought they might crack. Her fingers were now as numb as her toes. Her eyes were closed. She was on the point of pushing him away and telling him to forget it, when to her utter relief she heard him grunt. She turned around and let go of her skirt and petticoat. She fixed a smile on her face and moved out of the deeper darkness, holding out her hand for payment.

He stared at her open palm. 'I don't think so,' he growled.

Polly's smile vanished. 'You give me sixpence *right now* or I shout for the lads. Your choice.'

To her relief, he decided that his chances of outrunning Polly's "lads" were low. He took two threepenny coins out of his jacket and threw them towards her. Luckily, she caught the coins against her bodice as she would never have found them in the dark if they had fallen to the ground.

Since the lads were imaginary, it was time for a rapid departure. She slipped past him while he was pulling up his pants and fled into the main street. She knew he could easily give her a beating to get his money back or knock her senseless with one swipe of that brawny hand.

She ran across Brady Street and headed for the poorly lit entrance to Winthrop Street. If her client decided to do something about his complaint, she hoped he would look for her in the pub or think Bucks Row would be her escape route since that dingy street was directly opposite the alley. She did not stop running until she was half way along Winthrop Street. It was deserted and narrower than Bucks Row and even more unpleasant due to the fact that the south side of the street was taken up by Harrison, Barber and Company, a firm of horse slaughterers. It broke Polly's heart to hear the *whinnying* of the poor beasts awaiting their fate on the other side of the high brick wall.

She searched for an unlocked privy. She needed to clean herself up. God knows what diseases had been hitching a ride on her malodorous client, ready to attach themselves to her most intimate places. She needed to tend to herself and remove her sponge. She found an unlocked gate, slipped quietly into the privy, and slid the bolt home to lock it.

She leaned against the door, her fist still curled tightly around the precious money. She reached into her pocket and pulled out a drawstring purse that was firmly attached to it by a length of ribbon. She placed the two threepenny coins in it and tucked it carefully back in her pocket.

A candle in an old pickle jar on a shelf above the door gave off a dim light. Polly took off her shawl, skirt and petticoat - the garments got in the way of the task of washing herself. She did not wear drawers, the girls told her they got in the way. Keeping herself clean was a very particular process and Polly carried it out as solemnly as if it was a religious ritual.

She began by removing the sponge she had placed high up in her vagina at the beginning of the night. She was ever thankful for her sponge. Her friend, Lizzie, heard somewhere that French whores used them to prevent pregnancy and keep themselves clean. She had got one for all the girls.

She was a jewel was Lizzie; her best pal. She would do a good turn for anyone. Her man, Mickey, worked on the docks and acquired some soft, beautiful sponges that came from the Indian Ocean. How amazed the girls had been when Lizzie explained where they should put them.

'You mean you gotta stick them up the muff?' Suzette Le Fevre had exclaimed with such a tone of disbelief they had all laughed. 'Soaked in *vinegar*? Are you having a laugh, Lizzie? Don't it sting?'

'Not as much as the clap or another chavvy.' Lizzie replied fixing her with a stern look. 'What's your problem eh? They keep you clean and stop babies. What more d'you want?' The lilt of her Swedish accent became more detectable when she was getting impatient. 'You dilute the vinegar a little bit of course.' She rolled her blue-grey eyes with a sigh. A murmur of comprehension went around the group.

'Better up the muff than up the duff eh?' said Suzette, and their raucous laughter filled the pub.

Polly washed her sponge under the tap in the dirty, cracked sink until she was sure it was clean and free of all traces of her client. Then she rummaged in the pocket of her petticoat for the small jar of vinegar she carried with her. She put the sponge in the vinegar for three minutes while she carefully washed herself with the square of cotton she kept in her pocket. This complete, she squeezed the sponge to remove excess liquid and put it back inside her. Lizzie had been very particular to tell them that this was important. Leaving the clean sponge in place, according to Lizzie, was what did the trick. As far as she knew, Polly did not have the pox or any other filthy disease a punter could give a working girl and she was sure it was all down to her sponge.

The stench of urine and other unspeakable things filled her nostrils and she had long ago resigned herself to the fact that it was impossible to draw a clean breath anywhere in Whitechapel.

She took her silver comb from her pocket. It was small but fine, with ivory teeth enclosed by a silver spine engraved with trails of roses. It was all she had left of a set that also included a mirror and a brush her parents had given her for her sixteenth birthday.

She set about fixing her chestnut coloured hair which she wore with a centre parting and curled into a bun at the crown of her head. There was a grubby, scratched mirror on a hook on the door of the privy. Polly caught her reflection in its depths.

*Pleased with yourself are you, Miss?* She heard the words as clear as a bell, but they were nothing more than a memory. Her mother used to say it all the time whenever she caught her admiring herself in the silver mirror.

That was in another life when she had been a respectable young lady. How she longed to run into her mother's arms right now. She forced herself not to dwell on it. Despondency had already snaked its ugly coils around her, squeezing the self-respect out of her until she was too ashamed to look at her own reflection.

Like most of the other dollymops - women who took to prostitution only when they were desperate - she took other work when she could find it but there was very little to be had. There were few options open to poorest women in Queen Victoria's London; cleaning, service or sewing; that was pretty much it. Prospective employers also wanted references and Polly could offer none.

Her parents ran the smartest drapery shop in London. Their customers were the rich people of Belgravia and Kensington who came to the shop because her parents held the royal warrant. They were proud to be drapers to Her Majesty, Queen Victoria and had supplied all the sumptuous curtains and upholstery for Buckingham Palace and some of the other royal residences. Despite these exalted circles, she had nothing but disdain for her parents business while growing up, and had not been shy about letting them know it.

The unexpected glimpse of her own face had brought on Polly's miserable thoughts. She had looked into her own eyes and in doing so felt as if she was confronting herself with her situation. She was surprised how big and clear her eyes looked because she felt as weary as death.

*She'll break some hearts with those eyes.* Auntie May used to say when Polly was a little girl. Auntie May was her father's younger sister. She had been employed at the drapery forever. As it turned out, Auntie May was wrong - it was Polly's heart that broke in the end.

The day after her nineteenth birthday, she had eloped with a sweet talking travelling salesman, Thomas Swindon. *Stupid, stupid,*

*stupid little cow,* she thought as she remembered how she had crept down the stairs of her parents' home. She left them a note on the mantelpiece in the parlour.

Every time he visited the drapery, Thomas had encouraged her fantasies and passed her romantic notes. He talked about his uncle's business - the button empire he would one day inherit. He said he was working as a salesman just to learn the day to day running of the business he would one day own. It would be so exciting. They would live in Paris. They would ride in fine carriages. She would have all the beautiful, fashionable clothes she wanted and Polly believed it all. He had promised her a small church wedding the morning after their elopement, prior to them boarding a train for the Continent.

The wedding never happened and the train never appeared. She found out later that Thomas had already lost his position as a salesman. He was not the nephew of a rich businessman at all. He was lazy and lacked any of the drive and initiative needed to make his plans and wishes happen. He was a dreamer who blamed his lack of success on anyone or anything, rather than accepting the responsibility himself. Soon he turned the blame on Polly and drank them into deeper and deeper poverty.

Dismayed, she discovered that it hurt to pass water. Her client had bruised her. She would need a gin or two before she could face the thought of taking another one. There were too many like the charmer she had just been with and she cringed at the thought.

As she left the privy, she heard the brewery clock on Brady Street strike the hour. She counted the number of chimes. It was two o'clock.

She stopped a street vendor who had finished for the night and was making his way home. She got him to sell her a baked potato for the low price of a halfpenny. It was dry, small and overcooked but Polly was so hungry she ate it anyway.

Winthrop Street and Bucks Row ran parallel to each other until they merged into a wide, ugly boulevard in front of the four storey board school that occupied the end of the block. Polly moved cautiously towards the school just in case her disgruntled client had headed along Bucks Row looking for her. There was no way of predicting what he would do. By now, he could have rounded up some friends to get his money back and help themselves to a free sample. She needed to get back on the main street as soon as possible.

11

A moment of inattention could have terrible consequences and Polly lived in constant fear of being found by a gang. They preyed on women like her, taking most of the money from each client and dishing out terrible beatings to anyone who complained, or in their view, did not work hard enough.

Emma Smith, one of Polly's lodging house inmates had been savagely attacked last Easter Monday. People said Polly reminded them of Emma because she was more refined in her speech than was usual in Whitechapel.

What happened to Emma had sickened Polly. She had been gang-raped by a group of men who then raped her again with some sort of blunt object which the police thought might have been a pickaxe handle. Emma died in the London Hospital two days later on the morning of the 5th of April. Her injuries were so severe there had been no hope of recovery.

Polly and Lizzie had tried to visit Emma in the hospital. The nurses had been strict about no visitors.

'She's in a very bad way,' a nurse told them, her voice gentle and sympathetic. 'It won't do any good to see her. We want to keep her sedated and settled, you see. It's better for her that way.'

'Couldn't we just see her for a minute?' Polly asked. 'She has two children and-'

'You need to understand,' the nurse interrupted gently. 'What those brutes did to her, well, it ripped her apart. The... *object* caused multiple ruptures of her female parts and tore a hole in her bowel. I've been nursing for ten years and I have never seen anything as shocking as what those men did to Emma. How that poor woman managed to crawl from the corner of Brick Lane to the top of George Street with all that pain and the injuries she had.... There's not a nurse in this hospital that doesn't feel for her.'

'Can't they do something? Can't they operate on her?' Polly said, her eyes as round as two saucers and shiny with tears.

'They have... They had to remove her womb because it was so badly damaged, and they've done as much as they could with the rest. But when things rupture, especially the bowel, it's rather hopeless. Everything leaks into the belly and infection sets in. It's excruciatingly painful. I've seen big, tough men cry for their mothers when they have a ruptured bowel and Emma has all those other shocking injuries as well. That's why we want to keep her sedated.'

She looked at each of them in turn. 'You do understand, don't you? These injuries… I'm so sorry, they're fatal I'm afraid.'

The nurse went on to tell them that they had loaded Emma with as much laudanum as they dared. Despite the huge quantity of opium in the medicine, the pain had continued to break through. While she was sleeping, they did not want her to be disturbed. The nurse's words still haunted Polly and she was terrified of meeting the same fate.

From that day, Polly had altered her accent to blend in with the people of the east end. She was careful not to draw attention to herself or stand out from the crowd in any way. She was feisty by nature and there were times when she struggled to keep her opinions to herself, but she was always mindful of the gangs.

The rain came at her horizontally as she continued along the street. Her feet were soaked even though she took care to keep her skirts out of the deeper puddles that had accumulated across the uneven pavement.

The gas lamps gave off nothing more than a feeble glow. In the back streets, they were poorly maintained and often damaged.

The Board School loomed out of the darkness. At the same time, a train rattled through the deep cutting behind the school. The terrible din made Polly wince. Smoke billowed from the engine stack and swirled in huge clouds over the high walls that hid the train from sight. The acrid smell made her cough and stung her eyes until they watered. She took a thin rag from her pocket and blew her nose. The train rumbled away as Polly wondered how anyone ever got any sleep.

A cold wind blew along Bucks Row and Winthrop Street. Once past the school, it formed a vortex that almost knocked her off her feet. Old newspapers and bits of straw that had escaped from the stable yard were sucked into the air. The stench of manure and boiling render from Harrison, Barber and Company made her want to vomit. This part of Whitechapel was surely the vilest in the whole manor.

Polly headed towards the short passageway known as Wood's Buildings. This was a covered footpath through a three storey tenement building and was a short cut to Whitechapel Road. She turned left into the narrow alley that led to the underpass.

As she looked into the darkened passage, a feeling of dread seized her. She had used this shortcut many times without a second thought; this time was different. As she reached the entrance she jerked to a halt.

Though it was always gloomy, right now she could barely see the path. The dismal gaslight at the half way point was not lit. It did not make sense. She could see they were all served by the same gas pipe that ran along the wall of the passage.

The light at the end of the passage on Whitechapel Road burned with its usual flickering flame. The light above her head was also lit, yet the middle section of the passageway was in almost complete darkness.

Polly screwed up her eyes and squinted into the passage. She could see nothing amiss, even though her instincts warned her to go no further. She tried to make sense of the uneasiness that made the tiny hairs on the back of her neck stand up.

This was not an idle fancy nor fear of the bogeyman. She had an inexplicable certainty that someone was lurking in the dark. The iciest of chills rolled down her spine.

'Who's there?' she said. Her eyes were fixed on the darkest part of the passage. She strained to hear the slightest sound. She knew without a doubt, if she turned her back, whoever was there was going to pounce. She took a step back, unaware that she was holding her breath until a lack of oxygen made her take in a gasping breath.

Then, a faint sound came towards her on the cold air. It was a long exhalation; a sigh. After this, there was silence. Unnerved by this eerie sound, she was afraid to turn and run.

A small cloud of vapour drifted towards her. It was a physical manifestation of the sigh she just heard. It had condensed on the cold air and was proof that her instincts were correct. Polly stared at it, hypnotised as it swirled and spiralled towards the roof of the passage. Her own breath seemed to freeze in her lungs. She was riveted to the spot. 'Sh... Show yourself,' she called out, her voice bouncing off the shiny brickwork.

Her heart pounded. She pushed every straining nerve to its limits trying to pick up any hint of what she was facing.

'I know you're there,' she said, trying to sound braver than she felt. 'Stop your teasing, it ain't funny.'

Wood's Buildings was known to everyone as *piss alley*. Polly knew if a man was relieving himself in the dark, he would usually whistle. He would also have replied with *ahoy hoy* when she called out.

Then, just for a split second, she saw two pinpoints of light - fleeting, glowing sparks in the darkness. She knew for certain that they came from another pair of eyes. Someone was staring at her, watching and waiting. She was barely breathing. Sweat rolled down her back. Like any animal being hunted, she sensed she was prey.

She heard something brush against the brickwork; it was soft and rasping; perhaps caused by something chafing and scuffing. There was nothing else to be heard now, but there had been a definite chafing, grating sound. It had stopped, yet she knew her stalker was moving closer. She could hear no footsteps. Then came a faint scratching sound that might be the hem of a cloak scraping against the brickwork. Polly listened until she thought her ears might bleed with the strain. There was no other noise until she heard a *click*. It was like a thunderclap exploding in her brain. It was enough to snap her from her fear filled stupor.

*Run!* The command screamed along her nerves. At first, her legs would not move. Sweat stood out on her skin. She was incapable of moving. She heard nothing except her frantic heartbeat. *Run!* She saw a glint of metal as it reflected the gaslight. This broke the spell and she ran. She ran for her life. She fled back towards the school. On reaching it she turned and tore along Winthrop Street. She almost fell as she made a right turn onto Brady Street and headed for the high street.

She knew he had chosen her. He had some foul purpose in mind and she was to be his plaything. With a sob of horror, it dawned on her that he could easily lie in wait for her on Whitechapel Road. Once on Brady Street, she had no option, she had to continue. The other direction led only to a manure works and a disused cemetery. Daring to look neither left nor right, she ran across Whitechapel Road and bolted towards the maze of streets behind the London Hospital.

## CHAPTER TWO

Sergeant Alf Cruikshank ran the back of his hand across his mouth. This was shocking to behold at four o'clock in the morning. First of all, there had been a fire down Shadwell docks and he had been forced to deploy most of his men to control the sightseers and looters. Now as if they weren't hard pressed enough, right at the other end of the manor, a woman had been found dead. Closer inspection showed her throat was cut and they had a murder on their hands.

It was a rum do, he thought. Bucks Row was an ordinary back street behind Whitechapel Road and an odd place to commit a murder. It was quiet and poorly lit, but the lady had been found lying on the pavement. She had been killed bold as brass in front of Brown's stable yard, her head only a single stride from the front door of the end cottage.

He looked left and right. The spot where the poor woman lay was overlooked by a warehouse on the opposite side of the street. Men worked there twenty-four hours a day, yet no one had seen nor heard a thing. Alf rubbed his chin. What could he surmise from this? Perhaps she had been brought to this place and laid out by her killer?

The victim was not well to do, her clothing looked shabby, except for the jacket she was wearing which was better quality than her other garments. A prostitute maybe? Possibly - out in the middle of the night wandering the streets, a mixture of old and new clothing. It was definitely possible. If that was the case, she might have been the one who brought her killer here. Yet, it was still an odd place to do her in.

It was an unusual murder in other ways. At every other murder scene he had attended in his time with H Division, there had always been an argument, a fight or at least some sort of uproar before the deed; that was not the case this time.

If she was a prostitute, and he knew a lot of them worked *The Roebuck* on the corner, she might know that the stable yard would be deserted. Could it be that she was going to take a client there? She might also have known that the small pedestrian gate was never locked in case of fire, which made the stable a handy place to take a client. Before she could reach out to open the gate, her killer had pounced.

He went over what he knew. Constable John Neil, a young Irishman from J Division, had found the body. He was not one of his own men but he was a solid copper Alf had heard. Neil would not have let anyone move the body to this location from elsewhere.

Neil had immediately sent Constable John Thain to get the local doctor. Quite the right thing to do as they could do nothing until the lady was pronounced dead. He crouched by the body and turned his bull's eye lantern on the victim's face. No noise, no rumpus of any kind, yet this was a savage, violent attack.

Her throat had been cut from ear to ear, all the way back to the bones of the neck. The blood vessels on each side of the neck had been severed with brutal force. There were two cuts. One, he noticed, appeared to be quite shallow; this cut must have been a false start. Perhaps the poor woman struggled then he managed to overpower her.

He gently moved her head to the right. It flopped over as if barely attached. The sight of it made even his cast iron stomach twitch. He swallowed hard. A lot of force would be needed to cause a wound of such severity. On the left side of her neck, he found another gash, much shorter in length.

So, you botched it to start with, did you? Alf thought. In fact, he could see that the killer had three tries to get it right. This suggested there had been a cold-blooded intention to kill despite the unsuitable location.

He cast the beam of his lantern about the scene. There should be great arching sprays of blood all over the place - both arteries having been severed like that. Each artery was as thick as a man's thumb. With the force of the pumping heart behind it, blood should have been propelled quite a distance; yet there was no sign of it.

Next to the stable yard was a high wall that concealed a very long drop to the railway line below. Alf weighed the situation. He was convinced the victim was about to lead her killer into the yard when he struck. Why didn't he wait until they were in the yard? He pondered this for a moment. It was an enclosed space, if someone had come in, or the victim had caused a commotion, he would have been trapped.

Cold-blooded and calculating, he thought. Why? Not robbery; this poor soul wouldn't have a penny to her name.

He shone his lantern on the lady's face. She had a bruise on the right side, across the lower jaw. He gently turned her head back to the left and grimaced at the way it moved, confirming that it was barely attached to her neck.

He saw a circular bruise on her left cheek. Maybe someone had given her a slap, or more likely in his view, these were finger marks where her murderer had grabbed her from behind and clamped his left hand over her mouth and chin, positioning her so that he could get his knife to her throat. There was no obvious motive for such a shocking crime. There was just no accounting for it, he thought as he stood up.

Doctor Rees Ralph Llewellyn arrived at five past four and pronounced the woman dead. Alf hated dealing with the local medics. It had taken Llewellyn twenty five minutes to come three hundred yards from his house on Whitechapel Road.

Alf watched as the doctor gave only the most cursory examination of the body. He felt the victim's hands, which were now turning grey. He listened for heart sounds and found none.

'Based on the fact that her legs and body were still warm, I'd say she had been dead for approximately thirty minutes,' said Llewellyn. 'I'd say there is about a wine glass and a half of blood lost.'

What did he say? A wine glass and a half? That was about six fluid ounces. Couldn't he see that lady's throat had been cut from ear to ear? Six fluid ounces was next to nothing for an injury like that. It wasn't possible. Not with both arteries cut right through and her head hanging on by a thread. He kept his opinion to himself. There was nothing to be gained by disagreeing with the doctor.

'Move her to the mortuary,' the doctor said. 'I have confirmed that life is extinct and I'll make a further examination there. Take her to Eagle Place.' He turned to Alf. 'If it transpires that she has people, she can always be moved somewhere better later on. I will invoice you separately for that.' He walked off.

Alf let out a long breath as he watched him go. The Metropolitan Police had their own doctor but he was only called out to special cases and despite her violent death, this poor woman did not qualify as a special case. He wished *The Met.* would use him as a matter of course, rather than any old quack that happened to be handy.

Constable Mizen arrived with the ambulance which was little more than a covered stretcher on a cart. Neil and Mizen detached the stretcher from its wheelbase and laid it beside the victim.

'Be careful, lads. You'll find her head ain't all that well attached. We don't want it coming off, now, do we?' The dead woman was lifted gently onto the stretcher and Alf's questions about the lack of blood were answered.

Beneath her there was a huge amount of semi-congealed blood. He could see that her clothing was soaked in it. When she was lifted up it was as if a dam had been breached and blood poured into the gutter. More blood sat on the paving flags in jelly-like lumps. Constable Thain turned chalk white.

'She's going to Eagle Place just off Old Montague Street' said Alf. 'It ain't far. Neil, you and me will accompany the victim, Thain, you stay here and keep an eye on the scene. As soon as this gets out, the gawpers will be arriving by the cartload. We want to keep them at bay. I'll ask Sergeant Kerby to send a few men over from J Division to help,' he said. 'And ask Mrs. Green at number two for some water to wash all that blood away, will you? The less there is to see the better, once the crowds start turning up.' He looked at the mess on the pavement and then turned away. 'A glass and a half of blood,' he muttered. 'Of course there had to be more. It stands to reason.'

They moved off with the so called ambulance, pushing the cart slowly in an attempt to extend a bit of dignity to the woman. Alf looked at the inert heap that less than two hours ago had been a living, breathing person. Blood was already coming through the thin sheet that covered her. He wondered who she was. Why had she met her death in such a ghastly way and more mystifying, why had the killer carried out such a brutal attack that it had almost severed her head from her body?

# CHAPTER THREE

There was a pink glow in the east above the rooftops, putting the time at about four o'clock. Shivering and soaked by the relentless rain, Polly finally reached the junction where Whitechapel Road met Commercial Street.

After Wood's Buildings, she had fled into the streets south of Whitechapel Road, keeping to the back alleys and dark places, terrified that whoever had been lurking in the alley might find her.

She felt a little easier when she saw *The Queen's Head* pub a hundred yards away on the corner of Commercial Street and Fashion Street. This was familiar territory.

She took out the small square of cotton from her pocket and wiped her face so as to erase any traces of the tears she had shed. She had been unable to stop herself from crying, even though she was disgusted at herself for giving in to self-pity.

*Feeling sorry for yourself don't change a thing, girl, so there ain't no point to it*, the girls often said. *You just got to get on with it and get by any way you can...*

A lamplighter was damping down the gaslights and turning off the gas. He was cursing the stubbornness of a gas tap that was giving him particular trouble. Since none of them gave off a decent light it hardly seemed worth his efforts. There was never more than a dim pool of light around each lamp post, with a black void in between that looked all the darker by contrast.

She hurried along Commercial Street passing the rows of grim streets. Drizzling rain turned into yet another torrential downpour. She pulled her shawl over her head and wrapped it around her slight frame. She was glad to pull open the door of *The Queen's Head* a couple of minutes later. The air was thick with smoke and the whole place smelled of stale beer and wet wool, but the pub was warm and dry.

The girls were in, as she predicted, and she made her way towards them. The piano player was playing a melancholy tune and some of the customers were singing along with gloomy voices and even gloomier expressions on their faces.

Her friend, Annie, budged along the wooden bench that lined the wall so that Polly could sit closest to the fire.

'Good God, you look like a drowned rat,' she laughed. 'Here.' She pushed a shot of gin towards Polly. 'I already got two lined up. The lads over there are buying.'

'Thanks, Annie, I only got enough for my lodgings tonight.' As long as she had a drink in front of her, the barman could not ask her to leave.

'There's plenty of business in here if you want it. The lads have got a forty-eight-hour pass before they ship out to Zululand at the end of the week, poor sods. They're keen as mustard.'

Polly looked at the red-coated soldiers propping up the bar. They were laughing and slapping each other on the back. Most were so drunk they could hardly stand. Their imminent departure for Africa was good for business. They would spend all their time drinking and going with as many of the girls as they could.

Polly knew that many of them had only just come back and the look in their eyes told the real story.

The newspapers had reported the final bloody battles of the Zulu wars in May and June. They had declared a glorious victory yet it was easy to see these lads had no appetite for it. Whatever it was they had seen and done, it had not been glorious, nor the romantic adventure they imagined it to be.

Polly wondered what that did to their minds to experience such things. You could always spot a couple of them in the crowd, sitting quietly, staring into empty space, lost in their thoughts.

Less than a month ago there had been a terrible murder. A woman, Martha Tabram, whom Polly knew well enough to pass the time of day, had been found dead on a dark landing off Whitechapel Road. She had been stabbed thirty-nine times.

Polly wondered what sort of person had enough fury inside them to keep stabbing at someone until they had thirty-nine separate wounds. Whoever it was would have to be a madman. There was a rumour going around that a soldier had done it, though it was never proven. Polly had been very cagey about going with soldiers ever since. On the other hand, this was a good opportunity to make some money and she was reconsidering her position.

'You seen Lizzie?' Polly said, turning to Annie.

Annie quirked her mouth and shook her head. 'Not tonight. According to Pearl, Mickey has her chained to the bedpost to stop her from coming out.'

'*Chained?* I swear I'll swing for Mickey Kidney one of these days,' said Polly.

Lizzie's partner of three years was a violent brute of a man and Polly knew Lizzie was afraid of him.

'A real prince, Mickey Kidney, ain't he?' said Annie.

'She should leave him, Polly. You should tell her.' Millie, who was sitting next to Annie, joined in the conversation.

'I do, Millie but she's scared of him.' Polly took a sip of gin. She did not like the taste, although she was thankful for the delicious feeling of warmth that spread through her and the way it lifted her melancholy mood.

She wanted to find Lizzie and ask her if it was true that she was being chained up by the tyrant she lived with. Polly knew Mickey Kidney was a bully. This, however, was a new level of control and domination even for him. She also wanted to tell Lizzie all about her frightening experience at Wood's Buildings. Lizzie would know what to say and she would make her feel better.

Polly longed to find a big comfortable chair and go to sleep, though she knew this was impossible. She had the choice of selling herself and having some food and a bed for the night or being cold, hungry and on the streets.

Pearl, Millie, Cathy and Louisa were already working the room. Polly watched them; they were good, she decided - if good was a suitable word to use to describe a whore. Even though they would ask the lads, all drunk, for double or even triple the going rate, they would make sure they had a good time.

Polly knew she would need at least another sixpence. It was still dark outside. She looked around the pub. Annie was right, there was plenty of business, but first she would have to build up her nerve before she could go with any of them.

She should have stayed over this end of Whitechapel and left the hard-bitten punters to the experienced dollies. This had not even crossed her mind when she went to *The Roebuck.* As a result, the whole thing had been a nightmare and she trembled at the thought of whoever had been lurking in that alley.

Polly could not find the will to take another customer. She had made a mistake with her last client. Everyone knew that sailors were heavy drinking and hard as nails and let's face it, she was terrible at being a whore.

It was obvious that she had a lot to learn. She often chose the wrong client and had no clue as to what she was taking on or how to please them. She relied on her looks.

The steady drone of voices lulled her into a stupor. She was quite happy listening to the conversation without joining in.

She had been as cold and wet as meat on the slab at Spitalfields Market when she came through the door of the pub. Now after an hour, the gin and the blazing fire had combined to warm her and dry her clothes.

'Hey Polly, was that Lord Nelson I saw you going off with at *The Roebuck*?' Pretty young Suzette called to her across the table. She put on a French accent with the punters but she was no more French than Polly. Her real name was Francis Kemp, though no one ever called her that anymore.

'Lord Nelson? What d'you mean?'

'That what we call him. He's a sailor. A blue jacket. I was gonna warn you about him.'

'What about?'

'It's a specialist dolly what does him.' Millie chimed in. 'All the girls know him. He's a regular when he's in town and far too much for a sweet little jam tart like you.'

'Oh that's nice, that is.' Polly replied. 'You should have warned me, Suzie. I can hardly bleedin' walk.'

They laughed even harder. She thought how shocked her parents would be if they heard such talk. Why should she care? These women were her family now and she needed to fit in with her new sisters.

Feeling better, she looked up, straightened her spine and pushed her shoulders back. She had been told that her breasts were full and shapely. The girls had taught her how to use them to get a punter interested.

She caught the eye of one of the soldiers and decided he would be her mark. A moment later he brought over a shot of gin and put it on the table in front of her. This was the code that indicated she was his choice. She gave him her brightest smile. She needed to keep him interested, though she did not want to go outside until the rain stopped.

There was a sudden blast of cold air. For a few seconds, there was a reek of soot mixed with gas from the street lamps outside. Charlie from Dawson's lodging house was standing in the doorway.

'There's been a murder. Buck's Row. A woman. They say it's terrible!'

The pub was instantly in an uproar. Polly froze. *Bucks Row*?

'Who is it?' Suzette asked, springing to her feet 'Charlie, for the love of God, who is it?'

The noisy pub fell silent.

'I don't know.' Charlie replied. 'But they say it's bad. Really bad.'

There was a stampede for the exit as sightseers rushed to view the gruesome scene.

Like Suzette, Polly wanted to know the name of the victim. She jumped to her feet and squeezed past the soldiers who were the only ones to stay seated. Perhaps, she thought, they had already seen enough gore for one lifetime.

# CHAPTER FOUR

**P**olly pushed through the door of the pub and stepped onto the pavement.

'Charlie?' she said. 'D'you know anything else?'

'No,' Charlie shook his head. 'All I know is they found her in Buck's Row.' He turned away to direct the crowd towards the murder scene.

Polly lurched into the alley next to the pub. Waves of nausea cramped her stomach. She reached out a hand and steadied herself against the wall. Her whole body heaved and she threw up an acidic combination of gin and the remnants of the baked potato. She coughed and gasped as vomit burned her throat. Panting, she reached into her pocket and pulled out her square of cloth. She dabbed her mouth and then feeling dizzy, leaned back against the damp wall, shivering with cold. It had stopped raining, but the bricks were saturated with rainwater.

She was sure it had been the murderer who was hiding in the darkness of Wood's Buildings. She knew she had not been mistaken when she saw the gleam of two eyes watching her and heard the *click* of a flick knife. She could hardly breathe as she recalled the long sigh that drifted towards her on the air and with it, the terrifying realisation that someone was waiting for her in the dark.

She was certain he had been creeping towards her when she had finally gathered her wits and ran. At the time, she was convinced he had given chase, but now it seemed that any woman who just happened to walk into his trap was doomed to be his prey. He had taken his time and lingered there, waiting for another unsuspecting woman to cross his path.

The casualness of his choice of victim was even more chilling. Her heart thumped against her breast bone. She knew she had to calm herself or have the shock of it be the death of her. It was easier said than done, when, if it were not for her keen instincts, she would be the poor soul lying dead in Buck's Row.

Polly tried to remember who had been in the pub. There had been quite a few of the girls – Annie, Mary-Ann, Eliza and Tilly. She trembled as her stomach tried to turn itself inside out. She gulped in another deep breath to quell its contortions.

Polly pressed a hand to her forehead, then wiped her eyes with the piece of cloth and mopped sweat from her clammy face.

Suddenly, a beam of light blinded her. Dazzled, she lifted her hand to shield her eyes.

'Hey! Get that out of my face.' The light was immediately lowered as spots danced before her eyes. She blinked. 'You just blinded me with that thing. Oh, you're a copper,' she said making out the shape of a policeman's helmet and uniform.

'What you doing there?' said Alf Cruikshank.

'You really don't want to know,' said Polly.

'Who you with? Stand aside and let me see in there.'

She shielded her eyes with the back of her hand. 'All right, all right. Don't be so bossy about it. I ain't with no one.'

Alf shifted his lantern and scanned every inch of the alley with its beam. They were fairly sure the Bucks Row victim had been a whore. He returned the beam to her face. This woman was dressed like one of them, yet he did not recognise her as one of the dollymops they locked up in the cells on a regular basis.

'You sure?' he demanded, using his torch to scan the whole area again.

'Course I'm bloody sure. I *said* get that out of my face. That light is making me see spots.'

He lowered the lantern again. 'Right then. You go about your business.'

'I *was* going about my business until you stuck your oar in,' she complained. Footsteps sounded on the pavement behind them and another beam of light and a policeman wearing a rain cape came into view.

'Who's there? Oh, sorry, Sarge...'

'Anything to report, Foggin?'

'No Sarge.'

'Keep looking.'

'But Sarge... I'm off duty now.'

'No, you ain't. I just put you all on a double shift. There's a maniac to be caught.'

'A maniac?' Polly repeated. 'D'you know anything about the murder?' The young constable looked at her as Polly looked from one man to the other. 'Tell me. Please? Who got done in?'

'Some woman.' The younger man shrugged. He turned to the sergeant. 'Sarge I-'

Polly grabbed the young constable's arm.

'Everyone knows that. Who is she? I want to know her name.'

'She's just some whore,' he answered, shrugging his arm from Polly's grasp. He turned away from her. 'Sarge, Inspector Spratley went to the mortuary an- '

'Just a minute.' Polly persisted, glaring at Foggin. 'She might be *just some whore,* but she has a name and she was flesh and blood like you,' she snapped, blinking to stop tears from forming in her eyes. 'And she could be my friend.'

'What d'you know, Foggin?' said Alf. 'Have they come up with a name for the unfortunate victim?'

'No, Sarge... Like I was saying,' he glanced at Polly, 'Inspector Spratley was at the mortuary and he thought her clothes didn't look right so he had a look. Sarge, she didn't just have her throat cut. The killer had a right old go at her. She's been gutted. He said her guts were all over the place. And get this Sarge, the murderer took a knife to her lady parts something shocking. He stabbed and stabbed at her.'

Polly gave a whimper, causing the sergeant to glance in her direction.

'Foggin, you dolt. There's a lady present.' The sergeant jerked his head towards her.

Polly felt heat flood through her in a wave that started at the top of her head and spread throughout her entire body. Her legs seemed no longer capable of supporting her. Her head began to swim and suddenly she was shaking as sweat cooled on her skin. Her vision blurred and her knees buckled.

'Now look what you did,' said the sergeant. His voice was far away, echoing somewhere in the distance. 'What have I told you about running your mouth? Help me get her into the pub.'

Polly groaned as she was half carried, half dragged back into the warmth of *The Queen's Head.*

'We're shut.' One of the barmen called as the odd trio came through the door.

'Don't you try and hoodwink me.' The sergeant pointed a warning finger at him as he fixed him with the kind severe stare that kept his constables in line. 'You have to stay open on account of the market. It's the law. Or would you rather I wrote the landlord up for a summons?'

The barman slouched off and Sergeant Cruikshank lowered Polly onto the bench by the fire. The swimming sensation began to subside but now she was shivering.

'Wilf?' he called to the other barman. 'Let's have a brandy, if you please? The lady's had a shock.'

The two barmen looked at each other and Wilf responded with a stubborn expression.

'Now! Or should I tell your boss you water it down and pocket the difference?'

Wilf slouched over to the table and placed a small shot of brandy on its scarred surface.

'Here, Ma'am, take a sip of this,' said the sergeant.

Polly raised the glass to her lips with two trembling hands. She took a swig and found its warmth pleasantly bracing.

'She ain't no *Ma'am*' Wilf muttered. 'She ain't nothing but a whore.'

'She is, Sarge.' Foggin agreed.

'Watch your mouth, Wilf. And no one asked you, Foggin so keep your trap shut.' Such was the sergeant's air of authority that Foggin's shoulders hunched. 'Anyhow,' he continued, 'you're late for check in. I want fifteen-minute patrols on the beat until I tell you to stop. Double shifts. Let them all know.'

'Aw, Sarge.' Foggin moaned.

'Go on. Get along. Mind you tell them I'll be checking up and I better not find any of you gambling in some pit on Brick Lane.'

Foggin put on his helmet and mooched out into the smoggy early morning air. Wilf moved behind the bar and continued his task of drying glasses with a very grubby looking towel.

The sergeant turned to Polly. 'Feeling better yet, Ma'am?'

'You don't have to call me Ma'am.' said Polly quietly.

'Alright then, would you prefer "sir"?' he replied, wiggling his eyebrows.

'No,' she gave a little laugh, 'but I could see the way the lad was looking at me. I am a whore, you know?'

'That don't mean you weren't a damsel in distress,' he replied. 'Especially after what that half-wit said about the victim.'

'It sounded really bad,' Polly's face contorted. 'He said she was gutted. And he stabbed at her... her...'

'Yeah,' he replied. 'I'm afraid it seems he did.'

'What kind of monster would do such a thing?' She shook her head and glanced at Wilf, who was still sullenly drying glasses. Then she looked at the door through which the young policeman had departed. 'Those two think she deserved what she got.'

'Well, they're wrong. No one deserves that.'

'No, they don't. Not even a whore.' She looked up. 'Listen, I don't do this unless I have to. Just when I'm out of luck and I ain't got nothing to keep body and soul together. I get other work when I can but there's nothing. The other girls, they're the same. Most of them do it to feed their kids.' She wondered why this bluebottle's opinion mattered to her.

'Ain't you got no family to help you?' he asked. 'Despite your manner of talking, I can still detect something better bred in your tone.'

'None so you'd notice,' she replied.

'Take some more of the brandy,' he said.

Polly complied, finishing the drink. She looked at him.

'How did you know he waters it down?'

'They all do.'

He took off his helmet and placed it on the table. He sat down on the chair opposite Polly. Now that she could see his face properly, she saw he was not as old as she had first thought, in his late twenties, she guessed. He was a big bear of a man, with side whiskers that were so neat they might have been trimmed using a ruler. He had a mop of copper coloured hair which was also trimmed at the back and around his ears with perfect precision. He could never be described as handsome, she decided. With that broad forehead and large nose, he looked tough and hard-bitten. Polly had a feeling that any felon would think twice about crossing him, as had the young constable, but, Polly noticed, if you looked more closely, there was something friendly in his warm brown eyes.

'How you feeling now?' he asked.

'Better. I ain't never done that before, I always thought I had a strong stomach.'

'I wouldn't think you'd heard anything like that before.'

'You're right there.'

'What's your name?' he asked.

'Polly,' she said. The brandy had done the trick and taken away the dread that had made her swoon.

29

'I've been studying on it. You ain't one of the regular dollymops around here and yet I think I know your face. Did you live in Morris Street? About two years ago?'

This made Polly look up. 'Yeah,' she said guardedly. Her eyes narrowed. 'What about Morris Street?'

'Morris Street was on my patch. Your old man were far too free with his fists.'

She was winded by the sudden recollection. She preferred to keep the part of her mind that contained all her worst memories, firmly closed.

'Yeah, that's right,' he continued. 'It's coming back to me now. Polly Swindon. The neighbours came to get me. Your man knocked you down the stairs. You were badly hurt. You were in the family way as I remember, and-'

'Yes, that was me.' Another spasm gripped her and this time, the pain must have shown on her face. He looked at her, his eyes were so filled with pity she could hardly stand it. It was as though he was holding up a mirror and saying *Look at yourself, look at the state you're in.* There was a long silence that seemed to embarrass him.

'Of course, I had just been promoted back then and still wet behind the ears.' He gave a small, forced laugh.

'Newly promoted or not, you sorted my old man out.' Polly replied.

'He had it coming.' he growled.

'I'm surprised you remember.'

'I'll never forget it. I ain't never seen nothing like it in my life. A pretty little slip of a girl lying there bleeding and screaming in agony, turning grey and shivering with shock. Your fella, shouting abuse, the neighbours after his blood when they seen what he done.' He shook his head. 'I can't say I blame them. The state you were in. When I caught up with him, it was all I could do not to rip his head off.'

Polly watched him intently. She had raked over too many bad memories this night.

'Small world eh?' she said trying to shrug it off. 'I ain't never forgot what you did.'

'You ain't back with him are you, Mrs. Swindon?'

'Thomas? No. I ain't seen him since he went inside. I don't think he wanted me around anyway. And I definitely don't want to be around him.' She looked down at her lap. 'He didn't actually get around to marrying me. My name is Polly Wilkes.'

'Oh. Well, I'm relieved in my mind that you ain't with him. Some of them go right back to men like him.'

Polly shook her head. 'Not me. It brought me to my senses. Better late than never eh?'

'He should have hanged for what he did. He took a life; you survived but your little baby didn't. The judge took that into account when he sent him down and gave him the maximum sentence but I don't think it were enough.'

'Neither do I.' Polly steeled herself, only just managing to hold back her tears. He was reviewing the worst moments of her life and she didn't want to think about it.

'What happened, Miss?' he asked. 'How did a nice young lady like you, end up like this?'

Polly gave a shrug. 'Same old story.'

'Where did you go? When you left the hospital?'

'The Whitechapel and Spitalfields,' she said.

'*The workhouse?*'

'What' d'you expect? I was in there nearly eight months. That's what happens when you ain't got nowhere to go. It ain't unusual.'

She had still been in the hospital when Thomas was sent to prison. Her friend Lizzie had rescued some of her things from their lodgings. The small amount of money she had kept hidden in the bible she had intended to carry at her wedding, was gone. She was weak and destitute. She had no choice but to apply for admittance to the workhouse.

'So, you're a sergeant?' she changed the subject.

'That's right. Three years gone February. Sergeant first class now,' he said.

'Like it, do you?' she asked, even though she had no idea what a sergeant first class was.

'It keeps me clothed and fed. Yeah, I like it. Except for nights like last night.'

'How does your missus feel about it?'

'I ain't married.'

'A fine fella like you?' He looked at her and raised one eyebrow. Polly blushed. 'Sorry, it's a bad habit… But I actually mean it. You're a good bloke, Sergeant. I thought about you sometimes after that night. I don't remember much about it. One thing I do remember was that you sorted everything out and you were very kind to me.'

'The workhouse,' he murmured, shaking his head. Polly gave a harsh sigh.

'Well, what did you expect? My man was in prison. I couldn't earn a living and even if I could there ain't no work to be had for someone like me.'

'Surely anything?' he said.

'There ain't anything,' she replied, becoming aggravated. 'Except this... and you know what? Even this is better than that terrible place.' She shuddered. 'I would chuck myself in the Thames before I'd go back in there.'

'But to be a dollymop...'

'D'you think anyone would do this if they weren't desperate? I don't live in a posh whore house with fine clothes and fancy bathing rooms, you know?'

He paused as if he was giving careful consideration to what she said. He looked as if he was about to speak but was thinking carefully before revealing his thoughts.

'You know what I noticed about you that night?' he said at last. 'You had the look of a well brought up young lady about you. You stuck in my mind cos of that. I'm shocked this is what became of you. I thought your mother and father might have come and took you.'

Polly gave a short derisive laugh. 'So did I. Unfortunately for me, they disowned me the moment I eloped with Thomas.'

'Oh... that's how it happened,' he said. 'But your parents, *surely* they-'

'No.' she shook her head.

In the workhouse, Polly had been told to write to her parents again and explain her plight. She received only one letter from Auntie May in reply. The letter said that she had written in secret because she was going against the wishes of Polly's father.

Auntie May warned her never to come back. The scandal of what she had done would have ruined them so they had already told everyone that she had died abroad. Auntie May had included two, one pound notes with the letter. This kindness by her aunt, at least allowed Polly to leave the workhouse. She rented a room and eked out the money as long as possible, finding work when she could. Five months ago it had finally run out and she was on the streets, sleeping in doss houses when she had the money.

The letter had taken away her last hope and it was the last she ever heard from her kin. She forced back the painful memories and shut them out of her mind once again. There was no point in dwelling on such things.

'Oh, Sergeant,' she said, 'this ain't a rare story. I ain't the only one by a long chalk. Look, I told you, I don't dollymop if there's any possibility that I can get other work - there just ain't none.'

He looked at her intently. Polly felt another surge of irritation at his expression. 'Don't look at me like that. When Thomas went to jail I had nothing. Not a penny... Anyway,' she changed the subject, it's been a long time since anyone regarded me as a lady.'

He shook his head slowly. 'I thought I'd done you a good turn, getting that good-for-nothing mutt away from you.'

She managed a smile. 'You did. I'm sure he would have killed me the next time. He was drinking too much and it was getting worse.'

'Yeah, the likes of him tend to get worse and worse until...' he sucked his teeth. 'Let's just say I ain't seen any reformed characters, on the other hand, I've had cases where the lady has ended up dead.' He looked at her. 'So was I right? You weren't brought up to this? How d'you end up eloping with him?'

'It's a long story,' she said, 'and you've heard it all before.'

'I'm a very good listener.'

'What's your name, anyway?' Polly asked.

'Cruikshank,' he said.

'Ain't you got a first name then?'

'Alf.'

'Well, Alfie, don't fret. You did the right thing. You got me to the hospital and you looked after me. I'm glad to be able to thank you for that.'

'Like I said, I ain't forgot it.'

'All water under the bridge now, ain't it?'

'Listen.' He leaned forward confidentially and rested his forearm on the table. 'You don't want to go out dollying. It ain't safe on these streets at present.'

'It never has been,' Polly replied.

Alf lowered his voice. 'No, I mean it. They think there's a real lunatic running around.'

'A lunatic?'

'This lady tonight, she weren't the first, there's been other attacks and now he's started killing. What was done to the last two… well, he'd have to be a stark staring nut-case and we ain't nowhere near finding him. This one is getting his jollies from killing and then doing stuff to the unfortunate woman. So you make sure you get off the streets.' He looked at her. 'You got somewhere to go?'

'I'll find somewhere,' she answered vaguely, knowing that she had to make a choice between doss money and food. The news of the murder had interrupted her plans to earn another sixpence.

'You sure?' Alf Cruikshank eyed her carefully, detecting a lie.

'Yes, I'm sure, Officer.' Polly smiled, mocking him.

'Polly?' Another voice cut into the conversation. 'Oh thank God. Thank God. I heard there was a murder and the victim was called Polly. Oh, I'm so glad I've found you.' Polly's friend Lizzie rushed towards her. She braked when she noticed the uniformed policeman sitting at the other side of the table.

She looked from Alf to Polly and then back to Alf. 'What's going on?' she demanded, hands on hips. Her eyes narrowed and she glared at Alf. 'Hey, Copper, leave my daughter alone. She is a virgin and I'm keeping her that way.'

Polly started to giggle. Alf was looking at Lizzie with a mystified expression. He turned to Polly for an explanation; there was the faintest hint of a smile on his world- weary features.

'Trust me, Lizzie.' Polly gave a little snort 'The sergeant knows a lot more than you think.'

Lizzie's blue-grey eyes turned to ice. Her expression was deadly as she looked at Alf.

'Did you make her go down the alley?' she demanded, hands still on her hips as she leaned towards him in a surprisingly intimidating manner.

'What d'you mean? What alley?' Alf replied.
Lizzie gave a derisive sniff. 'You're all the same. *En annan gris snut på take,*' she muttered.
Alf stiffened. He looked disconcerted as he turned to Polly. 'What was that? Some sort of curse?'

'No...' she laughed. 'She's Swedish. She reverts to her native tongue when she gets annoyed.' Polly was sure that the word *gris* meant "pig" in Swedish.

'Another copper on the take,' Lizzie translated, her words dripping with contempt.

'What'd 'you mean? I ain't on the take,' said Alf. 'Who's on the take?'

'Go figure it out,' she said with a wave of her hand.

'Lizzie. This is Sergeant Alf Cruikshank. He's one of the good ones, honestly. He was the policeman who helped me the night I lost baby Daniel,' said Polly, in response to Lizzie's suspicious look. 'Sergeant, this is my friend, Mrs. Stride.'

'Ma'am,' Alf nodded.

'She was my neighbour at Morris Street. You might remember?'

'I think I do. She was the one with your man's head in an arm lock.'

Polly laughed. 'She's very protective. We've been pals ever since I moved to Morris Street.'

Lizzie's eyes followed Alf's every move like a guard dog.

'That's nice. Call her off,' he said.

'Down, girl,' Polly laughed as Lizzie kept Alf in a steady gaze and sat down while continuing to view him with suspicion.

After a long moment withstanding her scrutiny, he stood up and put on his helmet.

'Well, I suppose it's time for me to be getting back to the station.'

'Which one you at?' Polly asked.

'Leman Street,' he said. 'Good morning ladies. You mind what I said, Miss. And warn the others to do the same.' He doffed his helmet at Lizzie. 'Ma'am,' he said. 'Miss Wilkes,' he nodded to Polly again and turned and left the pub. Lizzie moved to the now vacant seat, looking at Polly with narrowed eyes.

'What did he say to you?'

'He's alright, honestly. I think he's nice,' Polly grinned.

'Tell me what he said.'

'He said to be really careful and get off the streets cos this murder ain't the first attack that's been done by the same lunatic.'

'I knew there had been others,' said Lizzie. 'Annie Millwood and Ada Wilson were attacked last winter.'

'Now they think all of them were done by the same person, and he's started killing them. That's what he said,' Polly nodded. 'When you think about it, there was Annie and Ada but he must have meant Martha, perhaps even Emma as well. Listen, d'you know who it was that got killed?'

'That's why I was looking for you. I heard that she's called Polly. I knew you were over there tonight. I was having a fit until I found you.'

Polly's sick sensation returned. 'It might have been me, Lizzie,' she said. 'I'd had enough after the first punter. You know how they are sometimes. I was making my way back and I was gonna cut through Wood's Buildings. Something made me stop. I could feel someone watching me. Whoever it was, they were loitering. Wood's Buildings is right beside Bucks Row. I think it was the murderer. If I'd gone into that alley, he would have had *me*.' She gave a little sob and wiped away a tear with a trembling hand. 'I know it sounds stupid, sitting here now but I was unnerved, Lizzie. I never felt anything like it. It was as if he was the devil himself.'

'Now, now, Polly, shush, shush. You're safe.' Lizzie produced a clean white cotton square with forget-me-nots embroidered on one corner.

Polly opened it out and looked at it. 'It's lovely,' she said as she wiped her eyes.

'You keep it. Mickey got a big box of them from Shifty Jimmy to sell on the market, so I took a few. Now dry those tears.'

Another sob escaped from Polly's throat and tears welled up in her eyes. 'I was so scared.'

'You're safe, Polly.' Lizzie placed her hand on hers. 'The reason you didn't go down that alley was because your little angel is looking after you and whispering in your ear. Baby Daniel won't let you come to any harm.'

'You always make me feel better,' Polly sniffed. 'Even if you do talk a lot of bloody rubbish.' Then, a thought occurred to her. 'Hey, how come you're out? Annie said that Pearl said that Mickey had you locked in?'

'His latest idea is to chain me to the bed post to stop me going out at night while he's at work.' She sighed and frowned as she told Polly. 'Then he lets me out when he comes home in the mornings.'

'Oh he's a charmer ain't he, Mickey Kidney? Why are you with him, Lizzie?'

'I think perhaps I won't be soon. He's *översittare och en häst ass*'

'You're doing Swedish again.' Polly said.

Lizzie thought for a moment 'He's a bully and a horse's bottom.' she translated.

Polly laughed. 'Yes, that's exactly what he is, and not nearly as handsome. We told you what he was like. All of us.'

'I know. But you know me, I need to experience the pain before I listen well.'

'Ain't that the truth? Speaking of pain, don't think I ain't noticed that bruise on your cheek and the torn earlobe.'

'We had a big fight.'

'Oh, Lizzie... He's gonna kill you one of these days. Let me tell you, if it weren't for that sergeant, I'd be dead because of a man like Mickey. They don't change. They just get worse and worse. Ask the sergeant, he knows.'

'I just need a little money and then I'll leave him. He's been much worse since he came out of prison.'

'Blimey, he was only inside for three days. You had to go to the police after a beating like that. You were a mess.'

'He was angry when he came out. Now he's angry all the time.'

'You should press charges every time it happens. You keep letting him off. The problem is he's just a natural-born arsehole. The more you let him off the worse he'll get. You have to leave, Lizzie.'

'I know.' Lizzie sighed. 'I have cleaning work today; Betty Tanner will pay me sixpence for doing the lodging house. I've already saved a little and if I can take some money from him when he's drunk. I can get away soon.'

'What about the church? Did you ask them for help?'

'The Pastor gave me a beautiful hymn book.'

'What good is that? You can't eat it or sleep in it can you?'

'It was nice to see all the hymns I knew as a girl - and in Swedish.'

'I'm sure that was lovely, but is the church going to help you?'

'They said they might give me some money. They're thinking about it. We can save and start our tea shop, Polly. Wouldn't that be wonderful?'

'Yeah, that would be something. Me and you running a business eh?'

'For today, I need your help.' Lizzie told her.

'Anything darling, you know that.'

Lizzie produced a small key, the kind that fitted a padlock, from her pocket.

'I took this from Mickey this morning when he fell asleep.'

'What? He'll go mad if he finds out,' said Polly. 'What d'you want me to do?'

'Will you take it to the market and get another key made for me? Then bring it to my lodgings. I'll put the key back in his pocket before he wakes. Here's a shilling - that's how much it will cost.'

'Consider it done.'

'Then, when he locks me up each night when he goes to work, I can unlock it and get out.' Lizzie smiled.

'And lock yourself back in before he gets home in the morning so he's none the wiser?' Polly said. 'Lizzie, you're a genius.'

'I can't get the key myself because he gets his friends to spy on me. They tell him everything I do.'

'Ain't it a risk to unlock yourself, then?'

'It's worth it. I may find another gentleman,' she grinned. 'After all, I'm good for thirty-six.'

'You're forty-four,' said Polly. 'Alright, give it here,' she said taking the key. 'What time does he usually get up?'

'He gets up at eleven o'clock. He goes out and then returns to sleep off the drink before going to work.'

'So you need this delivered before eleven. Right then. It's ten to seven. I'll get down the market straight away.'

'Thank you.' Lizzie smiled, looking pleased with herself. Then the smile faded and she looked at her friend. 'Are you alright now?'

'I'm fine. Lizzie. Don't you worry. You know me, I bounce back.'

# CHAPTER FIVE

Number 36 Devonshire Street was the latest in a line of addresses for Lizzie - all of them close to the docks. The frequent changes of address were due to the fact that Mickey didn't see the need to pay the rent. He got regular work as a labourer, loading and unloading cargo in the new Royal Albert Dock, but he preferred to spend his wages on drink.

At half past eight, Polly knocked on the filthy, crumbling door. She could hear a baby crying, no doubt startled by the angry voices raised in a bitter argument in the room on the left.

A child who looked about five years old answered the door. She may have been older; it was hard to tell as she was thin and hollow-cheeked. She stared up at Polly with large blue eyes.

'Hello, sweets. Have you seen my friend, Lizzie? Mrs. Stride? D'you know her?'

The child continued to stare. The shabby grey dress she wore hung from her skinny frame. Two children of her size could have fitted inside it.

Polly put her hand in her pocket and brought out a small brown paper bag. It contained her precious cachous. The small purple candies were her protection against the foul odours of her clients. 'Here have these.' She handed the bag to the child. 'They're supposed to be for making your breath smell like a bouquet of violets but they're nice and sweet,' she smiled.

The girl took them and immediately put a few in her mouth. She stared silently at Polly, who fancied she saw a glimmer of pleasure in the child's dull eyes. It warmed her heart and made her want to scoop her up and take her away from this vile place, though she knew she could do no better than whoever was raising her.

Number 36, like all the others in the street, had once been a decent family house. There were four rooms on the ground floor - two on each side of a long passage that ran from the front door to the back. Each room was nothing more than a damp, crumbling hovel.

Polly looked around her. Even if she was able to afford the outrageous rent of three shillings a week, these vermin infested holes lacked the basic comforts. They had no running water and probably harboured foul diseases to boot.

Polly smiled at the girl. 'Cat got your tongue has it?' She touched the child's dirty hair in a brief caress before noticing the ringworm sores. 'Not to worry, I know where she lives.'

Polly moved along the dim passage towards the staircase at the back of the house. She came across two more tiny tots, filthy and shoeless with large sores on their purple toes and crusted scabs at the corners of their mouths.

They were playing with a piece of wood that had fallen off the staircase. They were oblivious to the rat droppings and squalid danger of their playground.

A baby swaddled amidst a bundle of rags, was asleep in a corner under the stairs. At least this baby was covered up, Polly thought. With heartrending frequency, babies were often left semi-naked in the filth, under the supervision of brothers and sisters who were far too young for the responsibility. She knew that their mothers had no choice. They had to go out to seek meagre work, sell themselves to buy food or steal it. Others escaped their misery by drinking themselves into a stupor.

This was a level of deprivation she had never even dreamed of in her old life. Now, though she was still appalled, she was no longer surprised to find children living like this. Too many people and not enough work. It didn't take much to create these conditions and now she was in the same situation as the rest of them.

She climbed the stairs at the back of the building. She was conscious that she was disturbing the rotted wood and filth between the risers that would now be falling like snowflakes on the sleeping baby. Her heart gave a tug as she heard the infant give a wheezing cough. It did not cry, despite the fact that the cough must have shaken its entire body and turned the little mite blue.

The truth was, the child was probably too weak to cry. Many did not make it past a year old and any strength they were born with soon drained away.

The first floor of the dilapidated house had the same layout as its lower counterpart. There were two rooms on each side of a narrow corridor. When she reached the top of the stairs, Polly moved towards the room at the end of the passageway that was shared by Lizzie and Mickey.

She tapped lightly on the door. It opened a few inches almost immediately and Lizzie peeped through the gap. Polly saw straight away that she had a fresh cut on the right side of her lower lip and a bruise was forming across her cheek.

'Has he found out about the key?' she whispered.

'No.'

'Then what the hell-'

'Come in.' Lizzie whispered putting a forefinger to her lips. She opened the door and Polly stepped into the room. Kidney was a motionless bulge on the bed in the corner. He had covered himself with his jacket and was snoring loudly. The pretty handkerchiefs had been thrown from their packing case and were scattered across the floor. There was a pile of them on the battered old table next to the window.

'Was that for taking a couple of the hankies?' Polly whispered jabbing her finger towards Lizzie's new injuries.

'Never mind' Lizzie replied.

'It was, wasn't it?'

'I didn't think he would notice if I took three or four of them.'

'Oh Lizzie, you gotta get away from him.' Polly fumed. She threw a venomous glance towards the lump on the bed. 'Give me that skillet. A few good whacks to his thick head and that'll be that.'

'Ssshh…' Lizzie grinned then winced and touched the cut on her lip to see if it had started bleeding again. 'Do you have the key?' she whispered.

'Yes. I got you some change too - I beat him down to ninepence.'

'I need to get it back into his pocket,' said Lizzie.

Polly placed the key and the new duplicate in Lizzie's hand. She watched as Lizzie edged towards the bed. A medieval looking length of chain with one end padlocked to the bed frame, the other with a wrist shackle attached to it lay beneath the bed. On seeing it, Polly felt a surge of rage. She looked at Mickey, who was lying on his back, window rattling snoring sounds emanating from him. She longed to put a pillow over his head and sit on it.

Lizzie was not a timid person and yet, Polly noticed, she changed when she was around the ignorant waste of skin she lived with. Right now, she looked more nervous than she had ever seen her.

'What you doing?' whispered Polly. 'Don't he take his pants off to sleep?'

'No.' Lizzie replied.

Polly made a disgusted face and watched as Lizzie knelt down beside the bed and slowly moved her hand inside Mickey's trouser pocket.

Mickey, still asleep, made noises of appreciation. Polly started to giggle. She stifled it as Lizzie threw her an anxious look.

Gently, Lizzie pulled out a thin, pocket watch style chain. One end was held in place by a button attached to the inside of his pocket. The other end had an empty metal ring that usually held the key.

Lizzie had almost succeeded in putting the key on the ring when Mickey gave a grunting snore and rolled over, trapping her hand. Both women froze. Polly saw at once that Lizzie was scared and prayed that he wouldn't open his eyes.

Any movement would risk waking him up. Lizzie had no choice but to remain there, trapped by his body. Mickey was made of solid muscle from years of toting goods to and from ships. Polly knew it would be painful for Lizzie to have her arm trapped beneath him.

The raised voices from downstairs were now getting louder. The argument, which seemed to be between a man and a woman, was threatening to break into outright violence. Mickey could awaken at any moment. The two women stood motionless as two long minutes passed.

'This is ridiculous.' Polly whispered.

Lizzie shrugged helplessly and mimed a *"what can I do?"* gesture. Polly crept to the side of the bed.

'What are you doing?' Lizzie whispered, wide-eyed as Polly leaned close to Mickey's ear.

'Mickey, roll over,' she said in a pleasant tone next to his ear. He gave a loud snore then rolled away from Lizzie, freeing her hand. Polly grinned as Lizzie quickly hooked the key to the end of the chain and very carefully slipped it back into his pocket. As her hand re-emerged, she was clutching a half crown coin and a big smile lit up her face.

Polly quirked her mouth. 'Nice work,' she whispered as Lizzie put the duplicate key in her pocket. 'Just like a man,' Polly grinned. 'The only time he'll do what he's told is when he's asleep.' Mickey snorted and began to stir. Polly, who was still by the side of the bed, dropped to the floor and rolled underneath it.

Mickey squinted at Lizzie who by then was standing innocently by the washstand on the other side of the room.

'What time is it?' he said groggily.

'It's only quarter to nine.' she said. 'Go back to sleep.'

'I would if you didn't make so much bleedin' noise,' he growled and then tutted irritably. 'See? Now I gotta go and have a piss.'

He cursed under his breath, rolled out of bed and stumbled to the door. Lizzie moved in front of the bed so that her skirt hid Polly from view. Mickey, scratching himself, headed in the direction of the privy which was in the yard at the back of the property.

As soon as he was gone, Polly slid out from under the bed. Lizzie pulled her to her feet and they stood there for a moment, laughing. 'Polly you're as nimble as a cat.'

'Quick as a flash that's me.' said Polly, brushing dust from her dress and shawl. 'That was close, though, weren't it?'

'But now I have my key,' said Lizzie cheerfully. 'Let's get something to eat.'

'That would be great. I'm starving.'

'Betty will let us sit in the kitchen at Flower and Dean Street and give us some hot water for tea. We can get some bread and a stick of butter.'

'Sounds wonderful.' Polly said. 'I could definitely go for that.'

Lizzie picked up her woollen shawl and swung it around her shoulders.

'Let's go,' she said.

'What you doing here, Slag?' said a voice behind them.

The two women span around to see Mickey in the doorway. He was glowering at Polly.

'Mickey I-' began Lizzie.

'Who you calling a slag?' Polly cut in, glaring at him, hands on hips.

'I'm looking right at you. It ain't difficult to work out, even for a stupid cow like you.'

'I ain't no cow and I ain't stupid. You, on the other hand, are an arsehole. I seen what you done to her, Mickey,' said Polly squaring up to him. 'And you better keep your hands to yourself.'

He took a step towards Polly. 'Or what?'

'I ain't afraid of you,' she said, though her heart was hammering. 'Go on. I dare you.'

Mickey looked at her, a malicious smirk on his face.

'You think I wouldn't?'

43

'Oh I think you would try,' said Polly scathingly. 'Proud of yourself are you? Big Man? Knocking a woman about who's half your size? You ain't nothing but a bloody coward you are. A coward and a bully.'

'Polly, come on let's go.' Lizzie said her voice sounding small and scared.

'If you *ever,* lay a finger on her again, I'll have you, Mickey Kidney!' Polly blazed as Kidney gave a short laugh. 'Oh that's funny is it?' she said. 'Well go on, have a laugh, except you know what? You better sleep with one eye open cos you never know who's biding their time waiting for the chance to send a coward like you to hell, and I'm at the front of the queue!'

'Who do you think you are? You filthy little whore.' Kidney lunged at her, circling her throat with a large hand. He raised the other to hit her.

'Mickey don't!' Lizzie shrieked. Polly reacted instantly. She closed her hand around his crotch and dug in her fingernails. With one smooth action, she twisted and squeezed. Having a way to defend herself was the first thing her sister dollymops had taught her and very useful it proved to be.

Kidney made an attempt to carry on with the attack, however, this little trick had dropped bigger and tougher men than him. After only a few seconds, his eyes bulged, he gave a squeak and released her.

'Next time, I'll pull them off and smack you in the eye with the soggy bit.' said Polly through gritted teeth.

She let go. Kidney dropped to the floor, groaning, dry heaving and calling her every filthy name she had ever heard.

Lizzie pulled Polly towards the door. 'Come on,' she urged.

They stepped out onto the street and headed in the direction of the lodging house.

'I got to wash my hands.' Polly pulled a face and took a tentative sniff. She glanced at her friend and saw her worried expression. 'I'm sorry, Lizzie,' she exhaled sharply. 'He's such a pig. You have to see that.' Then she saw Lizzie's face. 'You're really afraid of him ain't you?'

'I worry what he might do if he gets in one of his rages and the drink is on him.' Lizzie admitted.

'And so you should. God, Lizzie, he sounds just like Thomas. You know what he was like, the problem is, sooner or later there ain't gonna be a time when the drink ain't on him and I'm scared for you. You got to leave.' The look on Lizzie's face told Polly that her friend had made her mind up. 'Listen, when he goes to work tonight, why don't we go and get your things? You got some money off him just now and you can get a bed in Crossingham's for a while.'

'Yes,' Lizzie sighed. 'I know, you're right. He's disgusting when he is drunk and he has filthy habits.'

'Not to mention the fact that he knocks you into the middle of next week on a regular basis. You change when he's around, Lizzie. You act all nervous, not at all like yourself. And look at the state of your face. All for a few pretty hankies? He should have been letting you take your pick not giving you a hiding for taking a few.'

'There is no reason for me to stay with him now. He used to be amusing and kind, now he's neither. I just want my hymn book and the roll of green velvet cloth I have been saving; I can sell it or use it to make some fine things to sell on the market.'

'Right then, that's settled.' She linked her arm with Lizzie's as they headed along the street in the direction of the shop where they could buy some bread and butter. 'You know what's funny? I'm the draper's daughter yet you're the clever seamstress.'

'What is funny about that?' asked Lizzie.

'Never mind. You Swedes, you got no sense of humour.'

'Yes we do, that's just not funny.'

# CHAPTER SIX

Someone had opened the back door of the lodging-house. Polly felt a blast of cold night air hit her in the back of the neck, sending a chill down the length of her spine. She turned around and peered into the dim passage next to the kitchen.

Annie nodded and wiped away tears with the heel of her hand. 'I miss her, Pol. To lose her like that is just so wrong.' Her bottom lip trembled and more tears overflowed onto her cheeks.

'I know,' Polly sighed. 'It was a terrible thing.'

'She could have made something of herself, you know? Marrying Billy Nichols was the worst thing she ever done. Twenty-four years she stuck with him.' *'Brrrr...* Annie darling close the door. Come in here where it's nice and warm,' she said to the middle-aged woman who was about to step out into the dismal night. 'You don't look at all well.'

Crossingham's kitchen always had a good blazing fire. The regulars were able to sit around the cooking range in the comfort of its cosy glow. Annie closed the door and came into the kitchen. She squinted and seemed dazzled by the single gas light on the wall above her.

'I don't feel well, Pol,' she said as she placed her hands on the back of a wooden chair to support herself. 'But I ain't got my doss money. Evans has already been around and clocked me in here. He's told me to get out.'

'Huh, he's only the night watchman.' Polly replied with a flick of her hand. 'I thought Timmy Donovan lets you stay in here in the warm if you ain't got money for a bed?'

'He does. Now he wants my doss money cos he says I've been boozing and spent it. I swear, Polly. I ain't touched a drop. I had a glass of porter off Willie Stevens earlier at the funeral. I had a bit of fancy for it and I didn't want nothing to eat.' She put her hand to her head. 'I got a thumping headache; it's got me dizzy. And before you ask, I ain't been on the drink.'

Annie flopped down on the chair and massaged her forehead. Polly put her hand on Annie's shoulder. 'I weren't going to ask. You never mind. We can put Evans off for a bit.' Polly felt a sob shudder through Annie's skinny frame. She patted her shoulder comfortingly.

Annie whimpered, got out a very clean handkerchief and held it to her nose. 'You would have thought he would have had more consideration on account of it being Polly Nichols's funeral today,' she said. 'To be murdered in that terrible way. How she must've suffered.' Annie's eyes filled with tears as a raspy breath caught in her chest.

'She were a good friend of yours weren't she, Annie?'

Annie nodded and wiped away tears with the heel of her hand. 'I miss her, Pol. To lose her like that is just so wrong.' Her bottom lip trembled and more tears overflowed onto her cheeks.

'I know,' Polly sighed. 'It was a terrible thing.'

'She could have made something of herself, you know? Marrying Billy Nichols was the worst thing she ever done. Twenty-four years she stuck with him.'

'Was she a widow?'

'She wished. He's a waste of skin, that man. I mean, what sort of husband has an affair with the woman what's attending his wife's confinement? There was terrible atmosphere at the funeral cos Billy Nichols turned up. The eldest lad, Edward, who's twenty-one now, would have nothing to do with him. He told the other four kids to do the same. But little Henry, Polly's youngest, is still only nine years old, bless him, what's he to make of all this? Then Billy kicked off about them parting due to her being a drunken whore.' Annie shook her head. 'That's shocking, that is, to say such a thing at somebody's funeral. Mr. Walker, Polly's dad, said it was Billy what drove her to drink and a few words were exchanged. Mr. Walker is built like a blacksmith. He could have knocked Billy's block off if he wanted. At least he had the decency to hold back on account of the occasion. I wish he'd flattened him, Billy said he kept the kids with him but he's a liar. He didn't want them, he was with his fancy piece. Now she's got a child by him. Then he said Polly got maintenance money off him for the kids. No she didn't, he paid up for less that year then welshed on it. She sent the Parish Officer after him and everything. He made up some yarn about her being on the game and said that's why he refused to pay her anything and they believed him. Just cos he's a man, they believed him and not her.'

'That ain't a rare situation, Annie. Men come up with all sorts of excuses for not paying and because it's a man's word against a woman's, they're believed.'

'You know how it is, Pol. Once he stopped paying what was due to her, she had nothing. Five kids to feed and not a single penny coming in. It's a powerful instinct to want to put food in your child's stomach. What else was she supposed to do? Her going on the game was a consequence of Billy not paying, not the cause of it and he knew it. He had no right to say that.' Annie sniffed back tears. 'My John never done that. He sent me a ten shilling postal order every week until the day he died.'

Annie gave Polly a long account of her life in Windsor with her husband and family. Annie and her husband worked for a member of parliament and some of her sisters worked for royalty. Talking about it brought up memories that upset Annie.

'There, there, you got to stop distressing yourself,' said Polly as tears ran down Annie's face. She rubbed her shoulder sympathetically. 'You both had your trials ain't you? It's a terrible thing to be told something like that was done to your friend. But you know what, Annie? I think she was already gone before he did those awful things to her and she knew nothing about it.'

Despite her comforting words, the same thing had preyed on Polly's mind. Fate had swapped Polly Wilkes for Polly Nichols and she was having difficulty coming to terms with it.

'I hope so.' Annie bowed her head.

'Well, you just think on it like that. You look poorly tonight. You ought not to be weighing yourself down with melancholy thoughts. You got to look after yourself.'

Polly took a good look at her. She could feel every bone in Annie's shoulder. Although the sickly glow of the gaslight was hardly flattering to anyone, her skin looked like wax and she was very pale.

Annie's eyes seemed to have sunk back into their sockets and there were dark circles beneath them. One eye, Polly noticed was also sporting a purple bruise. She patted Annie's hand. 'So, where's Eddie Stanley tonight? Ain't he usually good for your doss money?'

Annie looked up.

'He's with that cow, Eliza Cooper. She's trying to take him away from me. I can't get to him, Pol. He would give it to me but she's making sure I get nowhere near.'

Polly could see that Annie was having trouble catching her breath and took short wheezing gasps between sentences. She could hear a definite rattle as Annie exhaled. She was in a poor state.

'Where did you get the shiner, Annie?'

Annie looked penitent. 'I had a fight with Eliza.'

'You? Fighting? I ain't never heard of such a thing.'

'I'm telling you, she's got Eddie down as a meal ticket. She's ripping him off all the time. I seen her do it, the brazen mare. She had the cheek to take a two bob bit off Eddie's table and put a penny in its place. I collared her about it down *The Britannia* on Tuesday and she had a go at me when we got back here. As it turned out, she beat the hell out of me. Look at this...'

Annie undid her bodice and revealed a spectacular blue-black bruise on her chest. Polly could see swirling colours of purple, cranberry and dull yellow around the edges.

'That's a shocking bruise, Annie. It looks like you burst a blood vessel or something. It looks serious, that does. It needs looking at.'

'I went up the infirmary and they kept me in until yesterday. To tell you the truth, I feel really rough. My chest don't feel too good neither. Never mind,' she sighed. 'It don't do to give in, do it?'

'What'd they say to you up the infirmary?' Polly asked.

'They gave me some pills for my headache and some liniment for my chest,' she said. Then a thought occurred to her. 'Here, where's Lizzie? We don't often see one o' you without the other.'

'She'll be down any time now.'

'She's left Mickey ain't she?'

'Yeah, she has. Keep it under your hat that she's here, alright?'

'Course I will. We all told her what he was like.'

'Yeah.' Polly replied vaguely. 'So, has the medicine helped?'

'A bit. Listen, tell Lizzie I'll see her later.' Annie stood up.

'What? You ain't going out are you?'

'I have to Pol. I have to get my doss money somehow.' She started to cough. It was an endless, deep, phlegmy, rattle. Polly had a bad feeling about it. She had heard such a cough many times when she was put to work in the workhouse infirmary. She had never forgotten that raw, rasping sound and the putrid smell on the breath - it meant Consumption - a disease that filled a person's soul with dread. It was well named. It was a flesh-eating disease that went for a person's lungs then spread to other vital organs. Poor Annie. No wonder she looked so ill.

'You had anything to eat?' Polly asked.

'No.'

'Annie, you're hopeless. I'll get you a baked potato. There's some in the oven. They're just what was left behind after the market. We cut the bad bits off and they're alright.'

'To tell you the truth I ain't really hungry, Pol.'

'Come on. You have to keep your strength up, don't you?'

Polly frowned. Annie's loss of appetite could be another sign of that dreaded disease. She was as thin as a reed and looked as if a strong breeze could snap her in two. They heard footsteps on the staircase and Lizzie came into the room.

'Lizzie, talk some sense into her will you?' Polly said as she moved to the fireplace and opened the oven door.

'What's the matter?' Her accent was more noticeable this evening. It always was after she had been to the Swedish church.

'She ain't at all well and she planning on going out dollying.'

'I have to, I tell you. I must pull myself together and get my doss money.' said Annie.

'Yeah, that's right, she does.' John Evans the night watchman strode into the kitchen. 'Come on Annie, pay up or get out,' the roughly shaven old man insisted.

'Hey, Evans. Have a heart, will you? She ain't well.' Polly replied.

'Rules is rules. This ain't the casual ward.'

'She ain't taking up a bed. She's just sitting in here keeping warm.' said Polly.

'Rules ain't made to be broken, come on, Annie. Get out.'

'What if the murderer is out there? She don't have to have a bed, just somewhere safe. The police said you ain't got to be so strict.'

'The police ain't here. Are they?'

Polly shot him a look of disgust and her eyes narrowed. 'God forgive you for loving your job so much.'

'I don't make the rules, I just make sure they is followed.'

'Come on, look at her. She ain't well. And it's close to midnight.'

'Take her down the infirmary, then. She ain't my problem.' He looked at Annie. 'You better have your doss money by the time I've been 'round and done the checks, Annie or you hit the pavement. Alright?' He stomped off.

Annie hauled herself to her feet. 'See? I have to go out.'

Lizzie opened her purse and took out four pennies.

'Annie, take this. I made some money today.' Lizzie pressed the coins into Annie's hand. 'Get yourself a bed and get some rest.'

'Here's two from me. Don't go spending it on rum.' Polly said firmly.

'You two are my guardian angels.' Annie replied with a smile.

'Yeah, regular bloomin' cherubs, we are. Now do as you're told,' Polly replied.

Annie beamed, revealing a row of perfect teeth that looked odd and out of place against the hollow-cheeked, washed-out face that looked so sallow and sickly.

'I won't forget this.'

'Don't worry. We won't let you,' Polly said. 'Now get along.'

They watched Annie as she headed for the dormitory area. She swerved and veered off to the left, putting an arm out to steady herself as she picked her way down the corridor.

'She ain't very good,' Polly said quietly.

'She looks worse than when I saw her last week. Her face seems pinched and she looks grey. It's like she has no blood,' said Lizzie.

'I think she's got the Consumption,' said Polly. 'She's been swaying like she's drunk except she swears she ain't touched a drop.'

'Annie has a reputation for being under the drink most of the time.' Lizzie replied.

'I know but what if she ain't?' Polly turned back to the oven and closed the door. 'What if she's like that because she's sick?'

'If she's dizzy and stumbles about and isn't drunk, then she's very sick.' Lizzie replied.

'That's what I thought.'

'If this happened to a beast on our farm, they were killed and their carcasses had to be burned. They said it was a disease of the brain and could be passed onto people.'

'Funny you should say that because I was just thinking about the workhouse infirmary. I saw people do the same and the doctor said it was to do with their brains being infected with the Consumption. They used to stagger about like Annie does and sweat up terrible at night. They would say they were too hot and fling their blanket off, then five minutes later, they would be shaking and say they were freezing cold again. I would go and cover them up and next thing they'd be red-hot again. I think that's what's happening to Annie, god help her.'

'I've often seen her shivering.' Lizzie agreed.

'Yeah, me as well. And, with brain fever, a person can't stand the light or any noise. Some folk call her *Dark Annie,* don't they? Cos she likes to sit in the dark on account of her headaches.'

'She prefers the dark, and quiet places. She often complains the pub is too bright and noisy.'

'Someone should be looking after her, the state she's in. She shouldn't have to go out dollying for the want of four pence or walk the streets all night cos she ain't got it.' She looked at Lizzie. 'We should make sure she goes up the London Hospital tomorrow. They might help her a bit more than the workhouse infirmary did.'

'Yes. She needs a proper place to stay, so she can rest. This place is no good.' Lizzie sighed. 'It is such a pity she can't sell her work and get herself some nourishing food. She's a beautiful needlewoman.'

'So I've heard,' said Polly.

'Her crochet work is so good she can work the finest yarns. She can crochet roses that stand out like real ones, even tiny ones for a bridal veil. There aren't many who can do that.'

'Well, being the former daughter of one of the fanciest drapers in London, I can tell you they would sell like hot cakes. She can't make them because she ain't got money to buy the yarn and she can't buy the yarn cos she ain't made any.'

'Maybe you could get your family to give Annie some yarn and pay her for her work?'

'Fat chance of that. I'm dead to them remember?' Polly replied. 'My Auntie May's letter made that made very clear. Anyway, it was a good thing you grabbed a pile of those hankies of Mickey's to sell. Thanks to you, Annie's got a bed tonight and so do we.'

# CHAPTER SEVEN

'Move along, please. There ain't nothing to see.' said Alf Cruikshank in his most authoritative tone. A large crowd had accumulated outside number 29 Hanbury Street. 'Come along, now.' He raised his voice to the ear-splitting volume he reserved for such occasions. 'Go about your business. Move on.'

It never ceased to amaze him how fast word of an incident spread through the neighbourhood.

'We want to know what's going on.' A voice in the crowd called out. There were murmurs of agreement from the rest. Alf sighed, he was going to need some help. He ploughed forward and although the crowd did not disperse, a path was made to the door.

Like the rest of the street, number 29 was riddled with woodworm. The strong, mushroom smell of dry rot grabbed Alf's nostrils before he reached the door. The door frame was peppered with tiny wormholes, it looked as if it might fall apart if ever slammed shut.

He looked around him.

It was a miracle these places stayed up, he thought as he stepped inside.

Alf knew this was a respectable house owned by a widow, Mrs. Amelia Robinson who had a reputation for being a deeply religious woman. He also knew that she was fussy about her tenants and only let rooms to families that met her standards. There had never been any trouble at this address - until now.

Once inside, Alf was faced with a long passageway crammed with more people. Many were standing on the staircase to the left of the door. Alf wondered if the woodworm ridden structure was strong enough to take their combined weight. If the staircase went, it would bring the whole building down.

'Excuse me, please. Make way,' No one moved. He was growing impatient. 'Do I have to start taking names? I said, make way.'

The crowd then parted as if controlled by a single mind and made a path along the passage that reached the back door. 'Thank you,' he said, each pair of eyes fixed on him as he moved towards the rear of the property.

The rear door was open and Alf could see uniformed officers in the backyard.

He paused on the threshold at the top of three steps that descended into the yard. Dawn had broken an hour ago and the area was filled with light. He took in all the details of the scene in an instant. He saw a high wooden fence that surrounded a small enclosed yard. In the top right corner was a privy, in the top left, was a shed.

Alf's stomach rolled and he held his breath. The smell of faeces was overpowering. Only a week ago, he had been at the scene of a gruesome murder. Now, again, he was looking down at the mutilated body of a woman.

She lay with her head a few inches to the left of the steps, her legs towards the fence that separated the property from next door. Blood had flowed from her wounds and flooded the area around the base of the bottom step. A deep, crimson rectangle had formed, picking out the shape of the uneven ground where a paving stone was missing.

Alf blew out his cheeks and looked away to the surrounding rooftops. He braced himself, took a breath then looked again at the body.

Her knees were drawn up and her thighs spread apart so that her genitals were displayed to the world. It was a final sick indignity perpetrated against the unfortunate woman. Alf felt fury begin to burn in his chest. Not satisfied with killing her, the fiend had done this to humiliate her after death and shock those who saw his work.

Alf had a bad feeling about these killings. His copper's instincts told him this murder was the work of the same deranged individual who had killed Mrs. Nichols last week and probably Mrs. Tabram at the beginning of August. The level of violence in each crime was increasing and it seemed unlikely to be a coincidence.

Joe Chandler, an inspector at Commercial Street station was standing at the foot of the steps, a few inches away from the pool of blood.

'Alf, good to see you old man. How's your Mother?' It was the first thing Joe asked whenever he met up with Alf.

Ten years ago, Alf's mother, Temperance Cruikshank had gone to Mrs. Chandler who was suffering a labour that was rapidly going wrong. As the young doctor shook his head at the developing situation, Mrs. Cruikshank had taken over. Like many midwives, she had far more experience than the average medical man when it came to delivering babies. Her skill saved both mother and child. Chandler, who was then a sergeant, had never forgotten how grateful he was. He had encouraged Alf to join the force and written the letter of recommendation that helped him get into the Metropolitan Police.

'Not too bad, sir. Can't complain.' Alf replied vaguely.

'This is a bad business,' said Chandler, looking down at the corpse. 'I happened to be passing the end of Hanbury Street coming off shift this morning and three extremely agitated gentlemen caught my attention. When I got here...' he paused 'Well, you can see for yourself. It's shocking.' He cleared his throat. 'Bagster-Phillips is on his way. Nothing we can do until he gets here and formally certifies her.'

Doctor Bagster-Phillips was one of *The Met's* own medics. Alf thought of him as a bit of a complaining windbag, on the other hand, he would give a more informed opinion than Doctor Llewelyn.

A young constable snapped to Chandler's side.

'This is all I can find, sir.' He held up a piece of sacking.

'Then it will have to do... Cover her... lower area, Hastings.' He turned to Alf. 'I just wanted to afford the poor woman a little dignity,' he said.

''Do we know who she is?' Alf asked. 'Someone suggested she's a well-known dollymop by the name of Annie Chapman,' said Chandler. 'That isn't official yet, of course.'

Alf glanced back at the crowd inside the house. They had better get rid of them before Bagster-Phillips arrived. If not, there would be a lot of belly-aching from the dour, straight-laced man. Alf beckoned to the two constables who were standing to attention by the fence. They came to his side in an instant.

'Get the names of them that's standing in that passageway. Find out who lives here and tell them to return to their lodgings. Then get rid of the gawpers outside in the street. Oh, and make sure we know how to find the men who found the body. We'll want statements.'

As the two men shot off to do Alf's bidding, Chandler put his handkerchief to his nose. 'There's obviously no doubt that she's dead. That pile of disgusting offal beside her left shoulder is most of her bowels. Hence the smell. However, we must follow procedure; the death has to be recorded officially.'

Alf crouched down beside the corpse. The face was swollen and the tip of her tongue protruded through her blue lips. There was a ghastly injury to her neck where the monster had ripped open her throat.

On the fence, he saw splashes of blood about fourteen inches from the ground. She was lying on her back when he started on her with his knife, Alf surmised. He knew blood spurts from the carotid artery could travel several feet. Though the splashes on the fence were feeble, it meant she was still alive when he inflicted the long ripping wound.

'Holy mother of God...' he murmured. Alive but not conscious, he prayed.

He lifted the piece of sacking that Hastings had placed over her abdomen and held his breath. As far as he could tell, the woman's abdomen had been ripped open from vagina to breastbone. Alf looked away from the glistening coils of intestine, blood vessels and membranes that lay beside her shoulder. The gaping abdomen was an empty cavity, drained of blood by the severing of the great vessels of the abdomen. A pool of blood two or three inches deep surrounded the body. Alf blinked, taking in a sharp breath as he took in what he was seeing.

'He's taken stuff away from her, sir. You can see daylight through her quim.' He looked up at Chandler. 'Her internal lady parts have been taken out. What kind of beast are we dealing with here?'

Chandler, grey-faced, shook his head and looked as if he could vomit at any moment.

The victim's face was turned towards them. It was grey and swollen giving a chubby appearance. It was grotesquely at odds with her skinny, undernourished body. Her eyes were not completely closed. The whites of her eyes were speckled with blood from tiny haemorrhages and her tongue was swollen and blue. Alf rubbed his chin. These were signs of strangulation so why did he also cut her throat from ear to ear?

The gash to her neck was so deep the end of her windpipe protruded through the wound. It was as if he had been trying to decapitate her. The severed blood vessels had contracted like purse strings in response to being cut. The stumps of arteries and veins in the victim's neck looked like bloody sausages in the vicious wound. Alf replaced the sacking and stood up.

'She's been strangled *and* her throat is cut,' said Chandler. 'Why do that? I've never seen a murder victim where more than one method has been used so thoroughly. As for that abdominal wound… it beggars belief. She's been eviscerated. And as for the damage to her genitals… It looks to me like he did it for jollies.'

Alf nodded in reply, it being exactly what he was thinking. 'Yes, sir. I seen things done on a man for revenge. Why this poor creature?'

Chandler looked at the corpse, an expression of pity on his face. 'She does look dirt poor, doesn't she? Poor woman. What a state she's in.'

'The lady at Bucks Row had her throat cut just like this. Once they got her to the mortuary, they found she had been disembowelled. Her insides hadn't been pulled away in this fashion; apart from that it's all very similar. Same day of the week and similar time.' Alf shook his head. 'We've got a maniac on our hands, sir.'

'Yes. It does look like the work of the same killer. There's no obvious motive for such butchery. I mean for whatever reason he killed her. He might have strangled her, or cut her throat, or stabbed her, - not all of them surely? And look at the location, Alf. He seems heedless of being caught in the act.'

'Yes, sir.' Alf looked up at the grubby windows of the house. 'This yard is overlooked a considerable amount by the houses on either side and over the back. Wouldn't you have thought someone would have heard something and come to see what was occurring?'

'As far as we know, no one heard a thing. We'll have to interview the residents of all the surrounding houses.'

'We couldn't make sense of Bucks Row neither,' said Alf. 'It weren't a place you would pick to do someone in. It transpired that the lady was a dollymop called Polly Nichols. It looked like she was about to lead him into the stable yard for the business. She only got as far as the gate before he struck.'

'He would have been trapped in the yard if there had been a commotion,' said Chandler.

Alf nodded. 'Exactly, sir. It could suggest premeditation. D'you think he goes out hunting for women to kill?'

'It's possible. And if he does, he's a singular type of killer, Alf. Apparently, the victim doesn't live here. Perhaps she was also looking for somewhere dark to take a client - as they do.' Chandler scanned the yard. 'Look at this place, if the woman had raised the alarm he would have been trapped.'

'Perhaps that was an error, sir. He might have thought there was a back gate into the alley through which he could escape. It's the case with most of these type of houses. Here, there ain't one. It's completely surrounded by other yards as you can see.'

Chandler rubbed his chin. 'So, he must have left through the front door.'

'Must have. It's the only way out. Unless he climbed over half a dozen high fences like this one.'

'Mr. Davis, the resident who found her, said the front door was wide open when he came downstairs,' said Chandler. He sighed. 'Similar victim, similar injuries, similar circumstances. This is a bold and arrogant killer, Alf and I think he's doing it for the pleasure of killing.'

'That's my opinion too, sir.' Alf agreed. 'And it appears he's developing a taste for it.'

## CHAPTER EIGHT

In the relentless drizzle, Polly and Lizzie had walked the three miles from Whitechapel to Forest Gate. They found square number 148 on the southern edge of Manor Park Cemetery. Within that square, it didn't take long to find grave number 78. Annie Chapman had been buried there the day before, on Friday the 14th of September.

'It is hard to believe her life ended that way.' said Lizzie.

'I know. Would you credit it? With all the struggles she had with her health?'

'There were times she was so sorrowful about her boy having to go in the home for cripples. I thought she might throw herself off London Bridge. Did you know, she sometimes walked from Whitechapel to Windsor to visit him?'

'All the way to Windsor and back? That has to be thirty miles each way.' Polly replied. 'And to top it all, she has to come across the Whitechapel Killer. That was just Annie's luck weren't it?'

'Yes,' Lizzie sighed. 'Poor Annie.'

Polly stopped and picked up a newspaper that was lying on a nearby park bench. 'Look at this. The whole front page is about Annie's murder.' She began to read. '"*Whitechapel is at the centre of a commotion that is unprecedented.*" Look, they've drawn pictures of Annie.' Polly tutted. 'Not flattering nor much of a resemblance I must say. It says the murders were done by the same maniac, just like that sergeant said. Then it talks about Annie being found behind 29 Hanbury Street and what was done to her. I don't want to read that.'

Lizzie placed the bunch of forget-me-nots they had brought with them in an old pickle jar on the slab that covered Annie's grave as the rain eased off to a misty drizzle.

Polly took a page from the middle of the newspaper, folded it into many layers and then tore it in half. She took off her boots, removed soggy, wet newspaper from each one and replaced it with the folded paper.

'That's better.' she said, tying the string that served as shoelaces, into bows. She put the soggy paper and the newspaper into a waste bin at the end of the path. Then she returned to Lizzie who was still beside Annie's grave. 'Annie got killed last Saturday. She must have been out dollying to get her doss money like the other night when we saw her. I hope Evans is ashamed of himself. He should be locked up for the way he treated her.' said Polly.

'Yes,' said Lizzie. 'If she had no money and no work, she would have had to go out.'

Polly crouched by the grave. 'You're the talk of London, Annie. You're in all the papers.' She stayed there for a moment and then stood up. 'Look at this...' she said to Lizzie. 'It's pitiful ain't it? It looks more like the covering of a cellar than a grave.'

'It will be like a cellar. It's a communal grave. Annie is in there with who knows how many other people and more will follow.'

'Bloody rozzers. How dare they? How dare they arrange Annie's funeral without telling anyone?'

'The murders are frightening for people. They wanted to avoid a fuss,' said Lizzie.

'It ain't right,' said Polly. 'There was none of us there for her. Hardly any flowers for her and only her brother and one of her sisters at her funeral. It ain't decent. A pauper's funeral is what she had.'

'Did Annie's family refuse to pay for a funeral?' Lizzie asked.

'No, according to Suzette, it was quite the opposite. When her brother found out, he wanted to pay for it and do it all proper, and the police wouldn't let him. Annie used to live well at one time, you know. Her husband John worked for a 'sir' somebody what's the Member of Parliament for Windsor who rubs shoulders with the royal family and she had a cottage on the master's country estate, a good wage coming in and a nice family. Some of her sisters work for royalty.'

'I didn't know that.'

'I think her family is well thought of. Her oldest girl died but the youngest girl goes to a very good school in Windsor. She was took in by Annie's sister.'

'That must have been after Annie was sent away,' said Lizzie.

'It was an odd state of affairs. Annie told me her husband still gave her ten bob a week after they parted. No kids to support nor nothing so he must have thought a lot of her to do that. Ten bob would be a hefty lump out of his wages.'

'In that case, why did they split up?'

'That's the thing. The master said she had to get off the premises on account of her being an embarrassment. They said it was due to her drunkenness.' Polly quirked her mouth. 'That didn't sound right to me, Lizzie, Annie always denied that she drank a lot.'

'Yes, she did, even when she was staggering along the pavement.'

'After that talk I had with her last week, I'm beginning to wonder if she were telling the truth. I think a terrible wrong might have been done to her, Lizzie.'

'Apart from being so brutally murdered, you mean?' said Lizzie raising an eyebrow.

'I mean during her life.' said Polly. 'Think about it. Her little Emily died of a brain fever five or six years ago, not long after John got the job with this toff. Then, shortly after that, Annie starts staggering around slurring her speech. She was always complaining of headaches, weren't she? Everyone took them to be hangovers due to her reputation for being drunk.'

'Yes.'

'What if little Emily had the Consumption and it went to her brain and that's what caused the fever? Who would be the one nursing her and giving her kisses and cuddles? Annie of course. What if Annie caught it off her? They say it can turn chronic and last for years in some people.'

'Yes, it can. I've heard of that,' said Lizzie.

'When John and Annie separated he gave her enough to live on out of his wages. Why would he do that if he thought she was a useless drunk what made him look bad in front of the master?'

'If the master said she had to go, then she had to go. Either John would have had to give up a good position or make arrangements for Annie.'

'So he made arrangements to give Annie ten bob a week. That would be enough to pay for a nice room and all her needs. Unfortunately, he died a couple of years later. That's when it all started to get bad for her. Once he'd gone, she had to go on the game, then she took up with that Eddie Stanley and he looked after her until Eliza Cooper muscled her way in.'

'Poor Annie had a lot of setbacks in her sad life.' Lizzie looked down at the grave, her eyes brimming with tears. 'Your suffering is over now, Annie. Sleep eternal peace.'

'Rest in peace, Annie,' Polly added. 'God bless. We won't forget you.'

They made their way down the long path towards the cemetery gates, their arms linked. It began to pour with rain again and they took shelter under the grand arched portico of the main entrance.

'You've been very quiet,' Polly glanced in Lizzie's direction. 'This is really getting to you ain't it?'

'They need to catch this murderer, and soon.'

'Well, I don't know how. The Protestants blame the Irish Catholics and the Irish Catholics blame the Jews. The Jews are sure the murderer is a protestant or a catholic and the police don't seem to have a clue. *The Star* has had a real go at them and you heard how that paper I found in the cemetery reported it. They implied the police won't put any effort in because the victims were *unfortunates*. Did you know that's what they call us, Lizzie? They said they weren't trying very hard to catch him. Worst of it is, it's probably true.'

'I worry for you and the other girls. He might kill again. If anything happened to you...' She shook her head. 'I don't know what I would do.'

'I can look after myself. Don't you worry.'

'I wish you wouldn't go out until he's found.'

'You know I try to get other work. If I can't find any I have to go out, Lizzie. It's either that or the workhouse. I'd rather take the risk with the murderer than go back in there.'

'I would rather you were safe.'

'You're not usually this melancholy. What's the matter?' She looked at her friend and sighed. 'It's him again ain't it?'

'Mickey thinks he can make me go back to him. He still thinks he's the boss of what I do.'

'It's been nearly two weeks. I thought he'd got the message?' said Polly. 'Does he know where you are?

'I think so.'

'Then you got to move, Lizzie. Straight away.'

'I'll go back to the Swedish church tomorrow. They'll have decided whether to give me some more money. I can move away, somewhere he won't find me.'

Polly pulled her shawl more closely around her and linked her arm tightly with Lizzie's in a one armed hug. 'Maybe I could come with you? Perhaps we could get on one of those big boats and go to America?'

'I looked into that. The cheapest ticket would cost four pounds.' She patted Polly's arm. 'I would never go so far away without my Polly.'

'We could open our tea shop in America. What d'you think? An English teashop might go down well in New York,' said Polly.

'It would be a dream come true.'

'Why not, eh? One day.'

'One day.' Lizzie replied.

'Blimey it's cold. You'd think it was winter already. What happened to summer this year d'you think?'

'When we get back, let's go to *The Ten Bells*.' said Lizzie. 'I got a shilling ironing for Mrs. Jones at the bakery yesterday.'

'Yeah. A nice ginger wine would just hit the spot and they'll have the piano man in for the Saturday night sing-song.'

'As long as Pearl doesn't get up and sing again. It made my ears bleed.' said Lizzie.

'It was funny though, weren't it? She was so off key but she really belted it out. *The boy I love is up in the gallery...*' Polly mimicked, which made Lizzie smile. 'We could do with a good laugh and the girls should be in.'

They were weary after their long walk and were thankful to reach *The Ten Bells* on Commercial Street. The pub was crammed with people. George, the piano player, was nowhere to be seen - neither was the piano that was usually brought into the bar on Saturday nights.

'It's much busier than I expected,' said Polly as they sat down at a table by the door.

'There are a lot of new faces here tonight.' Lizzie pointed out.

'You're right and it's a bit miserable ain't it?' Polly whispered. 'I was hoping for a bit of a laugh but they're talking about the murders.'

'He's a Jew! The papers say he's a Jew,' bellowed a man who was standing so close to them, he startled both women. 'Listen to this in *The Star*. *"There is a maniac haunting Whitechapel. His expression is sinister and seems to be full of terror. His eyes are small and glittering. His lips are parted in a grin which is excessively repellent."*'

'I thought nobody alive has seen him?' Polly whispered. Lizzie shrugged in reply as another man jumped up.

'It says here, "*Whitechapel is half mad with fear.*"'

A third man stepped forward. 'The police confess that they don't have a clue. What they waiting for? Another murder? People are even too scared to talk to a stranger in the street and Commissioner Warren is doing absolutely nothing.'

'Oh here we go...' Polly muttered.

The murmuring grew louder.

'They don't care about us,' continued another man, stepping forward with his thumbs hooked inside the pockets of his waistcoat 'These women were killed for the want of four pence for a bed in a common lodging house.'

Polly recognised the voice of the well-known local businessman, George Lusk. Lizzie leaned towards her confidentially.

'He did repair work for the church. Even Pastor Sven says he makes trouble,' she whispered.

Lusk now had everyone's attention. 'All they want is to keep us quiet and know our places,' he said. There were murmurings of agreement from the crowd. The young man who had read out the newspaper report was standing beside Lusk as he continued. 'They want us kept out of sight. They want to keep us away from the fancy folks in the West End. All they think we're good for is scrubbing their floors and emptying their chamber pots.'

There were more noises of agreement from the crowd.

'When was the last time he emptied a chamber pot?' Polly whispered. 'Ain't he got a big fancy house with a dozen servants up Mile End?'

'Well, we ain't going to stand for it.' Lusk continued. 'We are going to protect our own. If the police can't catch this fiend; we will.'

The young man beside Lusk suddenly jumped onto a table as if he was about to burst into song. He had a pencil behind his ear and he was wearing a billy-cock hat tilted towards the back of his head. He held a newspaper in his hand.

'Listen to this in *The Star*,' he said. '"*The woman was ripped up from groin to breastbone. The viscera had been pulled out and scattered in all directions. The heart and liver had been placed behind her head. She was covered with blood and lying in a pool of it*"'

Someone in the audience whimpered. The reader, it seemed to Polly, was relishing the gory details far too much as he continued. '"*The knife was jabbed into the deceased at the lower part of the abdomen and then drawn upward, not once... but twice. The first cut veered to the right, slitting up the groin but the second cut went straight upward along the centre of the body reaching to the breast bone.'"*

Several women shrieked.

'Are we going stand for this in our community?' said Lusk. 'Where are the police? What are they doing about these horrific murders? We should get rid of the imbeciles in charge.'

The crowd roared and began to applaud.

'The Star said he was a Yid,' someone reported. 'It says here, *"He is a Jew or of Jewish parentage and his face of a marked Hebrew type"*'

Polly's head snapped around towards Lizzie. 'How the hell can they know that? No one knows who he is.' she murmured.

'Well, I heard he was a Mick. Probably from Dublin,' said another man.

'No he ain't. He's a doctor,' said a third.

'Let's get out of here,' said Polly. 'All this talk is terrible. That's our friend they're talking about.'

'*The Britannia* should be quieter.' said Lizzie.

They left *The Ten Bells* and crossed Commercial Street. Ignoring the rain, they paused on the corner of Brushfield Street.

'Annie didn't get far after she left the doss house, did she?' said Lizzie. 'Poor Annie. She must have turned down the side of Crossingham's into Little Paternoster Row and come out there.' Polly looked where Lizzie was pointing which was to the narrow alley that connected Dorset Street to Brushfield Street.

'She would have stood right here and if she couldn't find a punter, she would have walked up past the market, crossed over the road, went into Hanbury Street and just like that, she's gone.' Polly snapped her fingers.

'I wonder where she met her killer?' said Lizzie. 'It could have been right here.'

Polly felt her stomach clench. 'He's in our midst ain't he, Lizzie?' she said. 'He must be. And he could be anyone.' Like the other girls, she knew she was playing Russian roulette. Her very next client could be him.

'That's why I worry about you. Listen to me Polly. You mustn't go out. Promise me you won't go out? I have a constant feeling of dread.'

'If I can't get work I'm on the streets anyway, Lizzie. What else can I do?'

'I don't know, we'll have to think of something.' she replied. 'Even if you get yourself arrested you'll get a place to sleep and a cup of tea off a friendly policeman.'

'They ain't all friendly. You know some of them demand a free one. I've kept out of trouble so far and I want it to stay that way.'

'There's always the workhouse.' said Lizzie.

'No. Never. I'd rather take my chances with the killer than go back there,' said Polly.

Lizzie's brow creased into a worried frown. 'Listen,' Polly continued. 'That George Lusk just wants everyone to be scared. Lusk's only doing it because he wants to get on the new council. He's stirring things up and I bet he's using that newspaper to do it. I think that young man who jumped on the table was a reporter. The people at *The Star* wrote things no one could possibly know. How the hell can they know his eyes are small and glittering or what his expression is like? It's a disgrace they write such things. It's all made up.'

'Polly Nichols and Annie are dead. Someone did that.'

'That's true, except it don't mean it's going happen again, does it?' said Polly. 'You know what? I bet George Lusk would love it if it did. He's revelling in it and using it to try and get himself elected.'

'Mickey admires George Lusk.'

'That says it all don't it?'

'So did that young man.' said Lizzie.

'That young lad was probably in his pay. I bet him and Lusk are in it together.' Polly replied. 'Come on let's get to *The Britannia*. A couple of gins and you'll soon cheer up.' They walked the short distance to the next corner.

The next morning Polly returned to *The Britannia*. She had made a deal with Sid the barman to take the morning delivery from the brewery.

'Hey, Sid, I've shifted dozens of these crates. You ain't paying me enough.' She heaved another crate of beer bottles from the pavement where they had been left by the dray-man.

'I told you it was men's work.' Sid replied from the open cellar hatch. He was sitting on a beer keg and reading a newspaper.

'I didn't say I couldn't lift them, I said I'd shifted dozens of 'em and I ain't even getting a penny a dozen.'

'Alright I'll throw in a gin when you've done,' he said.

'Don't overdo the generosity will you?' Polly muttered. Then loud enough for Sid to hear, 'I'd rather have a ginger ale,' she said as she struggled with the crate she was carrying and dumped it on top of the stack.

She paused for breath and went to the outside tap to rinse her face. She dried herself with her shawl then stepped out onto the pavement.

In the shadow of Christ Church, partially concealed in the disused graveyard, a figure caught her eye. She would not have thought twice about him except that he was acting in a comical, shifty manner. As she watched, he pulled up the collar of his coat, looked left and right and moved around the side of the church. He positioned himself behind one of the buttresses.

The disused graveyard at the side of Christ Church was a known meeting place for prostitutes to meet rich customers. This man was about as discrete as a charging bull, Polly thought, laughing at how theatrical it looked. Then she saw George Lusk. Suddenly she was curious rather than amused. Was Lusk a sodomite?

As the young man stepped out to greet Lusk, Polly could see his face. It was the young man she had seen reading from the newspaper in *The Ten Bells* the previous night.

She pretended to adjust the bottles inside one of the crates as she surreptitiously watched the two men. Lusk gave the lad a shove, indicating he should stay behind the buttress.

Polly saw the younger man take a brown envelope from Lusk and place it in the breast pocket of his jacket. Lusk seemed to be doing all the talking, then a moment later they walked away in opposite directions.

She had heard rumours that George Lusk was involved in all sorts of shady deals. There was talk of a more sinister side to his good works. He put on a squeaky clean appearance to the world, a pillar of the community. Despite this, Polly had been warned by some of the girls, to stay out of his way. People who invited his disapproval tended to have nasty accidents.

Sid paid her sixpence and gave her a bottle of ginger ale. She sat down in a quiet corner of the pub, shielded from the door. Sid would leave her alone and it was warm and dry. She might even manage a short nap.

She had enough money for a bed in Crossingham's. Though hunger gnawed at her, she would wait until the end of the day when they sold off the bread. She would get a loaf for a penny to share with Lizzie. Polly was still thinking about this when Lizzie ran into the bar and headed straight for the counter.

'Give me a brandy, Sid. Where's Polly?' she said, slapping two pennies on the counter. She was shaking. Sid complied and she downed the brandy in one gulp.

Polly rushed to her side. 'I'm here. Whatever's the matter?'

'Oh Polly...' she said clutching a hand to her chest.

'Come and sit down,' Polly put a hand to Lizzie's back and guided her to a seat on the side of the bar that was hidden from the door.

'What's happened?'

Lizzie tried to calm herself enough to continue.

Polly called to the barman. 'Sid, give her another brandy on the house, eh?'

She took Lizzie's hand in both of hers and rubbed it vigorously. The hand was cold and trembling. 'There now, darlin'. Calm yourself.' She looked up to see Sid glaring at her.

'Come on, Sid. I shifted enough of them crates for you.'

Sid scowled and mooched over with a very small glass of brandy. He placed it on the table. Polly looked at the tiny measure. 'Show a bit of class, will you? Look at the state of her.'

Sid ignored her and slouched off as Lizzie picked it up and downed it like the last one. She tried to place the empty glass on the table; her trembling fingers seemed unable to let go. She looked into its empty depths as if she could do with a third measure.

'C'mon. Tell me what happened. Didn't you have some cleaning work today?'

'Yes, I did. Betty Tanner gave me sixpence to clean at Flower and Dean Street. Mickey found me there,' she said. 'He came to the back door. He said he was sorry and things would be better now. I told him it was over and I wasn't ever going back to him. He got angry. He told me I wasn't leaving him. I told him I already had. We argued. Then he pushed me through the curtain into the store room and got me against the wall.' she lifted her hand to her neck. 'He put his hands around my throat.'

'Let me see...' said Polly, carefully moving aside Lizzie's collar. There were some vivid red marks on Lizzie's neck. She was bleeding where Mickey's fingernails had dug into her flesh. Lizzie winced. 'Sorry...' said Polly.

'I couldn't breathe, Polly.' Then he got up close, right in my face and he said. *I'll see you in the ground first, bitch.*' Tears filled her eyes. 'There was a knife on a box right beside him. I saw him looking at it. I thought he was going to pick it up and finish me there and then.' she wiped away tears.

'How did you get away?'

'I kneed him in the balls.'

'The whirligigs again? He'll be singing like a choirboy before long.'

Lizzie began to giggle. 'His eyes nearly popped out of his head.'

'His old bawbels were probably still a bit tender after what I did to them.'

Lizzie kept laughing until her pale face became crimson. She finally took a breath.

'I kneed him so hard, I think I hit bone.'

Polly let out a splutter of laughter. Sid the barman looked at them curiously.

'Then what happened?'

'He dropped to his knees and I ran. He started to puke or I think he would have followed me. I didn't stop running until I got here.'

Lizzie's laughter turned to tears and she started to cry uncontrollably.

'There now. It's alright, you showed him. You're safe.' Polly put a hand on Lizzie's shoulder. The touch made her wince again.

'You'll have some lovely bruises there in a day or two, but nothing broken eh? And you fought back. I'm proud of you.'

Lizzie started to shake her head. 'He'll come after me, Polly. He had a crazy look in his eyes...' A sob came from somewhere deep in her chest. 'If he finds out where I am, he'll come.'

'Then we had better not let him find you.' said Polly. 'You'll be alright at Crossingham's tonight. I ain't letting you out of my sight.'

'You're a good friend, Polly. Lizzie put her hand on top of Polly's and give it a squeeze. 'I need to see Betty Tanner. I said I would sell her my roll of green velvet for one pound.'

'A quid? It's worth three times that.'

'I know,' Lizzie sighed. 'It's too hard to keep it safe in a lodging house, and she puts cleaning work my way.'

'Whatever you think is best. Promise me, once you've seen Betty, you'll stay away from Flower and Dean Street, alright?'

# CHAPTER NINE

'Feel that chill, Lizzie?' Polly pulled her shawl more tightly around her. The two women emerged from Crossingham's lodging house into an early morning fog. Polly shivered. 'I don't know what's going on with this weather, it should still be quite warm out at this time of year.'

A chilly north wind blasted its way through the narrow streets. It funnelled along Dorset Street, scouring everything in its path.

'This is nothing. You should-'

'Don't tell me. Try a winter in Sweden.' Polly finished the sentence with a grin. 'It must be bleeding cold in Sweden that's all I can say.'

'Not always. The summer is shorter, but the days are longer,' said Lizzie.

'I bet you got cleaner air in Sweden. If a bit of a breeze don't get up and make this fog lift, it'll be a pea souper by the end of the day.'

The year had been the coldest anyone could remember and the summer had never arrived. Polly dreaded the winter and walking the wet, grimy streets looking for work. Trying to find some respite from the cold was her ever present thought.

It was at the end of last winter she had sold herself for the first time. The money sent to her by Auntie May had finally run out and she had been unable to find enough work. Frozen to the bone, tired and hungry, she had reached the point of utter desperation. A night on the streets between October and March was out of the question.

'I got to find some work today, I ain't got nothing left.' said Polly.

'I can give you money for lodgings.'

'That's nice of you, Lizzie, except you got to keep your money. You have to stay one step ahead of Mickey.'

'Pastor Sven found me some work today.'

'That's good,' said Polly. 'What doing?'

'Cleaning for Mrs. Jones.'

'The lady from the bakery? She's nice, Mrs. Jones.' Polly replied.

'Yes, she gives me bread and sometimes cake.' Lizzie added. 'We can share it tonight.'

'I'll look forward to that,' said Polly.

The Swedish church had given Lizzie some money and, so far, she had been able to find lodgings and stay away from Mickey Kidney. It had been almost a week since he attacked her and Polly was anxious about him trying again. The man had fewer refinements than an ape and some of the girls had passed on warnings to Lizzie that he was looking for her. Lizzie merely shrugged her shoulders.

Polly was afraid that Mickey would bully Lizzie into going back to him. His bullying ways had succeeded before. As long as she had money for a bed, she knew Lizzie could stay away from him. So far she had managed to do this thanks to the money she received from the Swedish church each week and because Pastor Sven put work Lizzie's way whenever he could.

'Maybe I'll have some luck today.' said Polly.

She said goodbye to Lizzie and headed south on Commercial Street towards Commercial Road. Unlike most of the others, she was not completely resigned to a life of prostitution.

Some women made a living by going with enough punters to earn a good amount of money to live on; some even saved enough to get out of this life. It meant at least a dozen customers most nights, the thought of which, horrified Polly. Women resigned themselves to this life because there was not the slightest reason to believe that it could be better. Polly had not yet been on the streets for long enough to kill off all hope, even though she could see no way out of the place they called the abyss.

When they thought their miserable lives could get no worse, a madman had come to prey on them. The word was that the murderer was only killing prostitutes. The police had pinned up notices advising the girls to stay off the streets. Polly couldn't think of a more pointless piece of advice. As she reached the corner, a policeman was putting up another of the notices on the wall of *The Queen's Head.*

'Why don't you get them to open up the church halls and community halls as refuges so we got somewhere to sleep? How can we get off the streets if we ain't got no money, nowhere to go and nothing to eat?'

The policeman ignored her. Like the rest of the "respectable" people, he probably believed the victims got what they deserved.

There was as much talk about loose morals as there was about the killer. People talked about the consequences of sin as much as they talked about the murdering maniac. It was more comfortable to believe that the women brought their terrible deaths on themselves.

Polly was outraged that the murders were held up as examples of the penalty for immoral behaviour. *The wages of sin is death,* they said, rather than admit the women were pitiful victims of their circumstances as much as their murderer.

Polly tried every shop and business she came across on Whitechapel High Street and was turned away at each place. It was harder than ever to find work because many of the dollymops were doing likewise. By eleven o'clock she was footsore and weary. She had walked the length of Whitechapel from Aldgate to Mile End and back again - without success.

She crossed the road where Whitechapel Road, Commercial Street, Commercial Road, Aldgate and Leman Street converged into a wide junction and began her search all over again.

Many reasonably well-off Jewish people lived in the area around Commercial Road. She could sometimes get some cleaning or laundry work. The first shop she came to was a tailoring shop owned by a Jewish couple, Mr. and Mrs. Abrahams. Mrs. Abrahams had given her cleaning work before. Polly stepped inside as the bell on the door tinkled gently.

'Good morning, Ma'am. Do you have any work you could give me today?' Polly asked her, grateful to be in the warmth of the shop for a while.

'I am sorry, not today. I have nothing.'

Polly nodded a respectful greeting to Mr. Abrahams who was at the back of the shop pressing garments. The huge ironing press hissed as he brought down the lid in a cloud of steam.

'Please, I'll do anything. I'm a hard worker.'

'I am sorry,' said Mrs. Abrahams. She took a good look at Polly. 'Let me give you some hot coffee before you go out in the cold again.'

She took a cup from a stack on a tray that appeared to be kept for customers and poured out a cup of hot, sweet coffee from a trivet on the fireplace. She handed it to Polly.

'Thank you. That's very kind.'

The lady nodded and continued with her task of folding some shirts. She put them in a pile and wrapped them in brown paper, tying the parcel with string. 'You badly need work?' she asked, looking at Polly with sympathy as she tied the string. For Polly this was a pleasant change. Most people dismissed her without a second glance as though she was something less than human. She was touched by this small act of kindness.

'I need to pay for lodgings each night,' Polly told her. 'The police say that women should be indoors at night after the terrible murders, but it's hard to find work.'

Mrs. Abrahams gave Polly a concerned look.

'A woman should not have to face such a thing. Where are your people?'

Polly hesitated; she was always reluctant to discuss her past but she responded to the other woman's sympathetic nature. 'My people had very strict standards. When I was a young girl, I made a mistake.'

'What kind of mistake?' Her tone was wary.

'Oh, nothing dishonest,' said Polly, quickly. 'I... let's just say I followed my heart instead of my head.'

'And for this, you were banished?' said Mrs. Abrahams, sounding shocked.

Polly thought about it then quirked her mouth. 'I suppose you could call it banishment, yes.'

'By your own parents?'

'Yes.' Polly cast her eyes downward.

'The...' Mrs. Abrahams struggled for the right word. She looked at her husband for help. *'Co to jest slowo Okrutny?'*

'Cruel,' he replied.

'I am sad at this cruel act.' she said. 'Even your mama agreed to this?'

Polly could feel her throat tightening. 'She would have had no choice in the matter.'

Mrs. Abrahams held Polly in her kind expressive eyes. 'I have seen these lodgings, they charge four pennies, do they not?'

'Yes.'

'I can give you four pennies if you will take this package to my sister,'

'You will?'

'One moment,' Mr. Abrahams stopped what he was doing. Steam rose into the air from the pressing machine. 'How do we know you will not take the shirts and pawn them?' he said, looking at Polly.

Mrs. Abrahams glared at him. 'Husband. You and I know what it is like to be afraid and without a safe place to sleep at night.'

Polly looked at Mr. Abrahams. 'I wouldn't do that, I'm an honest person.'

Mr. Abrahams was unmoved. 'Give her a note and ask Tilda to pay her the four pennies. I will pay Tilda back tomorrow at the wedding,' he insisted.

Mrs. Abrahams sighed, chewing her cheek as she stared at her husband. 'Very well,' she said finally and wrote out the note as commanded.

'My sister *will* pay you, I promise,' she told Polly. 'The shirts are for the men of my sister's household. Our cousin is getting married tomorrow.'

'A wedding? That's nice,' said Polly. She turned to Mr. Abrahams, straightening her spine. 'I wouldn't have stolen them, sir. I'm not a thief.'

'Here, take some of these. I made them this morning.' She handed Polly a paper containing two small sweet pastries.

'Thank you' said Polly.

Polly finished her coffee and ate the two cakes which were delicious and light as angels wings as Mrs. Abrahams carefully wrote the name and address on the parcel 'It is not far,' she told Polly.

Polly read the address. 'I know where it is, she nodded. She put down her empty cup and picked up the parcel. 'Thank you for the coffee and the pastries.'

Many of these Jewish families had fled the pogroms in Russia. Many had settled in this part of Whitechapel and had brought skills with them to set up businesses. They became shoemakers or tailors like Mr. Abrahams.

Several Jewish shoemakers had set up businesses on Greenfield Street. Polly marvelled at the craftsmanship and sighed as she hankered after the beautiful shoes and boots on display in the shop windows. She was pondering the fact that she could never afford boots as fine as these when she came to the address half way along on the street. She stepped inside and her senses were immediately assailed by the wonderful smell of leather and boot polish.

Polly smiled at the pretty, kind-faced, pregnant woman who met her at the counter. She handed over the parcel and the note.

'Wait, please,' said the lady and disappeared into a room in the back of the property.

When she reappeared she was with a tall, stout man with very dark hair and brown eyes. A tape measure was draped around his neck like a scarf.

'This is my husband, Mosiek,' said Mrs. Lubnowski as she handed over four pennies.

'How do you do?' Polly nodded to him. She looked at the other woman. 'I wonder, do you have any other work I could do? I'll work hard, and I'm an honest person. I'll do anything. Anything at all.'

Mr. Lubnowski said something to his wife in their native language which Polly thought might be Polish or perhaps Russian. After a further couple of minutes of discussion, Mrs. Lubnowski sighed and then shrugged her shoulders. Polly did not need to speak their language to understand the gesture - it was common to wives everywhere and it said *Fine, do what you want.*

'Come with me, please,' said Mr. Lubnowski.

Polly followed him to the back of the house, through a door and down a flight of steps into a basement. It was cold and there was a strong, fusty smell that was probably caused by damp in the walls. The area she was being led towards was well lit by two gas lamps. Mr. Lubnowski turned them up to their fullest setting so that even the corners of the basement were filled with light.

She reached the bottom step before it occurred to her that this could be a dangerous situation. She had no path of escape. Mr. Lubnowski was between herself and the staircase. She continued along the corridor on the strength of her belief that her instincts were not screaming warnings at her.

Mr. Lubnowski directed Polly towards a door at the rear of the basement. The wall and door looked newly constructed. It was sturdy and well made, but Polly wondered why they would go to so much trouble to section off what was nothing more than a cellar.

Polly waited for Lubnowski to speak.

'Our brother is sick,' he said. Polly could hear the tension in his voice. She looked around and wondered why a sick person would be kept in such an unpleasant basement.

'Ain't it bad for him to be down here? What's wrong with him?'

'No one knows,' Lubnowski sighed. 'The sickness, it is in his head; his body is strong like an ox.'

'His head? You mean he's got some sort of growth or damage?'

'Who knows?' he shrugged regretfully. 'He saw very bad things as a child. The clearance of my people from their land was violent. The soldiers were cruel. They showed no mercy. Men, women, children, all the same, no mercy.'

'I'm so sorry. That's horrible,'

Lubnowski paused. 'We could not prevent him from seeing these things. Ever since then... He is not right.' Lubnowski pointed to the door beside her. 'He hurts himself. He does things that are very bad for him. He refuses to eat his food and yet I find him eating rubbish out of the bin.'

'He ain't the only one 'round Whitechapel who has to do that,' Polly said.

'We feed him well, he does not have to,' said Lubnowski. 'Tomorrow my wife and I are to attend a wedding. We need a person to watch over him because it is difficult when he is left alone. The neighbours have made comments. He makes noise. They are not happy.'

'What would I have to do?'

'Just persuade him to eat, if you can, and keep him safe.'

Lubnowski opened the door. The room he showed her was completely different to the rest of the basement. It was warm and lit by two paraffin lamps that were securely bolted to the wall. There was a small table and a chair, a plump sofa and a bed. It seemed to Polly that the Lubnowskis were doing their best for their troubled sibling.

In the corner, on a grubby bed, was a pathetic figure of a man. He had two days growth of stubble on his chin. His shaggy, matted hair made it difficult to judge his age. It was a muddy brown colour, though it might have been a few shades lighter if washed.

A powerful smell emanated from him. Polly recognised the odour of semen. He was curled up with his knees against his chest. He was completely focused on plucking the hair from the back of his hand. It made Polly wince as she watched him. Over and over again he plucked at it, making the flesh bleed. It must have been painful, yet he seemed oblivious to what he was doing to himself.

'Aaron? This person will care for you tomorrow,' said Lubnowski. 'You must be on your best behaviour. You must not disgrace me by your actions.'

Aaron did not react to his brother's words and kept on plucking at his hand.

Polly walked towards him. She could see there was intelligence in his eyes. He was not an imbecile, however, he was a pitiful sight. She held her breath at the stench, then after a moment or two, she concluded that he didn't smell as bad as some of her customers.

He lifted his head and looked in Polly's direction. He squinted to focus on her and then looked away, staring at the featureless wall opposite.

'If you would give him some food and keep him here.' said Lubnowski. 'That is all we want.'

Polly did not speak until they were at the top of the stairs.

'Is he always so quiet?' she asked.

'Yes. He only hurts himself, not others. He only makes a disturbance if he is alone in the house.'

Polly looked doubtful. 'Mr. Lubnowski, believe me, I need the money, but I don't think I can do this. He could be a handful for a stranger to-'

'We have had many doctors to see him. When I say he hurts himself, I do not mean he is violent. I am referring to…' he heaved a sigh then cleared his throat. He pulled a face. 'My wife insists I tell you this, I'm sorry, I find it very difficult.' He shook his head and gave a low groan as if appalled at what he must say. 'He only ever harms himself. He....' Again, Lubnowski hesitated. 'He often engages in.... personal abuse. This is how he hurts himself. You may find that you are the unfortunate witness to this.'

'I see,' said Polly. She had already guessed this by the smell of him.

'What if I gave you one shilling on account?' said Lubnowski, 'and tomorrow when we return home I will give you another.'

Polly hesitated, 'I don't know, sir. Don't you think he needs someone bigger and stronger than me to look after him?'

'I promise you he is very quiet. We will provide some food for you also.'

Polly hesitated. Mrs. Lubnowski came towards them. 'You have asked this woman to look after him?'

'Yes, I have, wife. And I have said what you insisted I say.'

'Mosiek-'

'How else are we all to attend the wedding?' he interrupted. 'We are expected, and cannot offend the Cohens. They are important to our business.'

Polly turned to Mrs. Lubnowski. 'I've seen worse, honestly.'

'He will behave himself,' said Lubnowski.

Once again the couple began to converse in their own language.

Lubnowski turned to Polly. My wife says I must give you two shillings tomorrow. Three shillings is a good wage for this work.'

'Three shillings?' Polly's jaw almost dropped. She thought about it. If playing with himself was the worst of it, she could deal with it. Heck, she *had* dealt with it and been paid a lot less. She would consider her life to be easy if all a man wanted her to do was watch.

'Yes, three shillings. On the understanding that if he does… what he does, it is impossible to stop him. If we restrain him he becomes agitated. It is easier to leave him alone. The doctors say this is what caused him to be an imbecile.'

'Did they?' Polly replied eyebrows raised.

'Will you take the job?'

Polly hesitated. 'All right,' she said, 'I'll do it for three shillings.'

Mr. Lubnowski relaxed. 'Good.'

'What time d'you want me here?'

'Please be here at eight o'clock. The wedding preparations will be taking place at my brother-in-law's house.' He handed Polly a shilling coin.

'Thank you,' she said. 'I'll see you tomorrow; eight o'clock sharp.'

Polly was feeling pleased with herself as she made her way back to Dorset Street. She had four pence for her lodgings and a shilling to spare. She would go there straight away to pay for her bed and pick out a bunk that was comfortable and in a quiet part of the dormitory.

She did not relish the prospect of spending the day looking after a malodorous man who played with himself a lot of the time. On the other hand, she truly had seen worse and had another two shillings coming her way.

The next morning she had to be out of the lodging house by seven o'clock as usual. It was cold, it was starting to rain again and it looked as if it was set in for the day. Today Polly did not care a jot. She would be in a warm kitchen all day and have some food to eat.

She arrived promptly at five to eight and the Lubnowskis left for the wedding at eight fifteen. There was some bread, some cheese and some sweet cakes on the kitchen table. There was a fresh pot of coffee on the stove. Some salted beef had been left for her on the cold shelf in the kitchen larder. The Lubnowskis had been generous.

First, she went to check on her charge. She made her way down the stone steps into the basement and very quietly opened the door to his room. He was lying on his side, asleep and buried in his blankets with his face to the wall.

She picked up two shirts that were lying on the floor, the cuffs were spotted with blood from his constant scratching and plucking at his hands. She would show some initiative and soak the sleeves in a basin of salt water to remove the stains. If they were pleased with her she might get more work. She closed the door very quietly and crept back upstairs. The longer he slept the better, by the sound of things, she decided.

Yellow flames licked around the red hot coals on the fire making the kitchen warm and cosy. She filled a second very large kettle with water and swung it on a hook over the fire to heat beside its twin. When Mr. Lubnowski awoke, she hoped she would be able to persuade him to wash and let her put some ointment on the sores on the back of his hand which she had noticed had chunks of flesh missing.

Then she took some of the bread and salted beef and poured herself a cup of coffee. She sat down at the table to eat. This was fine; it was the easiest work she had ever done.

She finished her breakfast and sat with her elbows on the table. The clock on the fireplace told her it was only ten past nine. She drummed her fingers on the table top. She looked around the room and blew out her cheeks in a long sigh.

Steam jetted from the spout as the kettle began to boil. She stood up, picked up a cloth and swung the kettle away from the fire to slow the boiling down to a gentle simmer. She turned back to the table and almost let out a scream. Lubnowski was standing in the small lobby between the kitchen and the door to the basement. He was as still as a statue and was quietly, fixedly watching her with intense dark eyes. She recovered quickly from her fright and slapped her palm to her chest.

'Goodness, you gave me a start,' she gasped, composing herself. She wondered how long he had been standing there, staring at her in that disconcerting way. 'Remember me? I'm Polly. I'm here to look after you today.' She looked at him more closely. He was wearing a long grubby shirt that left Polly in no doubt that he was naked beneath it. She studied him passively as her eyes swept the length of him. He was covered in bruises. 'You've been having a go at yourself ain't you?' she observed.

His silent stare was disturbing. She stood up, picking up a blanket that was folded on the arm of a chair. She walked slowly towards him and opened it out. His unblinking eyes followed her like a cat. 'Cover yourself with this,' she said putting the blanket around him. He was so thin he could have wrapped it around himself twice. 'Why don't you come and sit down?'

He was clean shaven today, though the razor he used must have had a dull blade as his face and neck had numerous nicks and cuts.

She guided him to one of the chairs. He did not resist. He was like a puppet with a heartbeat. 'Fancy some breakfast?' she asked in a chatty tone. 'That's nice salt beef your sister- in-law left for us.'

He sat down heavily on the chair after some pressure on his shoulders from Polly.

She poured him some coffee and put the cup on the table in front of him. He looked at it as if carefully studying the steaming brew. Still, he did not utter a word.
'I'm going to make you something to eat, all the same. If I'm looking after you, I got to earn my money don't I?'

As she prepared the food she had the chance to observe him. He was pitiful. He would not touch the coffee and shifted his stare from Polly to the wall above the fireplace.

Polly thought of the things his brother had told her. He had seen bad things as a child in his homeland. No wonder his mind had snapped. He was a poor soul affected by seeing terrible sights and experiencing fear that no child should. The personal abuse was probably *because* of his trauma, not the cause of it.

Polly cut him two slices of bread, spread them generously with butter, sandwiched several thin slices of salt beef between them and placed the plate of food in front of him.

Polly sat down at the table at right angles to him. He was staring at the wall, his eyes unfocused as if his mind was a blank slate.

She studied him, after a moment or two and decided that far from being a blank slate, his mind was working hard. There was something in his eyes that told her his head was teeming with thoughts.

'Aaron?' she said quietly. 'That's your name ain't it?' For the first time, he glanced at her. 'Try and eat something. You need feeding up a bit. You're far too skinny.'

He sat very still, so much so that she found it chilling. He moved only his eyes. He made no attempt to eat. An unspeakably foul smell emanated from him. Polly sat quietly next to him as she tried to get the measure of the situation and wondered what was going on with this man.

By the look of him he seemed to be in pain.

The agony she saw in his eyes was not just from the cuts and scratches he inflicted on himself, she decided. This pain came from his mind, and for him, it was as excruciating as anything physical a body could inflict on its owner.

'What you thinking about?' she asked him gently. 'Can you tell Polly?'

He did not reply. Then, after about ten minutes, Polly gave a start as he looked at her and spoke as if no time at all had passed.

'Your breath smells like violets,' he said.

'Er… thank you,' she replied. Several more minutes passed before he spoke again and when he did he was still answering her question.

'I hear many voices.'

She took a slow breath in. 'Right now?' She listened for several seconds. 'I can't hear anything. Are you hearing the voices now?'

'I hear them always. They give me no peace.' He closed his eyes wearily.

'Well, that's not very nice' she replied in a sympathetic tone as it dawned on her that the voices he heard were in his head. 'What do they say to you?'

He turned to her, his expression very serious. 'They say I am bad. I am evil. They tell me when I am to sleep and they scream at me to wake up. They tell me what to do every moment.'

'That doesn't sound fair. Who are they? Who do they belong to, these voices?'

For the first time, he made eye contact with her. His eyes were large and the irises as dark as black olives. His gaze was intense. 'They are the voices of departed human spirits who are in the immediate vicinity of this earth.' He replied in a whisper.

His hands tightened into fists.

'I see,' Polly blinked, feeling anything but in the know. She paused, drawing her brows together. She brushed some breadcrumbs aside and leaned forward placing her forearms on the table.
'These spirits, are they your relatives? Are they good spirits?' her eyebrows arched in curiosity. 'Do they nag you and try and make you a better person, like a conscience?'

'No.' he said shaking his head. Then he lowered his voice to a confidential whisper. 'These spirits are bad. Their evil ways prevent their ascent to the life beyond.'

'To heaven you mean? Is that paradise for Jewish people too? Well, that ain't good… They sound like the kind of spirits that ought to be minding their own business.'

He shook his head slowly and looked at her. 'Humanity lives in darkness. These souls hide in this earth plane instead of remaining in their dark realm.' He stared at her intensely. 'I have been shown all this.'

'Have you?' said Polly, not understanding what he meant. He spoke excellent English, better than his siblings, but his train of thought was difficult to follow. 'So, what else do these spirits say to you?'

He struggled to reply, he was out of touch with reality and the voices in his head were the cause. Polly understood that for him, these spirits *were* his reality and it might help if she could understand his strange world. 'Tell me what they say,' she asked.

He turned his dark eyes on her. 'They tell me the world is full of sin. That mankind is evil and I am the most evil of all.'
Polly thought about this. 'Well they ain't wrong about the world being full of sin, but they're wrong about you ain't they? You ain't evil.'

'I do my best to please them,' he said, sounding weary. 'I distract them with physical pleasure or I punish myself to make them stop.'

'I see.' Polly said again, 'Well, that explains a lot.' She leaned towards him. 'You know what? I think you should tell them to shut up and go away. Tell them you ain't going to listen no more.'

He stared at her in surprise, as if this had never occurred to him.

'Those voices have got no right to say those things to you,' said Polly. 'You know what they remind me of? There was a preacher who used to come around the workhouse and he was full of that kind of talk. Mankind was doomed, mankind was rotten and were all going to cop it one day and pay up for our sins.'

She smiled at him. 'That might be true. Who knows? And there is a lot of bad in the world that's for sure. Yet that kind of talk doesn't help, does it?' Now he was looking at her with his penetrating dark eyes, his bushy eyebrows drawn together in confusion. 'What I mean is, it makes things worse.' Polly cut his sandwich into smaller pieces in the hope it would encourage him to eat some of it. 'That old preacher in the workhouse thought he was doing the right thing, putting us all right. Telling us straight what we were doing wrong. The thing is, it doesn't help anyone and sometimes it has the opposite effect.'

She could see that she had piqued his interest and her instincts told her to keep talking. She nudged the plate of food towards him. 'In the end, the people said: You want rotten? We'll show you rotten. He made them feel so bad, they considered they had nothing to lose, so they turned to crime and violence. You see, he was doing more harm than good because he frightened the people and taking away their hope of better things to come. It doesn't work like that. Even if you frighten them into doing what you want, they aren't doing it out of goodness and so it does harm in the long run. They do what they're told because they're afraid of going to hell, but that doesn't save their souls does it? And besides, when you think about it, who was he to say the people were bad? He didn't know what was in their heads. His job was to make them feel better not condemn folks to hell on his own authority.'

'I do not understand,' he said.

Polly guessed as much, nevertheless, he appeared to be opening up. She had no idea what he was making of her chatter, but he seemed to be listening, so she kept talking.

'Take the workhouses… In the beginning, they were put up to take in the people who were destitute and had nowhere else to go. That's a good thing, right? Unfortunately, they were built by people who thought they had to do good deeds if they wanted to go to heaven, not out of compassion for the poor. Problem is they treat the people who have to go in them very badly. They seem more afraid of giving the poor something for nothing than they are of going to hell. It's so awful in those places that most folks would rather be on the street than stay there. They separate man and wife because God forbid they should make even more hungry mouths to feed. You might think that's fair enough, but why separate mother and child as well? There ain't no excuse for that.' Polly continued. 'They talk all the time about the poor being wicked - just like your voices tell you. They tell them they're worth nothing and they're bad just because they're poor. *It's to save their souls*, so they claim, that they work them like dogs. It's not about the money they make out of them, oh no, it's not that. No, no, toiling from dawn 'til dusk on the poorest rations you could imagine is for their salvation. The fat profits they make out of it is neither here nor there. They set them to work on horrible jobs like unpicking old rope. D'you know what that's like? It's like having lots of little needles pricking the ends of your fingers all the time and it makes them bleed. If they're not doing that, they have them cleaning unspeakable filth off things. They make them pray all the time and tell them they got to repent their sins. They don't show a morsel of kindness, not even to the smallest child. Their lives are more wretched than before and without their families it feels ten times worse. All the while these so called good people are telling them they're bad – just like your voices tell you. So, what happens? The people start to think they are bad when they're not – and neither are you. If those voices are telling you bad things, you tell them to shut up and leave you alone because you are *not* bad.'

She could see that her voice was having a calming effect on him. The frown lines between his eyebrows had relaxed, though his piercing eyes still regarded her.

'I am afraid to talk to them,' he whispered. 'If I do, they will know that I can, I do not want that.'

Polly nodded sagely. 'Hmm. I see your problem,' she replied, also in a whisper. She made a big play of apparently pondering the problem. 'Well then, how about you completely ignore them? Just pretend they are on the other side of a brick wall and they can hammer and shout all they like and you still can't hear them. They've got no right to talk to you and they've definitely got no right to tell you

you're bad. Who do they think they are? They ain't of any consequence so you ignore them.'

He looked at Polly as if this was a revelation to him.

Polly smiled. 'Eat a little breakfast eh?' she said. 'If you eat some, I'll read to you.'

'They put poison my food,' he whispered.

'This ain't got no poison in it. I made it for you myself and it's never left my sight. Look?' she picked up a piece of the sandwich and ate it. 'I'll be your official taster like Kings and Queens have. See?' she said. 'There's some Charles Dickens over there on the shelf. He wrote some cracking stories.' A strange expression crossed his face. 'You're listening to them again aren't you? You ignore them, Aaron.' His body tensed and she could see he was struggling. 'Tell me what they saying to you.'

'That you are an evil woman,' he said in a low voice.

'I'm not evil. I'm your friend.' Polly replied, doing her best to cover her uneasiness at the remark. He closed his eyes as if wrestling with his thoughts.

'We're friends aren't we?' she prompted.

He didn't reply but picked up a piece of the sandwich and put it in his mouth.

'That's the ticket. I'll get you some hot coffee to go with it.' she said standing up.

He finished the sandwich and the coffee. 'That's good. You need some nourishment inside you. Do you the world of good that will.'

'You will read to me now?' he said. He sounded so like a little boy that her heart warmed to him.

'Yes, I will, but first, you need to have a good wash.'

'Why?'

'Because you stink.'

He looked up at her in surprise. 'I do?'

'Not half. You're like sweaty cheese on a hot day.' she said, smiling at his bemused expression. 'Tell you what. I'll get that tin bath out of the lobby and put it in front of the fire. I already got the big kettle hot and there's some nice *Pears* soap under the sink. I'll read to you while you have a nice long soak. How's that?' She filled the bath with two buckets of cold water then added boiling water from the big kettle. She filled the kettle again and set it on the fire to boil. 'Right then, take off your shirt and in you get.'

When he hesitated, Polly smiled. 'It's too late for modesty. You ain't wearing no draws. I already seen what the stork brought.'

When he took off his shirt she saw a deep scratch that ran diagonally from the side of his neck to the top of his breast bone.

'That looks sore,' Polly tutted as he eased himself into the water. 'You got to stop listening when those voices tell you to hurt yourself. Look at your hand, you've made it bleed now.'

He was so thin, Polly could see his ribs and the chain of bony protuberances down the length of his spine. He was also wiry and Polly knew she should not underestimate his strength.

Once he was in the bath, he seemed to enjoy the sensation and began sluicing himself with water. He poured the water over his head and Polly gave him the bar of *Pears* soap to wash with.

She found an enamel jug, filled it with warm water and gave it to him to rinse himself. She warmed up the bath with hot water from the kettle then took *Hard Times* by Charles Dickens from the shelf and sat down in the armchair next to the fireplace.

'Right then. Let's see what you make of Mr. Gradgrind. He could easily become the voice in someone's head, the old goat.'

He listened avidly as he soaked in the bath. Polly read for almost two hours, stopping to scoop out the very dirty water from the bath and adding more hot water from the kettle. She could see he was enjoying getting himself clean. She read to him for another hour.

'You're going to have to come out soon or you'll turn into a prune,' she smiled. 'Where are your clean clothes? I couldn't find any in your room.'

She found some clean long-johns, socks and some towels in a cupboard in the other room. 'If these are your brother's clothes it's just too bad.' She helped him out of the bath and wrapped him in the towels.

'Sit there while you dry off,' she said pulling out a chair. She emptied the bath using a bucket. There was a film of scum and dirt all across its surface.

'Look at all this muck that's come off you,' she said as she poured the last of it down the sink. She wiped the bath dry with a towel. 'There, that's better.' She put the bath back in the lobby and then looked at him and picked up the long-johns. 'This will keep you nice and warm,' she said as she helped him put on the all in one undergarment and then the socks. Next, she found some clean black woollen trousers and Aaron obediently put them on.

'My word you look like a different fella now. You're so handsome.'

'Please. Read more now?'

'All right. Will you eat something if I read?' She put a few lumps of coal on the fire.

She made him a plate of bread, cheese and salted beef. 'There, you sit and eat that and I'll read to you.' She sat down and picked up the book. 'That Mr. Gradgrind don't half remind me of your spirit voices. He thinks he's right about everything and folk have got to do what he says. Someone should have told him to shut up, shouldn't they?' she gave a little laugh.

Polly kept reading. She sensed that it was giving him relief from the turmoil in his head. She was well into the spirit of the story, entertaining him by doing different voices for the different characters. She was glad to give her own voice a rest when he fell asleep on the couch by the window.

She ate some bread, cheese and some salt beef, then lubricated her dry throat with more coffee. She looked at the poor tormented man. When he was asleep he looked like any other man. No one would guess how troubled he was.

She hoped Mr. and Mrs. Lubnowski would be pleased that he was clean and fed. If so, she might get regular work when they needed help. While he slept she found a cupboard that was stacked with perfectly laundered bedding.

The Lubnowskis must be doing well, she thought. The sheets had the mark of a commercial laundry on them and they were snowy white and perfectly ironed.

Guessing that his bed sheets would be as smelly as he was, she went down to his room in the basement and stripped the bed. She was right, his sheets were stained with blood and an assortment of disgusting things.

She made the bed up with fresh linen and left the room neat and tidy. She hoped that Mr. and Mrs. Lubnowski would notice her efforts. She had done her best to earn her three shillings. She took the two shirts whose sleeves had been soaking in the salt water and added them to the dirty sheets in a bundle next to the door and went back upstairs. He was still sleeping. She read more of Hard Times for the pleasure of it.

Suddenly, a scream split the silence. Startled, Polly jumped to her feet; her first instinct was to run from the room. Aaron lay on his back, screaming. He was clawing and punching the air, kicking as if he was fighting off an invisible attacker. He gave out a loud, high-pitched howl. It was pitiful, he sounded like a wounded animal. He breathed like a rampaging bull. He snorted, his nostrils flaring. Polly stared at the sight; she had no idea what to do.

Her mind raced. In the workhouse, when someone had a paroxysm, two of the biggest, strongest assistants dragged them off to be submerged in an ice-cold bath. Perhaps she had caused this by allowing him to have an extra-long hot bath? Afraid that she had created this frenzy and caused his nightmare, she moved cautiously around the kitchen table. Mr. Lubnowski had told her that it was important to keep him in the house. She made sure she had a clear run to the door if she needed to escape and would be able to lock him in if he turned violent.

It was painful to watch him writhe in what looked like terrible agony.

'It's alright!' she shouted at him from a few feet away. 'Listen to me, it's alright! Listen to Polly. It's alright. You're dreaming. Wake up!' She took a step closer to him. 'Aaron! Wake up. You're safe. Polly's here.' He clutched at his head. He seemed to be coming out of whatever seizure had possessed him. He rocked himself back and forth, grunting and breathing through his teeth. Despite being scared, she moved closer and saw that he was shaking. Sweat stood out on his brow. She quickly rinsed a cloth and moved to his side. She mopped the sweat from his face and used the cloth as a cold compress for his head. Finally, after several minutes, he settled down.

Polly, her own heart racing, stayed beside him for a long time, until she was sure he was over it - whatever it was. 'That was quite a nightmare,' she said watching him carefully.

He looked as if he was still in pain. He did not answer. Instead, he whimpered and curled into a ball. Polly again thought about what Mr. Lubnowski said he had seen as a child. She dropped the cloth on the table and sat down on the couch beside him. She placed her hand on his shoulder. He flinched but did not shake her off. 'It's alright.' she soothed. 'You're safe here. You're away from those terrible soldiers. You put that dream out of your mind.'

'Read. Please,' he asked, his voice cracking.

'Course I will.' Polly said picking up the book.

'My God. I cannot believe it.' said Lubnowski. 'He is clean and he is calm.'

'He's had a bath and we've been reading,' said Polly. Matilda Lubnowski was smiling. 'I am astonished at the change in him.'

'He hasn't eaten much. He's had a couple of sandwiches and some coffee. He likes to be read to. We've been reading Hard Times by Charles Dickens.' Polly indicated the book in her hand. 'We've read over half of it. Your brother seems to like Dickens.'

'Those books? They were in the cellar when we came here,' said Lubnowski.

'Well, that was most fortuitous because Aaron is quite partial to them.'

'Perhaps you should go downstairs now, Aaron?' said Lubnowski as the children came into the room. Two adorable little girls, one no older than seven the other no older than five, wore pretty green velvet dresses each with a flowery and very beautiful Belgian lace collar and a big bow at the back. A boy of around nine wore a suit like his father's and was holding the hands of a toddler who was just learning to walk.

'You have a beautiful family,' Polly smiled.

The boy and both girls looked at their uncle warily. It was obvious to Polly that they were afraid of him. She stepped forward.

'Here's the book, Aaron. It was very nice meeting you I'm sorry we didn't finish the story.' Aaron moved meekly away. 'Can he read English? I mean I know he understands talk but reading it off the page is another matter.' Polly said.

'Possibly not.' Lubnowski shrugged.

'Well, there are some pictures, perhaps he can look at those,' said Polly.

'Come, Aaron,' Lubnowski guided him towards the door of the basement and escorted him downstairs. Polly knew that he was getting Aaron away from the children.

'Was everything alright?' asked Mrs. Lubnowski.

'He was a good as gold,' said Polly. 'Listen, Ma'am, I know this is not my place, but he says he hears voices. They tell him all sorts of bad things. If he's down there in the basement all the time he ain't got nothing to do except listen to them.'

'He is not always in the basement. He spends time with our family. And on good days, he goes out.'

'That's good because he will not have many good days if he's listening to bad things in his head all the time. He was great when I was reading to him. It distracted him better than.... the usual way he distracts himself. If you want I'll come and read to him anytime.'

'I will ask my husband.'

Lubnowski came from the basement a moment later. 'His bed is clean and his room has been made good.'

'I had a bit of time to spare when he fell asleep.' Polly explained.

'We are very grateful for your efforts. Here are your two shillings,' said Lubnowski.

'Thank you, I'd better get going or they might give my bed away.'

Polly stepped out onto the dark street. It was only nine o'clock yet she was uneasy. She hurried along Greenfield Street walking close to the road. She was afraid, like all the other women in Whitechapel, of the dark recesses and alleyways. The Whitechapel killer could be lurking in any of them. She turned left onto Fieldgate Street and saw the glow from the bell foundry.
She could feel the heat coming off the bricks.

She rounded the corner onto Whitechapel Road. Normally, she would take the back streets to avoid the gangs. Tonight, after Lizzie's dire warnings, she was just as worried about coming face to face with the killer.

Alf Cruikshank had called him a maniac. The way Polly Nichols and Annie Chapman had been killed made it seem so. She was thankful to have made some money without having to take a stranger down a dark alley. The street was well lit and there were still people about who were moving from pub to pub. She was relieved when she finally reached Dorset Street.
She hid her money deep inside her bodice and then went inside Crossingham's lodging house. She lay down gratefully on her bunk. It had been an exhausting day but a good one. Her stomach was full and she had three shillings all her own. She rolled onto her side and fell asleep.

# CHAPTER TEN

'Millie, what the hell did you do that for? He's one of my best customers.' Suzette followed Millie into *The Queen's Head*, demanding an answer.

Millie looked at her, an apologetic smile on her face. 'Sorry Suze. I thought he had a knife. I was sure I saw something shiny.'

'It was just the buttons on his sleeve.' Suzette replied, folding her arms.

'Oh...' Millie gave a nod of comprehension. 'Never mind. Better safe than sorry eh?' she dropped the ten-inch length of solid lead, with which she had just bludgeoned Suzette's client, on the table with a loud thud.

Suzette put her hands on her hips. 'Can't you tell the difference, Millie? Cos if not, we've got a problem. You can't keep knocking the punters out. It ain't good for business. What am I supposed to do with him now? He's lying unconscious in the alley.' She jerked a thumb back towards the door.

'Don't worry about it, Suze.' Millie dismissed the problem with a flick of her wrist. 'He won't remember what happened. Let's go and get him. We can prop him up on a seat in the corner over there. When he wakes up with a headache, he'll think it's a hangover.'

'How are the two of us gonna get him in here?' Suzette demanded. 'He must weigh two hundred pounds... Honestly, Millie. I think you like whacking men over the head with that lead pipe.'

The two women walked off, still arguing about how to get Suzette's unfortunate customer back inside the pub.

'How about a wheelbarrow?' suggested Millie.

'You got a wheelbarrow on your person, have you?' They heard Suzette reply as the women moved out of earshot.

Polly laughed. 'That's the third time this week.'

'Millie is right. Better safe than sorry.' said Lizzie.

Having little faith in the police to protect them, the girls had taken matters into their own hands. They were now usually seen on the streets in pairs. They looked after each other because no one else would - each becoming a parody of a chaperon.

Suzette had acquired some lengths of solid lead from the men building the bridge. These cudgels were passed around the girls and carried by the chaperon. Their purpose was to cave in the skull of a client if there was any sign of a knife.

The atmosphere was tense and the women were nervous. Because of this, they had been used a few times in error, especially by Millie. Fortunately, not with sufficient force to kill the recipient, but unfortunately with enough force to knock him senseless.

The fear of being mistaken for The Ripper was keeping the punters away. Vigilantes roamed the streets, roughing up any man they considered suspicious. There had been dozens of attacks on innocent men and business was slow.

Chaperoning her friends forced Polly to face the sordid world from which she longed to escape. She traipsed the streets for hours each day, looking for work. This gave her too much time to think about how dangerous her life had become and what she must face each day to survive.

Polly also worried about Lizzie. It had not yet sunk into the dim, alcohol pickled brain of Mickey Kidney that Lizzie was done with him. Mickey was under the impression that he had the right to control Lizzie's movements. He had not got the message that it was over, even though it was nearly three weeks since she had moved out of Devonshire Street.

Mickey's dockside mates were everywhere. They made no secret of it to Lizzie that they reported back to him about everything she did.

When Polly recognised two of Mickey's mates in *The Queen's Head*, she insisted they move to the Northumberland Arms further along the street. She was uneasy. In her opinion, Lizzie was no longer taking the threat seriously enough. She suspected this was down to Lizzie's reckless streak. There was a wild side to her character that could lead to impulsive acts. Most of the time she had this demon under control; occasionally, impetuosity won.

Polly worried that a tiny reckless part of Lizzie was flattered that Mickey wanted her back and she was using his mates to make sure he heard that she was out having a good time. She was pretty sure that Lizzie would never go back to Mickey but it worried Polly that Lizzie considered it good sport to tease him.

Polly was relieved when Pastor Sven found Lizzie a night sitting job caring for an elderly Swedish gentleman who was near death. Someone who could speak his native language was needed and Lizzie was glad to have the chance to speak Swedish.

She was to meet Pastor Sven at eleven o'clock at the corner of Fashion Street and Brick Lane. He would take her to the address and introduce Lizzie to the gentleman, his wife and sons. Polly was relieved. Lizzie would be safe and out of Mickey's reach for the entire night.

The twelfth of September was yet another rainy night in the wettest year on record. The soldiers, who provided the girls with plenty of free gin and a good income, were now on their way to South Africa. There were always sailors looking for women but there was a new rumour that the killer was a sailor, meaning Polly was much more wary of them these days.

She still had half the money she had earned when she looked after Aaron and had no inclination to look for customers. She and Lizzie stayed in the pub until it was time for her to meet the pastor. Once Lizzie was safely in the company of Pastor Sven, Polly made her way back to the lodging house.

As she hurried along Fashion Street, a sense of apprehension crept over her. She tried to dismiss it; Whitechapel was a jittery place and everyone was feeling the tension. It took strong nerves not to get carried away with anxiety over the murders.

Polly glanced over her shoulder and saw no one behind her. There was a potato vendor across the street and two people were talking outside the Northumberland Arms. It was a perfectly normal scene, yet she had the same sensation in her gut as the one she had felt at Wood's Buildings. She shivered, feeling as if icy water was dripping down the back of her neck. Something was pricking her sixth sense.

It was a moonless night and the gas lamps, as usual, were of little use in penetrating the darkness. She kept moving, the thudding of her heart sounding loud in her ears. She glanced over her shoulder again. There was still no one around. She tried to dismiss the feeling. After all, this was an open street, not a deserted alley, yet the sense of dread would not be quelled. She quickened her step and did not bother to dodge the puddles that had formed on the uneven paving stones. She ploughed forward, feeling the need to reach her lodgings as quickly as possible.

Through the corner of her eye, she caught a glimpse of the shadowy depths of Harriot Place - a small blind ended lane between numbers 55 and 56 Fashion Street. She shuddered and kept on walking.

There's no one in the alley, she told herself. Most women talked of the same feelings of apprehension and unease.
Suddenly, a hand grasped her shoulder. She gave a shriek and turned around, her heart leaping into her mouth.

'Aaron?' she squeaked. 'Flaming heck, I just jumped out of my skin.' She put her hand to her chest and took a couple of deep breaths to recover. 'What you doing here?'
She took a good look at him and saw he was soaking wet. His face was impassive but he looked at her with eyes that as ever, gave away his pitiful inner torment. He stared at her for what seemed like a long time. He did not seem to understand that he had just given her the fright of her life. Polly tutted. 'Aw... Look at you. You're soaked.'
He seemed oblivious to the fact. Then quite childlike, he pulled the copy of *Hard Times* out of his pocket.

'Polly? You read to me?'

'Oh, Aaron. It's very late.'

Aaron pushed the book towards her. 'You read?'

'I told your brother I would come and read. I know you want to know what happens at the end of the book, but you shouldn't come out looking for me at this time of night.' She scanned the street left and right. 'Don't you know there are gangs 'round here that would hoist you from the nearest lamp post just because you're Jewish? Come on. I'll take you home.' She took hold of his arm at the elbow. 'This way.' She turned him around 'We'll go along Brick Lane. That way you might not get beaten up. You have to stay away well away from here and Dorset Street over the other side. They would lynch you soon as look at you. D'you understand?' She walked him back in the direction from which she had just come. 'You're really wet. You been out all day?' she tutted in disapproval. 'They really should keep a closer eye on you.'

They turned onto Brick Lane and headed south towards Whitechapel High Street. Greenfield Street was not far. As they reached number sixteen Polly saw that all the lights were out and the household appeared to be in bed. She frowned. Surely they must know Aaron was not home? Weren't they concerned that he was wandering the streets? Angry at their neglect, she began to pound on the door.

After a few minutes, Mosiek Lubnowski opened the door. Matilda was standing behind him, a paraffin lamp in her hand.

'Miss Wilkes?'

'Look who I got here,' said Polly.

Tight-lipped, Mr. Lubnowski stood aside and Polly pressed her fingertips to Aaron's back to nudge him into the house. 'He's completely soaked to the skin.' she said 'I found him on Fashion Street or rather he found me.'

The couple passed each other a look and Polly hoped they were feeling guilty.

'He should really have a mustard bath… I suppose at this time of night, some dry clothes will have to do. He came looking for me to read to him. He wants to know how the story ends.' The Lubnowskis looked on in silence. Polly's brow puckered. 'Mrs. Lubnowski, Aaron needs something to dry himself with and some dry clothes.'

Matilda Lubnowski put the paraffin lamp on the table and went to find a towel.

'Come on Aaron, take your jacket off,' said Polly, pulling it from his shoulders.

'You will you read now, Polly?' he replied.

'You need to get dry and go to sleep now, Aaron. I could come back tomorrow and read to you if you like?'

'That will not be necessary,' said Lubnowski stepping forward. Matilda returned with a towel and a nightshirt.

'He likes me to read to him, sir. I don't want any money. I'll do it for nothing.'

'It will not be convenient,' he replied. 'Please do not let us detain you further.'

'Would it do any harm?' said Polly.

'Thank you for your time,' he said.

She was being shepherded towards the door. Polly stood her ground and turned to Matilda. 'He needs more than he's getting. If it calms him when I read and distracts him from the things in his head, where's the harm in it?'

Lubnowski opened the door. 'Goodnight,' he nodded.

Polly glowered at him and then looked at Aaron.

'Goodnight Aaron. Remember what I said. Stay away from all them streets beside Spitalfields market. The gangs around there would string you up - if the police don't find you first and put you in the cells. Alright? You behave yourself and maybe your brother will let me come and read to you. I'll see you soon.'

'Go downstairs to your room, Aaron.' said Lubnowski, dismissing him rather too abruptly for Polly's liking.

She turned to the couple. There were things that had to be said.

'Look, you might think I'm speaking out of turn but this is not on. There are things he don't understand because he ain't got the capacity. He can't be left to wander like this. He could come to all sorts of harm.'

It dawned on Polly that perhaps the Lubnowskis knew Aaron was out of the house. It could be that getting him picked up was their intention. Perhaps they saw it as a way of ridding themselves of their burden.

Matilda Lubnowski was pregnant and the couple also had young children. It couldn't be easy to have Aaron in the house. Though looking after Aaron day in, day out must be a terrible trial, this was a cruel way of dealing with the problem. She could see that Lubnowski was far from happy to see him. She had not exactly been thrown out, but she had been shown the door.

Once again Polly was hurrying along a deserted street late at night. Anyone would think she was determined to run into the Whitechapel killer. She quickened her pace.

She was soaked by the time she reached Crossingham's and had to dry off before going to bed. She dozed on one of the angular wooden chairs in the lodging house kitchen in front of the fire; steam rising from her damp clothes.

She was safe, she had money in her pocket, and a bed for the night.

# CHAPTER ELEVEN

The 29th of September was a warm, dry day at last. Polly sat down to rest for a moment on a low wall behind a coffee shop on Whitechapel High Street.

She had traipsed the length and breadth of Whitechapel and Spitalfields all morning. Her feet throbbed. She had hoped for work in the coffee shop perhaps washing dishes or cleaning. As usual, she had been turned away with hardly a glance by the owner.

She lifted her face to the sun and closed her eyes. She savoured the golden rays that only rarely managed to peep through the built-up landscape.

She sighed. The weather would soon become much colder and damp as winter closed in. The biting wind would blast through the narrow streets. There were few places to find shelter. The narrow alleys seemed to whip the winter winds into an eddying frenzy. She had barely made it through her first winter in Whitechapel. Once Auntie May's money ran out, if it had not been for Lizzie, Polly was sure she would have fallen prey to a gang or been found frozen in some filthy alleyway, trying to keep warm beneath a wet canvas or potato sack.

Perhaps she could spend the winter in the workhouse? She dismissed the idea immediately. The exhausting toil they expected bordered on inhuman and some of the overseers were less than the good Christians they were supposed to be. Looking at some of them the wrong way could result in callous punishment. Young girls and women like Polly were often used as unpaid whores. She would rather throw herself in the Thames than enter that terrible place again. This left her with two choices. – find work or try to be a more successful dollymop.

Her dress and shawl were threadbare and had holes in them. Her boots were worn out and fastened with string. It was no wonder she could not get regular work.

Prostitution was the one profession where there was always plenty of work. On a good night, her sister dollies could manage a dozen clients or more. At sixpence each, six shillings was good pay for a night's work. That amount would be more than enough to see her through the week. It sounded simple so why was she unable to do the same? She was desperate, so why would she turn away from a reliable way of earning some money?

It was not so much about the clients, who were lust filled and completely indifferent to her. It was her own demons that gnawed at her. The other women had found a way to cope. They could shrug their shoulders and distance themselves from the deed.

Suzette had tried to teach her.

*I told you. You got to treat it like it's business. Keep your feelings out of it.*

She told Polly she should touch the punter, unbutton his pants, flaunt herself, use what Mother Nature gave her.

*It's what you gotta do, Pol. It's business and you're selling them a service. So flash your bubbies at 'em, show a bit of leg, then a bit of thigh... You know the kind of thing I'm talking about. Do everything you can to get them excited.*

Polly's eyes had grown wider and wider the more Suzette had talked. *It gets them done quicker so it's better for you,'* she said.

Polly had been appalled and repelled by the advice before Suzette had finished speaking. If that was what the other girls were doing then her last punter was right, he had not got his money's worth.

*Listen. If you can't stand it with men, there are always ladies who like girls.* Suzette had suggested after reading Polly's horrified expression. *You know your way around a woman's body, don't you? That might be better for you... I can show you the places they go to get girls.*

*WHAT?* Polly's jaw had dropped so far it almost dislocated. *Women? Wanting other women? Was Suzette having a laugh?*

There had been whispers, sniggers and rumours about some of their teachers at school. Polly had been sceptical, believing it to be the imaginings of overheated school girls.

*A lot of them are married and got rich husbands,* Suzette had continued, *and it ain't even a crime. It's only illegal for a man to go with a man, not a woman to go with a woman.* She then casually explained how to go about satisfying a woman. *You're young and pretty. That's what they want.*

Polly was aghast. Then, on reflection, it did not sound any worse having to satisfy a man and there would be no risk of pregnancy. *Could she do it? Probably... and it might be easier than trying to satisfy a man.*

The things Sergeant Alfie said to her started to prey on her mind. She straightened her spine. It was all very well him saying those things, but she had to face reality. She was alone and had to fend for herself. No point in harking back to what she used to be - that was then and this was now.

Her dollymop sisters long since told her to pick one night and take as many clients as she could. They said that compared to taking a client most nights, it lowered the chances of falling pregnant, while her sponge gave her some protection against diseases. *It's even safer if you've got Eve's curse. The sponge will stop the blood and the punter will never know the difference.*

Polly heaved a sigh and knew their advice made sense. She had never managed more than one customer per night. Six shillings a night was a princely sum. The men on the docks earned a single shilling for a night's work. On the other hand, a dolly risked filthy diseases, violence, gangs and childbirth.

She wriggled her toes inside her boots. These had been her favourite pair in her former life. They were not intended for walking miles and miles of pavement. The kitten heels were now half their former height. The soles were worn into holes beneath the balls of her feet. She had lined the boots with newspaper but still they let in water. Newspaper turned into papier-mâché once wet. The mushy mess squeezed between her toes and set like concrete as it dried.

The pain from the blister on her heel told her the skin had rubbed away again and it was probably bleeding. She had already been to the casual ward at the infirmary for some salve and a bandage which had not helped much.

Someone knocked on the rear window of the coffee shop. Polly turned her head and saw the owner glowering at her. He gave an upward flick of his index finger. He didn't want her type hanging around his property. She stood up and limped wearily along the alley towards the main street.

If she had a shilling, she could buy a pair of comfortable boots off the stall on the market. If she had two shillings, she could buy a jacket and a hat from the same stall. A jacket would look a lot more respectable than her tattered old shawl. If she could earn three shillings, she could have a bed in a lodging house, get warm and have something to eat. If she made a regular income, she might rent her own room like Suzette.

She knew what she had to do if she wanted that kind of money. She made up her mind. This time, she would take as many clients as she could, make some money and buy the things she needed. She would even ask Suzette about where to find ladies. She was not doing this for her own pleasure, her own feelings had shut down a long time ago, so why should it matter? It was business and she desperately needed money.

Lizzie came hurrying towards her as she emerged onto Whitechapel High Street. 'Polly, thank goodness, I've been looking for you for an hour.'

'What's up?'

'Betty Tanner will give us work cleaning the dormitories.'

'Both of us?'

'Yes. Some labourers off the new bridge were in last night and there's a lot to do.'

'Are the labourers still there?'

'No. Betty threw them out. She'll pay us sixpence each and let us use the washroom.'

'Oh, that's a life saver.' Polly replied. 'Wait a minute. Ain't you staying away from Flower and Dean Street on account of Mickey finding you there the other week?'

'I think it's fine now. I haven't seen him since.'

'Well let's hope so. Maybe it's finally sunk into that thick skull of his. Looks like standing up to him done the trick eh?'

'Perhaps.' Lizzie replied. 'Never mind him. My heart was in my mouth when I couldn't find you.'

'I'm always around here somewhere,' she said. 'I've been calling at every shop to see if I could get any work - there's nothing.'

'You shouldn't go down back alleyways, there's a killer about. I worry you'll be found in some dark place with your throat cut.'

'He only comes out at night. You worry too much. Anyway, there ain't been a murder for a month. He's gone, Lizzie. I, on the other hand, am like a bad penny, I always turn up.' she grinned. 'Right then, let's get along to Flower and Dean Street.'

They walked arm in arm as they always did. They headed west on the high street taking a short cut through a long narrow alley known as George Yard.

'That's where Martha Tabram got done in, back at the beginning of August.' Polly murmured. They each glanced into the stairwell of George Yard Buildings.

'Now they saying Martha was a victim of the Whitechapel killer,' said Lizzie.

'So I heard,' said Polly. 'Stabbed like a pin cushion, thirty-nine times.

'Poor Martha, they said it was the 39th stab wound that killed her as it went through her heart,' said Lizzie.

'I prefer to think the first one cut something vital and she went quickly,' Polly shivered. 'They think it was a soldier that killed Martha. To be honest, some of those lads don't look quite right. It's in the eyes. They've seen too much out there in Africa.'

'The Whitechapel killer is a soldier?'

'That's what I heard.'

'A soldier, a sailor, a doctor, a butcher, a man with a leather apron, they have no idea.' Lizzie huffed. 'We have to protect ourselves and poor Martha made one fatal mistake.'

'She took him to a place with only one entrance.' said Polly. 'One mistake and she paid with her life, God rest her soul.'

Lizzie nodded. It was a golden rule for dollymops – always choose a place with more than one exit. That way, the customer couldn't get between you and an escape route if things took a nasty turn. When Martha's killer pulled a knife, she was trapped.

They emerged from the alley, crossed Wentworth Street and headed along George Street, at the top of which was Flower and Dean Street. They arrived at number 32 and immediately set to with the cleaning. If they cracked on with the work, they would be able to pay for their lodgings early. This meant they could get the pick of the beds with the best mattresses in the smaller dormitory where the nightmares of boozed up drunks, the hacking coughs of the sick and grunts of those set on satisfying their base instincts did not disturb a good night's sleep.

'It is so nice when we work together.' Lizzie smiled. 'We laugh and the time goes so quickly.' She poured the last bucket of filthy water down the drain in the scullery, then turned on the tap to blast away any remaining scum from the bottom of the bucket. Polly began to rinse the washcloths and scrubbing brushes in the sink.

'You're right there. We can always find something to laugh about can't we?'

'Just think how good it will be when we have our tea room.' Lizzie smiled.

'I'll be great.' Polly replied. 'We'll be laughing every day won't we?' She put the wet cleaning rags on the hot water pipe to dry, then dropped the brushes into the empty bucket. 'Right,' she sighed, 'that's that.' She dried her hands on her skirt. 'Now we can have a nice wash; there's still plenty of hot water.'

'And, I still have some lavender soap,' said Lizzie.

'Ooh, what a treat. That'll get the smell of this place off us. Come on then. I'll wash your hair for you. Your fair hair don't half suffer in the smoggy air.'

The best thing about cleaning a lodging house was being able to use the washrooms before the hordes of inmates drifted in for the night. The building was empty during the day and there was always endless amounts of hot water from the coal-fired boiler. Lizzie had taught Polly how to use steam to clean her clothes, rather than water so they didn't become soaked and take hours to dry. Lizzie also steamed herself clean. Polly had been incongruous when Lizzie insisted it was the Swedish way. Polly watched her make a tent around a section of the hot pipes using a washing line, some sheets and some clothes pegs. She placed wet towels on the scalding water pipes so that steam filled the small bivouac.

Lizzie would sit inside completely naked. Her long curly yellow hair bushing out around her shoulders. She would chat away to Polly, stark naked yet completely comfortable with her bare beam. Polly had been nothing short of stunned the first time she saw Lizzie do this.

'Don't be so bashful, Polly. When you sweat you clean the inside as well as the outside,' Lizzie had told her. 'It's very healthy and steam cleans your skin better than water.'

Polly had choked at the word "sweat". 'Pigs sweat, ladies glow,' she had replied.

'Nonsense.' Lizzie snorted. 'Of *course* ladies sweat. It's good for you. Besides, pigs and people have similar skin. Have you ever touched the skin of a pig? A living one, not in a butcher's shop.'

'Of course not,' Polly said with mock hauteur. 'I was brought up a proper young lady, you know.'

'Well, Miss La-de-da, I was raised on a farm. The skin of a pig is similar to ours. They burn in the sun like us. They also sweat. Therefore, if pigs sweat, so do ladies. This is a fact, so no more English nonsense. Get in here and enjoy the steam.' Lizzie was so serious when it came to her sauna bath as she called it. 'Cleaning the inside and the out is a good thing, don't you agree?'

'It does feel wonderful,' said Polly.

'You must stay in the steam until you are the colour of the Echinacea flower.'

'I've never heard of the Echinacea flower, I wouldn't know what one looked like.'

Lizzie held out an arm. 'This colour,' she said.

'Lobster coloured, you mean?' She giggled when Lizzie muttered something in Swedish under her breath, then shrieked when Lizzie ambushed her by pouring a bucket of freezing cold water over her. Polly refused to believe it was the final part of the process until Lizzie did the same thing to herself and then washed herself down with cold water.

'The douche of cold water invigorates,' she explained. 'It also helps to keep the girls nice and firm,' she said, looking down at her breasts. 'Yours are good. They are an asset. You should take care of them and keep them firm.' Lizzie never got embarrassed, she would talk about anything. Polly had lost her shyness these days and was content to sit stark naked in Lizzie's bivouac and talk about breasts.

The final treat was to wash their hair using a little of the precious lavender oil soap. Then, wrapped in sheets, they would sit next to the boiler to dry their hair. It was their tiny oasis of luxury in the middle of all the filth and poverty they endured each day.

Polly looked at Lizzie 'Your hair has gone wild. You look like Lady Macbeth.'

'Who?'

'Don't they do Shakespeare in Swedish schools?'

'Perhaps,' she shrugged. 'I didn't pay attention. School was tedious and I was needed on our farm.'

'C'mere, Give me your brush…' Lizzie's hair, which was very fine and curly, became a pale yellow frizz after washing. 'We got to tame this mop of yours somehow.'

Lizzie sat down on a small step stool as Polly teased out the knots and tousled curls.

'You're getting some silver in here, girl,' said Polly.

'Oh thank you for pointing that out.'

'Actually, it looks nice, it makes you look fairer rather than older. Unlike the gunmetal grey I'll have one day.'

'You have a pretty face that will make up for it. We'll be two old ladies together in our teashop, still attracting the gentlemen.'

'Wouldn't you like to call it a day by then? Settle down with someone nice?' Polly asked.

'Perhaps, if I find the right gentleman and he is rich enough.'

'Honestly Lizzie you are a card.' Polly laughed.

Taking between her teeth the four hairpins Lizzie always used to pin up her hair, Polly began shaping it as best she could. 'Blimey, it really is curly when it's loose ain't it?' She smoothed it with the brush and then rolled it into a chignon at the back of Lizzie's head, finally securing it with the four pins.

'There.' She made some adjustments to the front of Lizzie's hair with her own silver comb. 'That looks nice.'

'Thank you. This morning when I was looking for you, I called into *The Britannia*. A gentleman from the bridge asked me to walk out with him tonight. I'm meeting him in the *Bricklayers*.' There was a glint in Lizzie's eyes, 'They got their wages today.'

'I'd hardly call them gentlemen after what we cleaned up this morning, but they'll be throwing money about tonight if they got their pay.'

'And I want to have some fun now that I am free from Mickey.'

A shadow crossed Polly's face. 'Lizzie are you sure? If Mickey finds out that you're with another man…'

'Mickey will be working.'

'His mates will be around and you know they'll tell him. You watch yourself. If he finds out you're with another bloke it might set him off again.'

'It'll be fine, Polly.' she smiled. 'You worry too much. I must start living my life again, otherwise, I might as well go back to Mickey. '

'Just like you worry so much about me coming across the Whitechapel killer? Just be careful, that's all I'm saying.'

'I will.' She turned her eyes on Polly, her expression grim. 'But the Whitechapel killer is a different matter. You're the one who has to be careful. I know you plan to go on the game tonight and I would much rather you didn't.'

'You know I have to, Lizzie. I walk the streets and get no work. My boots kill my feet,' she inclined her head towards the place where they were drying on the hot water pipe. 'This blister ain't healing cos it rubs all the time. And I want a jacket so I look more respectable when I go asking for work. I have to do something before the winter comes.'

'Promise me you won't go out alone.'

'I promise,' said Polly, gently mocking her, 'and you be careful not to make Mickey jealous.'

'Perhaps being jealous will do him good.'

'No, Lizzie.' Polly said firmly. 'You know the clay-brained, fat headed, muck snipe can only react one way and that's with his fists.'

Lizzie laughed. She put on her bonnet and tied the bow under her right ear. Polly watched her. Lizzie had a knack for tying a perfect bow, which was just as well as she was never satisfied unless her bonnet was perfect. 'I'll see you later,' she said, standing up. 'Please be careful.' She gave Polly a hug and then hurried down the stairs.

'Never mind me. You be back by midnight young lady!' Polly called after her.

Half an hour later, Polly went to pay for their beds at Crossingham's lodging house. It had started to pour with rain at six o'clock. All this rain was getting her down and she was grateful she would not be on the street tonight. She hurried along the pavement towards *The Britannia* on the corner, keeping her thin shawl over her head.

It was early and the pub was quiet. Inside *The Britannia*, Polly was glad to find Suzette and Cathy. Polly handed over the last of her earnings - two pennies for a ginger wine which she would make last an hour or two. When she joined her friends, she found them talking about the murders.

'It's been three weeks since poor Annie,' said Suzette. 'Cathy thinks there won't be any more murders. D'you think that's an end of it, Pol?' she asked her as she sat down.

'Lizzie's convinced he's still out there. Who knows? There are so many rozzers on patrol and the vigilantes are all over the place. Maybe he ain't had the chance.' said Polly.

'I don't think he's gone either. I think he's just biding his time until the next one,' said Suzette. 'I don't know what's worse. The murderer out there making us scared to go out, or all the bleedin' coppers on the prowl frightening off our gentlemen.'

'Well my Johnny only made one and four pence this week.' said Cathy. 'That ain't enough to pay for our lodgings and feed us. If we don't get any punters in here soon, I'll have to go and find some,' she sighed, looking around the pub. There were only four other customers and they were playing cards.

'I thought you just come back from the hop picking in Kent?' Suzette asked. 'You should be rolling in it for now.'

'No, it was terrible, Suzie… it was so wet. The blossoms were going rotten on the plants. It were slim pickings and we was up to the eyes in mud. Terrible it was, it weren't worth going really so I have to get some money somehow. My Johnny had to pawn his boots yesterday.'

'How did you convince him to let you come out dollying?' Polly asked.

'I don't tell him. If I did, he'd have a fit.''

'Then how you going to explain the fact that you've suddenly got a bit of money?' Suzette asked.

'Sometimes I can do a bit of busking. If I can draw enough of a crowd I can do a poem or a story that brings it a couple of bob on a good day. As it's raining cats and dogs, I told him I've gone to Bermondsey to get some money off my Annie. She's the only one of my kids that might have a little to spare,' said Cathy. 'She don't even live there no more, so I hope he don't remember or I'll get a right earful when I see him.' She heaved a heavy sigh. 'How else we gonna manage unless I can pull in a few punters?' she said finished off her gin. 'Right, I'm off down Aldgate. The workers off the bridge got paid today. We could sit here all night with nothing doing and I ain't got no money for another gin.'

'Cathy, don't go out on your own, it ain't safe,' said Suzette. 'Give it another half hour.'

'No, my mind is made up, Suzie. I need a good night tonight and there ain't no one in here.' She grinned and produced a *Colman's* mustard tin from her pocket. She opened it and pulled out a pawn ticket. 'I got this off Emily Birrell when we was hop picking. It's for a shirt,'

'Don't she want it?' Suzette asked.

'No, on account of her heading over Cheltenham way instead of coming back here. She said it's a nice one to fit my Johnny. And only tuppence to get it out of hock. I want to get it for him as a surprise, so I need to earn a few bob. He was so melancholy when we was in Kent. He's a hard worker you know, but there was nothing for him to do. He's normally one of their best earners. It hit him hard that we made nothing.' She held up the ticket. 'This will cheer him up a treat.' She stood up. 'Ta-ta for now.'

'Take care.' Suzette called after her.

'Don't you worry about me. The Whitechapel killer ain't gonna get me. It's all just a made up yarn by the papers anyhow. See you later.'

'A made up yarn?' said Suzette as the door of the pub swung shut behind Cathy. 'If that ain't her attitude all over? Who the hell does she think killed Polly and Annie?'

Polly shrugged 'That's Cathy, *devil may care*. She's so easy going ain't she?'

'Oh yeah, she's a scream. It's her most endearing quality - always up for a laugh and telling some tall tale or other,' Suzette replied. 'She ought to watch it, this killer ain't no joke,' said Suzette.

'You got that right,' said Polly. She took a tiny sip of her ginger wine as heavy rain continued to pummel the grubby window. The four card players had gone and they were the only customers left in the bar.

'You waiting for Lizzie, Pol?' said Suzette.

'No. We've been cleaning for Betty Tanner today. Lizzie found a new gentleman friend,' said Polly.

'You gotta hand it to her. She don't give up,' Suzette laughed. 'That's Lizzie.'

'So you had some work? That's good.'

'Thanks to Lizzie. She does quite well, finding work. The place was such a mess she talked Betty Tanner into taking me on as well. It was just sixpence and it's already gone on my lodgings and this glass of ginger wine.'

'You worked all day for sixpence?'

'Not all day. We had one of Lizzie's Swedish style sauna baths after.'

'Lizzie and her sauna baths,' Suzette smiled.

'They're smashing actually, they make you feel really clean.'

'She's always coming up with something ain't she? If it ain't sponges, it's saunas. So, you going dollying tonight to make yourself a dirty girl again?'

'I'm just thinking on it Suze. I'm desperate.'

'I told you, Pol, it's easy money if you get it right. Fair enough it ain't exactly pleasant but you do what you got to do. Besides, it don't last long and you get money in your pocket and food in your belly.'

'You make it sound easy.'

Suzette quirked her mouth. 'Hmm, perhaps… Listen, if you're desperate, it'll be easier to make money tonight than other nights.'

'Yeah?'

'They always go a bit mad when they get paid. If there's a lot of them wanting our services the price goes up. And, chances are they'll be drunk and not so demanding.' Suzette looked around the pub. Four more customers came in, they also showed no interest despite Suzette turning on her French accent. She sighed. 'Listen; d'you fancy having a walk down there? Cathy might have a point. They'll be staying down by the bridge in this weather.'

'All right,' said Polly, 'Let's go before I lose my nerve.'

They left the pub and walked south, heading in the direction of the river.

'Where is this bridge they're building, anyway?' Suzette asked.

'Don't tell me you ain't seen it? It's right by The Tower at St. Katharine Dock. You can't miss it, there are two enormous stone islands sticking up out of the water and a building site on each embankment. They ain't done the middle bit yet so it don't look like a bridge at present but I understand it will be a marvel when it's done.'

'Oh, *that's* what that is… So Southwark and Bermondsey will be handy once it's up?'

'Suppose so,' Polly replied. 'More streets to walk.'

'And the inside of a different nick, eh?'

'Don't jinx me, Suzie, I ain't never been arrested.'

Suddenly Polly shivered. 'Tell you what, Suze, let's not go as far as The Tower. That place gives me the creeps. I don't like going near it at night.'

'Honestly, that sixth sense of yours. What's the matter? D'you think all the ghosts are gonna come out and GRAB YA!' Suzette grabbed her arm and Polly gave a shriek.

'Suzette! I nearly wet myself,' Polly laughed, once she had caught her breath. 'It's bleedin' spooky that place. It's like there are scary things watching from the battlements.'

'It's the living you need to worry about, Pol - not the dead.'

'You know Suze, tell you the truth, I got the *heebee geebees* most of the time. Let's only go as far as Aldgate and see if we can find

Cathy. I keep getting a feeling someone's watching me and it's scaring the hell out of me.'

'Yeah, me too. But we're bound to feel that way ain't we? There's a lunatic on the loose.'

Instinctively, the two women looked behind them. The dark street seemed deserted. Then, Polly felt Suzette squeeze her arm.

'Did you see someone pull back into the alley just then?' she whispered.

'Oh leave it out, Suze, I'm already on edge.' Polly scanned the street. She could only see as far as the last dimly glowing gas light, though what she could see seemed empty.

'I did, Pol. I saw someone. I swear.'

'Come on, keep moving.' Polly whispered, trying to sound calm when every tiny hair on her skin was standing on end. She linked her arm in Suzette's and the two women quickened their pace towards Aldgate.

# CHAPTER TWELVE

'*Bonsoir mes amis,*' said Suzette as they stepped through the door of *The White Swan* on Aldgate High Street. Polly was partly amused and partly impressed at how easily Suzette slipped into her fake French accent. She seemed to take on another identity when she was working. Polly wondered if that was how she coped with selling herself to strangers half a dozen times a night.

They soon got the attention of a group of labourers in the bar. Cathy had been right, their potential clients had stayed close to their lodgings because of the rain and the pub was full of men with money in their pockets.

Polly spotted a quiet, ordinary looking chap and made him her mark. She was in no hurry. The gin was flowing and it was warm and comfortable in the pub. Other punters bought her drinks just to have her company and she had two glasses of gin lined up. She caught the eye of another man on the other side of the bar. She had learned how to keep them interested.

Polly had been to *The White Swan* before, though she had never picked up a client there. Suzette told her that Fred Davis, the landlord, turned a blind eye, as long as the girls were discrete and the customers were happy. There were a few other working girls in the bar apart from herself and Suzette. She could see that business was good and there was no shortage of customers. The men were spending well tonight. She could ask for more money and have as many clients as she liked. If she kept her nerve, she could earn enough money to see the week out. Seeing that the girls taking clients outside were back in less than five minutes, she steeled herself to make a move and find a customer. She swallowed a mouthful of gin and summoned the courage to go through with it.

It did not take long. After five minutes she was leading her first customer along the high street towards Half Moon Passage a few yards away. This was a long and convoluted back alley with several possible escape routes should she need one. Suzette followed her out with her own client. The girls made sure they went out in pairs or groups and were taking all the punters to Half Moon Alley. They made sure they kept within shouting distance of each other.

Grimly, Polly focused on getting through the next few minutes and barely registered the shambling figure who was walking towards her.

'Polly?'

Her head snapped around and she looked into the face of the one who had called her name.

'Aaron?' she said. 'What you doing here?'

He had that same pitiful haunted look she had seen when she took him home the week before. It seemed clear that nothing she said to Mosiek Lubnowski had changed a thing.

'Read to me,' he said.

He was looking at the pavement. He never made eye contact. He thrust the copy of *Hard Times* towards her. Polly glanced at her client and then looked at Aaron.

'Oh, Aaron, I can't. Not right now.'

'Polly, read,' he said, fidgeting from one foot to the other. Once again he tried to make her take the book.

Polly turned to her client. 'Give me a minute. I just need to explain to him.'

'You go with Jews?' he said, his voice dripping with contempt.

'I read to him. He has trouble understanding things.' Polly grabbed Aaron's sleeve. 'C'mere.' She pulled him aside so she could talk to him.

'Aaron, listen. I would really like to read to you, but I have no money. Not a single penny and if I don't get some I won't have anything to eat nor a place to sleep tomorrow. D'you understand?'

Aaron's eyes narrowed. Polly wondered if the voices in his head were telling him differently. 'Aaron? Listen to me, not the voices. I don't have a home like you. I need to earn money just to get a bed in a doss house. If I don't, I have to walk the streets all night. I can't do that Aaron, not with a killer on the loose.'

'I pay,' said Aaron shoving his hand in his pocket.

Polly looked at him. 'You pay? Oh no, Aaron, I don't think so. I mean, I know you don't I?'

'I pay, you read. Mosiek paid and you read, so now I pay and you read. Two shillings.'

'Oh, you meant, read to you? I thought- Never mind.' She glanced over her shoulder and saw that her client had gone back into the pub. By now he would have told the entire crowd that she sold her services to Jews. With so much hostility towards Jewish people in the east end, it would not be wise to go back in *The White Swan*. She doubted she would get any clients if she did.

Suzette, after throwing her a quizzical look, had teamed up with one of the other girls.

'Alright, Aaron, I'll read to you,' she said. 'It's better than the alternative, anyway.'

Aaron opened his palm and showed her a fist full of coins.

'Put that away. You mustn't let anyone see that you got money. You have to be careful. You must have three of four quid in loose change, there.' She took her fee and another shilling. 'This is for drinks.' she said. 'We can go over the road to *The Bull*, it will be quiet in there and there's a little snug where no one will bother us.'

Aaron handed her the book.

'It's a bit damp, Aaron, you been carrying it around for a while?'

Inside *The Bull*, Polly bought a ginger wine for herself and the same for Aaron.

'Here you are, this is the same as what I have. There's no poison in it, I promise. No matter what the voices tell you. Polly wouldn't lie to you, would I?'

'Polly read,' he said in reply.

Polly opened the book. 'Right, let's see how horrible Mr. Gradgrind is getting on.'

She read to him for almost three hours. It was gratifying to see how it soothed him. He never seemed calmer and at peace with himself than when she read to him. Whether it was the story or the sound of her voice that kept his demons at bay, she could not tell.

Polly could see over the bar counter into the main part of the pub. Though no one had come into the snug, the main bar had filled up and was busy. There were some men standing at the bar counter. She could not hear their conversation but did not need her sixth sense to recognise the potential danger. She could tell by their scowling faces that they had a problem with her being with Aaron.

'It's time to go, Aaron,' she said as she came to the end of a chapter. 'I don't like the look of those men. I think they want trouble.' She looked at him. He was never rid of the tired lines beneath his eyes, but she thought his face looked less pinched and a little less sallow.

He had not touched the ginger wine and Polly had ended up drinking it, plus two more, in response to a *Buy more drinks or get out* look from the barman at the beginning of the third hour.

'We could do this again if you like.'

'I pay two shillings, you read tomorrow?'

'Yes, of course I will. We should come earlier next time to avoid the roughnecks, but I can't keep taking two bob off you every time'

'Yes, two bob,' he nodded. 'Two bob and you have a bed and food.'

Polly looked at him, amazed. It was the first time she had seen him show any understanding of someone else's needs. She wanted to punch the air. Up to now, he had been so out of touch with reality he could barely recognise his own needs let alone someone else's.

'Yes, Aaron. For two bob I will have a bed and food,' she smiled then glanced again into the bar. 'Come on, let's go.' She finished her drink and then knocked back the one that Aaron had not touched.

As Polly guided Aaron through the crowded bar towards the door, one of the men stuck out his foot and another gave Aaron a shove in the back. This sent him sprawling across the floor amongst the tables and barstools.

'Hey! There weren't no call for that!' said Polly.

'Jew loving whore.' One of them hissed at her.

Polly helped Aaron to his feet as two of the men squared up to him, ready for a fight.

'Leave him alone!' Polly put herself between Aaron and the ringleader. 'He ain't hurting no one. He likes me to read Charles Dickens to him. See?' She held up the book. 'How can anyone take offence at that?' She was afraid that Aaron would retaliate; if he did, it would not end well for him. 'Look, he's just a poor man with his own troubles, like the rest of us. He don't want any bother and neither do I.'

To her relief, her words had chiselled a small impression on the hard men. Aaron's body was as tense as a coiled spring. She was relieved that he didn't make eye contact nor answer back to his tormentors, despite the filthy names they were calling him. Once on his feet, Polly made sure he kept moving. It occurred to her that this was probably something he put up with on a regular basis.

When they reached the pavement outside, she took a calming breath and exhaled sharply. 'Are you alright?' she asked him. 'Aaron, I'm so sorry. They're arseholes, the lot of them.'

Whereas before she could see he was relaxed, now she could see his distress rising. He had turned pale. For a second he looked at her, then just as quickly he looked away. His face was contorted by an internal anguish and she knew that the voices in his head would be screaming at him. He took the book from her and quickly turned away.

'Aaron, those men were bad. You are *not* bad, understand? You are not bad. Don't listen to the voices.' He hurried away from her, a humiliated figure. Polly ran after him and caught up with him as he crossed Houndsditch. 'Aaron? D'you want me to take you home?' He kept on walking. She followed him to the next corner, acutely aware of his pain and embarrassment. 'Aaron?'

He did not turn around nor speak. She stopped at the corner and let him go. It looked as if he was heading for the synagogue in the next street. It was a place where he would feel safe and find comfort with his own people, while she felt ashamed of hers. It had been a completely unprovoked attack.

She heard the brewery clock strike one. She should have kept an eye on the time and left the pub earlier. Once those men were boozed up and the worse for drink, it was bound to get rough.

She headed quickly along Aldgate in the direction of Commercial Street. The men had given her a look of sheer contempt. She remembered what a gang of men had done to Emma Smith and she was frightened for her own safety. After the names she had been called, she knew she was in danger from the same louts. She needed to get away and stay away from Aldgate for a while.

Until those thugs ruined it, it had been an enjoyable evening. She liked reading to Aaron. She had two shillings in her pocket and her bed was already paid for at Crossingham's. Though she had not made the six shillings she had been aiming for, she was satisfied for now.

The men had destroyed the small amount of respite her reading to Aaron had given him. They should try and live with such turmoil inside their head, she thought, boiling with fury.

The cold night air hit her and she suddenly felt dizzy. The four glasses of ginger wine on top of the two gins she's had in *The White Swan* were making her head spin. She longed to lie down but she forced herself to move forward. The pavement felt oddly sponge-like, and to her surprise, she had to concentrate on placing every step with care. Every now and again she glanced behind her, just in case some of the men from *The Bull* were following her. She thought about taking a shortcut to Dorset Street via one of the back streets. Even in her tipsy state, she knew that it would be a stupid thing to do. If one of the louts had followed her, a dark back street was just where he would want to find her.

She ploughed ahead on the main street. It was still raining. As she glanced in the windows of each pub she could see they were full; people were staying put until the rain stopped. She paused at the entrance to Castle Alley, the full effect of the alcohol hitting her hard. She focused her eyes with difficulty, swaying a little as she looked at the road ahead.

She put a hand out to the wall to steady herself. Castle Alley itself was a wide lane used as a shortcut between Whitechapel Road and Wentworth Street. The entrance to it was narrow and very dark for the first few yards of its length. A jolt of fear had a temporary sobering effect as Lizzie's warnings echoed in her mind. Never mind the roughnecks, there was a killer at large on these streets and it would be foolish to linger in such a place. She shivered and moved on.

She could make out the outline of a man walking towards her. As he came closer, she could see that he was well dressed and wearing a long dark coat. Even in her alcohol-fuelled haze she sensed danger. Polly's heart rate quickened as she felt his eyes on her. Having some of her wits about her, she crossed to the other side of the street. She carried on walking and when she looked again, he had also crossed the road and was coming towards her, his stride purposeful.

Her heart thumping, she darted into the recess of a shop doorway, pretending she was looking for a door key in her pocket. She held her breath as she heard his footsteps getting closer.

Alarm shot through her as she was grabbed by the elbow and yanked out of the doorway.

'Hey!' she shrieked and tried to struggle free. 'Let go of me!' He was dragging her to the corner Leman Street where Polly knew there were two blind alleys. If he got her as far as either of them, she was as good as dead. No one would hear her cries for help.

She struggled with every ounce of strength she had. 'What d'you think you're doing? Stop it. I said let go!' She tried to fight him off. Her feet were hardly touching the ground. 'Get off me!'

She tried to twist out of his grasp. His grip was like a death trap. Terrified, she knew she was fighting for her life. She tried to scream but only managed a pathetic wail. Her heart was hammering against her breastbone. He was very strong. She grappled with him, she wasn't going down without a fight. She kicked, writhed and flailed. Nothing she did had any effect. She found it impossible to escape and panic began to snake its tendrils around her.

'Stop it!' she shrieked.

'No chance,' he growled as she continued to fight. She was weakening and no match for him. Then, he pulled her into the brighter light of a street lamp and stared into her face.

'Polly Wilkes? What did I tell you about being out on these streets?'

For a few seconds Polly was not able to comprehend what was happening, then something clicked into place in her brain.

'S-Sergeant Alfie? Oh, th- thank God...' she stammered. She stopped struggling and tears of relief flooded her eyes. She grabbed the lamp post to steady herself and clutched her chest with the other hand as if to slow down her frantic heart.

'I thought-' she stammered 'I thought I was done for-'

'And you are very fortunate that you're not. What did I tell you? *Stay off the streets.*'

Even in her inebriated state, still trying to catch her breath and her vision blurred by tears, she could tell he was angry.

'I- I...' She was unable to speak. She looked up and tried to focus on him. As Alf watched, she let go of the lamp post, swayed, tottered sideways and grabbed hold of it again.

'That's it. I'm locking you up. It's a simple as that. You're in for a night in the cells,' he said.

'What?' She was suddenly stone cold sober. 'I ain't going in no cells.'

'Yes you are. It's for your own good. Come on, it's Leman Street nick for you.' He took hold of her arm. Polly tried in vain to wriggle out of his grasp. His grip was vice-like.

She hugged the lamp post as if it was her best friend and held on as tightly as she could as Alf tried to pull her in the direction of the police station.

'This ain't fair, you ain't on duty. You've got clothes on.'

'Yes I am. I'm undercover.'

Still clutching the lamp post, she squinted at him.

'Undercover?' She looked him up and down. 'Not with those great big copper's feet you ain't.'

'Oh yeah? Well you didn't recognise me did you? You thought I was *him.*'

'What d'you expect the way you pulled me out of that doorway?' she said. 'Come on, Alfie. Don't lock me up.'

'No chance. What d'you think you're doing trying to pick me up on the street?'

'I wasn't trying to pick you up.'

'Yes you were. You crossed the road just when I did and you waited for me in that shop doorway. You were gonna follow me and try it on, weren't you?'

'No. You've misunderstood. I-'

'What if I had been him? You'd be dead by now.'

'Alfie, don't say that… I'm gonna-' she heaved, bent over, and threw up in the gutter.

'Oh, that's pretty,' said Alf.

Panting and eyes watering, she reached into her pocket for her piece of cloth. 'Well you ought not to say such things.' she gasped. Alf produced a clean white square of cotton and gave it to her. She wiped her face.

'I'm saying it cos it's true. You ain't in any fit state to look after yourself. I was watching you as you came along Aldgate. You were six sheets to the wind and weaving about all over the place. You might as well stop struggling, I ain't letting go.'

'And I ain't going in no cell.'

'Yes you are.' He tugged on her arm and found it was firmly hooked around the lamp post.

'No I ain't. Come on, Alfie. Let me go.'

'Sorry. No can do. It's for your own good.'

She gave a roar, released her grip on the lamp post and started to take swings at him to fight him off. 'I ain't going in no cell!'

'Stop that! You're just making it worse,' he said. 'Right now it's soliciting and being drunk and disorderly. Would you like to add assaulting a police officer to the charges? Because the number of 'em against you is starting to mount up.'

'I ain't going in no nick.'

'Yes you are.'

Polly gave another bellow and continued to fight. She caught him a hard kick on his right shin.

'Ow! Cut that out.' he said. Polly also yelped in pain. Her old boots were no match for his solid shin bone. She cursed and continued to struggle.

'D'you want me to put resisting arrest on the list?' he asked, dodging another swing at him. 'Right. That's it!' The sergeant swung her easily over one of his broad shoulders and began to carry her like a rolled up carpet.

'Put me down!' she bawled. Furious at him, she pounded his back with her fists. Alf strolled along the street, not at all concerned by her futile attempts to get free.

He carried her, kicking and cursing, the few yards to Leman Street Station. The last things Polly remembered was being lowered onto a narrow bed and the sound of a metal door clanging shut.

## CHAPTER THIRTEEN

Alf locked the cell with the sleeping Polly inside and went to the front desk. He hung the bunch of keys on a hook on the wall and then turned to the eighteen-year-old constable at the counter.

'Constable Harris? The lady I brought in needs to sleep it off. Do *not* discharge her if she wakes up no matter how much she complains. I don't want her out on the streets. She ain't capable and I ain't gonna risk having a murder resting on my conscience. There's no need to put her through the books but I want a word with her in the morning. Is that clear?'

'As crystal, Sarge.' The lad nodded. He was a brand new recruit and had no experience to speak of, but he was all they had left to man the desk. Every copper they had was out on the beat looking for the Whitechapel killer.

'Where's the Inspector?'

'He was over at Commercial Street but we had to telegraph him, Sarge. There's been another murder, in Berner Street.'

Alf pulled up short and stared at him. 'A murder? You mean the Whitechapel killer has done another murder?' Now he could see that the young lad's face was as pale as parchment.

The lad nodded rapidly. 'Yes, Sarge. Inspector Pinhorn is meeting Chief Inspector West and Inspector Reid at the scene. He went half an hour since.'

'Do they have enough men?' he asked. 'These murders attract a bloodthirsty crowd.'

'Yes, sir. Harry Lamb is there along with the reserve man Collins and Bill Smith whose beat it is. Inspector Reid is taking a couple of men from Commercial Street with him and Spitalfields telegraphed to say they could send some men if they was needed. Sir? I heard that the *Guvnor* is on his way to Berner Street. It's all a great commotion.'

'Superintendent Arnold will be in attendance?' Alf's brows lifted.

'Yes Sarge, Inspector Reid sent one of the lads from Commercial Street to Stepney for him. He said he wanted to be notified if there was another one.'

'So he did, lad,' said Alf. He was thankful that there were plenty of men at the scene and he would not be facing another mutilated corpse.

At that moment Constable Foggin burst through the main door. He was sweating and breathless and had obviously been running.

'Sarge, there's been another one.'

'We know, Foggin - Berner Street. Do try to keep up.'

'No Sarge, this one ain't on our patch,' he wheezed. 'It's in Mitre Square, and it's him alright. There's a commotion going on over there.' Foggin puffed. 'I think it must be bad cos City force is crawling all over it.'

It took Alf a moment to take in the implications of what Foggin had said.

'The murdering devil had done two?'

'Within the hour, Sarge,' Foggin panted.

Alf ran through the details. Berner Street, to the east, quite a respectable residential street, south of Commercial Road. Mitre Square, a grubby little square. Dimly lit, surrounded by tall warehouses, a synagogue and a couple of churches. The two places were as different as chalk and cheese. Foggin was right, Mitre Square was in City Force's territory. By the width of a few hundred yards, the killer stepped into another jurisdiction and that made all the difference in the world. Everything west of Houndsditch in a line that ran all the way to the Tower of London was City turf.

'You didn't get involved did you, Foggin?'

'No, course not, Sarge. I ain't that stupid. You know how they are about it.'

H Division constables walked the beat as far as that invisible line, then turned around and walked back again. They took care to stay within *The Met's* territory.

City was a tiny force that policed the square mile of old London town. The bosses were touchy about anything that might lead to them being swallowed up by the Metropolitan Police. They would love to show them up by catching the killer under the nose of Commissioner Warren, and the bigger, more experienced force.

Alf rubbed his chin. H Division on its own was almost as big as the whole of the City force. It stood to reason that they didn't have anywhere near the necessary experience to catch this killer. They could never measure up to the famous Scotland Yard - the headquarters of *The Met*. Alf also knew it would not stop them from trying.

So, it was game on - City Force versus H Division and Scotland Yard. Any clues and all the witnesses would be City's business. Knowing how the two chiefs felt about each other, there would be no sharing of information - not officially anyway.

'Who found the body?'

'It must have been Eddie Watkins, I saw him earlier and his beat takes him through Mitre Square,' said Foggin.

'What time?'

'I dunno; I heard the whistles start blowing at quarter to two.'

Alf looked at the clock on the wall. It was almost five past two. 'What time did the Inspector go out?'

'Just before you brought that woman in at quarter past one.' said Harris.

Alf weighed up this information. The Guvnor wouldn't know about this one.

Both victims had been found within the hour. Alf knew it would be helpful to know if there were any similarities between Mitre Square and the other murders. The killer might have left clues this time or something might shed light on the other murders. Above all, they needed to know if it was the same killer.

'I'm going to Mitre Square. I want to see what's occurred,' he said.

'Sarge, it's on City-'

'I know, but I seen the first two victims. I'll know if it's the same killer and if it's going to be worth all the paperwork it will take to get information out of them. And, maybe they've found something that can help us put this lunatic away.'

Alf headed down the corridor to the locker room to change into his uniform.

The two constables looked at each other.

'They ain't gonna like it,' said Foggin. 'You know how upset they get when we tread on their turf. Is there a brew going? I couldn't half do with a cuppa before I get back out there.'

Alf knew Foggin was right. If an inexperienced man happened to stray into City territory, stern memoranda were sent and harsh words were uttered. Nevertheless, this could be a chance to gather vital evidence.

'Foggin?' Alf called from somewhere out of sight.

'Sarge?'

'You got two minutes to swill a cuppa. Then get back out there. There's a killer to catch.'

'Yes, Sarge,' Foggin sighed.

Alf turned left at the top of Leman Street and headed along Aldgate High Street. As soon as he passed the end of the ancient lane known as Houndsditch, he would be in City territory.

He had scrutinised the large map on the duty room wall as he buttoned up his tunic. He would make it look casual. He was simply making a friendly inquiry. He just happened to be checking on his men on the beat and heard about the murder.

The lads on the ground in the two forces got along well and many of them knew each other; Alf was well aware that the top brass did not. Newspapers often attacked *The Met.* and made adverse comparisons with City Force.

Less than a year ago, the Metropolitan Police Commissioner, Sir Charles Warren had ordered a military-style horseback charge on civilians in Trafalgar Square. It was a gathering of the poor and unemployed who were protesting about the lack of work, low wages and poverty in the east end. They were asserting their right to freedom of speech and peaceful assembly.

Alf had been drafted in, as had most coppers on the ground, to control the crowd. It had been, on the whole, a good-humoured gathering. Then, Warren persuaded the Home Secretary, Henry Matthews to make such gatherings illegal.

At the stroke of a pen, peaceful assembly in Trafalgar Square became a crime. Warren ordered the charge, trampling and bludgeoning the crowd indiscriminately, and it had turned into a riot. Three people died, dozens were injured and even more were arrested. It had been a disgrace in Alf's opinion and since then, *The Met.* could do nothing right according to the press. Alf disliked Warren, it seemed to him that he had an arrogant nature and would have his own way regardless of the consequences.

This new murder created a delicate situation and Warren was already touchy about anything to do with the way the Whitechapel killer continued to elude them and the way the case was being investigated. Now that City Force was involved, it was a golden opportunity for the press to make Warren and the entire Metropolitan force look bad. Alf knew that Warren wouldn't want anything about the previous murders to be shared with City and in return, the acting City Commissioner, Sir Henry Smith would not give anything away to help Warren.

There was a murdering nut case on the loose and the two top men were likely to be more concerned with their petty rivalries and the things being written in newspapers. Before all that kicked off and the two commissioners got involved, he could have a look at the murder scene. He might gain information that could help them catch this devil and he could not pass up this chance.

Feeling like an intruder in his own neighbourhood, Alf made his way up Duke Street. It would make a lot more sense to make City Force a division of *The Met* - though he knew it would never happen. The post of City Commissioner was a gift the Home Secretary could hand out to whoever was in greatest favour with him. Running City was regarded as an easy number - little work and a lot of prestige – until tonight when a maniac dropped a murder victim in their laps.

Alf paused as he reached the entrance to the alley known as Church Passage which led into Mitre Square. He could see a collection of uniformed officers and men in civilian clothes on the far side of the square near the exit onto Mitre Street.

Extra lighting had been brought in. Alf could not see the body which had been screened off by an oilcloth frame. He nodded to the young P.C. who was standing sentry at the end of the passage. He deferred to Alf's more senior rank and allowed him to stroll into Church Passage.

Someone broke away from the group around the body and came towards Alf.

'Alf Cruikshank? Very nice to see you. How's your mother?' said Detective Constable Outram.

'Not too bad; can't complain,' said Alf automatically.

'Well give her my best and tell her that the little scrap she delivered is a head taller than me now.'

'I will pass on your regards, Robert.' Alf replied, thinking his mother must have delivered most of the population of the east end over the years. He scanned Mitre Square. It was gloomier than he remembered. 'What you got occurring?' he asked.

'A woman has been murdered,' said Robert. 'Frankly, Alf, I've never seen anything like it.'

Alf could see that he was almost gagging at the thought of it. Outram laid his index and middle fingers across his mouth as if using the gesture to hold back rising bile. He breathed out slowly and then dropped his hand to his side. 'It's quite horrific.'

If this murder resembled the others, Alf thought, there were no words to describe it. Judging by the grim party around the body and the grey faces of all the men in the square, Alf deduced that it must be every bit as bad. Even at this distance, he could detect the stench of faeces and shuddered at what that meant.

'Was she disembowelled?' he asked.

'Yes.' Outram gulped as if to regain control of his rolling stomach. 'Oh that's right you attended the other two murders didn't you?'

'I did. That smell ain't something I shall forget in a hurry.'

'The other women were disembowelled?'

'Yes, but he went to town on the second one more than the first.'

'This one is-' Outram paused again. 'I say, Alf, would you mind taking a look at this victim? We're pretty sure she was done by the Whitechapel killer. I would like to know if anything strikes you, compared to the other victims.'

'By all means, I'll do what I can, Robert. You're convinced it's him?

'I don't think there's any doubt,' Outram let out a long uneven breath as he indicated that Alf should follow him.

Though he dreaded the sight, Alf had been hoping Outram would ask. He followed him towards the group of people standing beside the corpse. Before they reached the scene, Outram stopped and turned to him. 'You should brace yourself, old man.'

'Understood.' Alf replied.

Outram introduced him to the three other men at the scene who were Inspector Edward Collard with Detective Constables Daniel Halse and Edward Marriott. Collard was the man in charge and had been on duty at Bishopsgate Station when the report of the murder came in.

'Sergeant Cruikshank attended the other murders, sir.' Outram told him.

'I see. Thank you, Robert.' He looked at Alf. 'Any observations you might have would be welcome, Sergeant,' said Collard.

A piece of sacking had been used to cover the victim as a token of respect. Alf crouched by the body and lifted one side of the cloth and almost let out a gasp.

The victim was on her back. Her clothing had been pulled up to expose her belly. She was not wearing any drawers.

Her right leg was straight and lay parallel to the ground. The left leg was bent at the hip and the knee was turned outward, spreading it apart to expose her genitals.

'She's in a similar position to Mrs. Chapman, the second victim.' Alf offered to the assembled detectives. 'She was found with both legs in the same spread out position. We felt he did it to degrade the victim and consternate those who found her. Positioning the body would likely have been the last thing he did to her. He's only positioned one of this lady's legs so perhaps he was short of time.' Alf looked away and glanced around the square to relieve his eyes from the ghastly sight.

'That's in line with our thoughts, Alf,' said Outram. 'Constable Watkins was here on his beat at one thirty and all was well. He returned at a quarter to two and found the unfortunate woman. Constable Harvey has the adjacent beat to Watkins. He was here at twenty minutes to two, he came into Church Passage, but not into the square as it isn't part of his beat. He saw nothing.'

'So the killer did all this in less than ten minutes?' said Alf. 'In near total darkness?'

'It looks that way.'

What had been done to this poor woman was unspeakable. Alf shook his head and wondered how anyone could do this amount of damage to another human being in such a short time.

It was hard not to think about the fear the victim must have felt as she realised she had fallen into the clutches of the Whitechapel killer. Just over an hour ago, she had been a living, breathing human being; now she was a disembowelled corpse.

Her dying moments must have been spent in unimaginable terror. She would have known what was going to happen as she looked into those murderous eyes.

Alf did his best to remain dispassionate. He fixed his attention on what the corpse could tell him. Perhaps she had tried to put up a fight. Her bonnet had come off and was lying behind her head in a pool of blood on top of the rusted iron cover of a coal hole.

Her throat had been cut more or less horizontally from left to right with only a slight deviation downward towards the right side. This severed her windpipe and prevented her from crying out. The cut on the left side was deep enough to sever the great blood vessels on that side of her neck.

Alf felt his stomach twitch. He gathered himself and using all his strength of will, pushed his emotions aside. He gritted his teeth, channelling his fury and disgust into studying the murder scene. It took every ounce of determination he possessed to concentrate on the evidence. The way to help this poor woman now was to catch the monster that did this to her and see him hang.

'The wound looks like his work, sir. Mrs. Chapman was cut from between her legs to the breastbone just like this lady, except,' he took in a breath. 'It looks like he's refined his technique. He had a couple of tries with the last victim. There were two shallower cuts to the abdomen alongside the one that did the damage. It was the same with Mrs. Nichols. He don't seem to have hesitated so much with this lady.' Alf swallowed. His lurching stomach would not be still. It looked to him as if the killer was getting more confident. He paused and cleared his throat. 'The neck wound is similar, the cut was made left to right. It was much deeper with Mrs. Chapman and both sides were severed. With this lady, judging by the size of the wound, the right side could be intact. There were signs of strangulation with Mrs. Chapman, I don't see any sign of that with this lady.' There was a bitter taste at the back of his throat. He swallowed again. There was a moment of silence amongst the men - they knew as well as Alf did, that she might not have been dead when he commenced his evil work. The pitiable woman's intestines had been drawn out as a ghastly rope of wet tissue that was pulled taut across her chest and torso. She had been ripped open from vagina to breast bone. The remaining coils of glistening gut had been dumped above her right shoulder in a stinking heap that was running with blood and faecal matter.

'He's done the same thing to the innards,' said Alf. The upper part of the gut was still attached to the stomach tethering it inside the woman's body. He exhaled deeply. 'Mrs. Chapman's bowels had been lifted out completely and placed beside her right shoulder. It looked as if the killer was trying to do the same with this victim only the bowel ain't come away so cleanly,' he said. 'You can see what he's done. When he found it wouldn't pull free he cut it away and cast the bulk of it over her right shoulder. In both victims, it's as though his object was to get rid of it so he could get at what lay beneath.'

The smell that emanated from the corpse was atrocious. Bile, tissue fluid and faecal matter had poured onto the pavement from the severed bowel. The killer had left a short pouch-shaped piece of large bowel attached to the end of the rectum. Alf weighed up what he was seeing. The killer must have pulled on the remaining length of bowel, stretching it like a piece of vulcanised rubber. When he cut it, the muscular stump had telescoped back into the rectum, giving it this bizarre pouch-like shape. He had cast away the severed piece of intestine, which was still lying on the ground to the left of the body. The casual way it had been discarded was sickening. Alf blew out his cheeks. Why in the name of all that was holy had the maniac done this? This was not just a murder; there had also been intentional violation of the corpse, for whatever twisted reason possessed him. Alf cleared his throat.

'He's done the same as what he did to Mrs. Chapman and Mrs. Nichols. He disembowelled them to empty the abdomen so he could get at what he wanted - the female organs.'

Alf had suspected all along this was the murderer's goal. He had studied his mother's midwifery books to better understand the post-mortem reports of the two previous victims. He knew that once the bowels were out of the way, the womb would have fallen back into the vacated space. Its smooth surface and firm muscular shape would have been recognisable by touch in the dark. It would have been possible for him to get hold of it. The organs of the body, he had read, were not fixed in place and attached to each other. According to his mother's anatomy book they could move and slide over each other despite there being little space between them. The organs were packed in protective membranes like precious objects in tissue paper, joined only by the blood vessels and nerves that supplied them.

Alf suppressed a shudder as he imagined how the killer grabbed hold of the firm peach-like womb and peeled it away from the tough outer sack of the bladder. The bladder was not a delicate structure; its outer coverings were as tough as sailcloth. He could see it lying in the pelvis like a small, deflated football. Once the maniac separated the two organs he could sever the womb at its base and take his disgusting trophy. This left its entrance or cervix as a crimson flower shaped bud at the top of the vagina. Alf was sure this was the object of his degenerate desires. Alf guessed that once he had this prize, he ceased his perverted work.

'He's taken her womb. This was also done to Mrs. Chapman,' he said, sounding more dispassionate and objective than he felt.

'Did he take Chapman's kidney?' Collard asked. 'It appears to be missing from this victim.'

'No, sir, just the womb.' Alf looked down at the empty cavity. All that was left within the lower abdomen was the bladder and the two huge blood vessels that ran either side of the spine. The killer's insane, wild slashes had cut into the layer of fat at the back of the abdomen and stabbed at the spleen and pancreas directly in front of the kidneys. This deranged killer had taken out her kidney by slipping his fingers behind the larger of the two great vessels which ran from the heart down the left side of the spine, and wrenched the left kidney from its moorings, popping it out of its torn capsule like a butter bean.

Alf rubbed his chin. Why a kidney? What would the lunatic want with her kidney? This killer seemed preoccupied with the sexual organs. In every case, he had stabbed at them inside and out. Out of everything he did to his victims, the sexual organs received the most attention and damage. Perhaps in the dark, he thought the kidney was one of the lady's ovaries and taken it for that reason? Until Alf read his mother's books, he had not appreciated how small the organs of generation were and what a tiny space they occupied deep in a woman's pelvis.

Was this sick objective his motivation and what drove him to kill? Alf was convinced the killer got his jollies by mutilating the sexual organs. Did he disembowel his victims just to enable him to plunder her womb? The bowels were cast aside as if they were of no interest to him. He swallowed hard. Her external genitals had been savagely attacked to the extent that Alf doubted his own sanity for looking at it. He had ripped all the women from vagina to breastbone. Was this lust the root of his insane appetites?

He concentrated on the facts and tried to fix them in his mind so he could relay the details to Inspector Reid, and Inspector Abberline, the Scotland Yard man on the case.

They could not shy away from the truth. This murderer was of a singular type. He was a carnal savage, though not in the sense it was understood, where a victim was ravished by the vile perpetrator. This monster got his jollies mutilating the female organs. He was truly a maniac and this poor woman had endured a terrible fate.

As Alf watched, a ghastly blood clot slithered like a giant glistening slug from the gaping maw in her neck. A vast pool of blood surrounded the corpse. Feeling a surge of pity, Alf could see that most of the blood loss had been via the neck wound.

He bowed his head, putting a thumb and index finger to his cheeks. No one knew what this poor soul had suffered but she had not died instantly as a result of the cut to her throat. The neck wound was the source of the large quantity of blood in which her bonnet lay. For a pool of that size to accumulate, her heart must still have been beating and pumping it out. It would have taken a couple of minutes for her to die. He thought with horror what might have occurred during that interval and his blood ran cold as he thought about that first long, ripping cut.

He looked at her face. It had been mutilated by small deep wounds that made patterns across her cheeks and looked like short strokes from a sharp, pointed blade. It was the type of knife that was used to make precision cuts in pieces of meat. The cuts lined up with the slashes to the abdomen as if he had caught her face with the tip of the knife as he made the deep, vicious incisions into her belly.

The casual, careless brutality of it was blood curdling. The wild slashes of his knife had severed the tip of her nose and sliced vertically through her left eye. They would never know if she had still been conscious and felt the pain of those injuries.

'The attack appears to be as callous as the other victims,' he said at last. 'Looking at this poor woman, sir, he's been in more of a frenzy this time.'

There was nothing to single out this sad little woman as the target for a maniac. There was nothing special about her, she met a terrible death for only one reason; she was poor and because of that, had walked into his clutches. The assembled group of officers listened carefully, hearing Alf out without interruption.

'That was a sound piece of observation and reasoning as I have heard from any detective, Cruikshank. Very helpful,' said Collard when Alf finished.

'Thank you, Inspector. I just tell it like I sees it,' he replied, keeping to himself his burning desire to join Scotland Yard as a detective and work on the big cases one day. 'I'd bet a month's wages, sir, that you've got the work of the same killer, here.'

'As would I. It's unlikely there would be two maniacs capable of doing this, on the streets at the same time' said Collard.

Alf quirked his mouth and nodded.

The assembled men looked up at the sound of voices coming from the direction of Mitre Street.

'Damn it. Here come the vultures.' said Collard to Marriott as a gaggle of reporters sprinted into Mitre Street, each trying to be first on the scene. Mitre Street happened to be closest to the body and they headed straight for the constables who were guarding the entrance. 'Excuse me, I need to have a word with the gentlemen of the press…' he said and moved off towards them.

Alf reckoned he would have done the same. A constable's pay did not go far and severe temptation was put in front of them by reporters who would pay handsomely for inside information. There was no doubt that the two murders would have stopped the presses. Every editor would be out of bed waiting to see what could be splashed across the next morning's front pages. They were making a fortune out of this terrible business; the more shocking it was, the more papers they sold.

'We ought to get her moved. That way there's nothing to see,' said Outram.

'We can't, we're waiting for the police surgeon,' said Marriott.

'We've already got a Doctor. This is Doctor Sequiera; he's pronounced her dead.'

Alf now noticed the pale-faced young doctor who was standing in the group.

'The *Guvnor* wants Frederick Gordon-Brown,' said Marriott. 'Foster and the Commissioner are also on their way.'

Collard sighed and returned to the group. 'I've ordered a door to door search for witnesses and dispatched the reporters to wait around the corner on Mitre Street. The gentlemen of the press seem to already have made up their minds that this was the work of the Whitechapel killer,' he said sourly.

'That ain't the worst of it, sir,' said Alf. 'I just heard an hour since, that he done one in Berner Street before this one. Pound to a penny they know about it.'

'There was another one *tonight*?' said Collard.

Alf nodded. 'She was found just before one o'clock, sir. My *guvnor* is over there right now.'

'The Berner Street victim was found at about one o'clock and this victim was found only forty-five minutes later?' said Collard.

'It appears so, sir,' said Alf. 'I'll return to Leman Street now. I don't think there is anything else I can tell you. I intend to tell my senior officers that I believe this lady to have been murdered by the same killer. If anything turns up that will assist the investigation, I will be sure to let you know.'

'Thank you, Sergeant. Would you let Inspector Reid know that we have started a search on his patch?'

'I will, sir.' Alf nodded, thinking that it was about time. It was a quarter to three, an hour since the murder. 'And be assured we will be doing everything we can to assist,' he added.

It had been a very long night. Alf had seen enough to recognise similarities with the other murders and Doctor Gordon-Brown would make a full written report which they would make a formal request to see.

He started walking back to Leman Street and came to the spot where Polly Wilkes had tried to pick him up. A cold sweat washed over him as he worked out that he had come across her shortly after one o'clock right here and the maniac had killed a woman only a few hundred yards away, less than half an hour later. If the killer had done the first one in Berner Street by one o'clock, he would have been coming this way and she had been walking directly into his clutches.

Alf stopped in his tracks and felt all the breath leave his lungs. It could so easily have been her. He unbuttoned a pocket in his tunic, took out a handkerchief and mopped his face.

What if he had gone to that scene and it had been her lying there, displayed in such a degrading pose? Ripped up like a pig for market as Constable Watkins, who found the victim, had put it. He pursed his lips and blew out a long exhalation. It took him by surprise that it tugged at his insides in such an intensely painful way to think about it.

He took comfort in the fact that she was safe in a cell tonight, but what about all the other nights? This monster was not going to stop his filthy business.

He began walking again. He knew she wouldn't take advice about staying off the streets and felt quite panicked at the thought. A determined expression came over his face. He would find her and lock her in the cells every night if he had to.

He rubbed his chin with his forefinger and thumb. She would fight him every inch of the way, just as she had done tonight, he smiled as he thought of how she had struggled and cursed. Let her fight me, he thought, my shins can take it.

She was no more than a spelk of a thing despite her feisty resistance.

Alf pulled open the door of the station and went directly to the duty room. Reid had returned from Berner Street and a few of the detectives were holding conversations about the murder.

'Sergeant?' Reid called to him. 'What can you tell us about Mitre Square?' The room became silent.

'It was another woman, sir, of similar class to the others, possibly on the game when she was murdered. They have not been able to identify her. It was bad, sir. There were similarities to what happened to Mrs. Chapman and Mrs. Nichols - but worse. I would say it was definitely the work of the Whitechapel killer.'

'Damn him to hell for moving into City turf.' Reid answered. 'There's no doubt?'

'I wouldn't think so, sir.'

'Well, that brings City force into the investigation. All the evidence from this case will be lost to us,' Reid sighed.

'That's why I went and had a look while the body was still insitu, sir. The place was swarming with officers. We should be so lucky I might add.'

'City is a small speck in the middle of our turf. They have six stations, yet pound to a penny, they will insist on being equal partners in this investigation.'

'They got an awful lot of manpower, sir.'

Alf was amazed by how many men City had managed to get on the ground at Mitre Square. As the situation unfolded, he found it difficult to contain himself at their incompetence. The three City detectives had arrived on the scene only a moment or two after the body had been discovered. By chance, they had been talking at the south end of Houndsditch near St Botolph's Church when they heard a police whistle. They had helped to cordon off the murder scene, but no one had ordered an immediate search of the surrounding areas, yet the killer *must* have been still in the vicinity. It might have been their best opportunity to catch him red handed carrying his obscene prize of body parts.

George Morris, a Metropolitan police pensioner who worked as a night watchman in the nearby warehouse, had been the first to come to Watkins assistance. The whistle that was blown to sound the alarm belonged to him. Not all City constables had been issued with whistles, which to Alf was a disgrace. It had taken them an hour to decide to take the search into Metropolitan territory and he would bet his best boots they had only extended their initial investigation two streets east of Mitre Square to the boundary.

As most of the murders had occurred well to the east, it was likely that the killer's lair was beyond that point and he would be heading for it, yet here seemed to be no sense of urgency amongst the City detectives.

'They're gonna try to outdo us ain't they?' said Inspector Pinhorn. 'They would love to catch him and take the case from under our noses. One confounded square mile, that's all they've got to police and they have plenty of men to do it. Unlike us; we're always scrabbling about for boots on the ground.'

'Collard asked me to inform you that they would be stepping into our turf, sir,' Alf told Reid.

'Did he now?'

'I thought diplomacy was the order of the day, sir. I also said *The Met.* would do its bit to assist.'

'And so we will.' Reid reached for the duty roster and looked at where their men on the beat were located. 'We need to get the word out to our lads to report anything unusual. He's out there somewhere and we're going to get him.'

'What of the Berner Street victim, sir?'

'A woman of the same class as the others. She had her throat cut with no additional mutilation. It's believed the killer was disturbed by the person that found the body. She's as yet unidentified.'

An hour later Alf knocked on Reid's office door. He felt weary; the events of this terrible night seemed to be going on and on. He peered around the doorjamb of Reid's office without stepping inside.

'Sir, Alfie Long found a blood stained piece of cloth in Goulston Street. He said it had been dumped outside Wentworth Buildings, next to a bit of anti- Jewish writing chalked on the wall.'

'And?' Reid replied.

'They think it could have been dropped by the killer, on account that Goulston Street ain't far from Mitre Square.'

'Show me.'

'Um, you won't want it in your office, sir. The exam room is probably best.'

Edmund Reid put down his teacup and followed Alf down the stone staircase to the exam room in the basement of the station.

The cloth had been spread out on a marble counter top, ready for Reid's inspection. It was a piece of cotton approximately one square yard in size. It was roughly rectangular in shape. There was a large blood stain, approximately fourteen inches across, close to the middle of the cloth. They could see that blood had pooled in the centre portion and soaked into the fabric.

'The killer took away organs, sir,' said Alf. 'It looks like part of an apron and could have been used to carry them away.' Alf looked up. 'I happened to notice that the victim was wearing an apron.'

'It's a reasonable assumption,' said Reid. 'The victim was disembowelled and the foul odour indicates that this other substance is probably excrement.'

'Undoubtedly, sir.' Alf agreed. 'These stains here...' Alf indicated blood and faecal stains towards the edge of the fabric. 'Looks like the blood didn't soak in; it was transferred onto it, perhaps from the murderer's hands.'

The two men looked at the cloth silently for a moment, knowing that they were looking at bloody hand prints from the killer. Though it was absolutely no use to their investigation, it was a chilling thought.

'I think we can safely assume this is evidence from the Mitre Square murder. The killer cut away a piece of the victim's apron, placed the victim's womb in it-' said Reid.

'There was a kidney missing too, sir.'

'God above...' Reid murmured. 'So, the womb and kidney were placed in this piece of cloth and carried away by the killer, for whatever deranged reason he might have to do so.'

'These stains here might have been caused by urine leaking from the kidney.' Alf pointed to a portion of the big stain which looked watery and a more dilute shade of red.

Reid's mouth twisted in disgust. 'Yes. There may be a blood trail somewhere if this ghastly bundle of his leaked. Tell the men to be vigilant. Document all this will you, Alf, and send notice to City to come and have a look at it? Who did you say found it?'

'Alfie Long, sir - on his regular beat round Goulston Street. It's to his credit. City detectives including Danny Halse, who we know in his view ain't never wrong about nothing, had a walk around there and didn't come up with nothing.'

'Whereas Constable Long, who had heard all the police whistles, but didn't know what was happening, it being a City matter, had the presence of mind to investigate.'

'Yes, sir. He searched the building and came up with nothing, then took the cloth to the nearest nick, which was Commercial Street. They sent him here.'

Alf knew it made them look more efficient than City force and Reid would be pleased.

'Excellent, Sergeant. We must not forget the professional courtesies of course. We will co-operate totally and completely with our brothers in City.'

'Oh, of course, sir,' said Alf. 'Every courtesy.'

'Every courtesy until Sir Charles Warren sticks his beak in.' Reid sighed.

'The body has gone to Golden Street Mortuary,' said Alf. 'I've sent word to ask them to confirm the victim was wearing an apron and if it has a bit cut from it. We'll be ready for 'em when they get here, all nice and efficient.'

'Very good, carry on.' Reid turned away and moved towards the door, then paused. 'I'd better go and show my face at Goulston Street. I hear there is a fight brewing over the writing found next to that unspeakable thing.'

'Sir? Would the killer stop and write something on a wall three streets away from the murder scene, while police whistles were being blown all over the place and he had that filthy bundle in his hands?'

'No. I think it was probably written by a reporter to stir up trouble as soon as people heard there had been two murders on one night. They really are a despicable bunch. They're making a fortune printing the so-called details of the murders, most of which is exaggerated or made up.'

'I've got a feeling someone on the inside is tipping them off – the whole of the London press were at Mitre Square by half past two. Collard sent them away. They didn't like it.' Alf shook his head.

'No doubt there will be wild accounts in tomorrow's papers and more criticism of *The Met*. The more gruesome they make it the more they sell,' he sighed. 'I had better get over there since it's on our turf and one of our chaps found it.'

'Good luck, Inspector,' Alf nodded. 'I'm sure Commissioner Warren will be pleased that the only decent piece of evidence was found by us and on our turf.'

'Yes,' Reid sighed. 'And tickled pink to have the last say on what happens to a vital piece of evidence in City's investigation.'

Alf left the inspector and went to the cells to check on Polly. She was on her side, fast asleep and snoring softly.

He gave a little chuckle and indulged himself by watching her for a few moments. She had a pretty, angelic face that mesmerised him, yet the words that came out of her mouth earlier had made his ears ring. As he watched her, he once again gave thanks that she was not the poor woman who had been found in Mitre Square that night.

# CHAPTER FOURTEEN

Someone was gently shaking her shoulder. Polly forced open her eyelids and needles of light drove themselves into her eyes. She closed them again quickly.

'Can you sit up?' The voice was as loud as a trumpet in her ears and made her wince.

She opened her eyes again and as her vision cleared she saw Alf standing over her. She sat up, her joints stiff from the hard bed. She groaned as pain shot through her head. He handed her a mug of tea.

'Ta,' she croaked as she took it from him. She took a sip. 'That's a good cuppa, that is. Oh...' She put her hand to her forehead.

'Hangover?' Alf enquired.

'My head feels like someone's breaking rocks inside it,' she croaked.

She could feel him watching her and braced herself for a telling off. She was surprised when it never came. In fact, she thought, as memories of what took place the previous night came back to her, Alf seemed surprisingly quiet.

She looked up groggily. 'What time is it?'

'Half past six... Listen, the Whitechapel killer did two women last night.'

'He's done it again?' Now she was wide awake. 'Where?'

'One of them was in Mitre Square, just 'round the corner from where I picked you up.'

It took a moment for the information to sink in. When it did, Polly's stomach turned over; fortunately, this time, it was empty.

'Two? He did *two?* Who are they, Alfie? What are their names?'

'They ain't been identified yet I'm afraid.' He looked at her intently. 'Did you hear what I said? One was right where I picked you up. It means the killer was there, right where I found you last night.'

'I- I heard. Where was the other one?'

'Berner Street,' he had not taken his eyes off her. 'You realise he was coming this way don't you? He did Berner Street first and you were walking right towards him when I picked you up.'

Polly felt a familiar wave of heat followed by a cold sweat as blood drained away from her head. She handed the mug of tea back to Alf and tried to put her head between her knees. She stayed that way for a moment before sitting up again. She clutched the edge of the iron bed frame beneath the thin mattress and stiffened her arms to brace herself.

'Alfie. Two of my friends were out dollying 'round there, last night.'

'Where exactly?'

'Um… Suzette Le Fevre was in T*he White Swan* and Cathy Eddowes was around Aldgate somewhere. I don't know where exactly.'

'Did you see any other women engaging in prostitution?'

'Er… Yeah, the bridge workers got paid so there was a lot of business. There were some others but I didn't know them.' She began to rock back and forth. 'Alfie, I have to know who they are. I got a terrible feeling-'

'Drink your tea. I'll see what I can do.' He gave her back the mug and then left her alone in the cell. She shivered as she sipped the tea.

Alf was right, they had all been gambling with their lives. It had been a matter of chance when and where the killer struck.

After a few minutes, she heard his big copper's boots echoing on the stone floor and he reappeared. He came into the cell. 'Nobody knows nothing yet, I'm afraid. The trouble is, if they're street walkers, no one never misses them for days.'

She looked up at him. 'Do I have to go up before the magistrate?'

'No.' He sat down next to her on the narrow bed. 'You would have, but I didn't book you. So technically speaking, you ain't under arrest. You just needed a safe place to sleep it off.'

'Why you so good to me, Alfie?' she smiled. 'Thank you.'

'You ought to know I wouldn't arrest you,' he said. 'It ain't good for a woman to have that on the record.'

'You *said* you were arresting me,' she said softly.

'No, I *said* you would have a night in the cells.'

'So you did. There's a crafty side to you, Alfie Cruikshank.'

He looked at her. 'I threatened to arrest you after you started taking swings at me.'

She pressed her lips together and bowed her head. Their eyes met and she gave a short laugh when she saw there was a glow of amusement in his eyes.

'You're still messing with me.'

'Just a bit,' he gave a wry grin.

Up to now, Alf would look away if their eyes locked, but this time he showed no inclination to shift his gaze. He kept staring into her big brown eyes and it was Polly who looked away. She fixed her eyes on the wall opposite. Much to her embarrassment, hot blood flooded into her cheeks. She pondered the wall thoughtfully, then took a deep breath.

'Listen,' she said, taking care to look straight ahead rather than at him. 'I'm sorry for that remark about your feet...'

'It's all right. I do have big feet.'

'And for kicking you in the shins. I'm sorry about that too.' She grimaced as she remembered what took place. 'Um... and for pounding you on the back.'

'Hardly felt a thing.'

She pressed her lips together and pulled a face as if she was in pain. 'And I'm sorry about the bad language.' She kept her eyes fixed on the wall. '...And the names I called you.'

'You certainly know a lot of curse words.'

There was an uncomfortable pause. 'You're still staring at me aren't you?' She knew the answer without shifting her gaze from the wall.

'I like looking at you,' he said.

She blushed to an even deeper shade of red. She placed her clammy palms on her knees and hoped her burning cheeks didn't look as crimson as they felt.

Alf cleared his throat. 'Listen, I saw what he did to the lady in Mitre Square. It were shocking. What if I went to that scene and it had been you? You have to stay off the streets, Polly Wilkes.'

'Would it have upset you if it had been me?'

'Of course it would.'

She glanced at him and found him gazing intently at her. She swallowed and looked away. 'As a matter of fact, I wasn't out dollying last night.'

'Come off it. When I picked you up you were tottering along from Aldgate to Whitechapel Road.'

'Yeah, but as it happens, I wasn't on the game. I'd been reading to a poor Jewish lad I looked after a couple of weeks ago.'

'Reading?' he reiterated incredulously.

'Yeah, reading, you know, from a book? I read Charles Dickens to him. It calms him down. He's a pitiful soul, Alfie. He's bad with his nerves and he likes to hear stories. We're reading *Hard Times* at present.'

'And *that's* what you were doing down Aldgate last night?'

'Yes.'

'So how come you were tipsy?'

'Cos they won't let you sit in a pub unless you buy a drink and ginger wine is the cheapest.'

Alf gave a throaty chuckle. 'You got drunk on ginger wine?'

'What's so funny?'

'Inspector Reid gives that to the vicar of St. Mark's when he comes in.'

Polly fixed him with a beady-eyed stare. 'Ginger wine is quite potent, actually.'

She heard the chuckle rumble through his chest. 'If you say so…' Polly cast him an indignant glance and Alf cleared his throat. 'Right then, I'll show you where the washroom is and you can do your ablutions. You can go as soon as you like.' He stood up and moved to the door of the cell.

'Alfie?' she called after him. He turned around.

'You should call me Polly,'

'I should like that very much.' he said, giving her the same long look as before. He gave a brief nod. 'Stay off the streets, Polly. You weren't on the game, but you were still in his hunting ground last night and he don't seem to be particular about his victims.'

She shuddered but nodded in a mollifying way. The fact was, if she had no money, she had no choice.


Polly went straight to Crossingham's and paid for a bed for herself and Lizzie for that coming night, then she headed to 16 Greenfield Street. She did not want Aaron to keep the arrangement they had made for that evening. It would be wise to stay away from Aldgate for a while until the roughnecks forgot about them.

Mosiek Lubnowski answered the door. 'Miss Wilkes… Again.'

'Mr. Lubnowski, I just wondered if Aaron is alright.'

Lubnowski's face hardened. 'Why would he not be?'

'I read to him last night and some rowdies roughed him up a bit in the pub.'

'Aaron was in a public house?'

'Yes, we went in the snug in *The Bull* and I read some more of the book to him. As we came away, some men had a go at him. Naturally, he was upset and I just wanted to know if he was alright and to tell him not to go down there for a while.'

'He is fine,'

'I made an agreement to read to him this evening. Would you tell him if he wants me to I'll-'

'That won't be necessary.' Lubnowski interrupted. 'He is fine, thank you for your concern. Good evening.'

'But it really upset him. I thought reading to him might help if--. Hmph. Well that was rude.' Polly muttered as Lubnowski closed the door before she finished speaking.

She headed to *The Britannia* bought a glass of ginger wine and settled herself there for the rest of the day, knowing that Sid the barman would leave her alone. Much later, Millie dropped into the chair opposite. 'Polly, have you seen Cathy today?'

'No, not since last night,' Polly replied. 'Apparently, she was doing an impression of a fire engine on Aldgate High Street and according to Pearl, she was last seen being carted off to Bishopsgate nick for being drunk.'

Millie started to laugh. 'She's a hoot that Cathy ain't she?'

'I don't know how she could have been drunk, Millie, she didn't have no money and was as sober as a judge when she left here at half past seven.'

'She's good at busking. I bet she thought if she acted the fool and made people laugh they might give her some money. She can spin a good yarn can Cathy - she should be on the stage.'

'You could be right. Pearl thought it was going well until the two coppers picked her up.' Polly grinned.

'She's such a card,' said Millie affectionately. 'When I heard the other one was in Mitre Square I was worried.'

'Cathy would have been locked up by half past eight and sleeping it off in the cells at Bishopsgate.'

'I'll let John Kelly know. He's been beside himself cos he ain't seen her since yesterday afternoon,' said Millie. 'Where's Lizzie?'

Polly shrugged. 'She'll turn up when she has a fancy. She might be at the Swedish church down by Prince's Square, as it's Sunday. Or, she could be with the new gentleman friend she met last night. If that's the case, she might not turn up for a day or two.'

'Here, Pol, it's all about the murders in here.' said Millie handing her a copy of *The Star* newspaper that had been left on an adjacent table. 'Read it will you? The newspapers have been quick to print the story. They say the poor soul murdered in Berner Street is called

Elizabeth Stokes. The woman in Mitre Square was too cut up to be identified.'

Polly took the newspaper and began to read. ' *"Whitechapel: The murdering maniac sacrifices more women to his thirst for blood. Two victims this time. Both women* swiftly *and silently butchered in less than an hour."* Millie, you sure? This paper don't half exaggerate.'

'Yeah, go on. I want to know everything what happened.'

'All right.' Polly unfolded the newspaper and placed it on the table. The story of the murders took up the whole of the front page. She began to read.

' *"The terror of Whitechapel has walked again and this time has marked down two victims, one hacked and disfigured beyond discovery, the other with her throat cut and torn. Again he has got away clear; and again the police, with wonderful frankness; confess that they have not a clue."* Millie, do you really want to hear this?'

'Go on,' said Millie, as more people gathered to listen.

Polly continued. ' *"Meanwhile, Whitechapel is half mad with fear. The people are afraid even to talk with a stranger."'* Polly tutted, 'Whitechapel ain't half mad with fear. I mean, people are scared but if you ain't a-'

'Go on, Pol. Keep reading,' said Millie.

*'"Near the spot where the woman in Mitre Square lay, two pawn tickets were picked up. It is not known whether they belong to the deceased or to her murderer. The tickets were in a small tin mustard box."* Polly stopped and stared at the page. 'Oh my-' She read on quickly *'"One was for sixpence and the other was for one shilling and dated the twenty-eighth of August. They were for a pair of boots and a man's shirt and in the names of Emily Birrell and Anne Kelly."'* Polly's voice faded away. 'Where's Suzette?' She pushed away the newspaper and jumped to her feet almost knocking over the table. 'Where's Suzette?'

Millie shrugged in reply.

'Oh my good God,' said Polly.

'It's alright, Pol. It ain't Suzette, I seen her this morning,' said Millie.

'No, not Suzette, it's Cathy. Cathy Eddowes!'

Polly ran from the pub. She held up her skirts as she tore along Commercial Street. It was almost ten o'clock and it was dark. Her first thought after reading the newspaper was to find Alf Cruikshank.

She dodged a carriage that had no lights on, ran across the junction into Leman Street and sped towards the station. She pulled open the door and darted inside.

A young constable was at the panelled oak counter. He gave her a hard look.

'Yes? Can I help you,' he looked her up and down, '...Miss?'

'Alf Cruikshank. Where is he?' Polly asked breathlessly.

'What's it to you?'

'Is he here?' she puffed. She held onto the counter supporting herself against its solid shape.

'I ain't saying until you tell me what you want with him.'

'It's about the Mitre Square murder. I know who she is.'

The words worked like magic. The constable immediately knocked on a door behind the counter and summoned Alf from the room.

'Miss Wilkes? What brings you here at this hour?'

'I know who she is; the woman in Mitre Square.' The words tumbled out. 'It's the pawn tickets. She was talking about them.'

'Slow down, slow down, before you give yourself a spasm. Roberts?' he said to the constable at the desk. 'Get the lady a drink of water.' Roberts obeyed the order instantly. 'Try and calm yourself, Polly,' Alf said quietly. 'Take a deep breath and tell me what you know.'

Polly complied and managed to compose herself before speaking.

'Last night my friend, Catherine Eddowes, told us about a pawn ticket she had from someone she met hop picking in Kent. It was for a shirt. It was in a *Colman's* mustard tin. I saw it. The paper says they found two pawn tickets in a mustard tin beside the Mitre Square victim. Her old man ain't seen her since yesterday afternoon. It has to be her. We heard she was in Bishopsgate nick - she must have been let out.'

'Catherine Eddowes?'

'It has to be, Alfie. It said in the paper the other ticket was for a pair of boots and she mentioned they'd had to pawn her old man's boots on Friday. That were the twenty-eighth, weren't it? She sometimes goes by Cathy Kelly on account of her man being called Kelly. I think they said the name was Kelly on one of the pawn tickets in the papers. It fits.'

'It fits well enough to investigate. Where does she live?'

'Usually in Cooney's lodging house on Flower and Dean Street. She lives there with her man, John. They've been together for years.'

Alf beckoned two constables who were beside him in an instant.

'Robinson, Godfrey, I want the two of you to go to Cooney's lodging house on Flower and Dean Street. See if you can find Mr. John Kelly. When you do, see if his wife has turned up and if not, bring him here. Don't tell him what it's about. This could be a false alarm and if it ain't, we will want to break any bad news to him gently... Have you got that clear? '

'Yes, Sarge.'

'Don't come back 'til you've found Mr. Kelly.'

'Right, Sarge,' they said in unison.

'Go on, lads. Go on. This is urgent.'

Roberts handed a cup of water to Alf. Alf turned back to Polly and guided her towards a small, austere room on a corridor to the right of the counter. Here, Polly, drink this,' he said handing her the cup. 'Would you wait in here for a little while? I'll need to take a statement from you.' He inclined his head towards the room from which the constable had summoned him. 'You see him in there? He's the big Scotland Yard man, Fred Abberline. I need to go and brief him about what you just told me.'

'Very well, Alfie. Can I use your washroom while I'm waiting?'

'Course you can. When you're done, I'll see about getting you a cup of tea.'

In the washroom, Polly took off her bodice and washed herself thoroughly.

The blister on her heel was bleeding after her mad dash down Commercial Street. It was becoming a crater and refused to heal. She cleaned it as much as she could and tore off a small piece of her petticoat to use as a dressing to protect it from rubbing against her boot. She combed her hair and pinned it up again.'

When she finished she headed for the room Alf had indicated. She caught sight of him through a slightly open door behind the counter. He was still talking with Abberline. They were looking at a map that was spread out on an enormous table.

'Right, sir,' Alf was saying as he took his leave, 'and in the meanwhile, I'll see to that other matter.'

'Excellent. Sergeant. Carry on. It would be a fine thing to identify the victim before City force eh?' said Abberline with a smug look on his face.

By the time Alf came into the room, Polly was staring out between the bars that covered the window, into a well-lit yard. She had watched a young lad uncouple a fine black horse from a carriage and lead him away to the stables at the back of the yard. It seemed even the horses and stable boys of the Metropolitan Police had to be on call twenty-four hours a day. She turned as Alf closed the door. There was a square table and two chairs in the middle of the room and nothing else. Polly supposed it was bare and featureless because it was used to interview criminals.

'How you feeling?' he asked.

'Better now I've had a wash. I fair sprinted here when I read in the paper about Cathy.'

'I've asked a constable to bring you some tea.'

She was too agitated to sit down. 'Thank you, Alfie.'

Just then, a constable knocked on the door then came into the room with a tray that contained a pot of tea and all the necessary accompaniments and placed it on the table.

'Ta, Roberts.' Alf said as the young man waited for further orders. Alf dismissed him with a jerk of his head and sat down on one of the chairs. 'Come and have some tea,' he said, reaching for the cups and saucers.

Polly complied as Alf stood the cups on the saucers and then poured out the tea. He put extra sugar in one of the cups and handed it to Polly. She stirred it then took a sip of the steaming liquid. The hot tea was comforting and reviving. She gave a little sigh and took another swallow and then another.

As she drank, she watched Alf, who was setting out some paper, a pot of ink and a pen on his side of the table. He took the pen out of the pot of ink and tapped it gently on the edge to remove the excess. He began to fill in some details – date, time, location and the reason for the statement.

His movements were precise and controlled. He looked in command and on top of things and it gave her reassurance that she was in safe hands.

He looked up and caught her looking at him.

'What's the matter?' he said.

'Nothing's the matter. Ain't I allowed to look at you?'

He resumed his task without a word, but his ears glowed red and she saw that he was blushing. Polly could not help but smile but decided it would be better not to draw attention to it.

She read the words *identification of murder victim* as the reason for the statement and her thoughts returned to the horror of why she was there.

'It's her, Alfie I'm sure. Poor Cathy. The Star said the things he did to her was… the injuries were horrific.'

'That paper is a menace. They're always setting off trouble. A lot of what they print is just made up lies.'

'Even if half of what they printed is true, it's a terrible way to go,' said Polly.

Alf thought about the murder scene and the chamber of horrors it resembled. Once again he gave thanks that Polly was alive and sitting in front of him.

'She was dead weren't she, Alfie? When he did those things to her?'

'Er… yes definitely, she was. She was definitely dead.' He scrutinised his papers intently to avoid looking at her. Polly was holding him in an unrelenting gaze. He set to writing again without meeting her eyes.

The fact was, the preliminary post-mortem report had come in and had identified the cause of death as haemorrhage from the left carotid artery, just as he suspected. The jugular vein was intact and the artery itself was cut into, not completely severed. On the right side, the outer sheaths of the vessels were cut; the vessels themselves were intact. Alf had already worked out what this meant. The poor woman did not die instantly.

Doctor Bagster-Phillips, the self-appointed guardian of decency had censored his findings. He said the neck wound caused "immediate death". Alf knew that *immediate* was not the same as instantaneous. The victim had suffered much more than the report indicated.

Alf had a theory that this killer struck like an assassin. His priority was to silence his victims. He had strangled the others first. This was a slow process and required effort on his part. He had refined his technique for this victim. He went straight for the windpipe, making sure he cut it below the voice box. It was a quick and efficient way of preventing any cries for help. A severed windpipe would not cause death as air could be sucked in through the gaping wound. How proficiently he severed the vessels of the neck to bring about death was of no consequence to him. He didn't give a damn about putting her out of her misery before beginning his foul work. He may even have enjoyed the victim's death throes.

Death by haemorrhage was not instantaneous. It required more blood loss than people thought before someone lost consciousness, and her brain would still be receiving blood from the intact vessels on the right side. It was probable that she was not dead when he started on her and she may even have had some awareness until blood loss deprived her brain of oxygen. Alf suppressed this terrible thought and kept his expression impassive.

There was no way he would tell Polly this and heaven forbid, the victims loved ones ever found out, but this was a horror he would carry with him forever. All the ill-fated women deserved to have someone know. They deserved to have someone acknowledge what they went through and say, *I understand, I'm sorry, I know that you suffered.* Alf sucked in a long breath and his broad chest expanded to almost full capacity. *You better hope you're dead when I find you, you bastard*, he thought.

'Something wrong, Alfie?' Polly's voice shook him from his contemplations.

'No, no, I'm just weighing up what to write,' He cleared his throat. 'As I was saying, we'll know soon enough if it's your friend. You have your tea while I write it all down. We need a record of what the lady said to you about the pawn tickets. You need to tell me exactly where and when that conversation took place.'

Polly told Alf about meeting with Catherine Eddowes on Saturday night in *The Britannia* and gave him all the details of the conversation. Alf carefully recorded it all in neat copperplate handwriting.

'You need to sign it now. There, at the bottom on the right.'

Polly hesitated. 'I'll need to sign my proper name, won't I? I ain't done that in years.'

'Polly Wilkes, ain't your name?'

'My name is Mary Victoria Wilkes. Polly's a pet name for Mary.'

'How's that then?

'Same way as Jack is for John, I suppose,' she shrugged. 'Funny, Annie Chapman used to say that. It was probably one of the last conversations I had with her. She used to prattle on, bless her. I think she might have had Consumption of the brain.'

Alf nodded. 'She did - it was in the post-mortem report.'

Polly gasped. 'Everyone assumed she was drunk because she was poor and homeless and all the time she was sick. She kept on telling us that she wasn't drinking and...and nobody believed her because she staggered about and slurred her speech.' Her voice faded away and dry sobs disturbed her breathing. Then, she covered her eyes with the heels of her hands to stem her tears. 'Oh, Alfie. It's all so awful.'

After a moment she felt him pat her arm awkwardly. 'There now, don't take on.'

'I'm sorry,' she said, a hitch catching her voice. 'Poor Annie, she must have felt so poorly and we didn't believe her. We used to take the mickey out of her for saying she wasn't drunk when she couldn't walk straight… and all the time she was ill.' Alf held out a handkerchief. Polly grasped it. 'Thank you' she cried. She dried her tears and then blew her nose. 'I got three of your hankies now,' she said brokenly as her voice snagged on every word. 'I-should-have-washed-them-and-given-them-back to-you-and-I-haven't.' This made her cry even more.

Alf gave a short laugh. 'Of all the things to think about when you're upset.' He looked at her. 'It don't matter. I got plenty. I've had a box of them in my Christmas stocking every year since I was a nipper. Have some more tea and try not to take on so badly, they say it ain't good for you to distress yourself.'

She regained control after a moment. 'I'm s- sorry,' she sniffed. 'It's two of my friends that… that monster has killed now. And neither of them would have hurt a soul. You say keep off the streets and I try every day but there just isn't any work and it's so bad if you can't get in one of the doss houses and the gangs are always on the prowl and it's been so wet this year.' She began to cry again. Just as awkwardly and self-consciously, Alf patted her hand.

Polly took a deep breath and pulled herself together, again wiping away her tears. 'I'm alright now.'

'Take a minute,' said Alf gazing at her. 'I know how hard it is, Polly and I fret over you about it. How you set for money?'

'I'm all right for now as it happens, I got two bob for reading to the Jewish lad.'

'Look, if you can't get work and you're skint. You must come to me. I don't want you out on those streets.'

'You can't go giving me money. How would it look?'

'I don't care how it looks, I don't want you to be next.' He reddened. 'If I turned up at a murder scene and-' he looked away, paused, licked his lips and then pressed his mouth into a thin line. 'It's not just the injuries, it's…. He degrades them, Polly. If you-' He shook his head again, this time to shake the image from his mind. 'No… I couldn't… I ain't having it. You must promise to come to me if you're stuck.'

She smiled through reddened, watery eyes, her mouth quivering. 'You're-always-so-kind-to-me,' she said, a sob hitching on every word.

He gave her a long look. Her hands were shaking and Alf placed his large hand over hers.

'Drink your tea,' he said gently. 'I don't want you distressing yourself like this. Take your time. I have to read this statement back to you but not until you feel composed about it.'

She drank a second cup and found that she did feel better. Her hands had stopped shaking and she was able to calm herself and think more clearly.

'Does that sound like a true account of what happened?' Alf asked after reading the statement to her.

'Yes,' Polly nodded.

'Right then Mary Wilkes. Sign your name.' He gave her the pen.

When she finished signing, she saw Alf was studying her, first tilting his head to the right and then to the left.

'What's the matter?'

'Nah, you ain't a Mary. To me you're Polly. It suits you.' He looked down at her signature. 'Right then, on behalf of the Metropolitan Police, I thank you, Mary Victoria Wilkes.'

'What will happen now?'

'This will be passed onto City. We'll get a statement from Mr. John Kelly and City will make arrangements for Mr. Kelly to view the body.'

Polly shivered. 'That's a horrible thing for him to have to do.'

'Yes,' he sighed, 'I feel for the man, but it has to be done I'm afraid. If it does turn out to be Catherine Eddowes, you'll probably be called as a witness at the inquest by City Force. They'll send you a letter care of Crossingham's.'

'It is her,' Polly grimaced. 'I wouldn't have said anything if I wasn't sure.'

'I know. All this is just procedure.' He stood up. 'Listen, it's almost two o'clock in the morning. Why don't you kip down in our sickbay? I'll tell them you're out of sorts after the bad shock of your friend and everything.'

'Can I? Thanks, Alfie. I didn't relish the thought of going out there.'

'Right then, I'll take you to sickbay and then I'll need to go back and speak to Inspector Abberline.'

Alf led her into the depths of the station past the cells to the back of the building.

Sickbay was sparse and clinical. It contained a full-sized hospital type iron-framed bed with a horsehair mattress that was firm and comfortable. She locked the door and stripped down to her camisole and drawers. It was quiet, safe, warm and comfortable and she fell asleep at once.

When Polly awoke the next morning she felt much better. The washroom attached to sickbay was a lot nicer than the one in Crossingham's lodging house. Joy of joys it had a bath, a proper porcelain bath with taps. It also seemed to be supplied with endless amounts of hot water and soap.

She took her time and used the opportunity to strip off. She washed her underwear and put it to dry on the red hot water pipes. Then she steamed some marks off her bodice and skirt. She filled the bath and sank into the gloriously hot water.

The public baths charged sixpence for this pleasure and she could never afford it. This was a rapturous luxury and it soothed her aching muscles. It felt so good to be clean. She lay back in the water and felt as if she was washing away all the misery and horror of life on the streets. She spent twenty minutes combing her hair with her silver comb. When it was dry, she pinned it up in a coiled bun at the crown of her head. She found some salve and a cotton swab for the blister on her heel.

She left sickbay and moved down the narrow, tiled corridor towards the corner where the building opened up into the large vestibule that contained the oak panelled reception counter. She could see Alf standing behind it. She was about to go up to him, but pulled back into the corridor when she heard a commotion.

'You're a band of fecking idiots!' Polly recognised the raised voice and distinctive Irish accent of Mickey Kidney who was at the counter.

'You mind your conduct or you'll find yourself in the cells,' she heard Alf say to him.
Stupid as ever, Mickey did not heed the warning.'I want to see some progress,' he said. 'You should be ashamed of yourselves. Are you listening?' He banged his fist on the counter top causing Alf's pen to jump out of its inkwell and splatter black ink all over the immediate area.

'You clot-pole.' Alf growled. 'You got ink all over my ledger. I don't like it when there's ink all over my ledger.' He began to soak up the mess with blotting paper while aiming a deadly glare towards Mickey.

If he had any sense, Mickey would have paid attention to the growl in Alf's voice and proceeded from that moment as carefully as if he was facing a grizzly bear. Instead, he pulled back his fist and threw a punch. The blow missed Alf, but hit the constable standing next to the counter on the side of the head, knocking off his helmet.

'Oi!' the constable exclaimed. He grabbed Mickey and wrestled him to the floor. Mickey bellowed and started throwing punches in random directions. The constable responded by landing some blows of his own on Mickey's torso. 'You had enough yet? Cos there's plenty more if you want 'em,' he said as Mickey emitted a stream of curses and threats that attracted the attention of other officers.

Polly rolled her eyes as Mickey started throwing more punches and yelling blue murder. He was still shouting and kicking as two more constables leaped on him.

She slipped past commotion and left through the main door of the station, A fine carriage was waiting outside and the most beautiful, glossy black horse Polly had ever seen, nodded in its traces. Its breath made billowing clouds on the cold morning air. She could not resist going up to the beautiful animal.

'You're a fine boy, aren't you?' she murmured, stroking his nose. One of the things she missed about her former privileged life, apart from having enough to eat and a roof over her head, was riding her pony in the park.

He really was a fine horse and both he and the carriage were far too smart for this part of town. Then she caught a glimpse of the passenger, who was reading a newspaper with intense concentration. It was George Lusk. She slid out of sight and moved away, wondering if his presence had something to do with Mickey.

She knew that Mickey had joined Lusk's Vigilance Committee. Not, Polly suspected, because he cared about the Whitechapel killer. Rather it was Mickey's style to play the big man. He would want to be part of something where he could act like a bully and feel important. Lizzie said Lusk was ambitious, and so was Mickey.

'Miss Wilkes?' Polly turned on hearing her name. Alf Cruikshank was behind her on the pavement. He moved to her side. 'I wonder if you would do something for me?'

'Just name it, Sergeant.'

'Would you come with me to St. George's Mortuary?' Polly looked at him, her brows drawn together. 'Blimey Alfie, I've had better offers.'

Alf coloured a little. 'I think you might be able to identify the Berner Street victim,'

'I thought the word was her name is Elizabeth Stokes?' Polly replied.

'We ain't sure now. It's all in doubt. The witness who identified her don't seem all there, to be honest.' He tapped the side of his head with his forefinger. 'We're pretty sure the victim is local. You know a lot of people 'round here and I trust you to give me an honest answer. They've had people traipsing in all morning. They're just sightseers wanting to see the body and they say the first name that comes into their heads.'

'Course I'll help, if I can.'

'Right then. You come back in the station and I'll sort the paperwork out and speak to Abberline.' He guided Polly back inside the building. She was glad to see that she would not have to face Mickey Kidney, who was already handcuffed and being frogmarched along the corridor towards the cells.

As the cab rolled along St George's Street, a main highway that ran from west to east. Polly thought about the task ahead. She bit her lip.

'Alfie? She ain't bad, is she? I mean, what they say he does to 'em...'

'Don't worry, Polly. I'll go in first and make sure she's decent to look at,' he said. 'These places ain't no picnic but it won't be too bad. She weren't... you know, she only had her throat cut as far as I understand.'

St George's church was a large, white, impressive building with high tower almost as big as a cathedral. The mortuary was behind the church in a public garden which decades before had been a cemetery. The mortuary itself was a small, anonymous, rectangular brick building. It was accessed via a discrete gate on a side street called Ratcliffe Street. People walking in the gardens were probably unaware of the procession of bodies that were constantly being moved in and out of the nondescript building.

Alf asked the cabbie to wait. He led Polly into a sparse waiting room that was lined with dark green rectangular tiles. It reeked of carbolic disinfectant. A long wooden bench lined one of the walls. Polly sat down as Alf knocked on a large, solid oak door and was invited inside.

When he emerged five minutes later, Polly stood up and braced herself to face the horror that was in the other room. Then she noticed Alf's complexion which had turned grey. He moved towards her and did not seem to be able to speak.

'My word, it ain't that bad is it?' she asked.

After a moment he found his voice. 'There ain't no need for you to go in, Polly. I was able to identify the victim.' He had a strange look on his face.

'Alfie? What's the matter? Why you looking at me like that?'

'Polly. I... I don't know how to tell you-'

'Tell me what? What Alfie?'

'You should sit down.'

'Never mind that. Tell me what?'

'Oh my good lord.' He replied, running his hand down his face. 'Polly, I'm so sorry...' He looked at her and placed his hand gently on her forearm. 'It's Mrs. Stride.'

'I don't understand.'

'I've had a look at the victim. I'm afraid it's your friend, Mrs. Stride.'

'The vic- Don't be silly. How can it be Lizzie?' The look on his face told her that he was not mistaken. 'It can't be her, Alfie.'

'I'm so sorry. It's her, Polly.'

'She was out with a gentleman and-' Polly froze. 'Oh God. Oh God. Oh dear God. Let me see her.'

'No.' Alf said catching her around the waist as she tried to dart past him. 'No. That's not a good idea.'

'I want to see her, Alfie.' She squirmed out of his grasp and wriggled away from him.

Alf grabbed her and pulled her back towards him. 'Not yet. Polly...No.... Listen. Not yet. Please, listen to me. Polly, Polly...' He held her tightly against him. 'Listen to me. Listen.... You don't want to see her like that. No,' he said as she tried to struggle free. 'Let them make her nice. Listen to me. Let them make her nice. You're not here as an independent witness now. You're here as her friend. All right?' He cupped her cheek with his hand. 'Right?'

'Alfie.' Polly began to cry. 'It can't be her.' Alf pulled her into an embrace and she collapsed against his chest. 'It can't be.'

Alf held her comfortingly without a trace of his usual awkwardness.

'I'm so sorry,' he said, holding on to her for a long time and letting her cry. Eventually, he spoke again. 'Listen, Polly, does Mrs. Stride have any kin what needs to be told?'

'Are you s- sure it's h- h- her?'

'I'm afraid I am. We'll need an official identification from someone with a proven connection to her and I would much rather it wasn't you...'

'It should be me. I'm all she's got except that stupid waste of skin she used to live with.' Her lungs were seizing up and her chest felt tight. She was unable to suck in enough air. 'I-don't-want-him-near-her.'

Her voice came in short gasps as tears poured down her face. Alf offered her a handkerchief.

'I-still-got-your-other-one,' she sobbed. She took the handkerchief and pressed it to her cheeks.

'Can you suggest someone who could identify her?' Alf asked her gently.

Polly looked up. 'Me,' she sniffed. 'She's my best friend. It's down to me to do it.'

'Polly-' Alf began.

Polly took a deep breath and dried her eyes. 'It has to be me, Alfie. I got to do this for her. She would do the same if the boot was on the other foot.'

Alf studied her carefully for a moment. 'Very well. You wait here, and I'll make sure they're ready.'

He went back into the post-mortem room as Polly, stricken with grief, began sobbing again. She could hear Alf speaking to the mortuary attendants in a raised voice. By his tone she deduced that he was berating them for something, though she could not make out his words. A few moments later he re-emerged from the room.

'Are you sure about this, Polly?'

She nodded and stood up. 'Yes.'

'Very well,' he said on a sigh. 'Hold on to me.' Alf hooked her right arm over his and led her through the door into the post-mortem room.

The first thing Polly noticed was that the room smelled like a butchers shop on a hot day and pungent odour of preserving fluid nipped the back of the throat. Like the waiting room, the walls were covered in dark green tiles and the floor was black granite. It was dirty. There were splashes of blood and other less identifiable fluids on the walls and floor. Some shallow enamel trays on a long bench against the wall had been covered up using a stained white sheet. On a table in the middle of the room, a shape that was obviously a body was covered with another grubby looking white sheet.

Alf led her to the table. She felt the strength of his left arm holding her up and his right hand clutching hers.

A dishevelled looking mortuary attendant with a two-day growth of stubble on his face stood at the other side of the table. Polly could not take her eyes of his apron which was covered in vile stains.

'Now, Polly. I'll ask you formally if the person here is Mrs. Elizabeth Stride and you must speak the answer *yes* or *no*. Alright?'

Polly nodded, feeling her knees growing weak.

Alf nodded at the attendant who pulled the sheet back to reveal the face of the corpse.

Polly's head began to swim. Lizzie lay on the table with her eyes closed. Her hair looked just the same as when Polly had styled it for her two nights ago. Only a few strands had come loose. She put out a hand and brushed them back into place with shaking fingers. She could see where blood had been hastily cleaned from the skin around her neck and face. There was a dark red gash that started beneath Lizzie's left ear and ran across her neck. It was deeper on the left side and more superficial on the right. Her face looked uninjured apart from the healed scar on her earlobe where Mickey had hit her for taking the pretty handkerchiefs the day Polly had brought the duplicate key to Devonshire Street. She stared at that scar, and another on her lip, which removed any doubt in her mind that the body was that of her friend.

She felt sick and her knees started to buckle. She heard Alf's voice far away. She thought she heard him ask the question and thought she answered him, but could not be sure the word had emerged from her lips. The next thing she knew, she could feel the sting of ammonia smelling salts pinching her nose and throat. Her vision cleared and she found she was in the waiting room, sitting with Alf, who was supporting her against his torso.

'Take your time, my dearest,' she heard him say through the fog of her grief. Her bones had turned to jelly and she was unable to support her own weight. Alf held on to her as reassuring and solid as a rock. She thought she felt him press his lips to the top of her head, but didn't know if it was real or if she was dreaming.

Gradually her mind cleared and she looked up at him wretchedly. 'You got to get him for this, Alfie.'

'We will, Polly,' he said gently, 'I promise we will.'

# CHAPTER FIFTEEN

Polly stared at the roiling water. The Thames was a mighty river; deep as well as fast flowing. The eddying fluxes of the incoming tide were deadly. She could see the sucking currents skating across the surface. The water swirled and churned, pulling everything under. Nothing escaped its grip.

Polly did not know how long she had been sitting under London Bridge, though it was time enough to become chilled to the bone. The loss of her friend was unbearable. The pain she felt was a physical thing. To make it stop, all she had to do was walk down the embankment steps into the muddy brown water. It was so simple. It would all be over in a few minutes.

She slumped against the cold, damp stonework of the bridge. Her knees were drawn up to her chest. She had tucked herself into a ball as meagre protection against the icy wind that barrelled down the Thames.

Some of the time, she placed her head on her knees and cried. Other times, she threw her head back and tore a howl from the depths of her soul. She held her breath so even that dreadful, desolate cry was made in silence. Wave after wave of tears blurred her vision. Tears soaked her cheeks and dripped onto her skirt. Every tear was shed in silent grief.

The tide came in fast. The water had already covered the lowest of the steps and was lapping against the second. All she needed was the nerve to take that gentle fall and the river would do the rest. The current would pull her under and take her out of this life. Once that mighty river had you, it did not let go.

Many had done it at this very spot, finding that single moment of courage. No one would miss her if she did likewise. It was so simple. One little step and then blissful oblivion.

She was tired of fighting for scraps. There was no point in trying to get through another hopeless day. She no longer had any courage. There would be no better life. Her body heaved with huge noiseless sobs that shook her small frame as she tried to summon the courage to walk towards the water.

Polly held her breath as she heard someone on the steps that ran down the side of the bridge onto the embankment. She did not move, she was hidden in the shadows and would not be noticed.

A young woman came into view. She was wearing a stunning royal blue velvet gown. It had a fashionable shelf like bustle with perfect swags and drapes around it. She wore a matching fitted jacket with a high collar that looked stunning.

Polly looked at her with admiration. The young woman's hair was styled into a pile of curls at the back of her head. Her gorgeous small brimmed bonnet was in the fashionable plant pot shape. Polly gazed at her, blown away by the exquisite outfit. The girl was perfect in couture and looks. She wore a matching pair of gloves that Polly could tell were good quality kid leather.

She was distracted from her grief for a moment as she wondered about the young girl with growing unease. What she was doing on the embankment alone and so close to the river? Then a young man appeared, and Polly's concern grew in a different direction.

The young man moved to the girl's side and they watched the swirling water for a while. They had not noticed Polly, who was huddled in the shadows close to the underside of the deck of the bridge. She was able to watch them as they laughed and talked. She surmised that the girl was probably only four or five years younger than herself; yet sitting there, watching them, Polly felt at least a century older.

The young man threw small twigs into the river for the girl's amusement. They watched them sail away for a short distance before turning on end and being sucked under by the strong currents.

As he searched for another stick with which to entertain the young lady, he noticed Polly. He straightened up, looked at her for a moment then turned and took hold of the girl by the elbow.

'Come along, dearest.' he said.

'Oh but, Thomas, this is such fun,' said the young lady.

The name made Polly wince and suddenly she saw her younger, stupid self in this girl.

'We can find another place.'

'This place is perfect,' she replied. 'Do throw another stick in the water.'

'Um, I'm afraid we are not alone, dearest. There is an indigent woman over there. Better to give her sort a wide berth, you know.'

'Oh, is there?' the girl answered. 'Do let me see her. What a hoot.' The young lady turned around and stared openly at Polly as if she was a specimen in a zoo. Polly, in return, was able to take a good look at her. Her guess was accurate, she thought. The girl was about seventeen or eighteen years old and she was regarding her with unabashed curiosity.

Her expression turned to one of haughty contempt when she saw that Polly was staring back at her. The look she gave her was like a poisoned arrow directly to the heart and it found its target. Even to this child, she was an insignificant nobody, an object to be gawped at as something less than human. Then it occurred to Polly that this girl was with the young man, unchaperoned.

'Bloody hell…' she murmured through gritted teeth. What did she think she was doing, the brainless little idiot?

Polly knew exactly what the little feather-head was doing. Hadn't she done the same thing herself? She was flirting with the young man and revelling in the attention he was lavishing upon her.

Polly knew what an intoxicating feeling that was. She had been just like her. She had been headstrong and craved excitement. She knew what the girl was thinking. She was having fun and to the devil with the consequences. The young man flattered her. He hardly took his eyes off her and did everything he could to amuse her and ingratiate himself into her favour.

The girl's stare hardened into an arrogant glare. 'Don't you dare stare at your betters you… you impudent nobody.'

A flash of rage overtook Polly. A blazing scarlet mist blurred her vision and at once she knew why people described rage as "seeing red". She jumped to her feet and charged towards them.

'You stupid little half-wit!' she shrieked. The girl froze and gaped at Polly. 'You think you're better than me? Do you know how I ended up like this? By doing exactly what you are doing right now. How *dare* you seek this young man's company unsupervised,' she blazed. 'Do you have any idea how much damage this will do to your reputation? Go and find your duenna and apologise to her this minute! THIS MINUTE! Do you understand? Go on! NOW!' Polly roared, jabbing a finger towards the steps. All the bravado and haughtiness vanished from the girl's face. 'And don't you *dare* believe a word he says,' Polly ranted, 'because it's all lies, every word of it. LIES! No decent young man would let you do this. Go on! Go home while the hour is still reasonably respectable and make sure you beg your duenna's forgiveness.' The girl's chin quivered as Polly turned her blistering rage on the young man. 'And YOU!' You are obviously older than this girl. Shame on you!' she raved as he looked back at her open mouthed. 'Shame! Shame! Shame! How dare you take advantage of her restlessness? You should be horsewhipped for luring her down here. You must know that, for her, there are serious consequences to this behaviour. That means you are either a gold digger, a roué or a complete fool!' She glared at the girl once again. 'Either way, unless you want to end up like me, disowned by your family. Living on the streets and selling yourself for a bed in a stinking lodging house, have nothing to do with this boy. Go on, get out of it! Now! NOW! I said!' She stamped her foot in their direction.

Polly had unwittingly shed the east end accent. The two were shocked that someone whom they had judged to be a low-born, shabby, common woman, sounded like a lady. She spoke as they did, had berated them with eloquence and authority and understood about duennas. This made any thought of answering back evaporate in the heat of Polly's blazing fury. The young girl's bottom lip stuck out in a trembling pout. The young man looked like a little boy being told off by his nanny. 'GO!' Polly shrieked. The two turned and fled up the steps. 'And you girl, go back home to your mother at once!' she screamed after her. 'AT ONCE!'

She sat down heavily on the steps and put her head on her knees. The exertion had made her light headed. That young girl had no idea what a short journey it was from there to here. The contemptuous look she had given Polly lingered like the pain of a hornet's sting.

She sat up and looked at the water again. It was running even faster as the tide reached its peak. She watched the powerful, swirling currents and burst into tears. Seeing that young girl was like having a window into the past and regret crushed her until she could hardly breathe.

The river looked cruel and terrifying but not as much as carrying on without hope. Why bother to struggle on each day, only to survive to struggle on again the next? Had she not met Lizzie, she might have done this right after she left the hospital. It was her friendship and wise advice that had made the difference.

A fresh wave of grief took her breath away. The shock of Lizzie's death had not abated. She could not remember leaving the mortuary. All she remembered was Alfie saying *"I'm very sorry, Polly."*

She had been incredulous at first. Don't be stupid. How could it be Lizzie? The look on Alfie's face had made the unthinkable true. She remembered a roaring noise in her head. The rest was lost in a dense fog that she was unable to penetrate.

She had the feeling that Alfie had been with her for a while. She had a vague recollection of Suzette or perhaps it was Millie, telling him not to fret. They told him they would look after her. The next morning, she had woken up in a single room in Crossingham's lodging house. She had left before six o'clock and wandered the streets all day, not knowing what to do with herself. She kept finding herself looking for Lizzie and then remembering that she was gone. Her brain had stuck in that pattern and the pain kept crushing her again and again.

This morning, she had woken up under the bridge. She supposed she had spent the entire night there yet had no recollection of finding this place. She had not moved all day. She had just stared at the water. Her limbs were stiff with cold and her muscles painful.

She shuddered. Death by drowning seemed a terrible way to die. Fear of the feeling of suffocation as water filled her lungs was the only thing that kept her on the embankment. It was getting dark, her teeth were chattering and she was shivering.

She wanted to drift into sleep and never wake up, but she knew the air was not quite cold enough for that. She had no desire to make her way back to Dorset Street to spend another night in a common doss house. Perhaps she would just sit right here until her broken heart finally stopped.

'POLLY?' She heard footsteps hurrying towards her. 'What the blazes d'you think you're doing?'

Her muscles had seized up in the cold and she was unable to move. She lifted her eyes and saw Alf Cruikshank standing in front of her, an expression of relief on his face.

'Alfie?' she mumbled. 'What you doing here?'

He crouched down beside her. 'What you doing sitting here? Good God, you're freezing.'

'Leave me alone. I ain't doing nothing wrong.'

He took hold of her hands and began to rub them between his. 'Come on. You need to get warmed up.'

'Please, go away and leave me alone. I don't want to go nowhere.'

'I ain't leaving you. I've been looking for you all day.'

'Why you been looking for me?'

'Cos nobody's seen you since first thing yesterday morning. I've been worried sick. I've been scouring the streets looking for you.' He took off his overcoat and wrapped it around her. The warmth of his body flowed into hers. 'You ain't been here all that time have you?'

'I dunno, I walked around a bit,' she replied in a lacklustre tone.

'I didn't know where else to look. I was scared witless. Then I heard someone yelling, and two kids shot out those steps as if their arses were on fire. I thought I'd take a look and here you are. Beg pardon for the language, but I've been frantic trying to find you.'

She looked at him. He was not in uniform. 'You undercover again?'

'Yes, though my shift finished hours ago. I made on I was looking for The Ripper, in fact, I was looking for you.'

She looked up groggily. 'Who?'

'That's what they're calling the Whitechapel killer; Jack the Ripper. Listen, I got to get you out of here. You're freezing. Come on, up you get,' he said gently. He placed her arm around his neck and hauled her to her feet.

Half carrying her, he guided her to the steps and they climbed towards the main road. There were three sets of ten steps with two rectangular landings in between. She was forced to pause on each landing, supported by Alf, until enough blood flowed into her frozen limbs to continue.

'Where you taking me?'

'I'm taking you home.'

'I ain't got no home, Crossingham's ain't a home, it's a doss house.'

'No, I mean to *my* gaff.'

'What? 'She shuffled to a halt and squinted at him. 'You can't do that it. It ain't respectable.'

'It ain't respectable - said the dollymop.' His bushy eyebrows lifted as he looked squarely at her.

'I meant for you,' she said.

'You let me worry about that. For now, it's all I can think of is to get you safe and warm. A doss house ain't no place for you. And you ain't sick, so there ain't no need to take you up the hospital. Besides, mother will be at home.'

'What's she gonna say when I walk through the door?'

'She's recently taken poorly. She won't even see you unless you go in her room.'

Alf got them a cab at the rank on Lower Thames Street. Polly had not eaten nor drank anything in over twenty-four hours. She felt sick and exhausted. The blister on her heel throbbed excruciatingly. For the entire journey, Alf held her in his arms and tried to keep her warm, while her head lolled against his shoulder in a semi-conscious haze.

Alf lived in a smart terraced house on Scarborough Street which was close to Leman Street, behind the police station.

As Alf helped her out of the cab and paid the driver, Polly could not miss the sharp contrast between this neat little street and Dorset Street. No broken railings, no peeling paint, no broken windows, no filth in the gutters nor destitute souls walking the pavements or lying drunk in the street. She had become so accustomed to seeing such things that she barely registered the awfulness of it. Seeing this street of comfortable well-loved and well-kept houses with shiny windows and glossy black doors, made her cry. She wiped away the tears thinking it was a stupid thing to cry about.

Alf's house was number eleven, half way along the south side of the street. Like all the others it had a shiny door-knocker and a brass letterbox. Alf opened the door and led her into a long narrow hallway.

'I'm home, Mother.' He called up the flight of stairs to his right.

There was a door on the left side of the hall which led to a parlour and another at the end of the hall that led to the kitchen.

A diamond shaped mosaic of tiles in terracotta, black and white covered the hall floor. They had a sheen on them in the gas light. A cream and brown patterned carpet ran the length of the stairs, held in place with brass stair rods at the angle of each riser.

'Come along to the kitchen. The fire will be on.'

The kitchen was cosy and warm, though it looked as if a whirlwind had passed through it. Alf snatched up some clothing from a chair by the fire and Polly sat down. He turned up the gas lamp until it gave out a decent amount of light.

'I'll just check on Mother,' he said.

Polly rested an elbow on the arm of the chair and wiped her hand across her face. What on earth was she doing in a copper's house? She was too exhausted to work it all out. The warmth of the fire felt wonderful. Heat began to thaw out her frozen limbs.

Glad that Alf had not yet returned, she took out the cotton square from her pocket, wiped tears from her eyes and blew her nose. The handkerchief Lizzie had given her fell to the floor. She picked it up and her eyes swam with fresh tears. She heard Alf's footsteps returning. She wiped her eyes, put away her handkerchief, smoothed her cheeks and sat up straight.

'Mother's all right, she just wants a cup of tea,' said Alf. 'And so do you, I imagine.'

Polly started to get up. 'No, you stay by the fire,' he said. 'You're absolutely soaked to the skin.'

He turned away and went to the sink to fill the kettle, he lit the gas ring and placed the kettle on the flame to heat. Then he set about putting three scoops of tea in the teapot and arranging three cups in their saucers. 'I'm sorry it's such a mess,' he said. 'Mother hasn't been able to cope since she's been ill. What with all the double shifts I have to put in, I'm not much help.'

'Have you told her I'm here?'

'There ain't no need for her to know. She's having one of her spasms so she's taken to her bed.'

'I'm sorry to hear that. Does it happen often?'

'With increasing frequency I'm afraid. It's been most of the time these last few weeks. She has medicine that makes her drowsy so she sleeps a lot.' He poured boiling water into the brown ceramic teapot then covered it with a woolly, knitted tea cosy to keep it hot. Polly watched him. Alf was obviously a man who knew how to make a decent brew. He put two scoops of sugar and some milk into a cup and then poured out the steaming tea before handing it to Polly.

'You know how to make a good cuppa, Alfie.'

'First thing a young constable learns,' he shrugged. 'Hang on…' he said, 'I just remembered something.'

He went into a lobby at the back of the house and she heard him descend some steps into what she presumed to be a basement. He returned carrying a leather travelling trunk. 'There are some of mother's things in here,' he grunted. 'They don't fit her no more.' He placed it on the floor. 'We need to take off your wet clothes. Oh my-' he gulped. 'I wasn't thinking about, um…' His ears turned bright red.

'Thinking about what?'

'Taking off your clothes.'

As Polly watched, his face turn as red as his ears.

'Alfie. I know that. You're always a perfect gentleman - even to a dollymop like me.'

'Don't call yourself that,' he said. He looked at her awkwardly then cleared his throat. 'Mother will be ready for her tea by now.' He gestured towards the trunk. 'There might be something in there you could put on. You'll catch a chill if you don't get out of...' He cleared his throat again instead of finishing the sentence. 'Anyway, I'll take mother her tea.' He added four scoops of sugar and some milk to a cup of tea then took it upstairs to his mother.

As she waited, Polly finished her own cup of hot sweet tea. It was like ambrosia of the gods and she felt the bone-deep coldness inside her begin to subside.

The trunk was neatly packed with good quality clothing that was as good as anything she would have worn in her old life. She could see that it had been well cared for.

It all looked too big for her by four or five inches, but she found a chemise, some drawers and a petticoat. All of the undergarments felt like silk. She pulled out a plain black skirt which she could pull in and tie tightly around her waist. She found a white blouse with a high collar and mutton chop sleeves and a black woollen shawl.

The blouse and chemise fitted her well because she apparently had bigger breasts than Mrs. Cruikshank. The drawers consisted of two separate legs held together by ribbons and a drawstring at the waist, they could be adjusted to fit, as could the petticoat.

She loved the feel of these clothes. She had been wearing her old dress for so long she had forgotten how nice it felt to wear good quality clothing.

Ten minutes later, Alf returned.

'She's settled- Oh my...' he said, stopping short when he saw what she was wearing.

'I hope you don't mind,' she said awkwardly. She pulled the shawl more closely around her shoulders.

'That's what I got 'em up here for.'

'I wanted to wear black for Lizzie.'

'You look... different.'

'Respectable, you mean?' she smiled, mocking herself a little.

'Well... yeah. I always said you had the look of a well-bred young lady. In that getup, you *are* a well-bred young lady.'

'Not any more, Alfie. I got no illusions.'

'It ain't an illusion,' he said, gazing at her. 'The fact that you've hit hard times don't change the fact of your upbringing.'

'Is your mother all right? It must be hard for you. All this going on and your mother poorly,' said Polly, changing the subject.

'Yeah, it is sometimes,' he sighed.

He moved further into the room. He saw that that her cup was empty. He took it from her and rinsed away the old tea leaves. He filled the pot with more hot water and then poured her another cup of tea. Automatically, Polly sat down before taking the cup from him, because a lady never drank tea standing up.

'Unfortunately, she took ill just after all this business started and what with the murders last Sunday, I ain't had much time for her,' he said.

Polly's eyes fill with tears.

'Sorry, I didn't mean to remind you.'

'It's alright.' She wiped her eyes with her fingertips. 'It's a fact and somehow I've got to get used to it.'

'When I found you, I had quite a turn. You were just sitting there staring at the river, as if you were thinking about chucking yourself in. I watched you from the steps for a while. You were oblivious.'

'To be honest, I thought about it.' She shook her head. 'I couldn't find the courage. I kept looking at the water and thinking that it seemed such a horrible way to go, 'course, compared to-' her eyes again filled with tears. 'Sorry.'

Alf crouched down beside her. 'I'm glad I found you,' he said. 'And for heaven's sake don't apologise. I know how close you were to Mrs. Stride.'

'I don't know what I'm going to do, Alfie.' she sniffed. 'I keep forgetting that she's gone. She's the one who would talk to me and make me feel better about something like this.'

He took hold of her hand between his and patted it. 'There now, don't take on, or you'll make yourself ill. Drink your tea. You must be parched sitting there all that time.'

Polly choked back her tears and then managed a swallow of tea. He gazed at her, a gentle expression on his face. 'What would she have said to you at a time like this?'

Polly gave a short laugh. 'She would have said '*It will be fine, Polly,*' she imitated Lizzie's slight Swedish accent 'As a matter of fact, that's one of the last things she said to me.' Her bottom lip trembled. 'She would also want me to make sure the bastard paid,' she said, her voice wavering.

He nodded. 'You leave that to us. Mind you,' he sighed, 'I don't know how we're gonna catch him, Polly. Four murdered women now, maybe more. The press is having a have a field day.'

Polly stared at him. 'You think the Whitechapel killer did Lizzie?'

'Well, yes. They're calling it a double event – her and Mrs. Eddowes. Why? What's up?'

'Lizzie was out with a gentleman the night she was killed. Everybody would have seen them together so I doubt he would be stupid enough to kill her and if she was with him all night, how could she fall into the clutches of this Jack the Ripper? Mickey Kidney, on the other hand, could have got her on her own for few minutes and done it in a fit of jealousy.'

Alf looked at her, the lines above the bridge of his large nose creased into a frown. He sat down on the chair next to hers. He was transforming into his policeman persona before her eyes.

'This Mickey is her husband?'

'They lived together until three weeks ago when she finally came to her senses and left him.'

'Why was that?'

'Because he's a pig. He knocked her about a lot. He even chained her to the bedpost when he went to work. He has a terrible jealous nature and a temper to match. Even though Lizzie ain't, *was*, no shrinking violet, he dominated everything she did and I'm pretty sure he pimped her out to his mates when he was short of money. About a week after she left him he found her in Clooney's lodging house on Flower and Dean Street and threatened her. He said he would see her in the ground if she didn't come back to him. She was in a right state. Of course it was him that killed her.'

'How often did he threaten her?'

'When *didn't* he threaten her, more like? He gets his mates to spy on her all the time. They let him know where she is and what she's doing.' Polly stopped abruptly. '*Was*,' she corrected herself again and moved on quickly. 'She had him in court one time because he beat her quite badly and she lost some teeth on the right side of her mouth when he smacked her a good one across her face. Another occasion he got away with doing time because she didn't turn up at court.'

'Why didn't she turn up? It would look bad. The copper what brought the case wouldn't like that. It would look like he hadn't got his evidence together properly.'

Polly sighed. 'Mickey might have threatened her, though I'm sorry to say Lizzie could be a bit dim that way.' She swallowed her rising tears. 'She was the best, kindest person in the world but when it came to men, she was as slow to catch on as a bag of snails. All Mickey had to do was put on a gushing, obsequious tone, say he was sorry, flatter her a bit, and she would follow him anywhere. He knew that and played her like a fiddle.'

Polly told him more about the day Lizzie had ran terrified into *The Britannia* after Kidney had threatened her in Flower and Dean Street. 'He's got a hell of a temper, Alfie. You saw how he went on the other morning at your nick. When I left, two of your constables were sitting on him and he was still putting up a fight. What chance would Lizzie have?'

Alf drew his brows together. 'You mean that idiot what spilt my ink and ran his mouth off was Mrs. Stride's fella?'

'Yeah, large as life and twice as ugly... What's wrong?' Polly took in his thoughtful expression.

'Now something he said makes sense. At the time, we thought he was just drunk and stupid.'

'He is, and he has a mean streak a mile wide.' She looked at Alf. 'What did he say?'

'Something odd. He asked for a detective to help him find his wife's killer. Then he said if he had been the detective on the case he would have killed himself.'

'Sounds like him. Talking rubbish and full of his own importance just about sums him up.'

'Why would he say a thing like that?' said Alf, drawing his brows together.

'He thinks a lot of himself. He's always making stupid claims about what he's got and what he's doing, or what he's going to do. At the bottom of it, he's just an arrogant, stupid man.'

'No, Polly, that ain't the point I'm making. You see, at that time, Mrs. Stride hadn't been identified, that's why I asked you.'

Polly took a sharp intake of breath. 'So how did he know she was dead?'

'I think he ought to be asked to explain that. The papers said she was Elizabeth Stokes,' said Alf.

'Yeah, so they did. Believe me, if the word was out that it was Lizzie, I would've been the first to know.'

'We had no idea it was Mrs. Stride. She was formally identified last night by a lady called Elizabeth Tanner. The inquest has been adjourned while we make enquires to confirm it.'

'I didn't identify her?'

'From your reaction, it was obvious it was her, unfortunately, it has to be done proper and formal like, and you fainted.'

'I did?'

'Yeah, you gave me quite a turn. You came over white as a sheet and down you went. Luckily I caught you and got you out of there.'

'Seems I got to thank you again, Alfie.'

'Not necessary…' he mumbled, dismissing her thanks with a shrug.

Sensing his embarrassment, Polly changed the subject.

'Betty Tanner runs the doss house on Flower and Dean Street. She put a lot of work Lizzie's way. I'm glad Mickey wasn't the one to identify her.'

'He might have, but no one knows where he is. He ain't been on the docks. I think I would like him to explain how he knew Mrs. Stride was dead when no one else did.'

Polly looked at him. 'There's only one way I can think of. As far as I'm concerned, the only way Mickey could have known she was dead was if he was the one that killed her.'

'Unfortunately, we need evidence. Listen, Polly, about the mortuary, I'm so sorry. I never would've asked if I had any idea-'

'I know that,' she said softly, reaching forward and placing a hand on his arm. Alf held her gaze but did not speak. 'What will happen now?' Polly asked.

'I'll let Inspector Abberline know. I think we should ask Mr. Kidney to explain himself – when we find him.'

'Alfred?' Polly heard his mother's faint call from upstairs.

'Coming, Mother.' He turned to Polly, 'I'll try not to be long. Make a fresh pot and have another cup of tea and then we'll have some supper.'

Polly set about making a cup of tea and thought about the information Alf had just given her. Only Mickey Kidney would be stupid enough to turn up at the police station demanding justice before anyone else knew Lizzie was dead. She needed no more convincing of his guilt.

'I'll get him, Lizzie. I promise,' she murmured. 'He'll pay for what he did to you.'

# CHAPTER SIXTEEN

One of the many things Polly's very expensive school taught her was how to tell if the servants were doing a good job. As she looked around the kitchen she could tell this house had been immaculately kept until recently but was now looking quite neglected. In the corner was a dresser upon which cups, saucers, plates and bowls were neatly arranged. They were dusty and looked as if they had not been touched in a long time.

There was a sink under a small window that was adorned with a pair of blue and white gingham check curtains. A cooking range surrounded the coal fire. It looked unused and a modern, grey and black, cast iron gas oven with a four ring hob had replaced it.

The dishes were washed and draining next to the sink and the everyday chores were being done, but she could see that the longer term household tasks were piling up. The entire house was dusty, there were things lying around and the floor had not been swept in a while. This was so unlike the meticulous Alfie she knew.

It must be difficult for him, acting as nurse to his sick mother, she thought. All the while putting in countless extra hours at the station as they tried to catch the lunatic who was murdering women.

She picked up the poker and plunged it into the fire, using it to separate the burning coals and get some air beneath them. Flames appeared and began to dance around the separated pieces. She felt good in the borrowed clothes and the silk was soft against her skin. Though she had played it down, wearing these clothes made her feel respectable. *Don't get carried away girl,* she thought, *you ought not to have any illusions about your lot in this life.*

She replaced the poker on its hook and noticed a journal on the shelf next to the fireplace. It was a Beeton's Christmas Annual from the year 1887. Polly, never able to resist a story, started to read the one that was featured on the front page called *A Study in Scarlet* by A. Conan Doyle. She was soon engrossed in the adventures of a detective called Sherlock Holmes.

She put down the journal, surprised at how much time had passed when Alf reappeared almost an hour later.

'Right, let's have something to eat,' he said rubbing his hands together. 'There weren't a picking on you before - you're skin and bone now.' He stopped himself as if he could hardly believe what he said. He swallowed. 'Not that you ain't a fine looking woman despite being so skinny.' He checked himself again and his face turned crimson as he dug himself into a hole. 'I don't want you to think there's any... I mean there ain't nothing underhanded in me bringing you here. Not that I been looking or anything.'

'I do feel hungry as a matter of fact, now that I'm not cold and wet through.' She looked at him, trying not to smile. She knew instinctively the best thing to do was ignore it when he fell over himself with embarrassment.

He recovered himself. 'Right then.' He opened the small pantry and took out a parcel of sausages and some eggs from the cool marble shelf. Several minutes later they were sitting at the table eating a meal which to Polly, was a feast.

'What will happen when you tell Inspector Reid about Mickey Kidney?'

'It will be looked into. We're still gathering evidence about both murders so I'll run it past Inspector Abberline as well.' Alf carved two slices of bread from the loaf at his elbow. 'After what you told me, Kidney is worth following up. The evidence is the thing, Polly. We'll have to get witness statements and to be honest, we ain't got the manpower to go searching for them. Every last man is on The Ripper case.'

'If you want witnesses, Sid the barman from *The Britannia* saw what a state Lizzie was in. And the girls all know what a temper Mickey has. They warned her he was looking for her and they all seen the bruises she had. The slightest thing set him off. She had a torn ear and a fat lip a month ago and there were terrible bruises on her neck from when he grabbed her that day.'

'It might be hard to prove,' said Alf.

'I'm going prove it,' she told him. 'I swear I'll see him hang.' She sighed, then glanced at the journal she had been reading. 'What would he have done?' she asked. 'I started to read this story while you were upstairs, about a detective; Mr. Sherlock Holmes.'

'You read *A Study in Scarlet?*'

'Enough to get the gist of it. I skipped ahead a bit in the parts about the Mormons wanting to control everyone but I read enough to follow the story and grasp the reason for the revenge.'

'What did you think of it?' Alf asked.

'I liked it. It was very dramatic. *Rache,* written in blood. Fancy that - it meaning revenge when everyone else thought the victim was trying to write a name.' She gave a short laugh. 'Holmes is a bit of a big head, but he gets the job done in a meticulous way.'

'He uses his brain,' said Alf. 'Observation and deduction. It's a marvellous story. I've read it lots of times.'

'I like how he does things. He's very methodical.' said Polly. 'He looks for clues and works things out. That's how detectives should go about things, isn't it? They should find out how to link all the bits together like a puzzle to work out who done it.'

'Yes, I think so too,' said Alf, clearly enjoying himself. 'I think Doctor Doyle hit the nail on the head. That's what true detective work is all about.'

'He's a doctor?'

'Apparently so. I think that might be what gives him the edge, I mean working out what ails someone is like detective work in a way.'

'I suppose so... Mr. Sherlock Holmes, with his magnifying glass. It's a good idea, isn't it? I mean all the clues might not be big ones, might they? A piece of thread here, a fragment there. I mean, a button off a killer's shirt or a piece of torn clothing could prove someone is guilty better than a witness, couldn't it?'

'Yes, it could.' Alf nodded. 'In fact, I would like to keep everyone away from a crime scene until we had the chance to look over every inch of it for clues; like Sherlock Holmes does. We got doctors at Scotland Yard but they don't specialise in studying the dead and they don't have to be particularly precise.'

'Well, I'm going to be precise and look for evidence that will send Mickey Kidney to the gallows.' She paused and looked at him. 'Will you help me, Alfie?'

Alf put down his fork and deliberated on the question. 'If he did it, I want to see him pay for it as much as you do, Polly, unfortunately, sometimes it ain't that simple and you got to be careful. You seen in the papers all the commotion about someone called Leather Apron?'

'Yes, they say he was the Whitechapel killer and the police let him go. People have been after his blood.'

'That's right, and that's what I'm talking about.'

'Tell me.' Polly rested her chin on her hand.

'Well, his name is John Pizer. He is a boot finisher and polisher by trade so naturally, he would wear a leather apron for his work. After Mrs. Nichols was murdered the word was from a number of witnesses we interviewed was that a man called Leather Apron had been mistreating prostitutes in the area. Then a leather apron was found in the yard where Mrs. Chapman was murdered. Detective-Sergeant Bill Thick, who incidentally, could not be better named, knew that John Pizer's nickname was Leather Apron. Armed only with this thought and nothing else, Bill saw fit to go and arrest Mr. Pizer. Just like that. No evidence, no positive identification, no chain of events that link him to the two women. The newspapers got hold of it and started writing stuff about him being the killer. Now it turns out beyond doubt that Mr. Pizer had nothing to do with the murders. The mobs and vigilantes don't care about that; they are still baying for his blood like a pack of hounds. So, we've had to protect Mr. Pizer, when we ain't got the men to do it. He's got himself a lawyer and he's going to sue us, the papers and anyone else who had a hand in accusing him. I don't blame him, he's in fear for his life and had to spend many a night in our cells for his own safety. He's in hiding with his family at the minute in the hope that it all dies down.'

'He really had nothing to do with Annie's murder?'

'Not a thing... Someone who lived at number 29 had washed their apron and hung it out to dry in the yard, that's all. *The Star* ran with it and made it a hundred times worse like they usually do. So what I'm saying is, you have to be sure of your evidence before you accuse someone. Be a bit cagey about it until it's rock solid. Don't tip off the suspect or anyone else and don't let them know you're looking into it. That's what Sherlock Holmes would do. Collect the evidence and keep quiet until you've got all you need and once you have it, pounce.'

'Understood. I won't go barging in. I promise,' she said, suppressing a yawn.

'You must be all done in.' said Alf. 'You can have my brother's room. You'll be alright in there.'

'Alfred?' his mother called.

'Coming mother.'

When he came downstairs he went straight out to the privy in the back yard with a chamber pot. He took the chamber pot back upstairs and then came back down and washed his hands. Then he took two thick slices of bread with butter and strawberry jam and a cup of tea upstairs to his mother.

While Alf was occupied with his mother, Polly washed the dishes, dried them and stacked them on the dresser with the rest. She collected the dirty clothes that were lying around into a basket and folded some sheets and blankets that were in a heap in the corner. Eventually, Alf came downstairs.

'She's gone off to sleep, now.'

'Where is your brother at present, Alfie? Won't he mind me having his room?'

'No, er... he passed away as a matter of fact.'

'I'm so sorry. Was it recent?'

'Five years, now. Mother hasn't been the same since it happened. I think that's when she started to decline as a matter of fact. Her health has been getting worse and worse ever since.'

'What happened?'

'He got brain fever. He was just a boy, fourteen.'

'What was his name?

'Daniel. He was named after father.'

Polly's brows lifted. 'I named my little boy Daniel. Not that he had a christening or anything, being that he was stillborn. Too little to come into the world he was, but I wanted to give him a name to mark the fact that he existed, even if it was just for a little while.'

'So, the baby you lost because of that brute was a little boy?'

'Yes,' she felt a lump rise in her throat. 'He was perfect you know, but so tiny, too tiny to live.' She swallowed, bowed her head and looked down at her lap.

'I'm sorry, Polly.'

She cleared her throat, looked up and forced a smile. 'We've both had our troubles, haven't we? Listen, won't your mother mind me being in Daniel's room?'

He lowered his voice. 'As it happens, I haven't told her you're here. She's a bit out of sorts tonight. Best to keep quiet about it, I think.'

'Whatever you think is best,' she said. 'And don't worry, I'll be out of here first thing.'

'No. Don't do that. I don't want to spend all tomorrow looking for you again.'

'What will she say if she sees me?'

'Don't worry, I'll think of some way of telling her if needed.'

Alf showed Polly to a small room at the end of the landing. It was a comfortable room with a brass bed, a wardrobe and a chest of drawers with a mirror.

Alf had found her a pillow and an eiderdown in the wardrobe. She stripped down to her drawers and camisole and got into the feather bed. In the doss house, she had to sleep in her clothes with her drawstring purse tied to her thigh, surrounded by the stench of cheesy feet, urine and vomit. This clean, comfortable and safe little room was a piece of heaven.

'God bless, Daniel,' she murmured as she fell asleep.


Polly was used to rising early. The bell rang in the lodging house at six o'clock on the dot and the occupants had to be out by seven. She opened her eyes and as drowsiness left her, she remembered where she was. She smiled, then yawned and stretched. The room was south facing and she could see sunlight making patterns on the ceiling where it peeped through the gap at the top of the curtains. She could smell bacon cooking. The divine aroma woke up her stomach - it rumbled and demanded food.

She sat up on the side of the bed. She reached over pulled aside one of the curtains and looked out of the window. The room overlooked a small tidy yard with a privy by the wooden gate. Remembering Alf's request, she dressed and crept very quietly downstairs.

She found Alf frying bacon in the kitchen.

'There's tea in the pot,' he said.

'Thanks.' She poured out a cup of tea and took a few sips as she looked around the kitchen. She noticed a white apron on the back of the door. She reached for it and put it on.

'Let me help.' she said as Alf turned to look at her. 'Nice apron for it.'

'Mother used to be a midwife. She still likes to use her aprons for her household duties. At least she did before she got so poorly.'

'She must have put them to good use. It looks like this has been a very orderly house.'

'Things have slipped since she got ill and what with all this forced overtime on account of the murders...' Polly was about to sympathise in reply when they heard footsteps in the hall.

'Who are you talking to, Alfred? Daniel? Is that you?'

Alf's jaw dropped as his mother appeared at the kitchen door. He looked like a little boy caught with his hand in the sweetie jar.

'Mother.' Was all he could say.

Polly turned to see a small, red-haired, hazel eyed woman in a stained nightgown.

She was holding on to the wall with one shaky hand. Her face was pale. Her skin looked dry and papery. Her long hair was in a messy plait that hung down her back. A sick old lady she might be, but when she saw Polly she fixed her with a steady-eyed stare.

'Who is this person, Alfred?'

Polly decided she must have been a tartar in her time. She looked formidable even now - all four foot eight inches of her.

'Um...er...' Was all Alf managed in reply.

'Answer me, Alfred,' she demanded.

Alf's mouth opened and closed like a startled goldfish. He looked, for all the world, as if he was afraid. This tough copper, who could sort out the hardest criminals without a second thought, had been reduced to a spluttering fool by his small, elderly mum.

Polly suppressed a smile. Alf looked at her and then at his mother. Polly thought he might be weighing up his chances of making it to the door and sprinting off down the street.

Taking pity on him, Polly stepped forward without missing a beat.

'Oh, Ma'am, you really shouldn't have come down those stairs on your own,' She went to her and gently took hold of the old lady's arm. 'Come and sit down, Ma'am.' She looked at Alf. 'I presume this lady is my patient, sir?' Alf's mouth was open but fortunately, he had the good sense not to speak. She eased Mrs. Cruikshank onto one of the kitchen chairs. 'I'm very pleased to meet you, Ma'am.'

Polly studied her; despite the fact that she looked as small and frail as a little bird, a strong personality shone through the fragile frame.

'Who are you?' Mrs. Cruikshank would not be deflected.

Polly knelt down beside her and placed her hand on hers. 'I'm Miss Wilkes, Ma'am.'

'Do I know you?' she demanded.

'Not yet, Ma'am. However, in a short time, I'm sure we will become well acquainted.'

'Why?'

'I'm here to look after you today.' She looked at Alf.
'Sir? Do you have a blanket for your mother?'
Without a word, Alf hurried off and retrieved a tartan rug from the parlour. Polly opened it out and placed it around the other woman's shoulders. 'Now, some tea and a little breakfast I think.' She stood behind Mrs. Cruikshank, her hand resting gently on her shoulder.

She stared at Alf who looked dumbfounded. 'Sir, if you would be so kind, please? I believe your mother would like some tea.'

Behind Mrs. Cruikshank's back, she looked at him pointedly and jerked her head towards the teapot.

Alf snapped out of it when he realised Polly had saved him and busied himself pouring his mother some tea.

'How about some buttered toast?' Polly suggested. 'Or would you prefer some bacon?'

'Both,' she replied, 'and a fried egg.'

'Very well.' Polly nodded, surprised at the older lady's hearty appetite.

'I still don't know who you are,' said Mrs. Cruikshank. She was like a little terrier with a bone and was not going to let it go.

'As I said, I'm Miss Wilkes. Sergeant Cruikshank has engaged me to look after you today and do some household chores.' She moved to the stove and began gathering the *accoutrements* for Mrs. Cruikshank's breakfast. There was some bacon already in the pan. Polly cracked an egg and cooked it in the bacon fat. She made some toast and then placed the plate of food in front of the old lady.

'If it's all the same to you, sir, I'll see to my patient's room while she is breakfasting here with you.'

Alf nodded, still sweating, but clearly relieved. Polly chuckled silently at his comical expression as she bustled off in a business-like manner, rolling up her sleeves as she went.
'Don't you worry, Ma'am. I'll soon have everything ship shape and Bristol fashion,' she called over her shoulder.

She went upstairs and found Mrs. Cruikshank's room.
'Blimey,' she murmured as she stood in the doorway and leaned against the door frame.

The room was a mess. It was obvious that Alf was struggling to cope. There was dirty laundry on the floor, piles of clothing on the furniture, dirty dishes scattered about the room and the bed was as smelly as anything she had seen in Crossingham's lodging house.

Without a moment's delay, Polly set to work. She owed Alf a lot. He had spent all day yesterday looking for her when he had all this to cope with at home.

She began by gathering up the dirty laundry and stripping down the bed. She put the articles in a bundle outside the door on the landing. She gathered up the dirty dishes and placed them in a stack on the little table near the door. She moved to the sash window and raised it to let in some of the morning air. She found some clean linen in the drawer and made up the bed. She continued working until the room looked neat and tidy.

She picked up the pile of dirty dishes to take downstairs and then saw Alf in the doorway. He was smiling. It was astonishing, she noticed, how a smile transformed his grim face.

'She loves the idea of me hiring a nursemaid,' he said. 'It's the first time I've seen her smile in ages.'

'Bit of luck I put this apron on eh?' Polly said in a low voice. 'Would you take these dishes? I'll bring the laundry.'

'You don't have to do all this.'

'Yes I do,' she said. She put her hand on his forearm. 'You've helped me so much. This is the least I can do. Besides, I'd rather be busy doing this than walking the streets thinking about things.' Alf looked down at the hand that rested on his arm as she gave it a squeeze. 'This is better, she thinks you got her a nurse to look after her. You get credit for being the good son that you are and she's non-the-wiser. Now, show me where your mother keeps the boiler and I'll get this laundry done. It ain't a bad day for drying,' Polly smiled. 'Come on, chop, chop; time to get cracking.'

'Wait a minute, Polly, doing laundry is hard work. I can't ask you to-'

'Of course you can, Alfie, and I want to do it. To be honest, this laundry *really* needs a wash.' She smiled at him. 'I'd rather be busy - honestly.'

She took the bundle of dirty washing down stairs. Alf brought out the boiler and two wash tubs into the yard. While the boiler heated up, Polly made a fuss of Mrs. Cruikshank.

'I'll help you to your bed, Mrs. Cruikshank. It's all made up nice and fresh.'

She escorted the older woman back upstairs and then helped her to wash and put on a clean nightdress.

'Where did Alfred find you?' Mrs. Cruikshank asked as Polly brushed the older lady's long hair. She could tell it had once been as copper coloured as Alf's. Now it was toned down by an equal amount of grey.

'It was a chance good fortune, Ma'am. I attended the station on another matter,' said Polly. 'The Sergeant was on the desk and following several conversations, he asked if I would come here and take care of you today.'

'What sort of conversations?' The old lady's eyes narrowed.

'The Sergeant was concerned about your welfare, Ma'am. He said he was having to do long shifts because of the Whitechapel killer and was concerned about you being on your own. I think you have a very good son, Mrs. Cruikshank.'

'Hmmph,' she replied, pursing her lips as if she agreed only grudgingly. 'When he's here.'

Polly looked at her. 'It must be difficult. This is one of the most important cases the police have ever handled and Sergeant Cruikshank is a vital part of it.'

'Hmmph,' she said again. 'Where did you learn your nursing?'

'Oh, I just picked it up by looking after people. All you need to do is keep someone clean, comfortable and well fed. It is not complicated.' She looked at Mrs. Cruikshank and gave her smile. 'Now, might I get you a nice cup of tea? Then I'll get on with the laundry while you have a little nap.'

A look of pleasure came over the lady's face. She had taken very readily to being looked after, which made Polly think the poor woman had needed it for a long time.

Polly went downstairs to find Alf at the table, finishing his tea. Seeing that the boiler was steaming, she went into the yard, added some laundry soap and plunged the sheets and Mrs. Cruikshank's underclothes and nightdresses into the hot water.

'D'you have any whites to go in the laundry? I might as well do a full load.'

Alf almost spat out his tea. His face reddened. 'No, no it's fine. Mother's is more than enough.'

'Suit yourself,' said Polly turning away because she was unable to suppress a grin. 'I'm going to take your mother a cup of tea and then she's going to have a little nap.'

When Polly came downstairs again Alf was in uniform.

'You ain't had any breakfast yourself, yet,' he said.

'I'll get something, soon as I've got the laundry sorted.'

'I can't tell you what a load off my mind this is, you helping mother, Polly.'

'It's my pleasure,' she nodded. 'Don't worry, I'll be the perfect nursemaid while you're gone. What does she like to eat?'

'I usually bring her in a bit of bread and cheese or a cake if I can get one. I'll be coming back for my dinner at about two, I usually give her something then.'

'She needs something more nourishing than that, Alfie. So do you for that matter. You got a shilling to spare?'

Alf produced a florin from his pocket.

'Two shillings? That's more than enough,' she said, taking the coin. 'Let me go to the shop. I'll see what meat they got and I'll get some veg. I promise I won't spend the whole two shillings.'

'It don't matter to me. Do what you think is best,' he shrugged.

'Can I borrow your mother's cloak?' she asked.

Later on, after Alf left for work, Polly checked on Mrs. Cruikshank and found her to be asleep. She crept back downstairs and set to work. She made some soup with a meaty ham hock she bought at the shop. She added onions, split peas, carrots, turnip and potatoes to the broth and let it simmer gently on a low heat. It smelled delicious. She found some flour, sugar and lard in the pantry. She made some pastry and leaving it on the cold shelf to rest, went out and bought some cooking apples. She made an apple pie and had just put it in the oven when Mrs. Cruikshank called for her.

'Nurse?'

Polly hurried up the stairs.

'Yes, Ma'am?'

'I need my medicine.'

'Right Ma'am,' said Polly. 'Which one is it?'

'The small brown bottle. Ten drops in a little water.'

Polly complied and handed the lady the concoction. The label said Laudanum which she knew was a powerful medicine made from opium. It was Polly's understanding that it was often abused and should therefore only be used for the most severe pain. Polly wondered if Mrs. Cruikshank was much more ill than Alf knew.

'May I ask what ails you, Ma'am?

'My head, my legs, my stomach. It all ails me,' Mrs. Cruikshank replied, closing her eyes and sinking back into her pillows.

'Well, I've made some nice broth. Do you think you could fancy some?' Polly asked. 'It's very good for you.'

'Perhaps a little bit,' she replied. 'And some bread.'

Polly prepared a tray and took it upstairs to her patient. This done, she sat at the kitchen table and ate a bowl of the broth herself. She was pleased with how good it tasted and delighted when Mrs. Cruikshank asked for a second helping and also accepted a slice of apple pie. It was satisfying to see the old lady eat so well and she herself enjoyed the sensation of having a full stomach.

Having boiled the laundry, Polly rinsed it in cold water, first in one tub and then a final rinse in another. She then put each item through the mangle to press out excess water. She was pleased how clean everything looked when she hung them on the washing line and they billowed in the breeze.

When she went back to check on Mrs. Cruikshank, she had fallen asleep. She had polished off her second helping of broth and the apple pie.

Alf came back at two o'clock. He sat at the table and enjoyed a large bowl of broth followed by a slice of apple pie.

'This is smashing Polly, a real treat. I didn't know you could cook.'

'Neither did I. Fortunately, your mother has Mrs. Beeton's cookbook over there on the shelf so I followed the recipe. Anyway, have you heard anything else about the murders?'

'Quite a lot, yes.' He reached for a newspaper that was in the pocket of his uniform tunic that was hanging on the back of a nearby chair. 'Look at this in today's paper,' he said.

Polly opened the paper and read the massive headline. '*Jack The Ripper.*'

'That's what he calls himself. Apparently, he wrote to the papers.'

'The murderer wrote to the newspapers?'

'I know, it ain't credible, is it? We ain't had anyone like him before. The result is, it's turned the whole thing into a ruddy pantomime.'

'Tell me. What's been found out?'

'Mrs. Stride was seen with a man at twelve thirty a.m. on Berner Street. The best witness is a young Jewish chap named Israel Schwartz. He said he followed a man down Berner Street from the Commercial Road end. He said this man seemed to be in a temper with himself and appeared to be slightly drunk. Schwartz said he made sure he stayed behind him because he thought he was spoiling for a fight.'

'What did he look like?'

'About five foot six. Dark jacket and trousers, black peaked cap, brown moustache. I know, that could describe Michael Kidney,' he said in response to Polly opening her mouth to speak. 'This man stopped and spoke to Mrs. Stride in the entrance to Dutfield's Yard and immediately started to quarrel with her. She struggled with him as he tried to pull her away from the yard onto the pavement. During this struggle the lady screamed. He said the screams weren't very loud - it was as if she didn't want to draw too much attention to their argument. From this Mr. Schwartz concluded it was a domestic, especially since after that, the man pushed Mrs. Stride to the ground. Mr. Schwartz don't speak any English and not wanting to get involved, crossed over the road. At that point, the man shouted *Lipski* at him.'

'Lipski?' said Polly. 'Why would he do that?'

'Ever since Israel Lipski was hanged last year, people been shouting it at Jews as an insult. I don't know why - especially since that poor little Russian was innocent in my opinion. Anyway, the assailant shouted Lipski at the same time as a man smoking a pipe came out of the pub opposite. This man saw what was occurring and shouted something at Mrs. Stride's attacker. Mr. Schwartz thought the man with the pipe might have been telling the other one to stop it. This scared the hell out of Mr. Schwartz, who thought he was going to be in for trouble and took it as a sign that they might pick on him instead. He moved out the way sharpish and was upset to find the man with the pipe was following him. Upon seeing this, Mr. Schwartz legged it and even though he lives on Ellen Street which runs along the bottom of Berner Street, he kept on going, all the way down to the railway viaduct on Pinchin Street. The man with the pipe didn't follow him all the way down there, so Mr. Schwartz went home. Meanwhile, Mrs. Stride had been dragged into the yard and either as she was falling to the ground, or while she was on the ground, her assailant held on to her and cut her throat on the left side. According to the medic, it would have taken only a couple of seconds to carry out the attack.' Alf looked at her. 'The rest of the report was about her injuries.'

'Did she die quickly?'

'Polly-'

'Tell me.'

'I really don't want to-'

'I have to know, Alfie. I want Mickey punished and I want to know exactly what he did. Please tell me. Was it quick?'

Alf sighed. 'She was found curled up on her side, next to the wall and that makes it look like it took a while. Her killer didn't cut deep enough, he cut the vessels that supplied the muscles of the neck but only nicked the main artery that supplies the brain and even then only on one side. I'm afraid she bled to death, Polly, and not quickly.'

'Why didn't she shout for help?'

He hesitated. 'Do you really want to hear this?'

'Yes. I want to know everything. I want to know what he did to her and why she died.'

'He cut her windpipe, Polly. You can't speak or nothing after that.'

Polly closed her eyes. Then she took a deep breath and stiffened her backbone. 'All that stuff this Mr. Schwartz described, it don't sound like a stranger does it? It was Mickey, I know it.'

'We need evidence. We've got men trying to find this bloke she was with. It ain't likely that we'll find him. Men don't want folk to know they were consorting with a prostitute. He won't come forward.'

'What about you? You're consorting with a prostitute.'

He looked at her for a long time. 'I don't think of you like that,' he said.

'That don't alter what I am.'

'Is that how you think of yourself? You consider that your limit? Is this your lot?'

'No, course not. I hate it, though I hate the workhouse more. I would rather die than go back in there. I try my best to find proper work.'

'I know it's bad out there and I don't blame you, Polly. In fact in an odd way, I think it takes a lot of courage for a woman to do that when they are out of other choices. It don't surprise me there has to be alcohol involved but you're better than that, so don't go calling yourself that.'

'It's what other people say that does the damage. It can't be repaired, Alfie and if you're seen in my company, it'll ruin you as well.'

'Listen, I got to go. Will you be here when I get back?' He stood up and put on his tunic.

'I need to make sure of my lodgings by seven at the latest so I can't be, unfortunately.'

'You could stay here…'

Polly stood up and moved to his side. 'You're a good man, Alfie Cruikshank but don't push your luck. We got away with it once but your mother is nobody's fool. If she weren't so frail she would realise that a nursemaid costs more than a copper can afford - no offence. Don't worry, I'll give your mum some supper before I go and make sure she's alright.' Polly put her hand on his. 'I'm really grateful, Alfie, for what you done for me. You came looking for me. You brought me back here, you fed me and put me up for the night.'

Alf flushed. 'I was worried about you. You'd had such a shock.'

'You saved me. If you hadn't found me, I might just have found the courage to walk into the river or died of the cold under that bridge.' He looked at her for an extended moment. He cleared his throat. 'Yes, well, I hope you won't think that way no more.'

'I'm set on bringing Mickey Kidney to justice now. I've got a purpose. I won't rest until he pays for what he did to Lizzie.' She looked at him. 'You'll tell me if you find out anything else, won't you?'

'Can I get in touch with you at Crossingham's?'

'Most of the time you can, yes,' she said vaguely. She could only stay there if she had the money.

'There'll be an inquest you see,' he looked at her intently. 'Listen, Polly, I been thinking on it. Will you come and find me first? Don't go out walking the streets. Come to me instead?'

Her eyes widened. 'W- What d'you mean?'

Alf studied her face and his jaw dropped. 'Oh, no…I… I didn't mean-' he choked. 'My word, Polly Wilkes, you don't half have a propensity for getting hold of the wrong end of the stick. I meant, I'll give you money for your lodgings. I don't want you out dollying. Not while this nutter is on the loose, not ever in fact. Anyone could be his next victim.'

'Alfie, you can't give me money, think how it would look. When you said that, even I thought you meant… you know…?'

'Never mind how it looks. I don't want to turn up at a murder scene to find you lying there all-' he did not finish the sentence. 'This ain't no normal killer, Polly. He's a true monster. He's deranged. So please, stay off the streets eh?'

Tears formed in the back of her eyes and she blinked to keep them away.

'D'you have money for a bed the next couple of nights?'

'I'll be all right.'

Alf eyed her suspiciously. 'Show me the money.'

She sighed and pulled a shilling from the drawstring purse in her pocket and held out her palm.

'Right then,' he nodded. He put on his helmet. 'Look after yourself, Polly.'

'You do likewise, Alfie,' she smiled.

'Right,' he said as they exchanged a long look.

Once Alf left the house she finished the chores and made sure the kitchen was clean and tidy and the parlour dusted. She ironed the bedsheets, Mrs. Cruikshank's nightgowns and underwear. She placed them in a neat pile close to the fire to allow them to air off so that they lost any traces of dampness before she put it all away.

Mrs. Cruikshank ate some more of the apple pie when she woke up, then asked for more of her medicine. This done, Polly knew the lady would sleep until Alf came home. Reluctantly she changed back into her own clothes, carefully washed the silk underwear by hand and set it out to dry, then she wrapped her old shawl around her shoulders and left the house.

# CHAPTER SEVENTEEN

Whenever Polly made her way along Dorset Street, one of the many terrible things she saw was half-starved waifs playing in the filth ridden gutters. The narrow streets and back alleys never saw sunlight so neither did the children.

She knew that here in the worst part of the poverty-stricken east end, many of the children were doomed to die before they reached double figures. If by some miracle these urchins survived, they were condemned to be the next generation of the lost.

The horror of it was that these children lived less than three miles from where she had been raised in abundance and luxury. Polly had been taught that if someone was poor, it was because they were defective and inferior individuals. She knew that her parents and everyone in their social circle believed this. It was the natural order of things and the inevitable result of weakness and a fault in their blood line. They were wrong.

Dorset Street was the worst of all. It was a sink hole of pitiful children and desperate woman. The people of this labyrinth, riddled with poverty and deprivation, didn't stand a chance. Yes, crime was rampant - because those willing to take the chance had very little to lose. Of course, drunkenness was commonplace – faced with hopelessness, many people turned to drink. The children were the helpless victims of both these things and it stabbed at Polly's heart to think of it.

Into this chaotic place swarming with people had come a madman. All the talk was of the murderer; Jack the Ripper - the latest addition to this hell.

Polly nodded at two women who were talking in the street, arms tucked inside the bibs of their aprons for warmth. She guessed from their troubled expressions that they too were discussing the murders. The feeling of tension was everywhere.

She walked across the entrance to an alley that opened out into a small grubby courtyard called Miller's Court. There were many such courtyards in the east end, and most were as grubby and dilapidated as this one. Two men loitered at the entrance, smoking evil smelling pipe tobacco. She could hear raised voices and the sound of a fight going on somewhere in the dingy alley. It was probably an organised affair and these men were watching out for the police who walked a Dorset Street in pairs - a constable alone on the beat was not safe. As Polly crossed the road to get out of their way, she heard someone call her name.

'Polly? Where the hell you been?' She turned around and found Suzette looking back at her. 'I was sure they were gonna find you dead in a back street somewhere,' she said as Polly's eyes filled with tears. 'Oh there now darling, I know.' she put her arms around her. 'We were so shocked about Lizzie.' She patted Polly's back to comfort her. 'And we were so worried when we hadn't seen hide nor hair of you for two nights.'

Polly was unable to speak. Suzette kept her in an embrace. 'Oh, there, there, now. Hush... We knew you'd took it bad. She was a diamond was Lizzie.'

Polly nodded, finally getting some control over her emotions. She pulled away and wiped her eyes with her shawl. 'I'm going to get him, Suze.' she said. 'I'm going to make him pay for what he did.'

'What? You're gonna catch Jack the Ripper?'

'Jack the-.No. Not him; Mickey Kidney.'

'What's it got to do with Mickey Kidney? They say it was The Ripper what did her in.'

'I don't care what they're saying. I *know* it were Mickey.'

Suzette looked left and right. 'Sssh, Pol. Keep your voice down. You gotta be careful what you say 'round here. Let's walk.'

They walked to the corner of Dorset Street. 'We better not go in any of the pubs, even the walls have ears in them places.' Suzette looked around. 'I know, let's go in the church.'

They crossed Commercial Street and walked towards Christ Church.

The needle spire of the white church stood out like a beacon to the surrounding streets. Suzette heaved open the massive door and Polly followed her inside. She had passed by the church countless times, though this was the first time she had stepped inside. The smell of Candle wax and paraffin lingered in the air. It brought back memories of Sunday mornings with her parents and Sunday school, which of course, Polly had hated.

'Won't they kick us out?' Polly whispered.

'It's a *church*, Pol.'

'Exactly.'

'Ain't you heard of Mary Magdalene?'

Polly quirked her mouth. 'Good point,' she said as they both genuflected and then slipped into one of the pews close to the door.

'Alright.' Suzette whispered 'What makes you think it were Mickey?'

'I don't think it: I *know* the bas-' she stopped herself as she remembered where she was. 'I know he did it,' she said. 'He already came after her that time in Cooney's and he's been spying on her since she left him.'

'Yeah, I heard that from Pearl.' Suzette nodded as Polly continued. 'That time in Cooney's, she only got away from him because she kneed him in the balls. He said at the time he would do her in and he has, Suze.'

'Mickey Kidney says a lot of things, Pol. Everyone knows he's full of it. Don't you think he's too much of a coward to do Lizzie in?'

'He's too much of a coward and too stupid to plan it, but if he lost his temper in the heat of the moment he would definitely do it. He's got about as much self-control as a two-year-old,' said Polly.

'And the strength of a raging bull, unfortunately.' Suzette added.

Polly nodded. She told Suzette about seeing Mickey at Leman Street station and what he said.

'Jesus.' She said, then she winced. 'Sorry,' she glanced up at the statue of Christ above the altar as if its expression might have changed to one of disapproval. She looked at Polly. 'So Mickey said that before anyone knew it was Lizzie?'

'Yes.' Polly nodded. 'Almost two days before she was properly identified.'

'Can you prove it? What about your policeman friend?'

'They all heard him say it and thought he was just a drunk with a big mouth. They didn't know he was Lizzie's ex at the time. Not until I put Alfie straight on who he was. He said he would pass it onto that Inspector Reid, and tell Inspector Abberline who's running the investigation.'

'Fred Abberline? He's all right, he is. A stand-up chap. He used to be a sergeant 'round here and he was always fair,' said Suzette. 'He knew what we was up against and he didn't judge.' She shook her head. 'You know, if Mickey went 'round the cop shop straight after it happened, he must be as stupid as he looks.'

'There's more, Suze. When I left the station, there was a fancy carriage waiting outside. George Lusk was in it along with some other man I didn't get a proper look at.'

'What's that got to do with Mickey?'

'Mickey is a member of Lusk's so-called vigilance committee. The news of the murders was the talk of Whitechapel. I think he went to Lusk and told him one of the victims was his wife,' said Polly. 'You know how he likes to make himself look important.'

'He would have heard *Dutfield's Yard* and *Berner Street*. He would have known it was Lizzie who had been found,' said Suzette.

'It never occurred to him that they didn't know who she was,' said Polly. 'Yet *The Times* printed her name the day after, on the Monday morning. Now, you tell me, how did that newspaper know her name when no one else did? Not the coroner, not even the police.'

'That's right, we weren't worried about Lizzie because they said her name was Elizabeth Stokes.' said Suzette.

'So you tell me, how did The Times know her name on Monday?'

'Beats me,' Suzette shrugged.

'If Mickey went to George Lusk on Sunday and told him his wife had been killed by The Ripper,' said Polly. 'Lusk could have tipped off a reporter on *The Times* and given them the story. Mickey would have been oblivious to the fact that there was a whole debacle about her identity going on and would have given Lusk Lizzie's name. Lusk would have given it to *The Times.* That's why they printed the right name when nobody else knew it was her. I think Lusk took Mickey to the station with a reporter on hand. It would be the little lap dog I saw him with 'round the side of this very church the other week. All set to rake up the muck about how this poor distraught widower got short shrift from the police. Instead, Mickey got himself arrested for getting obstreperous and throwing punches at the officers in the station.'

'The only way he could have known it was Lizzie was if he was the one what killed her,' said Suzette.

'Exactly,' said Polly, 'There's no other way I can think of to explain him knowing Lizzie was one of the two victims.'

Suzette nodded. 'Mickey probably thought if he went to Lusk and played the distraught husband, it would divert any suspicion from him.'

'And he messed it up in typical Mickey fashion,' said Polly.

Suzette gave a short laugh. 'It's almost comical, that is.'

'I wonder what Lusk will do when he realises Mickey's dropped him in it. It won't half make him look bad. It'll show him up as manipulative.'

'He's manipulative all right. He's up to all sorts of tricks to get himself elected.' A frown darkened Suzette's expression. 'Be careful, Pol. You should've heard Lusk going on about the police the other night in *The Ten Bells*. He's ruthless if anyone gets in his way.'

'As sure as I'm sitting here in this church, I *swear* I will make Mickey pay for what he did.'

Suzette looked up at the altar and the statue of Christ on the cross. 'Maybe you should ask Him for help? Cos it'll take a ruddy miracle.'

'If that's what it takes.' said Polly standing up and sliding sideways out of the pew. She genuflected again and avoided looking at the statue.

'You coming in *The Ten Bells*?' Suzette asked as they walked down the steps of the church.

'No, I'm going to Berner Street. I want to see where it happened, Suze - Lizzie's murder, I mean. I need to visualise it in my mind and find out what happened. Alfie says I have to play it stealthy and gather evidence before I accuse him of anything. I need to go there and see it for myself. '

'All right then,' Suzette sighed. 'I'm coming with you.'

'You don't have to.'

'I ain't going to let you do that on your own. Come on.'

Berner Street was a long, busy street that ran south from Commercial Road. It had a mixture of business premises and rows of cottage homes.

'It looks a lot better than Dorset Street, don't it?' said Suzette.

'Everywhere looks better than Dorset Street,' Polly replied. 'But you're right, it looks a respectable street; an ordinary, respectable street.'

'Marie said the word is that Lizzie was in the *The Bricklayers* on Settle Street with some bloke until eleven o'clock,' said Suzette. 'She said it was raining and they stood in the doorway for a while. It was commented on that they looked like they was eating each other - kissing and carrying on. Marie was sure some of Mickey's mates was in the pub at the time.'

'So it would have got straight back to him that she was with another man,' said Polly. 'Lizzie told me before she went out that she was meeting a gentleman. That sort of carrying on don't sound like her; not in full view of everybody. Unless...' said Polly, 'she wanted it to get back to Mickey that she had a new man.'

'Marie said Lizzie and this man hurried off out of *The Bricklayers* as soon as the rain stopped.' Suzette continued. 'So, they leave *The Bricklayers*, cross Commercial Road and wander down here. I wonder if anyone saw anything?'

Polly paid a penny for a posy of dried lavender at Sumner's greengrocers shop at the top end of Berner Street and then continued towards the yard where Lizzie was found.

'The sergeant said a Jewish man by the name of Israel Schwartz saw what happened,' said Polly. 'I want to speak to him. In his statement, Mr. Schwartz said he crossed the road to avoid an argument between Lizzie and a man who I think was Mickey. Just then, a man came out of the pub. This man shouted at Mickey. Mr. Schwartz thought he might be telling him to leave Lizzie alone. Mickey shouted back "Lipski" and pointed at Mr. Schwartz.' She looked at Suzette. 'Why would he do that?'

'Maybe Mr. Schwartz misunderstood?'

'I'm inclined to think he did,' said Polly.

'Who was this man, anyway?' Suzette asked.

'Mr. Schwartz thought he might be a friend of Mickey's on account of him shouting "Lipski". When he did, he thought they were both going to turn on him so he legged it - as did the man from the pub, which led Mr. Schwartz to think he was chasing him.'

'He was a bit of a nervous chap weren't he?' said Suzette.

'What if the man was Lizzie's new gentleman?' said Polly.

'Could be,' said Suzette.

'Mickey turns up. Mr. Schwartz said the man who spoke to Lizzie had come steaming down Berner Street a bit drunk and looking for a fight.'

'That sounds like Mickey,' said Suzette.

'He finds Lizzie who asks her new gentleman to give her a minute while she talks him.'

'In that case, why would he shout *Lipski*?' Suzette asked.

'What if he didn't? What if he was having a go at Lizzie for being out with a new man? What if he shouted something like *Who's he*? What if he was pointing at the man, not at Mr. Schwartz?'

'Demanding that Lizzie tells him who this bloke was?' Suzette added.

'Yes, it would fit with what Mr. Schwartz saw, but with a different interpretation.'

'You could be right, Pol. Especially since when Mr. Schwartz took off, so did the other man.'

'I reckon Mickey's mates told him where she was, and that she was with another man,' said Polly. 'That's why he came storming down here looking for her.'

'Sounds logical to me.'

'This man and Mr. Schwartz saw the whole thing, Suze. They might be able to identify Mickey as the man who had the fight with Lizzie. I need to talk to them.'

'Listen, Pol. If it was Lizzie's new man, he legged at as fast as Schwartz did. He ain't coming back, cos trust me, if he's off the bridge he'll have a wife and kids somewhere.'

'Then I'll knock on every door in Ellen Street until I find Israel Schwartz. They both saw him, Suze and I'm sure the man they saw was Mickey Kidney. If either of them can identify him, I might be able to prove that he killed her.'

'I know you want to get Mickey for this, Polly, but I got to be honest, you ain't got much chance. It might prove that Mickey and Lizzie had a domestic but it don't prove he killed her. And if that was Lizzie's gentleman, he ain't going to come forward. If it was Mickey's friend he ain't gonna grass him up, and this Israel Schwartz has already told the police everything he knows even if you find him.'

'But they both saw him, Suze,' said Polly in anguish. 'They could stop Mickey getting away with it.'

Suzette sighed. 'What about the fruit seller? It was in the papers that he sold Lizzie and her man some grapes. He might know something about this gentleman friend. You could talk to him, it must have been that shop over there.' She pointed to one of the corners Berner Street shared with Fairclough Street a few yards away.

Polly shook her head. 'He didn't sell Lizzie no grapes. She hated them, they gave her indigestion. It definitely weren't her.'

They arrived at the gates of Dutfield's Yard. On the right, set in the side wall of the International Club, was a door just as Alf had described.

'If you think about it, this big gate could have been left ajar and partially hid both the Lizzie and the killer in the dark. It would have

192

been pitch black at the time,' said Polly. 'There ain't no street lamps close by.'

'The paper said she was by the door near the gate. She must have been just here,' said Suzette, pointing to an area close to the wall.

Polly knelt down. 'Oh Lizzie.' she said pulling out the forget-me-not handkerchief and wiping away tears. She stayed there quietly for a moment, staring at the featureless cobblestones for a while, before placing the posy of lavender on the ground close to the wall. 'I miss you, Lizzie.'

'Come on, Pol. This ain't doing either of us any good,' said Suzette, blinking away tears. 'There's a pub on the corner. I'll buy us some grub.'

'Polly?' said John Evans, the caretaker at Crossingham's. 'Someone left this for you. It's been here since this morning.'

He turned the official looking envelope over in his fingers. 'You in trouble with the law or something?' he asked. 'We don't want no trouble.'

'You having a laugh? This place ain't nothing *but* trouble.' She gave Evans a hard stare. 'No, I ain't in no trouble and you mind your own business, John Evans.' Polly said as she opened the letter. She moved away from Evans so he could not read its contents over her shoulder.

'What is it, Polly?' Suzette asked 'It looks important. You been left a legacy or something?'

'No. I been called to give evidence at Cathy's inquest tomorrow.'

'Why?'

'When I read it in the paper about Cathy's pawn tickets, I told that sergeant what locked me up on Saturday. He took a statement.' Polly folded the letter and put it into her pocket.

'It'll be hard, Pol. You'll have to listen to all the horrible details,' said Suzette.

'I hope not. I've had enough of this lunatic's goings on. He might not have killed Lizzie, but he did Polly Nichols, Annie and Cathy. The bloody, raving maniac.' She sighed and turned to Suzette. 'Can you lend me one of your nice hats and maybe a jacket?'

# CHAPTER EIGHTEEN

Golden Lane City Mortuary was behind tall wrought iron gates. It looked like a workhouse infirmary. The smell of fermenting hops drifted on the air from the brewery nearby.

This was a strange place to put a brand new mortuary, Polly thought. Usually, these were to be found in graveyards or the attached to a workhouse. This one was in the heart of the city amongst the businesses and better-off streets. It was modern, purpose built and state of the art for all aspects of sudden death.

Polly passed through the imposing gates and found herself in a large crowded courtyard. In the middle of the courtyard and separate from other red brick buildings, was a fancy stone built structure with Doric columns that supported a flat roofed portico. Polly headed for this, assuming it would be the coroner's court building.

The area in front of the court building was crammed with people. A police officer stood beneath the portico in front of the door, blocking anyone from entering. The noise was deafening.

'The public gallery is full,' the policeman shouted, trying to make himself heard over the din of the crowd. 'There ain't no point in you trying to get in. Move along now please.'

The crowd ignored him and tried to push forward.

It was a quarter to nine by the brewery clock. Polly had arrived well ahead of the appointed time of ten o'clock: It seemed the crowds had arrived even earlier.

'Go on, get away with you. Go about your business.' The policeman bellowed. The crowd again paid no attention.

'Ahoy there!' he shouted at a man who was attempting to sneak past him. 'Where d'you think you're going? I'm gonna start taking names in a minute.'

Polly weaved her way to the front of the crowd. 'I'm a witness, where do I go please?' She showed the officer the letter.

'Down the side and around to the back of this building, Ma'am. There's a waiting room,' He whipped around and caught a couple trying to sneak behind him into the building. 'Oh no you don't! Get back! The public gallery is full I said.'

Polly nodded her thanks as the constable started to berate the couple and the crowd surged forward again. 'Right, that's it. I'm getting my notebook out,' she heard the policeman say. 'The next person what steps on this porch is going in the book.' He took his notebook out with a flourish and flipped it open. 'D'you wanna be first?' he said, pointing with his pencil at a man at the front of the crowd.

Polly followed the officer's instructions and made her way down the alley to the left of the court building. At the back, she found a yard where two carriages waited, each of the horses had nose-bags attached. She crossed the yard and could not resist going up to one of them.

'You're a fine boy ain't you? Yes… You're a beauty. Is that nice? You enjoying your breakfast?' she murmured. She placed her hand gently on the horse's neck and stroked it. 'Good boy. You're a good boy. I wish I had a sugar lump for you.'

Polly could see two buildings on the other side of the courtyard. One said "Mortuary" the other "Disinfecting Room". She peeped into a door at the back of the court and found a waiting room filled with people. Some were uniformed police officers, some well-dressed gentlemen and ladies. Polly decided to wait outside.

There was a privy at the back of the yard. She went to it and washed her hands. She removed the bonnet she had borrowed from Suzette and combed her hair, making sure the bun at the back of her head was smooth and tidy. She replaced the bonnet and tied the ribbon into a bow arranging it neatly beneath her right ear the way Lizzie used to do.

Suzette did not have a jacket to lend, but allowed Polly to borrow her new shawl as well as the bonnet. She looked in the mirror and checked that her face was clean. It was the best she could do and she had made herself as presentable as possible.

Back in the yard, she stood to the side of the door marked 'Mortuary'. She knew Cathy would be inside. They had brought her to Golden Street mortuary directly from Mitre Square.

The door opened and a group of people came out. None of them spoke and Polly noticed that some were pale and looked queasy. A few had dashed out through the door and were gulping in great lungfuls of air. Others were bent over, hands on their knees, as if trying to stop themselves from passing out.

It must be the jury, Polly thought. By the look of them she guessed they must have been viewing Cathy's body. She tried to be inconspicuous, staying against the wall as they filed into the court building.

The constable who had accompanied them slipped out of their view. He moved around the corner where only Polly could see him. He leaned against the wall and took off his helmet. He mopped his face with a handkerchief and blew out his cheeks. He stood there for a moment taking deep breaths. After a few minutes, he donned his helmet and walked back towards the door of the court.

Coming along the alley from the same direction was Alf Cruikshank. He was with two other gentlemen.

'Right, sir,' he was saying 'We have two witnesses giving evidence. Miss Wilkes and Constable Long. The rest are down to City force. I will escort our witnesses in as they are called before the court.'

'Very good, Sergeant,' said one of the men whom Polly thought must be Inspector Abberline. 'The Chief Inspector and I will go and make ourselves known to Mr. Langham.'

'Coroner Langham is in his office, sir. He's waiting for the jury to assemble and he'll call the inquest to order. I understand Mr. Crawford, the City Police solicitor, is with him. Major Smith is here as acting Commissioner as you know since Commissioner Fraser is on sick leave. He and Superintendent Foster are reviewing their officers' testimonies.'

'Excellent. Sergeant, you really are a marvel of efficiency.'

'Thank you, sir.' Alf nodded. He extended an arm towards the door. 'It's through there if you please.'

As the two gentlemen moved inside the building, Polly stepped forward. 'Hello, Alfie.'

Alf turned around. 'Polly,' he said. 'Hello there. I see you're giving evidence today.'

'Yes. I'm a bit nervous about it. What do I do? Do I just tell them about the pawn ticket?'

'Yes, tell them what you know just like it happened, like you did in your statement. They might ask you a few questions... Don't worry, it won't take long.'

'Good.' She exhaled a long breath. 'I'll be glad when it's over.' She looked at him 'How's your mother?'

'Not so well today, unfortunately.' Then he smiled faintly. 'You did me a good turn when you acted as if I had taken you on as a nurse. She liked that. She's been praising me up all week and has had a lot to say on the matter. She's not so fussed that it was only for one day.'

'It was my pleasure.'

'Listen,' said Alf. 'Can I see you later? I want to talk to you about something.'

'Er… alright. Where?'

'How about I take you somewhere proper? There's a smashing tea shop round the corner on Bridgewater Square, off Cripplegate. If you turn left as you come out of here, it's the next street down on the right. I gather they do nice afternoon tea.'

'That sounds really lovely, Alfie but you don't want to be seen with me. After I give evidence everyone in the court will know what I am.'

'They'll know nothing of the sort.' His expression darkened. 'Don't go calling yourself that. Just meet me there. This'll finish about two. Will you accept?'

'All right, Bridgewater Square.' she said. 'I'll be there.'

'Good,' he said. 'We had better get along, it will be starting in a few minutes.'

Polly and the rest of the witnesses were instructed to stay in the waiting room until they were called, after which, they could stay in court and listen to the rest of the evidence. A seat was positioned adjacent to the coroner's desk for the witness.  On the mezzanine above, the public gallery was crammed with people.

The coroner cleared his throat. 'Shall we begin?' He consulted a document on his desk. 'The first witness, Mary Victoria Wilkes, please.'

Alf opened the door that connected the waiting room with the court.

'Mary Victoria Wilkes,' he said. Polly's heart missed a beat. She had not expected to be the first witness. She stood up. 'This way, Miss.' He guided her to the seat next to the coroner's desk. Polly settled herself, conscious of all the eyes that were looking at her.

'You are Mary Victoria Wilkes?' asked the coroner.

'Yes, sir.'

'You reside at Crossingham's Lodging House, sixteen to eighteen Dorset Street?'

'Yes, sir.'

'How did you know the deceased, Catherine Eddowes, also known as Kelly also Conway?'

'She was a friend of mine, sir. Not close, we were friendly enough to have a conversation and pass the time of day.'

'I see,' said the coroner. 'When was the last time you saw her?'

'It was on Saturday night, last. She was in *The Britannia* public house where I met with my friend, Miss Francis Kemp.'

'What happened during that encounter?'

'She said she had been hop picking in Kent and it had been a bad year. She had not earned any money. She said that on the way home, a lady had given her a pawn ticket for a shirt. The lady had said she thought it would fit Mr. John Kelly. He was Catherine's... well, as far as we are concerned, he was her husband.'

'She showed you the ticket?'

'Yes, sir.'

'Can you remember how much the ticket was for?'

'It was for tuppence, sir. That's why she was so pleased. She was told it was a good shirt for the money.'

'What was the name on the ticket?'

'I believe it was Emily, Emily... something like Burton, or Barrel.

'Could the name have been Birrell?'

'Yes, sir, it could. That sounds like it.'

'Is this the ticket?'

The clerk handed a piece of paper to Polly. She looked at it, there were brownish- red stains on it. She swallowed hard. 'I believe it is, sir.'

'Do you know why Emily Birrell did not want this ticket?'

'I believe it was because she wasn't coming back to the area, sir.'

'Please record that this pawn ticket, that the witness has testified as being in the possession of Catherine Eddowes, was found on the victim.'

'Would you have a look at the other ticket please, Miss Wilkes?'

The clerk handed this to Polly. It was also badly stained.

'Do you recognise it?'

'I haven't seen it before, sir, though I see it is for a pair of boots. Catherine said that her man, John Kelly had pawned his boots because they needed the money to pay for a night's lodgings the previous evening. That would be the Friday.'

'Thank you, Miss Wilkes.'

She looked up and saw Alf standing at the back of the court. He gave her a brief nod and she felt better. Polly took a seat in a row that had been reserved for the witnesses and quietly breathed out a long breath. Several witnesses followed, all of whom verified Catherine's identity.

'John Kelly please.' said the Coroner.

An officer from City Force showed John Kelly to the witness chair.

Polly's heart turned over. He looked dreadful. He was hunched over and grief stricken. He sat down. Polly could see that he was pale and there were dark circles around his eyes. He kept his gaze fixed on the floor. The coroner gave him a moment to compose himself.

'You are John Kelly?'

'I am, sir,' he croaked.

'What is your address?'

'I live at a lodging-house, Cooney's at 55, Flower and Dean Street.'

'Have you viewed the body of the deceased?'

He paused as if the words had suddenly been snatched from his mouth.

'I- I have, sir and I recognised her as Catherine Conway.' He lifted his head for the first time and looked at the Coroner. Polly's heart went out to him; the sight of his drawn, wretched face was pitiful. 'She was my wife. We have been living as man and wife for seven years.'

'When did you last see the deceased?'

'I last saw her about two o'clock in the afternoon of Saturday in Houndsditch. We parted on very good terms. She told me she was going over to Bermondsey to try and find her daughter, Annie. Those were the last words she spoke to me.'

'Are you the father of Annie?'

'No, sir. This is a daughter I believe she had by Conway and is grown and married. Cathy promised me before we parted that she would be back by four o'clock and no later. She did not return.'

'Did you make any inquiry after her?'

'I heard she had been locked up at Bishopsgate Station on Saturday afternoon. An old woman who works in there told me she saw her in the hands of the police. Another acquaintance, Mrs. Pearl Bailey, told me the same which led me to believe it must be true.'

'Did you make any inquiry into the truth of this?'

'I made no further enquiries. I knew that she would be out on Sunday morning.

It distressed Polly to watch John Kelly. He was turning grey as the questioning continued and she could see the sheen of a thin layer of sweat on his face.

'Did you know why she was locked up?' the coroner asked.

'Yes, for drink, so I was told. I found this strange as we had no money for drink. She occasionally drank - not to excess, sir. They said she was impersonating a fire engine. I could imagine that, sir, for she was comical. I think she might have been hoping to get a few pennies from the passers-by if she made them laugh. That is what she was like.' His voice wavered and almost broke.

'Why was she seeking her daughter?'

'She went to find her to get a few pennies so that I shouldn't see her walking about the streets at night.'

'What do you mean by "walking the streets"?'

Polly stiffened. Typical of many well-off people, he had no idea that in his own city people were destitute and had no place to sleep at night.

'I mean that if we had no money to pay for our lodgings we would have to walk about all night.' John Kelly replied. 'I was without money to pay for our lodgings at the time. If I had…' His grief almost overcame him. He managed by sheer strength of will to hold himself together and was shaking.

'Did she have any quarrel with anyone?' Coroner Langham cut in.

John Kelly looked up. 'I do not know that she was at variance with anyone - not in the least. She is… *was* an amiable, agreeable soul.' His voice cracked and he took in a breath. 'She had not seen Mr. Conway recently - not that I know of. As a matter of fact, I never saw him in my entire existence. I know of no one who would be likely to injure her.' The poor man blinked rapidly to prevent tears from forming. The terrible strain had etched itself into his face.

The Foreman of the Jury cleared his throat. 'You say you heard the deceased was taken into custody. Did you ascertain, as a matter of fact, when she was discharged?'

'No. I do not know when she was discharged,' Kelly sniffed.

'One of the witnesses has testified that she had a pawn ticket for boots?'

'Yes, sir it was for my boots. We got two and sixpence for them.'

'Thank you, Mr. Kelly,' said the Coroner, then paused and looked at him sympathetically. 'Our condolences for your terrible loss.'

When he was excused, Polly noticed that John Kelly immediately left the court. Polly was glad, he ought not to hear the rest of the evidence.

A succession of witnesses followed. These were mostly police officers who had been at the scene of the murder, neighbours in Mitre Square who had come to the assistance of the police and others who lived within sight of where the murder was committed. Their accounts of what happened were very similar. No one had seen nor heard anything until the police whistles started blowing.

Doctor Frederick Gordon-Brown was called. As he sat down in the witness chair, there was complete silence in the room. The observers were like dummies, they did not move a muscle, nor did they seem to be breathing and the scene was like a still life painting.

'Please share what you know with us, Doctor Gordon-Brown,' said the coroner.

'I was called shortly after two o'clock on Sunday morning. I reached the place of the murder about twenty minutes past two. My attention was directed to the body of the deceased. It was lying in the position described by Constable Watkins. It was on its back, the head turned to the left shoulder, the arms by the side of the body, as if they had fallen there. Both palms were upwards, the fingers slightly bent. A thimble was lying near. The clothes were thrown up. The bonnet was at the back of the head. There was great disfigurement of the face. The throat was cut across. The upper part of the dress had been torn open. The body had been mutilated. It was quite warm - no rigor mortis and I estimated from that the crime must have been committed within half an hour - certainly within forty minutes from the time when I saw the body. There were no stains of blood on the bricks or pavement. There was no blood on the front of the clothes. There was not a speck of blood on the front of the jacket, but the body lay in a substantial pool of blood.' said the doctor.

'Doctor Phillips was asked to attend,' said Gordon-Brown, 'I wished him to see the wounds - he having been engaged in a case of a similar kind. He saw the body at the mortuary. The clothes were removed with care from the deceased. I made a post-mortem examination on Sunday afternoon. There was a bruise on the back of the left hand and one on the right shin; this had nothing to do with the crime. There were no bruises on the elbows or the back of the head. The face was very much mutilated. The eyelids, the nose, the jaw, the cheeks, the lips, and the mouth all bore cuts. There were abrasions under the left ear. The throat was cut across to the extent of six or seven inches.'

'Can you tell us the cause of death?'

'The cause of death was haemorrhage from the throat. Death must have been almost immediate.'

'There were other wounds on the lower part of the body?'

'Yes. Deep wounds to the genitals. These were inflicted after the throat was cut.'

Polly steeled herself as the doctor described the wounds inflicted on Cathy's body. She was glad that John Kelly had not stayed.

Mr. Crawford spoke up. 'I understand that you found certain portions of the body removed?'

'Yes. The womb was cut away with the exception of a small portion and the left kidney was also cut out. Both these organs were absent and have not been found.'

'Have you any opinion as to what position the woman was in when the wounds were inflicted?'

'In my opinion, the woman must have been lying down. The way in which the kidney was cut out showed that it was done by somebody who knew what he was about. It is hidden by a layer of fat.'

'Does the nature of the wounds lead you to any conclusion as to the instrument used?' asked the Coroner.

'It must have been a sharp-pointed knife, and I should say at least six inches long,' said the doctor.

'Would you consider that the person who inflicted the wounds possessed anatomical skill?'

'He must have had a good deal of knowledge as to the position of the abdominal organs and the way to remove them.'

'Would the parts removed be of any use for professional purposes?'

'None whatever.'

'Would the removal of the kidney, for example, require special knowledge?'

'It would require a good deal of knowledge. It is apt to be overlooked, being covered by a membrane.'

'The statement of the pronouncing physician at the scene, Doctor Sequiera suggests the killer had no specialist knowledge,' the coroner pointed out.

'On that point, we differ,' said Gordon-Brown coldly, and a tad irritably, Polly felt.

'Would such knowledge be likely to be possessed by someone accustomed to cutting up animals?'

'Yes.'

'Have you been able to form any opinion as to whether the perpetrator of this act was disturbed in his work?'

'I think he had sufficient time, however, it was in all probability, done in a hurry.'

'How long would it take to make the wounds?'

'It might be done in five minutes. It might take him longer; that is the least time it could take.'

'Can you, as a professional man, ascribe any reason for the taking away of the parts you have mentioned?'

'I cannot give any reason whatever.'

'Have you any doubt in your own mind whether there was a struggle?'

'I feel sure there was no struggle. I see no reason to doubt that it was the work of one man.'

'Would any noise be heard, do you think?'

'I presume the throat was instantly severed, in which case there would not be time to emit any sound.'

'Does it surprise you that no sound was heard?'

'No.'

'Would you expect to find much blood on the person inflicting these wounds?'

'No, I should not. I should say that the abdominal wounds were inflicted by a person kneeling at the right side of the body. The wounds could not have been self-inflicted.'

'Was your attention called to the piece of the apron found in Goulston Street?'

'Yes. I fitted that portion which was stained with blood to the remaining portion. This was still attached by its strings to the body.'

'Have you formed any opinion as to the motive for the mutilation of the face?'

'It was to disfigure the corpse, I should imagine.'

One of the jurors spoke up. 'Was there any evidence of a drug having been used?'

'I have not examined the stomach as to that. The contents of the stomach have been preserved for analysis. It was largely free of any food content.'

'Thank you, Doctor,' said the coroner.

Mr. Crawford stood up. 'The Corporation has approved a reward of five hundred pounds by the Lord Mayor for the discovery of the murderer.'

'Very good, Mr. Crawford. I think that is quite enough for today. We will adjourn until Thursday next, that is the eleventh of October, at ten o'clock.'

Polly was relieved to be out of the stuffy courtroom. The details of Cathy's murder had been harrowing. Her stomach clenched. She looked over at Alf who was holding open the door to the witness room. He had seen Cathy's body. He knew how bad it was. He was constantly warning her to stay off the street and now she understood why.

# CHAPTER NINETEEN

Jennings' tea rooms sat in the northwest corner of Bridgewater Square. It was only a two- minute stroll at most from Golden Lane Mortuary. Polly did not want to wait there for Alf. If she loitered in the square, she would draw attention to herself.

She had made herself as smart as possible for the inquest. She had steamed her dress the way Lizzie taught her, stitched the hem and the small hole in the sleeve. The bonnet Suzette had loaned to her was dark blue and it matched the shawl which was made of wool in a green and blue tartan pattern. Polly's dress was shabby and not the slightest bit fashionable. This would be considered a crime by those who frequented fancy tea rooms.

She knew Alf would have duties to attend to before he could leave the court. To kill time, Polly returned to the conveniences behind the court building. She removed the bonnet and washed her face. She combed her hair, put on the bonnet and made sure the ribbon was tied correctly in a neat, symmetrical bow.

She took out the scrap of lavender soap Lizzie had given her and washed her hands. Polly always made sure her nails were clean, this time, she made a special effort. Even so, she knew her hands were one of the many signs that would single her out as a lower class woman.

Respectable ladies manicured their nails into a rounded shape and used carmine cream to buff and polish them until they shone. Polly's hands were used to hard work and her nails had not seen a manicure in years. This was also a crime to the tea drinking classes.

She took the longest possible route to Bridgewater Square and instead of going directly to it she walked around the entire block by going south on Golden Lane turning right onto Barbican then right again past Aldersgate Street Station, right again into Fann Street and back to the mortuary onto Golden Lane. Opposite the mortuary, she turned right into Cripplegate Street, which led to Bridgewater Square.

The delicious smell of baking drifted along the street. Polly's empty stomach was tormented by the tantalising aroma of newly baked bread. Her mouth watered as she also detected the spicy, sugary deliciousness of fruitcake and, she fancied, cinnamon buns and apple pie.

Just as the brewery clock began to strike the hour she arrived in Bridgewater Square. To her relief, as she turned the corner, she saw Alf was waiting for her. He was apparently inspecting the small park that filled the middle of the square. As Polly drew closer she saw he was watching a robin red breast as it fussed around from tree to tree looking for morsels of food.

'You don't see many of them over in Whitechapel,' said Polly.

'Nice little fella ain't he? Looks well fed and all…'

Polly smiled. 'He's got the good sense to live opposite a bakery. He's bound to pick up lots of crumbs.'

'Yeah.' Alf gave a chuckle. 'Clever little bird.'

Alf guided Polly towards the door of the tea room. It was a small, elegant establishment and Polly felt a pang of apprehension. She knew what she would find inside. She was familiar with this sort of place. They prized decorum and respectability above all else. Just like her own family's business, they depended on it. Polly knew, had she not been with Alf in his police sergeant's uniform, she would not get as much as a toe across the threshold.

'Listen, Alfie. Why don't we just take a park bench and you can tell me what you what you want to say? They won't want me in there, I can tell you.'

'Nonsense, Polly. You're better than every single one of them,' he said. 'Besides, I promised you a nice tea. Don't you fancy a cup of tea and some sandwiches and cakes?'

Fancy it? Her mouth watered at the thought of it and her stomach ached for want of food.

'That sounds smashing, Alfie. But-'

'Well then, in we go.'

They were shown to a table at the back of the room. Polly knew this table was in the area reserved for customers they did not want to offend but preferred to keep discretely out of sight. Alf did not seem to notice as he sat down and placed his helmet discretely on the floor between the wall and the table. Nor did he notice the sideways glances and raised eyebrows of the other customers that stung Polly like a swarm of bees. She straightened her spine, held up her head and kept her eyes fixed on nothing in particular in the middle distance.

From the sparkling ceiling chandelier and thick carpet to the snowy white tablecloths, this tea room showed its elegance and approval of social aspiration.

Polly sank onto a plush velvet covered chair and immediately felt the pleasure of anticipation. She was quite at home and knew how to behave in such places. As a young girl, she had been in much fancier tea rooms than this one. It had been a regular thing during shopping trips with her mother and Auntie May.

She was aware of whispered comments and glances in her direction. One or two gave her direct looks that were filled with contempt. It was actually rather funny when you thought about it. She was surrounded by people who without a doubt, had less of a privileged upbringing and less of an education than *Scholaires pour Les Doué Filles*, her exclusive school gave her, yet they looked down on her and regarded themselves as her superiors. To them, she was low-born and uneducated; a poor person with the audacity to believe she belonged in a smart tea room.

Polly caught one of these looks and stared the woman down with her most haughty expression. Alf was oblivious to all of these subtle signals as he ordered a substantial afternoon tea of cakes, sandwiches and scones.

'This is smashing, Alfie,' she said looking around, determined not to let anything spoil this wonderful treat.

'Mother used to like to come in here,' he said. 'Mrs. Jennings and her daughter do all the baking. My conclusion is they must be good if they can satisfy mother.'

When the tea came, it was in a bone china pot. The fine-looking hand painted tea set was decorated with bouquets of roses. The silver knives, forks and spoons had been polished until they gleamed.

The waitress brought a three tier cake stand filled with finger sandwiches of ham, beef, cheese and egg. She returned a few moments later with another, filled with delicate pastries, feather-light cakes and scones.

Polly had not eaten at all that day and little the day before. It took all her willpower not to cram the sandwiches into her mouth and gulp down cups of tea. Instead, she forced herself to sip her tea in its pretty china cup and nibble delicately at the sandwiches and pastries.

'It's very nice,' Polly smiled. 'I feel like a lady.' Then her face grew hot as she saw a man and a woman, their heads close together, looking in her direction as they talked in whispers. She suppressed a sigh. She looked away and kept her back straight and her expression dignified.

At *Scolaires pour les Doué Filles* she had been taught the language of deportment. The placement of the hands and feet, the tilt of the chin and straightness of the back were crucial in conveying the right impression. The moment she sat down, it all came back very naturally, however, it seemed her fellow diners were not impressed.

'You have the look of a lady,' said Alf.

'Come off it, Alfie.' Polly gave a short laugh, thinking what a rare man Alf Cruikshank was.

'I mean it.' he insisted as Polly tilted her head a fraction of an inch towards the couple who were staring in her direction. Alf followed her cue and glanced to his left. They looked away a split second beforehand. He had no idea of the disdain that surrounded them.

'I've had a lot of experience,' he said.

Polly looked at him, grinning. 'Know a lot of whores do you?' she said in a very low voice.

He opened his mouth then closed it again.

'Not like that.' he said as his ears turned crimson.

She gave a little laugh. She found it endearing that this big, tough sergeant, blushed and stumbled over his words if the conversation got even slightly personal.

'I've arrested a lot of them,' he continued, 'I've seen them all, Polly. The sort that don't know no better. The ignorant, bawdy and common types. You ain't like that. There's something about you. It's in your face.'

'How can you tell?'

'Copper's instincts maybe? I can smell 'em.'

'Alfie.' Polly wrinkled her nose.

'Sorry, Polly. I don't mean literally. Although some of them-' He stopped and cleared his throat as he discerned this was not a conversation for a polite tea room. 'What I mean is, I got a nose for them.' He tapped the side of his nose. 'I can spot a wrong 'un a mile off.' He reached for another sandwich and put it on his plate. 'It's what makes a good copper and you either got it or you ain't.'

'Tell me some more about it,' she said, taking another sandwich. She liked to listen to him. A sparkle came into his eyes when he talked about the job.

'These young lads that join the force,' he said. 'You can't teach them it. They gotta have what it takes.'

'I've seen you at the station. The lads respect you. You give them an order and they jump to it.'

'All they need is a firm hand, Polly. Some of them come into the force as a way of getting out of a terrible life. Most are from families that are dirt poor. Tragic situations some of them. They ain't got any idea about respect. Mostly they ain't got a father on the scene to set them an example, so that's part of my job. I teach them how to behave. Show them that they have to respect themselves as well as other people.'

'You really like it don't you? Being a copper?'

'I do, Polly, though I would like to see it done better. All proper and professional like.'

'Like the detective in that story, Mr. Sherlock Holmes.' Polly smiled.

'I find him an inspiration,' he said, 'I knew you'd get it. I knew you would understand him and the story. You're educated.'

Polly lifted her eyebrows. 'Oh yes, I'm educated all right. Mother and Father spent a fortune on my schooling. No board school for me. For all the good it did.'

'Went to a posh school did you?' Alf put three lumps of sugar in his tea and stirred it slowly.

'The poshest,' said Polly. 'I was such a little madam,' she tutted. 'My parents wanted me to learn how to manage their drapery business before being married off to some penniless aristocrat. Of course, that didn't suit me at all. I used to call it the *dreary* business. What I would give now…' She shook her head as she gazed back in time. 'I must have been such a disappointment to them.'

'How was it you took up with that Thomas?'

'He was one of the travelling salesmen who came into the shop and father would order stock from him. Mother let him stay in one of the spare rooms in the attic because he used to travel all the way from Birmingham. She felt sorry for him I think. She also wanted to keep him sweet. He used to bring these special, hard to come by, buttons that she got for a particular customer. Father said they made a huge profit on them.' Polly shook her head. 'Just one of those buttons cost more than a year's wages for a man in the east end. It's shocking really. I thought he must be rich since he sold these expensive buttons.' She looked at him and could feel herself blushing. 'Yes, I really was that stupid.' Alf did not answer, he regarded her with a sympathetic gaze as she continued. 'He passed me secret love notes and spun a romantic yarn. I was dazzled. I hadn't met a boy like him before. All the ones I knew were horse faced, inbred and dull. At least back then I thought that. They were probably all perfectly nice looking.' she said. 'Anyway, he told me he worked as a salesman for the present and his uncle owned the business which he would inherit one day. He told me stories of the fine life we would have while he took liberties I ought not to have let him take. Just like those two kids down on the embankment. That's why I had a go at them. She was down there with him unchaperoned, just like I used to do. All the promises Thomas made. Can you believe I fell for it? Well, I did, hook line and sinker. I eloped with him and here I am.' She shook her head. 'Stupid, stupid, stupid.'

'You were just a kid, Polly. Don't be so hard on yourself.'

'I was eighteen and a spoilt little rich girl who thought she knew it all. That's what I was,' she sighed. 'When I made mistakes, Mother and Father were always there to sort things out. They were soft on me, really.' She gave a reflective sigh. 'Not this time. They outright disowned me.'

'Did you try to speak to them?'

'I wrote to them and I got the letter back unopened. Return to sender.'

Alf winced. 'That's harsh. They must have known the consequences that would have for you.'

'I tried again when I went in the workhouse. My Auntie May wrote back to me on the quiet. She's father's younger sister. She said mother had died a couple of months before and father blamed me. She told me father had said I was dead to him.'

Alf raised his eyebrows. 'Very harsh,' he said.

'Auntie May said they had told everyone I had been killed in an accident on the Continent and the shock had brought on an apoplexy which killed mother.' She blinked away moisture from her eyes so as not to allow tears to fall. 'She said they had received a card of condolence from Queen Victoria herself.'

Alf blinked. 'A card from Her Majesty? Really? That's very nice, but why did they lie?'

'The scandal.' Polly shrugged. 'Father holds the royal warrant. He provides all the haberdashery and drapery items for the royal palaces. It's worth a fortune to the business. You don't make money off The Queen, Her Majesty doesn't believe she should pay for anything. She's a shrewd old lady. She knows the upper classes follow her lead, and that alone is worth a lot of money. The Queen won't brook any sort of scandal and she can take her business away in an instant. She does it all the time. People have been ruined overnight because they fell out of favour with her for one reason or another. If she takes her business elsewhere, other customers follow suit and *poof* it's all over - it's all about snobbery, you see. Can you imagine the scandal of me eloping, then turning up months later, still unmarried with a bun in the oven? It would have ruined them.'

'Surely they could have done something. Come up with some plausible explanation.'

Polly paused for a moment. 'To be honest, so did I. It was a shock when they cut me off.' She shrugged her shoulders and picked up the teapot. 'Anyway, Alfie, I might be educated and had a nice comfortable upbringing but now, *I is what I is and I ain't what I ain't.*'

She refilled their cups from the pot. Alf put four of the small lumps of sugar into his tea this time. He stirred it with a delicate silver teaspoon that looked ridiculously small in his outsized hand.

'Mother said you were a very good nurse,' he said.

'Did she? That's nice of her.' Polly took a sip of tea, savouring the fragrance of a good quality brew. 'I just wanted to help and show you how grateful I was. A little bit of fuss seems to make sick people feel better doesn't it?'

'As a matter of fact, she's been asking if you could come back and look after her some more.'

'She has?' Polly smiled. 'Aw... I bet she feels quite lonely when you're on a long shift. I don't mind checking on her and fussing over her a bit. I could make her a bite to eat if you like.'

'Her saying that, set me to thinking, Polly.' Alf continued. He stopped eating and looked at her. 'With all this compulsory overtime I could do with some help with mother. I was wondering if you would come and look after her, like.'

'It would be my pleasure to look in on her.'

'That ain't what I meant. I meant a proper arrangement. I could pay you two shillings a week with bed and board included.'

Polly stared at him.

'You want to take me on?'

'Yes, as a housekeeper and nurse for mother.'

'Does she know about this?'

'It was her idea to have you as a live-in nurse. She even volunteered my brother's room, which took me by surprise. I know it don't sound much…but if you consider that it's with bed and board, it ain't all that bad an offer. What d'you say?'

'I don't know what to say, she said.

'Don't think I'm- I mean it's all as straight as an arrow.' His ears started to turn pink again. 'It would be respectable and everything. You would never be in the house with me without mother being present. She never goes out these days.'

Polly lowered her voice to a whisper. She could not help smiling at this dear man. 'Respectable? What will she say when she finds out what I am? What would all your neighbours say and your bosses?'

'Mother don't need to know about that does she?' he said. 'And no one else will know.'

'Oh, Alfie, of course they will. People gossip. Haven't you noticed all the dirty looks I'm getting in here?'

He looked around him vaguely. 'Can't say I have. No one knows you here or around where I live.'

'They don't have to know me, they can tell. Look at me.'

'They can't tell anything,' he replied emphatically. 'Maybe you look a bit poorer than some of them, that's all. They don't know you're... well it's two different worlds ain't it?'

'You'd be surprised. Lots of people saw me give evidence at the inquest, they know what I am. Then this one knows that one and that one knows another one. Someone will know me and that will be that. It is lovely that you asked me.' She bit her lip as she looked at him, 'I can't accept, Alfie. If I did, the gossip would ruin you. Your bosses would find out in no time and that would be the end of your dream to be a detective. I wouldn't want that to happen.'

'You would be mother's nurse, fair, square and above board.'

'With my past, they would never believe that there is nothing going on.'

Alf sat back in his chair and looked at her. 'Is that all you're worried about? Let them think what they like. We know it's respectable.'

'It's important. I don't care what they say about me. I do care that it could ruin you.'

'Polly, listen; one thing that's clear from that inquest is this lunatic ain't going to stop.' He lowered his voice even more. 'What he did to Mrs. Eddowes... well, it beggared belief... I felt for poor Mr. Kelly having to view her in that state. The papers made it sound bad, believe me, what they said weren't nearly as bad as it was in reality.' He looked at her. 'They think his nest is somewhere around Dorset Street... I want you off those streets, away from the doss houses. I don't want to turn up at a murder scene and find it's you lying there. Mother needs a nurse, it's the logical solution. Why should that be a problem?'

'You can't imagine how much I want to get out of this life,' she admitted.

'Then accept the offer.'

She shook her head. 'If you have me under your roof, you would be disgraced, Alfie.' she said. 'I would jump at the chance to help you look after your mother, except... living in your house?'

'It's mother's house and I'm hardly there at present, Polly. It would ease my mind considerable if someone was there for her through the night and you would have two bob a week all your own.'

'You would really pay me two bob a week?'

'Yes, and you would have all your food, your own room and everything.'

'Oh Alfie, it's very generous and I'm honoured that you asked.'

'No one would have any call to gossip.' He leaned forward in a confidential manner. 'You know something, Polly. A lot of the time it's about the clothes. That's what gets the respect. You dress like a nurse, sober and respectable, folks will take you at face value. The way you talked at the inquest this morning, that's more like how you were brought up to talk weren't it?'

'Did I talk differently? I was so nervous I can hardly remember what I said.'

'You spoke nicely. You do it all the time when you ain't around the other girls. You're doing it now and you did the same when you spoke to Mother. You bring out your proper accent and no one will ever have cause to doubt you.'

A tiny spark ignited in Polly's chest. Was it possible to be plucked from this miserable existence by a single chance offered by this big, awkward and very sweet man?

'Before I build my hopes up. Tell me… Why are you doing this?'

'You need a helping hand and Mother needs someone to care for her. You need a job, don't you? Ain't that what you've been telling me all this time? Mother likes you. It's simple.' He was blushing, she noticed. For all his big, hard headed appearance, he was a kind man and this was a very generous gesture. 'I told you, it will be all above board,' he said.

'Until she finds out I'm a-.'

'Don't use that word.' he interrupted in a whisper. 'You take on this work and you ain't that anymore are you?'

'Alfie, I…' she stared at him, pressing her lips together, lost for words.

'Come on Polly, what d'you say?'

She groped for the right way to say what she needed to tell him. 'You shouldn't have any illusions about me.' She lowered her eyes.

A look of concern crossed his face. 'Are you ill or something?'

'No. At least I don't think so…I don't want to deceive you, Alfie. I'm… I've done…'

'Have you done things I would have to arrest you for?'

'Isn't my "profession" illegal?'

'As a matter of fact, no.'

'Um? Why do the girls get locked up then?' she whispered.

'It's only illegal if a woman goes around asking for customers and bothering fine upstanding citizens -soliciting in other words.

'In that case, no. They've always come up to me and put a gin on the table. I hate gin.'

His face darkened to a deep shade of red. 'Listen, you can forget that now. This is a fresh start, Polly,' he said. 'Don't ever speak of it after today. You're Polly Wilkes, a respectable housekeeper and nursemaid. What d'you say?' Alf gave her the smile that Polly had started to grow fond of - the one that transformed his stern-looking mug into an agreeable face.

She stared at him. She opened her mouth. No words would come out.

'That's settled then,' he said.

It took her another minute to compose herself and blink back tears. 'I'm speechless.'

'Polly Wilkes? Speechless? Well I never,' he chuckled.

She shook her head. 'Fate was in a good mood the day you came into my life, Alfie Cruikshank. God bless her.' She picked up her teacup made a silly little toast to fate and then sipped the hot, fragrant, Darjeeling.

'When would you like me to start?' she said putting down her cup.

'There ain't nothing to gain by delaying. So, what about right away?'

'Whatever you say.'

'It will be a weight off my shoulders to know mother ain't on her own.'

Barely the width of a tea trolley from where Polly was sitting, were two middle-aged women who looked so alike they were probably sisters. In accordance with proper manners when one of them met her eyes, Polly nodded. Frowning the woman looked away, nose in the air and an affronted look on her face. It was a deliberate snub, and to Polly, it was as sharp as a knife to the stomach. She saw herself as this woman saw her and had a sudden feeling of panic. She looked at the dear man opposite, putting up with dolls house sized cups and nursery sized sandwiches because he thought she would like an elegant tea. He had no idea what having her under his roof would mean and what malicious gossip could do to his good name.

The snub she had just received was only a small taste of what was to come.

'Alfie, it's no use.'

'What's wrong with it now?'

'Your mother, your neighbours, your workmates, they'll all cotton on, no matter how I talk.'

'What d'you mean?'

She looked down at what she was wearing. 'I've got nothing else and they'll see me in this every day. They'll soon work it out.' Polly replied. 'And your neighbours, they'll wonder, won't they? What am I going tell them I've been doing for a living?' She thought for a moment. 'Maybe the girls can help me; only, their kind of clothes aren't-'

'I don't want you going back there.' He lowered his voice again, though the tone remained serious. 'That part of your life is over, Polly. I don't want you nowhere near Dorset Street.'

'Unless I borrow something from the girls, I haven't got-'

'I ain't seen any of them wearing anything worth having,' said Alf.

Polly bit her lip. She knew he was right.

Alf sighed, looking contemplative. 'However, I see your point. Ladies need things and you can't wear the same dress all the time.' He paused. 'How much is a new one?'

'Too much.'

'How much do you need for a new dress?' he repeated.

'A new one is out of the question. I might find one on the market for two or three shillings.'

'That's what you'll do then. I'll give you some money and you can go and kit yourself out.'

'What? But-'

'Oh, here we go.'

Polly narrowed her eyes into a hard stare. 'Think how it looks; me taking money off you for clothes.'

Alf stared back at her. 'It don't matter. I told you, Polly, looking respectable is three-quarters of it... Dress like a lady and no one will say a dicky bird. We'll tell the neighbours that you've been..... I know, nursing your auntie on the south coast. Bournemouth. That'll do.' He looked pleased with himself. 'You already have the manners and look of a respectable lady so we're home and dry. Now, let's enjoy our tea. I'll get the girl to bring some more.'

'Just like that?'

'Yeah. Just like that.'

Polly wanted to scream at the top of her lungs. 'Oh I really hope I'm not dreaming,' She gave a little laugh. 'I should pinch myself... I will be so upset if I am.'

'You ain't dreaming,' he said.

'I'll work hard and take good care of her, Alfie.'

'I know you will, Polly. Mother was a midwife for donkeys' years and you impressed her so much she thought you was a trained nurse.'

'We must remind her that I'm not. I don't want to lie about it.'

'We can tell her you picked it up as you went along.'

'Will she believe that?'

'No one trained Miss Nightingale and she's taught others how it's done.'

'I'm no Florence Nightingale.'

'You might be.' Alf wiggled his eyebrows in the way that made her laugh.

She took another sip of tea then put the cup down carefully in its saucer. 'You know, my first thought was to run and tell Lizzie about this. I keep doing that, then I remember she's gone. I keep thinking she's going to turn up safe and sound with some story about what she's been up to.' Her eyes grew bright as she blinked away tears.

'I think a lot of people do that. After my brother passed away. I used to think I heard him charging in through the back door after school like he always did.' He looked uncomfortable, as if he didn't know what else to say. 'I think you learn to cope that's all,' he said. 'You don't exactly get over it. Life will go on. And now our bargain will make things better for both of us so let's think on that.'

Half an hour later they left the tea shop. They walked south on Bridgewater Street and Alf hailed a cab when they reached Barbican. Once inside the cab, Alf discretely gave Polly two ten shilling notes. Polly's jaw dropped.

'Alfie this is far too much. All I need is a couple of bob for a dress. It's ten weeks wages.' she said in a whisper so the cabbie couldn't hear.

'I would imagine you need more than that, and it ain't wages,' said Alf. 'It's to buy your uniform so to speak. Take it and get yourself what you need.'

'You can't give me all this. Doesn't it leave you short?'

'I got a bit put by,' he said. 'And this nutter has put a small fortune in my pocket in overtime, so take it.'

'I'll only accept it if you'll call it an advance on my wages.'

Alf sighed. 'Confound it, Polly, you're wearing me out with all your objections and resistance. Take the money.'

'An advance. Right?'

'Take the money, Polly,' he sighed. 'You need to get yourself properly kitted out.' He put on his helmet.

'Very well, Alfie. Thank you. Are you going to come with me to the market and see what I spend it on?'

'I don't need to know the details. Besides, it's not a good idea. If I go wandering around the market in this uniform, most of them'll be away on their toes. If they do, I'll have to investigate and we just ain't got the time or the men available. You go and get your things and I'll check on Mother and give her the good news. I got to go back on duty at ten for another shift tonight so I'll need a couple of hours kip.'

'After you were at the inquest all day?'

'Unfortunately, that's how it works - not just for me, for the lads as well. To tell you the truth leaving Mother when I do double shifts has preyed on my mind. If you could be home before six I would be very obliged. Then we can have a bit of supper and I'll tell you what's what before I go.'

'In that case, should I bring something off the market for our suppers?' she beamed.

'That would be smashing, Polly.'

The driver slowed the horses and brought the cab to a halt as they reached Aldgate Station. Alf leaped from the cab and paid the driver. He offered Polly his arm as she stepped down.

'Good day, Miss Wilkes,' he nodded, touching the brim of his helmet.

'Good day, Sergeant Cruikshank.'

# CHAPTER TWENTY

As Alf strode off in the direction of Leman Street, Polly headed towards New Court, a grubby little offshoot of Dorset Street, where Suzette rented a tiny room. She returned the bonnet and shawl to a very groggy Suzette, who was hungover having been out all night, picked up her own shabby one, then headed for the market feeling elated that she no longer had to be part of that life.

Petticoat Lane was the biggest market around, weaving its way the length of Middlesex Street and overflowing into the surrounding streets. People still called it Petticoat Lane Market, even though the street name had been changed decades ago by those who thought it just too shocking for a place to be named after an undergarment.

Polly made plans as she walked. This was a dream come true and she felt like turning cartwheels right there in the street. Once Alfie was done with her services, she would have a proper reference and would be able to find another position. She would save up most of her two shillings each week and buy herself some nice, good quality clothing. Looking well dressed and respectable would improve her chances of getting further employment.

She kept a tight grip on the small drawstring purse in her pocket as she entered the market, knowing what easy pickings for thieves the place was. Many of them dossed at Crossingham's and in the night she sometimes heard them hatching whispered plans to steal from stall holders and relieve customers of their purses. She knew they sent out fledgling pickpockets to sharpen their skills at this market because it was always so crowded.

Polly took in the long rows of stalls and picked her way along the pavement towards the top of Middlesex Street. She had often looked longingly at the clothes on the second-hand stalls, wishing she could buy something. She felt a rush of pleasure. This time she had some money.

She began to sort through the jumbled pile of clothes on one of the stalls. She knew what to look for. Being raised the daughter of a draper was about to pay off. By touching the garments and looking at the weave, she could assess their quality. It was something she had been taught the whole time she was growing up. *With cotton, it's all about the number of threads per inch...* her mother had told her. *You want the highest thread count for the finest dresses. Over three hundred per inch or more. It feels like satin and you must make sure you handle the fabric very carefully, Mary Victoria. The threads are so fine they snag and snap easily. Then we would have to throw it all away.* Polly, bored as usual by drapery talk, asked what the point was of buying fabric to make a dress from such a delicate material.

Her mother explained that the fragility of the fabric wasn't a problem for their cosseted customers.

*The dress you're wearing is made out of that very same fabric, young lady,* her mother had pointed out. Polly had rolled her eyes, but now, she had a sudden insight into her own downfall. What her mother had called cosseted, she would call underused, underemployed and bored. In that stifling society, women, especially young women, were mercilessly controlled. They were permitted to do very little; especially outside the home. That kind of boredom was an invisible prison and she had rebelled. She wondered what kind of life it was, where even the most delicate fabric was not at risk of being damaged by any sort of useful activity.

Poor women, on the other hand, were worked to death and suffered the consequences of poverty. As she was now one of them, she needed a dress of good quality that would stand up to hard work.

Polly pulled a dress from the pile that looked just right. The cotton had been brushed to give it a softer feel and was probably two hundred threads per square inch. That was a good quality durable cotton. She looked at the stitching. She had already discarded a few that lacked the small even stitches she was looking for. This one passed the test and had a lot of wear left in it. The dress was navy blue with white pinstripes. A repair to the hem was needed; the rest of it was in good condition. Then Polly looked at the collar and could hardly contain herself. The dress had a Brussels lace collar - actual, beautiful white Brussels lace.

*Brussels lace is the best and most sought after, Mary Victoria. Look at the quality of the workmanship and the beautiful floral designs...* Polly had again rolled her eyes in a bored response to her mother's words. Now she could see how much the quality of this lace stood out from the others. A Brussels lace collar was a subtle sign of wealth and good taste. She carefully concealed her delight from the stall holder. She knew the price would go up if she showed keen interest.

This particular collar could be detached from the dress, meaning she could wear it with other garments. It was perfect.

She kept the dress close to her and began to rummage through the rest of the pile. She spotted another in lilac that was similar. It needed a repair to the sleeve. Her heart skipped a beat - this too had a Brussels lace collar. Trying not to seem too eager, she frowned at the defects on each dress and looked thoughtful.

'How much for these two?' she said to the stall holder. She held her breath.

'Two bob each.' said the bearded, flat capped proprietor.

Polly pulled out a wool skirt in a rich burgundy colour and another in pale blue - each for a shilling. 'I'll have them all if you knock a bit off the price.' The proprietor stared at her as if she had asked him to sell his first born child. 'Come on,' she continued, 'it's near the end of the day. You don't want to take them home just to bring them back tomorrow do you?' She beamed him a smile. 'How about five bob for the lot? They need to be repaired, look.'

The proprietor sucked his teeth as he considered the offer. Meanwhile, Polly picked up a white blouse with a lace yoke and stand up dog collar and a similar one in cream.

'Ninepence each,' said the man in reply to her inquiry.

'I'll take these two as well if you're prepared to bargain.' she said. 'Come on, you ain't going sell them to anyone else now are you? How about six bob the lot?' said Polly as the stall holder scowled. Polly grinned back at him. 'Go on, be a gentleman.'

'Six bob… and sixpence.' he said grudgingly. 'Then do me a favour; go and rob someone else will you?' He folded the clothes up into a pile.

'You're a funny man.' Polly replied. She handed over one of her ten shilling notes.

He looked at it. 'Blimey, found a rich punter last night did you?'

Polly glared at him. 'I'll have my change if you please.'

He handed her three shillings and sixpence change and she flounced off, pleased that she had bargained a whole shilling off the cost of her new things. She would burn the clothes she was wearing. She made up her mind that this would be the last time anyone would have her pegged her as a whore.

At another stall, she found a petticoat and two pairs of drawers along with two pairs of stockings, a chemise, two camisoles and two nightdresses. She haggled the price down to four shillings for everything.

Then, to her delight, further along the row of stalls she found her best bargain. A pair of good leather boots that fitted her small feet as if they had been made for her; even better, they were watertight. On the same stall, she spotted a leather suitcase. It would be perfect for carrying all her new things. She persuaded the stall holder to sell her the shoes and the case for three shillings and sixpence.

She had spent only fourteen shillings. She decided she would look for a bonnet and a warm winter cloak. She came across a stall where the clothes had become heaped into a tangled mountain. Sensing there would be a bargain somewhere in the pile, Polly set out to look for it. After a few moments of searching and separating the garments, she found a wool cloak in royal blue. She tried it on. It felt warm and soft, it was so much better than her old shawl.

'Hang on, I got a bonnet to match that to perfection.' said the woman who ran the stall. She produced it from a box at her side and handed it to Polly who put it on.

'Oh yes… That colour don't half suit you.'

'How much is it?' Polly asked her. She loved the cloak already and knew had to have it. The bonnet wasn't up to the minute fashion, having a wide brim, but she liked it all the same and the woman was right, it was a perfect match.

'It's three shillings for the cloak and a shilling for the bonnet. You can have them both for three shillings and sixpence on account of how well they look on you. How's that?'

'Thank you.' Polly gave her a big smile and handed over the money.

'You keep them on, dearie.' The woman smiled. 'They make you look like a proper lady.'

She thanked the woman again. She had all these things and she still had three shillings left. Polly finished her shopping by getting a washing sponge, some rose scented soap and a small bottle of eau de cologne for ninepence. All of it went into the suitcase. Despite the fact that it was scratched and the handle had been repaired, it was good quality and its latches closed with a satisfying *click*. Once she gave it a thorough polishing, it would look a treat.

She bought a straw basket for threepence. She would need one for carrying groceries now that she was a housekeeper. With the remainder of the money, she bought some cheese, a loaf of bread, potatoes and some mutton chops. She would fry the potatoes and chops for supper. This was more food than she usually saw in a week and her mouth watered in anticipation of a hot meal.

Polly left the market wearing the cloak and bonnet and felt as if she was floating on air. She felt proud as she carried her suitcase and her shopping basket. She was walking away from Dorset Street at last.

She emerged from the market and headed down Goulston Street towards Aldgate. She would have a ten-minute walk to Scarborough Street and into another life.

Then, her wonderful and most enjoyable day was interrupted. At the widest part of the street, outside the public baths and wash house, a makeshift platform had been constructed from several beer crates and some planks of wood. Two men were standing on it. Polly was amazed to see that one of the men was none other than Mickey Kidney.

Polly's heart sank and skipped a few beats as she identified the other man as George Lusk. She had been distracted by her good fortune. Seeing Mickey brought back all her grief and rage at Lizzie's murder. She had been waiting for the chance to confront him and tell him she wouldn't rest until she saw him hang.

Kidney was standing with his cap in his hand. His head was bowed and his shoulders hunched as though the weight of the entire world was upon them. Despite this, Polly could see that his beady eyes were scanning the crowd. Her new bonnet and cloak had transformed her, and his gaze passed over her without recognition.

If their eyes had met at that moment and he had recognised her, she might have flown at him like a cat. The fact that he had not, made her think again. She had been offered a new start in life today. A respectable lady would not spring out of a crowd to attack someone and call him a filthy murderer. She remembered what Alfie said; she needed to bide her time and get the evidence before she accused him of anything. Tipping him off would only make it more difficult to prove. She decided to stay, watch and find out what this was all about. Mr. Sherlock Holmes would have called it recognisance.

George Lusk was murmuring instructions next to his ear and Mickey nodded in response to whatever he was saying to him. They waited until a sizable crowd had assembled then Lusk stepped forward.

'Ladies and gentlemen or should I say fellow Londoners. I have come to speak to you today because I want to show you that it is within your power to make changes in your community. Yes, you sir, and you, sir.' He singled out members of the crowd. 'Why do you have this power? Because you have the power of the vote! A few nights ago, two more shocking murders took place within a quarter of a mile of this very spot. What are the police doing? Not much it seems. I see no evidence that they are close to apprehending this killer, this madman who is preying on our women, this lunatic who stalks our streets. Who will be next? It could be any woman. Wife, mother or daughter. This man here...' he took Kidney's elbow, 'is a victim of police incompetence.' Kidney stood with his head bowed. 'His dear wife was one of the women murdered those few nights ago.' The crowd murmured in response. 'His personal tragedy and terrible grief made worse by the incompetence of Commissioner Warren. There is no sign of a suspect nor an arrest to give him solace in his loss.'

Polly's jaw dropped as Kidney sobbed and wiped away a tear. 'My poor missus. She was devoted to me.' His voice cracked. 'I shall never find another like her.' The crowd made more sympathetic murmurings.

'This is a disgrace ladies and gentlemen. It's a disgrace that this poor man should have to live with this terrible loss. What you can you do?' He re-iterated a question from a man in the crowd. 'I will tell you, sir. Use your vote. Use this opportunity to show them that you will not tolerate their incompetence. Get them out! Vote for me, George Lusk. I will stop foreigners taking the jobs of Englishmen. I will make sure working men get a living wage and I swear to this poor man that I will ensure that the madman who took his wife from him is caught and hanged.'

Kidney gave a loud sob. 'Thank you, sir. I wish you would, sir, for I shall never know a moment of peace until the wretch pays for what he done to my Lizzie.' The crowd murmured again.

Polly could not stand listening to any more of his lies. She crossed to the other side of Goulston Street and quickened her pace slightly. She had to get away before she lost her temper. Lusk was a wealthy man and liked to think of himself as important. He was rumoured to be the richest man in the east end and it was obvious that he had high ambitions. He wanted to be elected to the new London Council. He wanted to be the man who ran the East End maybe even the whole of London. If Kidney was under his protection, proving his guilt would be more difficult.

'I know he did it, Lizzie,' she murmured, 'and I'll get him for you, I swear.'

# CHAPTER TWENTY ONE

Alf sat at the kitchen table. His collarless shirt was unbuttoned at the neck and he had rolled up his sleeves to the elbows, waiting with anticipation for the breakfast Polly was presently loading onto a plate from the frying pan. Their arrangement was working well. In three weeks, she had managed to get the whole house in order and establish a routine while caring for Mrs. Cruikshank.

Alf was obliged to take on hours and hours of compulsory overtime and Polly was surprised at how little free time he had. The strain on him when he was caring for his mother himself must have been intolerable, yet he had shouldered the burden without complaint.

'I know you're set on going, Polly and I have to say I'm uneasy about it. Michael Kidney will be there, guaranteed,' he said.

'I know he will. He wouldn't miss an opportunity like that to play the grieving husband. That play acting I saw him do at Goulston Street, sickened me.'

'See? That's why I'm uneasy. If he starts with all that rubbish, you'll have a go at him won't you?' Alf drew his eyebrows together into a frown.

Because of the earlier doubt over her identity, Lizzie's inquest had been adjourned so that more evidence could be gathered. Today was October 23rd, the fifth and final day. Polly wanted to be there.

'I won't lose my temper, I promise.' She placed the plate of succulent sausages, bacon that had been fried until the fat was crisp the way he liked it, two eggs with golden yolks, and fried tomatoes in front of him. Alf picked up his knife and fork and tucked into the food with enthusiasm. He looked doubtful as he weighed up Polly's promise and his expression was not lost on her. 'Lizzie was like a sister to me, Alfie. I can't miss the last day of her inquest. I want to hear it.'

'I wish I could go with you. I got to cover an extra shift again. There ain't anyone else on account of a few of the lads are giving evidence today.'

'You ought not to come with me anyway. It's best you're not seen in my company if some of your workmates will be there.' She put a plate stacked with slices of toast on the table then picked up the teapot and freshened the brew with more boiling water from the kettle.

'As will Inspector Reid, my guvnor.' He looked up. 'Why shouldn't I be seen in your company?'

'You already know why. You can't be seen keeping company with a former whore can you?'

He sighed. 'I ain't ashamed of you. And for the last time, I told you never to say that no more. You're a housekeeper and nursemaid – and a very good one at that.'

'People won't forget, Alfie, not in three weeks.'

'Listen, Polly. About the inquest, I know you want to do the right thing, but it would be better if you stayed away. You know it'll only upset you.'

'I can't, Alfie.'

'I really wish you would.'

'I have to be there for her.'

'Look, Polly-'

'Alfie, you're not the boss of me.'

'Yes I am,' he replied.

She thought about this for a moment. 'Oh, right, so you are. Anyway, that's not the point.' She put the teapot back on the table.

'Oh really? It ain't the point? How's that then?' There was a glint of amusement in his eyes.

'I'll keep quiet, that's the point. I promise I will sit quiet, listen to the evidence and hear the verdict out of respect for Lizzie.' she said. 'Now drink your tea while I take this up to your mother.' Polly picked up a tray with some bacon, scrambled eggs, toast and a cup of tea set out on it.

When she returned several minutes later, Alf was fastening his uniform tunic.

'Listen to me, Polly. If you insist on going, you can't go running your mouth. No matter what you hear. No matter what Kidney does or says, you say *nothing*.' He looked at her. 'It's serious.'

'I know,' Polly nodded.

'No matter what gets said. No matter what he does or how much he gets up your nose. Keep your mouth shut.'

'I got it, Alfie.'

Polly made her way to the Vestry Hall on Cable Street. It was crammed with people and the air smelled overused and stale. She had been one of the first to arrive and was glad she had found a seat close to an open window at the end of a row. At the back of the hall, it was standing room only.

Mr. Wynne E. Baxter convened the fifth day of the inquiry into Elizabeth Stride's death. The first witness was Detective Inspector Reid whom Polly surmised must be the one Alf had called his *guvnor.*

'Inspector Reid. Have you information on the identity of the victim?' said Baxter.

'Yes. I have examined the books of the Poplar and Stepney Sick Asylum. I found therein the entry of the death of John Thomas William Stride of Poplar. His death took place on the 24th day of October 1884 in the workhouse.'

'Thank you, Inspector.' Baxter nodded. 'Constable Walter Stride please.'

Polly thought this must be the son of Lizzie's hated brother-in-law. It was John Stride's brother who after a business dispute, had suddenly pulled out his one-third investment and caused them to lose their coffee shop in Chrisp Street, just off Poplar High Street. The loss of the business had resulted in John and Lizzie's first admission to the workhouse where they had been forced to separate. Couples were not permitted to stay together in such places. Lizzie was bitter about her brother-in-law and always said the distress it caused had contributed to John's death.

The young constable was shown into the room. Polly craned her neck to get a look at the young policeman who was walking towards the witness chair. Polly guessed his age as about nineteen or twenty years. He was pale and the hair that covered his forehead looked damp. He clutched his helmet to his side so tightly that his knuckles were white.

'Constable Stride, have you viewed the body of the victim?' said Baxter.

'Yes, sir.'

'Did you recognise the victim?'

'Yes, sir. The victim is the wife of my Uncle John Stride,' he said. 'I recognised her, I mean, the deceased,' he gulped, 'from a photograph. My Uncle John is dead four years since. The last I heard of them they were living in East India Dock Road. That was many years ago.'

'Thank you, Constable.'

The lad returned to his seat amongst the witnesses.

'Inspector Reid? You have evidence to add?' said Baxter. Reid stood up and moved to the witness chair once again.

'As you are aware, Mrs. Mary Malcolm caused doubt and delay about the identity of the victim.'

Baxter nodded. 'Yes. I have never before been moved to silence a witness, however, this woman identified her supposed mutilated relative with excessive and ghoulish relish. The record states that I considered this so unusual, as to doubt she was the deceased's sister.'

'Others were sceptical on the same point.' Reid replied. 'Not one word of genuine pity for the dead woman's shocking fate ever crossed Mrs. Malcolm's lips. Her own goodness and generosity to her poor sister was the never ending theme of her evidence and would have continued had you not cut her short, sir.'

Baxter nodded. 'What further have you uncovered, Inspector?'

'I have established, without doubt, Mrs. Malcolm's deceit.' Reid looked pleased with himself. 'I would like to call Mrs. Elizabeth Stokes, who is very much alive and well.'

Polly had heard Alf say that Reid took part in amateur dramatics and concert groups. She pressed her lips together. That pronouncement had been pure drama, she thought, as she shifted in her seat to get a glimpse of the woman who looked nothing like Lizzie.

The spectacle of the revelation and the subsequent personal appearance of Mrs. Stokes had distracted everyone from the point, which was, if until now, the victim's true name had not been known, how could Mickey Kidney have known that Lizzie was the victim the day after the murder, and how did one newspaper, *The Times*, print the correct name? Only one way, she thought, because he killed her and George Lusk paid a bribe to a reporter to print it.

'Michael Kidney, please,' said Baxter.

Polly was jolted back to the proceedings by the mention of the name. Every muscle in her body stiffened when she saw him. She held her breath. Perhaps this was where he would be confronted on that very point.

Mickey walked towards the chair, clutching a black bowler hat with both hands. His head was bowed. Somewhere he had found himself a brown check suit with a cutaway jacket and skinny leg trousers that were too short. He wore a black waistcoat with a watch chain and a white shirt with a black cravat. He was aiming for the look of a respectable citizen; he had achieved the look of a music hall comedian. Nevertheless, he was pulling off the demeanour of a bereft widower.

He settled himself in the chair and quickly ran his hand over his head to smooth his plastered down, heavily oiled hair. He wiped the hand on his trousers.

'Mr. Kidney would you please explain your relationship to the deceased.'

Polly's eyes burned from the strain of glaring at him. Mickey took his time, apparently making a valiant effort to compose himself and control his distress before finally speaking.

'For the last three years, she has been living with me, sir. We lived as man and wife though we were too poor to afford a proper legal ceremony.' He looked up sharply. 'I regarded her as my wife, sir, for in the eyes of God she surely was - ceremony or not,' he said looking at Coroner Baxter, who nodded as he continued. He heaved a sigh. 'I belong to the army reserve, sir. That has made me very disciplined in my habits.'

Polly's jaw had dropped but Mickey was not finished. 'My Elizabeth was a fine woman, sir, her only vice was that she liked to drink to excess.' He bowed his head and his face took on a regretful expression. 'At intervals during our association, she would sometimes leave me, sir, without any apparent reason, except a desire to be free from my restraining influence and to obtain greater opportunity of indulging her drinking habits.'

*The filthy liar.* Now Polly's jaw tightened as she clenched her teeth. Her blood began to heat up. She took slow, deep breaths. She could hear the sound of her blood sizzling through her brain.

'When did you last see the deceased?' asked Baxter.

'A week before, sir, at which time I tried to reason with her. She had left me to have one of her drinking binges. I tried to prevent her, sir. To my distress, she would have none of it. She was a determined woman, sir and would have her way.'

'You did not try to find her in the intervening period?'

'No point, sir,' said Kidney looking up. 'She was unreasonable when she was in that condition and kept bad company. I knew she would come back to me eventually.'

Blood pounded through Polly's head as Baxter studied Mickey.

'Several witnesses saw her with another gentleman, Mr. Kidney, one to whom she seemed much attached.'

Kidney bowed his head again. 'I would still have took her back, sir. We were very close and had hardly a cross word...' He cast a sideways glance at the jury. 'Except about her drunkenness. If only I could have impressed upon her the evils of drink,' he wailed, clutching the brim of his hat with tight fists, 'my dear wife might be with me today.' He pressed his lips together, bowed his head and shook it slowly.

Polly was incandescent. The words she was holding back almost blistered her tongue.

Baxter, now satisfied that Lizzie had been correctly identified and the facts surrounding her death established, had heard sufficient evidence.

'There is nothing to be gained by delaying the verdict,' he said. 'There is no point in prolonging this poor man's pain. Our condolences Mr. Kidney. You may step down.'

'Thank you, sir,' he replied.

What? Polly thought with a sinking feeling. Was that it? No mention of him knowing it was Lizzie before anyone knew who the victim was? No mention of his violent temper? Nothing about all the bruises and other injuries she suffered at his hands? No evidence from Israel Schwartz?

Baxter began to sum up. 'The victim was last seen alive by Michael Kidney in Commercial Street on the evening of Tuesday, September 25th. It seems she was sober, though she never returned home after that night. One witness, Mrs. Elizabeth Tanner, alleged that Mrs. Stride often times had words with Mr. Kidney, however, he has emphatically denied this and there is no evidence to support this assertion.' Polly's fury was making her ears ring. A woman's evidence counted for nothing and a man's lies were instantly believed. She clenched her fists into tight balls. So they had all imagined Lizzie's torn earlobe and split lip, had they? Had they dreamed up the bruising on her neck and frequent black eyes?

The coroner continued. 'She called at their home during his absence and took away some things.'

After which time he tried to beat the living daylights out of her at Flower and Dean Street. Polly seethed.

'With this exception, Mr. Kidney did not know what became of her.' Coroner Baxter continued. 'According to Mrs. Tanner, she cleaned the lodging house at 32 Flower and Dean Street on Saturday, September 29th, which was to be her last day on this earth.' He paused and looked down at his notes. 'When Doctor Blackwell's assistant arrived, the body and limbs, except for her hands, were warm. Blood was running from a deep wound in the neck. Even at sixteen minutes past one o'clock when Doctor Blackwell arrived he found her face slightly warm and her chest and legs quite warm. He estimated that she had been dead no more than thirty minutes.'

Polly's stomach lurched. Lizzie was still bleeding from the neck wound at ten past one? How could that be if she was supposedly killed at a quarter to one?

The coroner carried on. He discussed every detail of the crime. Polly was aware of only snippets as her distress soared. '…unlikely that a cry could have been raised without it being heard.… many people in the yard… editor of a Socialist paper was at work in a shed in the yard… families in the cottages only a few yards away… twenty persons in the different rooms of the club… No signs of any struggle… clothes were neither torn nor disturbed.' Polly felt as though she was floating, the coroner's words seemed to drift a long way off. Then his next remark brought her back to the present like a slap across the face. 'The position of the body suggested that she was either lowered without resistance to the ground or moved herself to the place where she was found. Only the soles of her boots were visible.'

What? Was he saying Lizzie might have placed herself where she was found? Did he mean she might have crawled to that spot after she was attacked? Polly felt as though a python was squeezing the air from her chest and another had wrapped itself tightly around her head.

She wasn't dead, Polly gasped for air at the thought. When he left her, she wasn't dead. She was still bleeding after one o'clock and now the coroner was saying she may have placed herself on her side the way she was found. She could have been trying to crawl to the side door of the club for help.

'Only one of the great vessels of the neck had been cut, nicked by the blade rather than severed,' said Baxter.

Polly felt her stomach heave. Couldn't they see that Jack would never have made that mistake? If Jack had cut her throat, he would have made a thorough job of it.

The coroner continued to unveil the horrific events. …No marks of gagging, no bruises on the face… the packet of cachous she held in her hand showed that she did not make use of it in self-defence… her right hand was lying on the chest, smeared inside and out with blood.'

Polly was distraught and could barely take it all in. Baxter went on to say that Doctor Phillips was unable to make any suggestion of how the hand became soiled. 'There was no injury to the hand, such as they would expect if it had been raised in self-defence to ward off her assailant, yet it was covered in blood.'

On hearing this, Polly sat up as straight as a ramrod. What was wrong with them? It was blood from her neck wound. They were all assuming she had died immediately like the others. Couldn't they see that she had died slowly? She had lain there bleeding. Her blood was still flowing at ten past one. Were they so fixed on the idea that she was killed by The Ripper they couldn't see it any other way. Mickey may not even have known when he left her, that he had inflicted a fatal wound. He was such a witless bully, he probably thought he had just shown her who was boss like he always did. Another attack to be added to the five punched out teeth, the broken jaw, the torn earlobe and the countless bruises she had suffered at his hands.

Polly stared at the back of his head with its stupid bowler hat. No one had mentioned him turning up at Leman Street station before anyone knew she was dead. No one took heed of the witnesses who mentioned that he knocked Lizzie around. Rage misted her vision. Even if he had not intended to kill her, the stupid, brainless, ignorant arsehole couldn't even work out a wound to the neck would be fatal if the victim didn't get help.

Polly imagined Lizzie lying there dying in that wet, pitch dark yard, hearing footsteps move close by, unable to cry out for help, hearing the singing that was going on in the club. Polly's eyes filled with tears. She must have put her hand to her cut throat to stem the flow of blood that poured from the gash in her neck. It was her last act as a living person as she lay there alone.

'Unfortunately the murderer had disappeared without leaving the slightest trace,' said Baxter as Polly tuned back in to what he was saying. 'There is no one among her associates to whom any suspicion can be attached.' Polly listened with astonished disbelief. 'She had recently left the man with whom she generally cohabited. This was so frequent an occurrence that neither a breach of the peace nor hard words accounted for it. She never accused anyone of having threatened her. She never expressed any fear of anyone and although she had outbursts of drunkenness, she was generally a quiet woman.

The ordinary motives of murder such as revenge, jealousy, theft, and passion appeared to be absent from this case.' Polly felt red mist blur her vision and rage descended. No *hard words*? Were they kidding?

'Madam, please be quiet and sit down,' said Baxter, which was odd because Polly did not know she had risen to her feet. She was delirious with fury and the words came pouring out.

'He's a liar! He used to beat her up all the time for the slightest thing. Sometimes he hit her just because he was in a bad mood. You should have seen the state of her sometimes. He's a pig! She was terrified of him. He came looking for her after she left him and she was scared stiff. He attacked her at Flower and Dean Street. He almost choked her. She still had the bruises the day she died. She didn't just leave him for nothing like you just said. She had to leave before he killed her in one of his drunken rages. Then he finally got her in the end because he heard she was with another man.'

'Madam, sit down or I will have you removed,' said Baxter.

'You have to listen to me. He got his mates to spy on her, he found out everything she did and he threatened her time after time. After she left him, he said he would see her dead. Mickey Kidney was after her. He killed her. She wasn't killed by The Ripper.'

The next thing she knew, Polly was being lifted off her feet and dragged by two very large policemen towards the door. She was pushed into the closed police carriage with tiny windows known as a Black Maria. She was taken to Leman Street Police Station and put into a cell.

Polly had braced herself expecting Alf to be at the desk when she was brought into the station by two Constables, each of whom had a firm grip on an arm. To her relief, he had been nowhere to be seen. She sat on the narrow bed, arms folded across her waist. She knew Alf would be livid when he found out. She had broken her promise to him. Perhaps he would even dismiss her.

She rocked herself back and forth. How could she keep quiet when they had talked about Lizzie as if she was nothing; a drunkard who led poor saintly Mickey Kidney, who never had a cross word with her, a merry dance with her dissolute ways?

When she looked up, Alf was standing outside the cell watching her with hands balled into fists on his hips. Polly could think of nothing at all to say as he continued to stare at her in silence.

'What you got to say for yourself?' he said at last.

In reply, she bowed her head, her eyes fixed on the concrete floor.

'Oh, *now* you keep your mouth shut,' he said. 'When the Inspector said we had a woman in custody who had a rage at the inquest, I knew straight away it would be you. What did I tell you?'

'You told me to keep my mouth shut,' she mumbled. 'I'm sorry, Alfie, you should have heard the things they were saying. Am I in serious trouble?'

'No,' he sighed. 'I explained to the guvnor who you were and why you did it. He was interested in what you said, as a matter of fact.'

Polly took a deep breath. 'Is he going to-?'

'We ain't got no evidence, Polly.'

'It's not right. He killed her, Alfie.'

She heard the clinking of keys. Alf unlocked the cell, entered it and sat down beside her. 'That's why I didn't want you to go. You weren't going to get nowhere standing up in the middle of a legal hearing, ranting and raving.'

'I just wanted them to listen. That inquest was a joke. I thought they were supposed to look at the evidence? They ignored all the women who said he knocked her about – even Betty Tanner's evidence. Unless you're a man they don't listen. They believed every lie Mickey told them. What was the point of all the adjournments?'

'I told you, Polly. All an inquest is supposed to do is establish the identity of the victim and the cause of death. It ain't like a criminal court.'

'They didn't even talk to Israel Schwartz. And he virtually saw Lizzie's murder.'

'They had his statement.'

'Maybe if he had come face to face with Mickey he would have recognised him.'

'Maybe. I heard Mr. Schwartz had death threats, so he weren't keen on coming to the inquest.'

'Death threats? I bet I know who threatened him.'

'We don't know.' Alf said gently. '*The Star* published what he knew about the murder. And with Mr. Schwartz being a Jew... *The Star* got a lot wrong. They twisted his words to suit their story because they love the idea of two murders by the same person on one night. Besides, we wanted to keep Mr. Schwartz's statement under wraps thinking his evidence might break the case.'

'You would never know it.'

'Listen, Polly. Nothing ain't going to bring your friend back, but that madman is still out there. An inquest is part of the process of law. It had to be done. All it does is establish the cause of death. It ain't the coroner's job to speculate on who done it. The evidence is still being collected and we're still looking. We don't want anything to spoil the chances of catching that maniac, do we?'

Polly heaved a sigh. 'Israel Schwartz didn't see Jack the Ripper. He saw Mickey Kidney. Lizzie's murder has got nothing to do with your stupid case. Israel Schwartz said he saw a domestic, and he did. Why do they say she was done by The Ripper? It's only *The Star* doing this. They delight in the idea of him doing two on one night because it sells more papers.'

'I can't argue with that.' Alf replied. 'That paper is a disgrace; the gorier the stuff they print, the more they sell.'

Tears filled her eyes. 'Alfie, Mr. Schwartz saw the attack at twenty to one. The doctor's assistant and two of the witnesses said her blood was flowing when they arrived at one o'clock and had just about stopped by the time the doctor came at a quarter past one. If her blood was flowing, she must have still been alive. She lay there dying for over half an hour while the blood poured out of her. Blood doesn't flow if the heart isn't beating, does it?'

'No, it don't.' said Alf gently.

'They were puzzled by Lizzie's hand being covered in blood. They couldn't understand why that would be, since there was no sign of a struggle. I know why. Lizzie wasn't dead. Why couldn't they see that? Mickey left her there with a gash in her neck and the blood pouring from it and her windpipe cut. She put her hand up to try and stem the bleeding. That's how she got blood on her hand the way they said. I think she tried to crawl to the door of the club for help. When she couldn't make it she just curled up where they found her in that pitch black yard.' Tears coursed down her cheeks. 'Feeling the blood pouring from her neck was the last thing she knew on this earth, Alfie.' Her voice hitched on a sob. 'He cut her throat and just left her there to die.'

'They thought she died just before one o'clock.'

'Well she couldn't have done could she?' Polly cried. 'If blood was flowing out of her and she was still warm, she must have been still alive at ten past one when the medic's assistant arrived. She was trying to crawl to the door and she didn't make it.' Polly broke down, her shoulders heaving.

Alf went into the cell and sat down beside her. 'Now then…. Don't distress yourself with such thoughts.'

'They've got Jack the Ripper on the brain. Why didn't it occur to them to look at the kind of injury she had? It wasn't deep enough to kill her outright. And if that's the case, the time of death isn't the same as the time she was attacked. Mickey's got an alibi and he ought not to have.'

'You could be right.'

'I am right. I went and had a look at the place she was killed. It would have been black as molasses behind that gate. I keep thinking about her, lying there all that time in the dark, dying, unable to cry out or get help.' Polly gave a shuddering sigh. 'Of course she wasn't killed by Jack. He's not some phantom that disappeared like smoke. Mr. Diemshultz didn't miss him by seconds at one o'clock and he wasn't hiding behind the gate in the dark. He had been gone for twenty minutes by then - right after Israel Schwartz saw him attack her, because it was Mickey Kidney who killed her.'

'We need evidence, Polly.' Alf said gently. 'The doctor said she had been dead *no longer* than half an hour, it's just a vague approximation.'

'If she was still bleeding at ten past one she hadn't been dead ten minutes never mind half an hour. The time she died is inconsequential, the time she was attacked is what's important. Her injury wasn't enough to kill her quickly and it *wasn't* Jack.'

'Polly-'

'Israel Schwartz saw her being attacked by someone who had gone steaming down Commercial Street spoiling for a fight with Lizzie. Jack wouldn't have done that, he wouldn't have stood arguing with her, Jack wouldn't have tried to pull her into the street, Jack wouldn't have picked a place as busy as that, and from what you've told me about the murders, Jack would have made a proper job of it. Besides, if it had been Jack who got hold of her, Lizzie would have screamed her lungs out and don't tell me that she was attacked by two different men in the space of ten minutes, cos that's just stupid.' She looked at Alf. 'I bet Mickey hasn't got an alibi for time between half-past twelve and ten to one. His break would finish at one o'clock and he was back on the docks by then. Nobody would suspect a thing. Because they think she was attacked shortly before she died, he's got an alibi and as long as they think Jack did it they aren't even looking for anyone else.'

'I see your reasoning, Polly. But it all boils down to the same thing. We need witnesses and we need evidence.'

'Then I'm going to find both. He killed Lizzie and he thinks he's got away with it - well he hasn't.'

# CHAPTER TWENTY TWO

Polly heard a loud crash and shot up the stairs. In Mrs. Cruikshank's room, the bedside table was on its side and the bottle of laudanum was on the floor. Its cork had fallen out and the syrupy liquid was soaking into the rug, leaving a reddish brown stain.

'Your medicine. What happened?'

'I knocked the table.' Mrs. Cruikshank was sitting sideways on the bed with her feet on the floor. Her face crumpled as if she was about to cry.

Polly knelt down and picked up the small brown bottle, scrutinising it to detect any remaining liquid. 'It's all gone I'm afraid.'

'I can't manage without it, nurse. You must get me some more,' Polly could hear a note of panic in her voice.

'Mrs. Cruikshank, it's quarter past eight. I don't even know where we could get any this time of night.'

'I must have it.'

'I'll get it first thing in the morning, I promise.'

'I have to have my evening medicine. How else will I sleep?'

'You had some, Ma'am - at six o'clock.'

''You know I take some more at ten. You know that.' Mrs. Cruikshank snapped. Her hands were trembling. The vile stuff seemed to have a grip on her mentally as well as physically. Her eyes were wide. This was genuine fear. It was unthinkable to her to be without the drug.

'What am I to do, Mrs. Cruikshank? All the chemist shops will be closed now. Can I make you comfortable and perhaps bring you some hot milk-'

'Hot milk?' she shrieked. 'Have you lost your wits? I need my medicine, not hot milk.' She was becoming more and more agitated. She took rapid, gasping breaths as if she could not suck in enough air. Polly could see this was not because of something physical, she had worked herself into a state because of anxiety.

It occurred to Polly that, other than overwhelming lethargy, Mrs. Cruikshank showed no outward signs of illness such as weakness, deformity or paralysis; yet it was obvious that she seemed to be in pain on a daily basis. This was an addict if she ever saw one.

'Dock Street,' said the older woman. 'There's a chemist on Dock Street. He lives above the shop. If you knock he'll usually let you in.'

'Dock Street?' Polly repeated. At this time of night, Mrs. Cruikshank was suggesting she go south of Cable Street - the acknowledged boundary beyond which lay the nests of thieves, robbers and all manner of debauched, ruthless types. It was much worse than anything she might have seen in Dorset Street where, if you were one of them and they knew your face, you were reasonably safe. These miscreants came and went on the hundreds of ships that berthed in the Port of London. They had no fear of discovery as they were gone again and half way across the ocean before their crimes were discovered. Polly was sure the lair of Jack the Ripper would be amongst the human detritus south of Cable Street.

'Yes, girl. 27 Dock Street,' said Mrs. Cruikshank, her hand shaking as she put it up to her face. 'I need my medicine.'

Polly considered for a moment. She knew Alf counted on his mother being settled for the night when he came home from a long shift as he was usually exhausted. By the look of her, his mother would be bouncing off the walls by the time he got home; unless she got some laudanum. There was nothing for it, she would have to go to Dock Street.

'Very well then,' she said. 'Now, you stay right here while I'm gone. Don't go getting out of bed; you might hurt yourself. I'll be as quick as I can.'

Polly put on her cloak and bonnet, took some money from the housekeeping tin and went out into the dark night. It was almost the end of October and it was cold. Polly wondered what the old lady had been doing to spill the laudanum. Perhaps she was sneaking extra doses between those Polly was giving her. If she was, her addiction was worse than they thought and therefore dangerous. When all the Jack the Ripper fuss was over, they would have to wean her off the evil stuff.

A train passed over the wide arched bridge at the south end of Leman Street. The heavy steam engine made a loud *boom* just like thunder as the train rumbled onto the bridge. Then there was a squealing of brakes as the driver brought the train to a halt at Leman Street station which was on the bridge. The monster waited there for a few minutes as another train, heading into the goods depot, crossed its path. They were a magnificent sight and Polly liked to see them - even though the noise made her ears ring. There was an ear-splitting hiss and a billowing cloud as the driver let off the excess steam from the engine, then *chug, chug, chug* as it took the strain of its loaded trucks and moved off. It was a powerful thing and a marvel. She liked seeing such things now, whereas previously she had been fixated only on surviving each day, too tired, cold and hungry to be bothered. As she walked, she thought about how much her life had changed.

She had grown very fond of Alf over the last few weeks, with his hair the colour of copper and his disarmingly awkward ways. He was hard faced it was true, but there was something about his less than handsome mug that made men with good-looking phizogs seem shallow and unmanly.

When Polly looked at Alf, she could see a genuinely fine man. The more she learned about him, the more she liked what she saw. Besides, she thought with an unexpected rush of delight, when a smile transformed his face, she defied anyone to say that he was not handsome. The trouble was, with that po-faced way of his, he rarely smiled. Polly grinned as she walked on with a lightness in her step, she knew she saw all she needed to see in his warm hazel eyes.

A choking smog had lingered over the streets all day. It had only dispersed when yet another sharp cloudburst dowsed the east end. She was becoming accustomed to seeing the streets black and shiny instead of dusty and grey. It had become second nature to avoid the puddles of water that accumulated between the uneven pavement flags and cobblestones. They never had time to dry up before the next downpour came.

After the station, Leman Street became Dock Street - the chemist shop must not be far Polly decided. Both trains had now gone on their way and her footsteps echoed as she walked beneath the bridge. All seemed eerily quiet and she felt a shiver scuttle down her spine.

Mrs. Cruikshank said that the chemist shop was beyond the railway bridge just past the entrance to the narrow lane called Hog Yard. Polly could see no sign of a chemist shop. The entire block consisted of a large tenement, the back of which was on Dock Street. Polly quickened her pace, hoping her opium-addicted patient was right about the shop. She had said it was just after the bridge. Perhaps she was mistaken and it was further along Dock Street.

Then, as she stepped off the pavement onto the cobblestones at the entrance to Hog Yard, someone grabbed her from behind and a hand covered her mouth. She had no time to struggle nor scream as she was dragged into the yard and slammed against the wall. The breath was knocked out of her lungs. Her attacker kept his filthy hand clamped over her mouth. She struggled against him. She was no match for his greater strength.

'I'm gonna finish you once and for all, Slag,' a malicious voice growled close to her ear. It was Mickey Kidney. The sour, disgusting stench of him filled her nostrils. He always smelled of fish. Lizzie always said his personal hygiene was non-existent. This close to him, she could also detect beer, tobacco and bad teeth.

'You just can't keep your mouth shut can you, Slag? Mouthing off about me is not clever. You think I wouldn't recognise you at the inquest in your fancy new clothes?'

Polly glared at him, his weight was crushing her against the brickwork. She could hardly breathe. Blood pounded like hammers behind her eyes. She kept them open, she wanted him to see the contempt in them. If these were her last moments on earth she would make sure he knew she would die cursing him and damning him to rot in hell.

Kidney got the message. 'You think you're so special,' he rasped, his brown teeth clenched, his lips pulled into a snarl. He circled her throat with his other hand and began to squeeze. He kept her pinned with his foul body so that she was unable to use the dollymop trick of grabbing his crotch and twisting the way she had done just a few weeks ago. She could feel the pressure in her head rising as his grip stopped the flow of blood through her brain. Her head was throbbing and felt as if it was going to burst. There was a buzzing sound in her ears.

She squirmed and struggled. She was not going to make it easy for him, though, in her heart, she knew he had her this time. She could see no way out. Mickey had won and like Lizzie, she would be called just another Ripper victim. Her eyes hurt, feeling as if they were bulging out of their sockets, still she forced herself to keep them open, damning Mickey Kidney to her last breath.

She stamped the heel of her boot into the top of his foot but his heavy boots meant she made no impression. She kicked out at him as hard as she could, which only made him tighten his grip on her throat.

He kept up the relentless pressure, his teeth tightly clenched, his eyes wild and full of hate. This was it. This really looked like the end. She couldn't struggle and she couldn't breathe.

Then, she was aware of another person beside her. She slid her eyes to towards this figure. By some miracle, Aaron was standing there. Sheer murder burned in his eyes as he looked at Mickey.

'You do not hurt Polly.' he said. His voice sounded flat, even though there was a chilling intensity about it. The warning in his tone seemed to evade Mickey. He looked at Aaron and scanned his length.

He saw a skinny, pale and tired looking man whom he apparently considered no match for his own heavily muscled frame.

'Piss off, Jew boy,' he snarled. He turned back to Polly. 'On first name terms with filthy Yids now are you?' he sneered.

'You leave Polly alone,' said Aaron, standing passively beside him.

Kidney laughed. Polly was running out of air and out of time. Her lungs were burning. 'Want to be next, do you? Shove off, Yid. Mind your own business.'

Polly was desperate. She managed a choking gurgle. Aaron reacted to the sound in an instant. 'You will not hurt Polly.'

Mickey did not even see it coming. Aaron moved like lightening. He jabbed at Mickey's neck with two fingers, just below his Adam's apple. Polly heard a noise like an egg shell cracking as Aaron got Mickey's windpipe in a pincer grip up and applied relentless pressure. She felt Mickey's body stiffen. Whatever Aaron did, pole-axed Mickey. He gurgled and his eyes rolled back his head.

Polly was amazed. Mickey had almost lost consciousness and it had taken only two swift, precise movements by Aaron. Mickey was unable to control his arms and let go of Polly. She slid down the wall gasping, gulping in air and coughing while Aaron, now in a blind fury, started to pound Mickey with his fists. He rained down blow after blow on him as Mickey sank to his knees. He was twice the size of Aaron but this did not seem to matter.

Mickey had a dazed look in his eyes. Blood poured from his nose and mouth. There was a gash on his cheekbone and another across his forehead. The bridge of his nose had split open and Polly wondered if the bones were broken.

The sight of blood seemed to work Aaron into a frenzy. She had seen him like this before. She had seen him fight in a similar way with an invisible adversary when she had witnessed his bad dream. Now he landed blow after blow on Mickey with steely determination and surprising strength. He seemed incapable of stopping. He kept on punching and pounding Mickey's face and torso.

Polly wondered if the sight of Mickey attacking her brought back bad memories. Perhaps this was a manifestation of the things he saw in his dreams. Whatever it was, a whirling dervish had been unleashed and Polly realised he was going to beat Mickey to death if she did not intervene.

'Aaron stop! That's enough,' she squeaked, her voice hoarse as she tried to draw in air through a painful, bruised throat.

'Aaron!' she croaked.

'He will not hurt Polly,' said Aaron as he continued to pound Mickey's face and body. Mickey was trying without success to curl up into a ball.

'No! Aaron, you have to stop. Stop! Believe me, no one deserves it more than him but I don't want you to hang for this piece of filth. Aaron. Stop it! Aaron, look at me. Please look at me.'

In a way that was bizarrely casual, Aaron turned his head and looked at her. 'Do what Polly tells you,' she said. 'Stop. I don't want you to hang, and you will if you kill him.'

The rage left him as suddenly as it had come upon him. Mickey was curled up and coughing. Then he rolled onto his knees and spat out a large jelly-like clot of congealed blood which made him gag. He vomited what must have been a bucket full of brown liquid that spread out over the cobbles and smelled sour, like beer. Polly watched as he tried to get onto his hands and knees. He was unable to manage it and slumped face down in his own vomit, heaving and gasping. She felt no compassion for this living, breathing piece of trash. She bent down to speak to him.

'I know you killed Lizzie and I'll see you rot in hell for it,' she croaked.

She turned to Aaron. 'Come on, Aaron. Let's get out of here before the copper on the beat or some of Mickey's mates from the docks turn up.' She grabbed Aaron's arm and guided him back along Dock Street towards the railway arch.

'What you doing this close to the docks? Don't you know it's very dangerous for someone like you? If any of the dockers catch you around here, they'll string you up just for being Jewish. And there's no mistaking you as a Jew.' Aaron did not speak but Polly was used to his tight-lipped ways.

Just before the railway arch at the end of Leman Street was the junction with Cable Street. 'Come on, this way.' She touched his elbow, guiding him towards Cable Street. Polly got the impression Aaron did not know where he was or how to get home. He stared down at the pavement as they walked. Providence had brought him to her at the time of her greatest need.

She stopped and looked at him. He glanced awkwardly at her smiling face and then looked down at the pavement once again. 'You know, you just saved my life.' she said. Her throat felt as if it was lined with broken glass when she swallowed.

Aaron looked up. 'You read to me, Polly?' he said.

'Is that what you were after? Were you looking for me again so I would read to you?' Polly smiled. 'Oh Aaron, I'll read you every book Dickens wrote. I'll read you a whole library.' She patted his bony forearm.

They turned onto Backchurch Lane. 'I wanted to come to see you, Aaron. Your brother wouldn't let me, remember? Thing is, I got a proper job now, looking after an old lady. Maybe now I'm respectable he won't mind me so much. And I won't take no for an answer. I know my employer, Sergeant Cruikshank won't mind me spending a couple of hours reading to you now and again.' She smiled up at him. As ever, his eyes were fixed on the ground. 'That man you saved me from killed my friend Lizzie. He's terrible, Aaron, an absolute waste of skin. The problem is, I know he killed my friend and he's got away with it. They're blaming Lizzie's murder on the Whitechapel Killer - this Jack the Ripper that's killed the other women.' She shook her head. 'I know it wasn't Jack who did it. Jack didn't kill Lizzie, that's rubbish.'

She could not tell if Aaron was listening to her or paying attention to the voices in his head, nevertheless, it felt good to unload her thoughts. She continued to tell him the story as they made their way along Backchurch Lane, heading towards Commercial Road.

He was quiet, staring at the pavement as they walked. Polly continued to chatter. He seemed to like the sound of her voice whether she was reading Charles Dickens or not. 'Anyway,' she said, 'Mickey came after me because I know what he did to Lizzie. He found out, you see. So now he's after me to shut me up, permanently.'

Polly decided to take Aaron a convoluted route just in case Mickey's friends on the docks had turned up and they were looking for them. They turned off Backchurch Lane, turning right into Fairclough Street which ran east to west and cut across the middle of Berner Street which ran north to south.

Polly paused at the corner. 'Down there, Aaron. That's where it happened, they're blaming it on The Ripper and they're wrong. I know it was Mickey who killed my friend.'

He glanced in the direction Polly had indicated as they walked on, seeming to pay scant attention. She never knew if he was listening to what she said or if it was the sound of her voice that soothed him.

After another few minutes they finally reached Greenfield Street. Number sixteen was dark and securely locked, just as it had been the last time she had brought Aaron home after she found him wandering the streets.

'How on earth do you get out?' she said as she looked at the dark house. 'Do they put you out with the cat or something?' She remembered the look on their faces when she brought Aaron home last time and wondered if it was exactly what happened. Well, she would see about that.

Once again she felt an overwhelming pity for this poor, tortured man as she rapped loudly on the door. It took more than five minutes to rouse the household. Finally, Mosiek Lubnowski came to the door. He sighed.

'Aaron,' he said. 'It worries us when you walk the streets.'

'Yeah, I can see how worried you are,' said Polly scanning the darkened windows.

Lubnowski looked at Aaron's hands. 'You have blood on you,' he said, as his wife Matilda came to the door wearing a woollen shawl around her shoulders. She stood behind her husband. By the look of her, she could not have long to go in her pregnancy.

Polly saw the alarm on her face as she saw Aaron's bloody hands.

'Don't worry, it's not his, Mrs. Lubnowski. Though you'll find his knuckles are a bit bruised, I'm afraid.' She looked at Aaron then at the couple. 'Your brother saved me from certain death tonight by beating up a man who was attacking me.'

'You should wash your hands, Aaron,' said Mosiek as Matilda Lubnowski's expression changed to one of relief.

'I'm sorry if that gave you a turn.' she said to Matilda. 'He's my hero. Aren't you Aaron?'

Obeying Mosiek at once, Aaron stepped inside the house. Polly followed without being asked. 'Let me help you, Aaron,' she said.

She was angry. They knew Aaron was out wandering the streets. They had ignored this fact and gone to bed.

'He was down Dock Street.' Polly continued as the Lubnowskis stared at her. 'I live over that way now; in Scarborough Street. I care for the mother of my new employer, Sergeant Cruikshank. It was lucky for me Aaron turned up.' She touched her neck cautiously.

'You work for a soldier?' Matilda Lubnowski asked.

'Not a soldier, no. A very nice police sergeant from Leman Street station,' Polly replied, trying to sound reassuring. With their terrible past, suffering at the hands of Russian soldiers, Polly could understand their nervousness.

They watched as she helped Aaron to wash his hands and then dry them. She patted his bruised knuckles gently. She looked at the other cuts and grazes on the backs of his hands. He had been hurting himself again. She knew this meant the voices in his head must be tormenting him. Aaron had told her he used physical pain and other distractions to appease what he thought were evil spirits talking to him. She felt a surge of pity for him. She turned to the Lubnowskis. 'A regular escape artist isn't he?' she said.

'He is not a prisoner,' said Mosiek.

'No, but he isn't responsible for himself either is he, Mr. Lubnowski? I think he loses all track of what's going on and he doesn't know where he is or how to get home. His clothes are soaked. He must have been out quite a while, it stopped raining two hours since.' She looked at Aaron and gave him a little smile. 'What are you like? You'll catch your death of cold in this weather.'

Lubnowski did not respond, he watched Polly intently as she helped Aaron clean himself up. 'Him wandering down by the docks isn't safe, Mr. and Mrs. Lubnowski. Believe me, some of the men who work down there are nasty characters. They would hang him soon as look at him just because he's one of your kind.'

'I will make sure he does not go out. Thank you for your time.' He took a step towards the door. 'Your neck is bruised and your eyes are red. You should go to your lodgings and rest.'

'Polly, you read to me?' said Aaron from behind Mosiek.

'Soon, Aaron I promise. My throat hurts at present. Look how red it is.' She turned to him. 'Listen, I live in Scarborough Street now. Number eleven. It's quiet and respectable. Quite a few policemen live around there, on account of it being behind the station, so all criminal types avoid it and it's nice and safe. You can come and find me there and if my Sergeant says it's alright, I'll read to you.' She looked at the Lubnowskis. 'Please don't stop him. It soothes him when I read and I owe him, big time. He saved my life tonight and all he wants in return is to hear the end of the story we've been reading. It isn't much to ask.'

'Aaron. Go and put on a nightshirt. You must sleep now,' said Matilda.

'Goodnight Aaron,' Polly said as Aaron did as he was told and went down the steps to the basement.

'Where is the man who attacked you?' asked Mosiek.

'Probably still rolling around on the cobbles on Dock Street. Aaron didn't half give him *what for*.' She gave a short mirthless laugh. 'Looking at him, you wouldn't think he could fight his way out of a paper bag, would you?'

'He could get into trouble,' said Matilda bunching her shawl close to her neck and holding it there.

Polly turned to her. 'Don't worry. There were no witnesses and I doubt Mickey will be able to identify him. He's a horrible man, Mickey Kidney. Aaron really did save my life, Mrs. Lubnowski.'

Mosiek pulled open the door. 'You need to get on your way. It is getting late.'

'Yes, I suppose I ought. My employer is working on The Ripper murder case so he's does long hours.' She looked pointedly at them. 'The household won't have gone to bed yet. I won't be locked out.'

'Good night,' said Mosiek.

Polly stepped out onto the street and the door closed behind her. She heard the door bolt shoot home.

# CHAPTER TWENTY THREE

Polly made her way back to Scarborough Street and let herself into number eleven.

Alf was sitting at the kitchen table. His tunic was hanging on the back of a vacant chair. He was eating some of the stew she had made earlier that day. His shirt tail was hanging out of his pants. He had taken his braces off his shoulders and they were dangling down as they always did when he was relaxing after coming off shift.

'Polly?' he said getting to his feet. 'I was getting worried. Mother said you spilled the laudanum and went to get more.'

'I spilled the laudanum?'

'What the-' Alf noticed the bruises on her neck and the pinprick haemorrhages in the whites of her eyes. He was at her side in an instant. 'What's occurred?'

'I'm all right.'

With great gentleness, took hold of her chin and looked at her face and neck.

'What's gone on?'

'Mickey Kidney had a problem with my little speech at the inquest.'

Alf let go of her. He moved back to the table, tucked in his shirt, put his braces on his shoulders, reached for his uniform tunic and began putting it on.

'Where you going?' Polly asked.

'I'm going to find Mickey Kidney and rip his head off,' he said with chilling calmness.

'What? No. Don't, Alfie,' she croaked. A resolute expression was fixed on his face and he continued to button his tunic. 'Please, Alfie, no. You'll get into trouble. Besides he's already had a good smacking.'

'From whom?'

'Remember I told you about the Jewish lad who likes me to read to him?' she said as Alf nodded. 'Well lucky for me he turned up. He came to my rescue and gave Mickey a right good hiding.'

'Then I'll have what's left of him before I throw his arse in the cells. Where is he?'

'I don't know. I think Aaron might have smashed his face and broken his nose. He could be at the hospital by now. '

'Right, I'll start there.'

'Alfie please don't.'

'I ain't going to let him get away with doing this to you.' He scanned her face and neck. 'Look at the state of you.'

'He didn't get away with it, honest. Aaron really laid into him. Please, you could get into trouble and lose your pension and everything. Isn't that what you're always telling your lads? Not to do anything stupid and mess up the chances of a pension? Stay here, I need you here. I'll do a statement and you can do it all properly if you like, so long as Aaron doesn't get into any trouble.'

'Polly, you look half throttled, I have to do something about it.' As if the implications of what happened suddenly sunk into her consciousness, she gave an involuntary sob.

'Your mother asked me to get her some more laudanum from the chemist on Dock Street.'

'Dock Street? She must have meant old Simpson's. That shop hasn't been there for years. She used to get her midwifery supplies from him. Anyway, I always keep a bottle or two on hand,' he told her. 'It's on the top shelf of the cupboard, look.' He pointed to the pantry. 'I gave her some when I came in and she's out like a light.'

'I wish I'd known. It's the only reason I went out. Mickey must have seen me and gone round the other way by the goods depot. He waited for me in Hog Lane. If Aaron hadn't been there tonight...' Tears filled her eyes and her bottom lip trembled. 'I would have been dead and you lot would have put it down to Jack the Ripper. Just like Lizzie.'

'And my worst nightmare would have come true.' Alf murmured.

She took a step towards him and laid her head on his wide chest. She felt his hand tentatively pat her back in an attempt to comfort her, but his body was rigid and she knew he was ill at ease. She sighed and looked up at him. 'Can't you at least give me a hug?'

His brow was furrowed. He blinked and put his arms around her in an awkward gesture, pressing her face against the rough fabric of his tunic. The buttons were cold against her cheek, but it was comforting to be in his arms and she stayed there for a while. Alf did not move. Then he cleared his throat.

'You want a cup of tea?' he asked.

'No. I just want you to stay here and hold on to me,' she said from the depths of his chest. Her breath hitched. 'I thought I was a goner, Alfie.'

They stood there for a moment more, then Alf pulled away 'I'll get you some tea,' he insisted.

Polly stared at him. 'Why won't you just stand here for a while?'

'I- um… You'll feel better if you have a cuppa.'

'Shut up about tea. I want you to embrace me, Alfie Cruikshank.'

Alf's face flushed as it always did when anything remotely personal was brought up.

'I can't, Polly.'

'Why not?' she stepped back and looked up at him. As she watched, he groped for an answer. It was obvious to her that he was having trouble coming up with one. He swallowed and stared at her dumbly.

She looked at him and a pain stabbed her heart. 'You don't have to explain. I know why. It's been plain enough since I came here. It's because I'm a whore.'

'Of course it's not.'

'Despite all your talk, you think I'm dirty.' Her bottom lip quivered.

'Stop saying things like that.'

'Then put your arms around me.' She wiped a tear from her cheek with the heel of her hand. His face contorted as if he was in pain. She could see that he was struggling with whatever conflict was going on in his head. Polly stared at him, determined not to let him off the hook. 'I thought not…What's going on, Alfie?'

'Nothing. Just drop it, Polly.'

'I won't drop it. Just admit it to yourself, it's because I'm a whore.'

'I told you. I don't think of you as a-'

'You say that but you won't even touch me, will you? Don't think I haven't noticed.'

'It ain't what you think.'

'Don't lie to me, Alfie Cruikshank. At the bottom of you, you think I'm dirty goods.' She sniffed and knowing she was about to cry in earnest, she turned away from him.

'No it ain't,' he insisted.

'Of course it is, I'm not stupid, I've noticed the signs. I told you this wouldn't work. Saying it's the past is one thing, living with what I was is a different matter-'

'No. It ain't that at all.'

'Yes it is, you can't even bear to touch me, can you?' she cried. 'Its fine, I understand. As a matter of fact I expected it,'' she said through her tears. 'Once you sink into that life they say it never lets you-'

'It's because I got feelings for you, Polly,' he blurted out. 'I get such strong longings when I look at you. If I was to touch you, I'm scared I could lose my head.'

He could not meet her eyes. His face was a deeper shade of red than she had ever seen it and he was looking somewhere over her head at the wall opposite.

Polly's jaw dropped. 'Oh,' she replied dully.

'*Oh?*' he murmured. 'Is that it? *Oh?*'

Polly stepped away from him and wiped away the tears from her cheeks with her fingertips. 'No, that's not all. In fact, I *am* stupid after all. I don't know why I didn't guess.'

'To be honest, Polly, I didn't know how you would react if you knew. That's why I ain't said nothing. I been trying to keep these feeling under control but it's beyond me. When I look at you, a fever takes me.'

'Is that right?' she replied coldly.

'So... how... how do you feel about it?'

'Fine.'

She began to calmly unbutton her bodice. She shrugged it off her shoulders and flung it aside. The thin chemise beneath it left little to his imagination. She started to untie the drawstring ribbon that kept it together. She straightened her spine and lifted her eyes to his face. Her mouth was tugged down into a tight line. It would have been no worse if he had called her a whore.

'You've already paid for me, Alfie. Help yourself.' Her voice shook but she kept up an aloof expression.

'Polly?' said Alf, aghast.

His face registered astonishment, but he was like a starving man at a banquet and seemed unable to tear his gaze away from her body. His eyes drank her in, taking in every inch of her soft skin and the sensuous curve of her breasts. He had a look of awe on his face which in a different situation, would have made her laugh with joy and affection. This was a very different circumstance.

'Will over here do?' she continued coldly. 'You better put the lights out, it's the rule for us whores, you know. We must only be used by a man in a dark place. Perhaps we could go in your back yard? That's what I'm accustomed to.' She could not prevent tears from forming in her eyes.

He gulped and continued to gaze at her body. The desire in his eyes was unmistakable and it crushed Polly's heart. She had seen that look in men's eyes. These men told her they had desires for her; the kind of desire they paid for and lasted a few minutes. In her old life, she had relied on it, but Alf's admission was a dagger to her soul. Discovering that there was a lustful side to him felt much worse than the things Mickey Kidney had done to her.

She knew that her breasts would be visible through the thin fabric of the chemise. She didn't care. She squared her shoulders, the way the girls had taught her, to show them off. Men liked them and it was obvious that Alf did too. She followed the line of his gaze and looked down at her chest.

'Like them do you? Yeah, punters always like my *bubbies*. What you waiting for?' she choked 'You want a better look? Should I take this off as well?' A tear rolled down her cheek as she continued to fumble with the ribbon on her chemise and loosened it to reveal the pink blush of a nipple.

Alf was mesmerised. His eyes were fixed on her. Then, finally, he tore his gaze away from her. He reached for her discarded bodice and handed it to her. 'Cover yourself,' he said hoarsely.

Polly blinked, then looked at him defiantly. 'Don't let the crying put you off. I used to do that all the time when I first started-'

Alf looked as though he was in pain. 'What the hell did you do that for?'

'I get the picture, I'm paid for fair and square.'

His eyes flickered in confusion. 'Why you saying such things?'

'You were the one who said you had desires for me.'

'*What?*' He had to think for a moment before the penny dropped. He inhaled sharply. 'Not that kind, you foolish little thing.' He sighed. 'Naturally, Polly Wilkes would get hold of the wrong end of the stick,' he muttered. 'Of course I have desires for you. I ain't made of stone.' He took hold of her hands, which were trembling. 'What red-blooded man wouldn't? But there's something about you that makes me mad for you, Polly. Ever since I saw you outside *The Queen's Head.*'

She blinked as understanding slowly dawned on her, a faint smile replacing the tears. 'I was throwing up in an alley.'

'I know,' he said softly. 'And the second time you kicked me in the shin and threw up in the gutter.'

There was a warm glow in his eyes. A flame had ignited within. Their eyes were locked together in an intense gaze that neither of them wanted to break.

'You threw me in jail.'

'But I didn't arrest you.'

'So, what are these desires, Alfie Cruikshank?' she asked softly.

'This kind, Polly Wilkes...'

He took her by the shoulders and pulled her small frame towards him and kissed her.

The touch of his lips was so sweet. Polly was stunned. Powerful feelings that she had buried a long time ago were instantaneously awakened. It was so unfamiliar that it took her a moment to understand that she was experiencing pleasure at Alf's touch. Her spirit soared. Wild emotions flooded her mind and body.

Alf quickly lost his awkwardness. With a confidence that until now had been dormant, he swept her into his arms. There was such enthralling passion in his kiss, Polly responded with joy. Her lips parted and she put her arms around his thick bear like neck and clung to him. The kiss went on and on. She felt his arms enfold her more tightly and he pressed her more closely to him.

Polly was delighted by her own physical reaction and to her amazement, felt a longing for him swell within her. She had assumed she could no longer react physically to a man. She thought her intimate feelings had been obliterated by the act of selling her body. She had reached this conclusion not because she felt nothing, no desire whatsoever for a client, but because she was capable of allowing them to use her, despite her revulsion. In Alf's arms, there was no mistaking her feelings of desire and delight.

Now she understood the difference that emotions made to the act of intimacy that took place between a man and a woman. This wonderful, awkward man had the power to make her feel loved. Finally, they parted and she began to cry.

'Now what have I done?' His awkwardness returned.

'Nothing,' she said. 'I'm-crying-because-I'm-happy.'

'Well, that's the queerest thing I ever heard...' Confusion filled his eyes.

She laughed at his expression through her torrent of tears. 'Oh, Alfie.' She kissed him hard on the lips, exhilarated by her newly awakened feelings.

Alf's large hand gently cup the back of her head and they kissed again more passionately. He pulled away, sighing long and low.

'Polly,' he murmured 'We got to stop.'

'That's not something I ever heard a man say.' She cupped his cheek with her hand. 'I haven't got any illusions, Alfie,' she said tenderly. 'You know the complete score. You know what I am.' She smiled softly and watched him, her face only a few inches from his.

'*Was*,' he insisted. 'And I already told you, stop saying that. I ain't never seen you that way. Even when you was one, I know you were driven to it by a desperate necessity.'

'I can't pretend I'm some innocent little virgin you just kissed,' she whispered.

'I wouldn't know the difference and I don't care about that. You're the sweetest pleasure I have ever known, Polly Wilkes, and I'm mad for you. I have such powerful feelings when I'm with you, it makes my head swim.'

'That doesn't alter things,' she said. 'And if you have desires for me, how can I refuse you when you know I've-'

'Of *course* I have desires for you,' he murmured. 'But this ain't the right way. It will be at the right time and in the right place of both our choosing.'

She started to cry again. Alf took off his rough tunic and cast it onto the chair. The blue-black dye was known to come off if the fabric got wet and her cheeks were soaked with tears.

He pulled her into his arms. 'There now. Don't take on. There ain't no reason to weep is there?'

'Perhaps, there is,' she sniffed. She rested her cheek against the smooth cotton shirt that stretched across his wide chest. She could feel the hard muscles beneath and the rise and fall of his chest as he breathed. She found this so very comforting as she listened to the beat of his strong heart. She knew this was true intimacy.

He produced a clean handkerchief from his pocket and gave it to her. He smiled. 'Here you are, soft girl.'

Polly dried her eyes. 'I'm not a soft girl,' she smiled. She lifted her face to his and kissed him. 'I never in my life felt this way, Alfie,' she said. 'Not even with Thomas.' She thought about this and then gave a short bleak laugh. 'Actually, especially not with Thomas.' She looked up at him. 'When you kissed me just then, it was a marvel to me. All the feelings that came from you. That's what a kiss really is, isn't it? It's what you give, not what you take.'

'It seems so.' Alf replied caressing her cheek with his giant hand.

She put her hand over his and gave a broken sigh. 'I'm hardly immaculate.'

'It don't matter,' he said gently, 'and I don't care. That's the past.'

She hesitated. 'In some ways, it's the past, yes,' she said. 'In another, it's still with me and it could prove to be an insurmountable obstacle.'

'I told you, people ain't going find out,' he replied.

'I don't mean that,' she said. She placed the palms of her hands against his hard chest and looked up at him. 'I've always been careful as I could be, Alfie. Only, the fact is, girls like me don't get to have proper relationships with good men like you, because we can have nasty diseases.'

Alf looked horror struck. 'You ain't sick are you?'

'Not that I know of - I'm as fit as a fiddle. It's… well, I worry that I could have something and not know it. Something that I could pass to you. I want to please you, Alfie, but it would be wrong to deceive you, or be on those kinds of intimate terms until I know for sure. Not that kind of intimate anyway.'

'I don't care about that, Polly.'

'You know better than that,' she said gently. 'Of course you do, but like you just said you're a red-blooded man and I know you have desires-'

'Come over here.' He tugged her in the direction of the large arm chair. He pulled her onto his lap and she looped her arms around his neck. The ribbon of her chemise was still hanging loose and she could feel the delight of his warm breath on her skin. He was suddenly very still. She looked down and saw he was looking at her breasts which were only a few inches from his face. She could tell he was holding his breath and struggling again with his natural urges.

She smiled and brushed his mouth with a kiss. 'It's not out of the question to touch me...' she told him softly.

Alf reached out but something stopped him from touching her. Polly kissed him. As they kissed, she took hold of his hand and guided it to her breast. She felt his whole body shiver. He pulled away from her, looking at her breast as he caressed it, an expression of fascinated pleasure on his face. His fingertips trailed across her skin and the breath caught in her throat. She had never been touched with such reverence. Desire swept through her. She slid her other arm around his neck and he kissed her with a passion that was new and marvellous to her.

The joy of it for Polly was that she felt this thrill and fervour as keenly as Alf. She was experiencing genuine feelings of passion and she craved him, she wanted him for the right reasons. This was not the silly girlish fancies of the young girl who eloped with a boy. It was a genuine womanly response to the man she was sure she loved. She ran her palms across his chest and took sensuous delight in the action. She could feel his muscles rippling against her. His body was lean and powerful. No wonder he picked her up as if she weighed nothing the night he put her in the cells, she remembered with affection.

He pressed his lips to her neck and covered it with gentle kisses, his breath hot against her skin as his firm mouth slid down to her shoulder and he kissed the soft skin he found there. She shivered on a sigh as he kissed her with a passion that left her weak.

'Polly,' he whispered. In response, she wrapped her arms around him and returned the kiss with equal passion. She felt his fingers lift her chemise as he sought more of her softness and cupped the swell of her breast. 'My sweet Polly,' he murmured against her skin. She inhaled the scent of him and tasted the delectable saltiness of him as her lips explored hard pectorals that quivered in response to her touch. He gave an agonised groan.

A second later, she found herself on her bottom on the floor.

'Alfie?' she yelped as she sprawled on the rug.

'I'm sorry, Polly. I had to get you off me. Another minute and I would have lost my head completely.'

'The word *stop* would have sufficed.'

'My head was saying stop, but the word wouldn't come out of my mouth,' he said. 'I had to take drastic action.'

She sat up and rested her arm across his lap. 'I could see you were getting carried away,' she said softly, 'and the marvel to me was, so was I.'

'Such remarks ain't helping me keep my composure.'

'They're not meant to,' she said. 'Listen, Alfie, I can see you have desires and you seem to be a quick study on the matter.'

'That don't matter to me,' he answered.

'Um… I beg to differ,' she smiled, eyebrows raised.

His face flushed a deeper shade of crimson. 'I didn't say I didn't want you,' he said. 'Of course I do. But it ain't the most important thing.'

He pulled her towards him. 'Come sit on my lap… only… put your bodice back on first.'

Polly complied. When she sat on his lap she sat astride him and put both arms around his neck.

'Not helping,' he breathed. She started to get up. Alf stopped her from moving by placing his hands on either side of her waist. 'I'll manage…' he said. He gathered his thoughts. 'Ever since I was a lad I've had Mother to consider. Father was a silversmith, you see. He bought this house and made a good living. Then new rules came in that forced him to move the business out of London on account that he used mercury.' Alf shook his head. 'It proved too much for him. He lost his business, took to his bed and then died when I was fifteen. My brother, Daniel didn't hardly know him since he was ten years younger than me. We did all right after father died. Mother had her midwifery and we had this roof over our heads.'

Polly tightened her embrace and kissed him which distracted him from the story for a while. He pulled away. 'I ain't never been no great romantic, Polly. It's a hard life in the force as an ordinary copper. The rules are very strict and you have to follow them to the letter.' He studied her face. 'When Daniel died, there didn't seem much of a reason to come home. Mother was at Auntie Ivy's in Bournemouth for a considerable time and the house was empty. That's why I did well and got promoted. If ever there were extra hours to be done they knew they could count on Alf Cruikshank.'

'It couldn't have been easy.'

'I did the extra hours willingly. I like it, Polly. I like sorting out the wrong 'uns and protecting people.'

She leaned forward, teasing him with her hot breath on the skin below his ear, raising goose bumps and kissing them away.

'What I'm saying is, I ain't had much time for finding a sweetheart. I mean, all the ladies I meet are thieves and prostitutes.'

Polly leaned back and looked at him. 'Is that a fact?'

He smiled. 'What I'm trying to say is I didn't think this was on the cards for me. Finding you is miraculous to me, Polly. And the fact that you seem to feel the same way, well it makes my heart turn somersaults.'

She kissed him again, not teasing this time.

. 'What I'm trying to say is, if we can never be together as a man and woman should, it ain't the end of the world to me. Naturally, I would prefer it to be different but it ain't the end of the world.'

'You deserve more, Alfie; much more. Would you really want a woman who can never be more than just affectionate towards you?'

His large hands spanned her waist. 'It wouldn't be ideal,' he said gently. 'But you're the one, Polly Wilkes, and if it ain't possible for it to be different, then that's how it is. I would worry if you were sick. The rest don't matter to me.'

She slipped her arms around his neck and curled her body against his.

'Again, I beg to differ,' she smiled, moving her position astride his lap.

'I ain't denying the urge is there, a powerful urge as a matter of fact. What I'm saying is, it ain't all that matters.'

'There are other ways I can please you, Alfie,' she said softly. 'I told you before, it wouldn't be taking advantage.'

'Of course it would. You have some notion that you don't deserve better - the fact is, you do. This should be about you and me, Polly. This is precious to both of us. If it carried on now, I would think you were giving yourself that way because you felt you should. It would be like I was one of your… your...' he let the sentence trail away. 'When you and me know each other intimately, it will happen the way it ought to and it will be the way a man is supposed to know a woman.' He looked at her. 'That's the way it has to be Polly. If you'll have me.'

Polly stared at him. 'H-Have you?' She jumped up. 'Alfie, you don't have to- You'll ruin your chances of – Alfie, you can't take up with a former whore.'

'How many more times… Don't call yourself that. What about it, Polly?' There was a confidence about him now. Gone was the man who blushed and stammered at anything remotely personal. 'It's you and me from now on, Polly,' he continued. 'It's up to me to look after you and provide for you. And if that means I can look at you, and touch you, then you can call me the happiest man alive.'

Polly burst into tears.

'My word. Your emotions really are all over the place, ain't they?'

Alf stood up and took her by the shoulders holding her at arm's length. 'Is that a yes or a no then?'

'Don't ask me that. Not yet,' she cried.

'Why ever not?'

'It all too quick and your head's in a spin. Your mother's off your hands, you're getting well fed, your laundry's done and your little friend down there has just woken up. I don't want you saying things in haste because you mistake all that for deeper feelings. I want you to think on things a while.'

'I have thought on it for a while.'

'But you haven't, Alfie, and you might change your mind.'

'Oh my dearest girl,' He scooped her up and swung her around. 'My dearest, dearest girl. As if I would change my mind about you.'

# CHAPTER TWENTY FOUR

Polly woke up early. It took her a moment for her mind to clear then she heard someone moving about downstairs.

She washed and dressed quickly, choosing a skirt and one of her two high neck, dog collar blouses to hide the bruises Mickey had inflicted on her. She crept along the landing and opened the door of Mrs. Cruikshank's room. She found the old lady snoring gently.

The door of Alf's room was ajar. His bed had been made neatly enough to satisfy a sergeant major in any army barracks. Polly hurried downstairs and found him seated at the kitchen table. He looked up when he heard her footsteps and stood up as she approached. She paused at the kitchen door.

'Polly,' he said, smiling. Polly launched herself towards him and flung her arms around his neck. She heard him laugh and she was lifted off the floor in a tight embrace. She put her hands either side of his head and pulled his face towards hers so that they could kiss.

'There you are,' he said pressing her tightly to him. 'My lovely Polly.'

She adored the feel of his arms around her and his solid bear-like strength. He kissed her neck and she winced. Alf looked at her and gently tilted her head. 'Those bruises have really come up,' he said. His voice rumbled from deep in his chest. 'I can see the imprint of his fingers on your neck.' Polly watched his expression change. 'When I get my hands on him I'm gonna make him wish he'd never been born.'

'Alfie? By the book remember?' Polly reminded him, though having him as her defender and champion was a delight to her.

'Very well, my dear,' he sighed. 'I'll wait until I get him in the cells before I beat him to a pulp.'

'You're not going to beat him to a pulp. You're going to do things properly,' Polly said, seeing the determined look on his face.

'As you wish,' he said. 'But he's going down for this.' His expression darkened. 'And I'm taking out what's due from him in pain, regardless of doing things right,' he growled. 'You'll need to make a statement.'

'Whatever you say, Alfie,' she said. 'Do I have to mention Aaron? I don't want to get him into trouble for beating him up.'

'It would be better if he came forward,' said Alf.

'I can't ask him to do that. I don't think he has the mental capacity to explain himself.'

'He must, Polly. There ain't much of a case otherwise.'

'Might he get done for beating Mickey up?'

'He was defending you.'

'It could put him in danger when word gets out; especially when that liar Mickey starts spinning a yarn. Aaron's Jewish you know?'

'I see your point.' He thought for a moment. 'You could say an unknown man came to your assistance.'

'That's what I'll do then,' she said. 'Right then, you had your breakfast?'

'No, I made a pot of tea, but I've been up pacing the floor since half past five. I've been thinking about you all night.'

'Oh yeah? What's on your mind, Sergeant?' she gave him a playful look.

He looked at her with none of his usual awkwardness 'As a matter of fact, I was thinking about you taking off your bodice last night.' He blew out his cheeks and shook his head.

'I was vexed with you.'

'Get vexed with me some more then,' he grinned.

'You only saw my chemise.'

'It's a very thin chemise, Polly Wilkes.' Alf said lifting his eyebrows comically.

'Really?' she folded her arms.

'It is, Polly,' he said. 'And I recall there was a little more than *looking* involved.'

'Well, Sergeant.' She moved towards him, pushing back her shoulders and looking down at her breasts. 'They ain't going nowhere.' She kissed him.

Alf pulled her over so that they both flopped into the large armchair. She gave a little shriek of laughter and pulling up her skirts moved astride him, pinning him to the chair. She kissed him again. The feel of his lips on hers was a new pleasure. They were firm and warm and the sensation was a delight.

'Leave off, Pol,' he groaned. 'I got to go and do a twelve-hour shift.'

She laughed and began to climb off his lap. He stopped her by spanning her hips with his big hands. 'C'mere…' He leaned forward and kissed her. Polly responded by wrapping her arms around him.

She stayed there for several minutes, enjoying all the sensations of being physically close and gloriously happy. There was no mistaking his desire for her.

She could feel the constraining effect of his clothing. Knowing that he wanted her for all the right reasons was intoxicating to her. She gave him a lingering passionate kiss. The feel of his lips on hers had become a gratification she could not do without.

'My sweet Polly,' he murmured. 'This is a revelation to me. The more you give me, the more I want. I ain't never understood what a man could be driven to, until now.'

She shifted her weight against him and she heard the breath catch in his throat.

She gazed at him feeling a pang of anxiety. 'I know how it is, my love. I would gladly release that prisoner down there, if-'

'Don't delay on my account,' he murmured unevenly.

She leaned back and looked at him.

'If it weren't for the doubt...'

Alf blew out his cheeks in a long exhaled breath.

'Right now, I don't care about the doubt.'

'I know,' she said watching him as she shifted her weight once again. 'And that gets a lot of men in a lot of trouble. It's a revelation to me too, Alfie. And it makes me keen as you.'

He gave a groan. 'That ain't helping the situation'

'I'll relieve your agitation if you want me to.'

She watched his face as he battled against the tyranny of his instinctive male urges.

'D' you want me to go blind?' he said.

'Trust me, Alfie, if that were really true, half the men in London would have lost their sight.'

'I don't know, Polly, I reckon there is a great deal of bad eyesight among the male population.'

'You are a card, Alfie,' she laughed and kissed him. 'Right,' she stood up. 'In that case, I'll save you from yourself and make your breakfast.'

She took out the frying pan and set to work. She could feel his eyes on her as she took the bacon and sausages from the cold shelf in the pantry and began placing them in the pan.

'Listen, Polly, I been thinking about... you know, what we talked about last night. It's preying on my mind that you might be ill. Should you see a doctor?'

Polly considered this for a moment as she gently pushed the sausages around the pan.

'I don't think it would help, my dearest. There's nothing to give an opinion on - except what I already know. I promise you I don't think I'm sick, but it's too important to take any chances.'

'What d'you know about this sickness?'

She turned the heat off the pan and sat down. 'A man doesn't usually have to have this kind of conversation with his girl. You really want to talk about this?'

'I think you might be surprised how many people have this conversation,' he said. 'You just tell me straight. What occurs?'

Polly composed herself. She folded her hands and rested them on the table.

She took a deep breath. 'Well, I'm told it starts with sores.'

Alf's eyebrows lifted. 'Where?'

'In an intimate place.' Polly shook her head. 'Cross my heart and hope to die, I'm not aware of ever having any such thing, Alfie, except I understand they aren't painful so they can be missed. After that, you get sick with what feels like a very bad bout of flu. I've had some coughs and sneezes but I don't think I've ever had the flu. I mean, the flu can kill a person. It's serious isn't it?' Alf nodded again as Polly continued. 'After that comes a rash, mainly on the hands and feet with more of the painless sores. The sores heal and they leave pockmarks; the thing is, they can also turn into ulcers.' she looked at him. 'You've probably seen them on a person's face before?'

'I have, Polly, horrific ones where it's eaten away the person's nose, mouth or eye socket sometimes,' said Alf gravely.

Polly nodded. 'Those ulcers can turn inward and make abscesses in the flesh and bones so you become crippled with pain and get putrid with infection. Then you die.'

'It don't sound like something a person would get and not know about it.'

'The trouble is, it can take a couple of years for a person to get these abscesses. In some people it takes a lifetime. What if I had the first part mild and didn't know it? Then one day these ulcers and putrid things start showing up all over me?'

'I'm inclined to think they don't appear in everybody,' said Alf.

'That's right. In some people, it all fades away.'

'And you're alright after that?'

'So I understand. The thing is, babies born within a couple of years of their mother being sick with the pox are very badly affected… it doesn't end well.'

Alf nodded. He knew exactly what Polly meant. 'Yes, I've picked a few of them up off the streets in my time, the poor little chavvies. You're right, it's pitiful how they suffer.'

'It's like they're born with the worst of it already taking place inside them. They say dying is the most merciful thing.'

'I think I would agree with that,' said Alf.

'If you get through it, which some people do, it's alright again and a child born would be as well as any other. On my life, I swear I haven't had any signs of it, Alfie, though I can't tell you how it gives me anxiety to think I might be mistaken. I would never forgive myself if I passed it to you, or… or to our babies.' Tears brimmed in her eyes. 'I couldn't lose another, Alfie.'

'I know, my dear, I know.' He took her hands in his. 'Listen, we have to think in terms that it's going to be all right. You're a sensible type of person. I think you would have known if you had those things.'

'Lizzie taught me to be very careful and I'm inclined to think I would.'

'That's how I see it inside my head. It's your nerves, that's all. Put it all behind you and we can start a new life.' A lustful grin curved his mouth 'And you better prepare to be loved like never before, my girl.'

She wiped away a tear from her cheek. 'It's obvious to me now that Thomas didn't love me, and I didn't love him. I was bored and he said things that appealed to my vanity.'

'C'mere.' Alf pulled her to her feet and gathered her in his arms. He held her tightly and she felt him kiss the top of her head. 'You paid a very high price.'

She looked up at him. 'Then this big, lovely copper came into my life. I'm so lucky.' She pulled his head towards hers and he gave her a long lingering kiss.

Reluctantly she pulled away. 'Right then, all this isn't going to get a murderer caught, is it? You got a double shift ahead of you and you need your breakfast.'

She moved to the stove and put the pan of bacon and sausages back on the heat. Alf followed her and put his arms around her from behind as she stood at the kitchen stove. He bent his head, buried his face in her neck and covered it with kisses. 'Hmm….' he murmured, 'you're a delight I can't get enough of, Polly Wilkes.'

Her stomach curled pleasurably. She turned around to face him. His hands slid down her hips and then grabbed each cheek of her bottom. Polly gave a little laugh.

'My, you *have* come out of your shell, Sergeant.'

'I have, Polly. I'm walking on air. I might even give the lads ten minutes extra for their break today.'

'Oh, don't go too mad will you?' she replied. 'Sit down and let me get you your breakfast.'

Alf complied. Polly took a plate from the dresser and set the bacon and sausages aside then cracked an egg into the pan.

He was becoming as enthusiastic as any other man about intimacy and she wanted to please him.

Pangs of anxiety made her stomach twist into knots. The truth was she could never know for sure. She had always followed Lizzie's advice about keeping clean and she was fairly sure she had never had any of the things Suzette told her about. Nor had she been on the game for long, just a few months after Auntie May's money ran out and even then, only when she was unable to get other work. That must cut down the risk, surely? Lizzie had warned her that it only took one infected client. Then what about children? After the traumatic birth of little Daniel, she didn't know if she could have more children. The doctors had not told her otherwise but what if it wasn't possible? That wonderful man over there deserved better than that.

She placed a fried egg on the plate next to the sausages and cracked the second one into the pan. No children. What kind of marriage was that? She added the second egg to the first and then placed the plate in front of Alf and only then was she aware that he was watching her.

'You put a lot of thought into frying those eggs,' he said.

She sat down on the chair beside him. 'I was thinking,' she said.

'I could see that,' he answered. He cut into the first succulent sausage and then speared it with his fork.

'What if I can't have kids, Alfie?'

'No couple knows that until they get married.'

'After what happened with my Daniel...'

'Did they say you couldn't have another?'

'They didn't say I could.' she frowned.

'Polly, my sweet girl, it's all nerves.' he said gently.

'I just want you to be sure of what you could be letting yourself in for.'

'I ain't never been so sure of anything in my life.' he said. 'All I want is for you to be healthy. Anything else would be icing on the cake.'

She bowed her head and felt tears flood into her eyes.

'Whatever is wrong?' Alf asked.

She could barely speak for the lump in her throat. 'You-c-called-me-your-sweet-girl,' she sobbed.

'Well, that's what you are.' Alf began to smile as she continued to sob. 'C'mere then, soft girl.'

'I-ain't-a-soft-girl,' she said unevenly.

'No, you're *my* girl.'

Polly let out a wail and cried even harder.

Alf put his arms around her. 'Silly goose,' he said fondly. 'Don't take on. You know what? You are fine and fit as a fiddle. One day we are going to enjoy all the privileges of being a bride and groom and then we'll have our very own brood of kids. Alright?'

She nodded tearfully. She took out the handkerchief with the forget-me-nots on it that Lizzie had given her. She looked at it. 'You know something? If I'm all right, it's down to Lizzie.'

'How so?'

'The night Thomas knocked me down the stairs, he would have started on me again if it hadn't been for Lizzie. She lived next door and I think she heard me fall. I was bracing myself for another kicking and suddenly Lizzie was there grabbing him by the neck from behind.'

'I recall having to pull her off him,' he said. 'Perhaps I should have let her choke the life out of him. The look on her face, she was set on killing him.'

'That was Lizzie. Right from the start, when I was on the street, she taught me how to protect myself and how to spot the wrong 'uns. She used to do everything she could to help me so I didn't have to go on the game. She used to impress on me all the time not to take risks even if I was desperate. She knew places to spend the night that were safe when I didn't have my doss money and whenever Mickey was working away, she let me stay with her.'

'Then I owe her more than I can ever repay.' Alf replied.

'Get the man who murdered her.' said Polly.

'I'll do my best, Polly. I promise. First I want you to come down to the station and make that statement. It would be better if you would name the Jewish chap that saved you.'

'I can't, Alfie. It would do no good anyway. He's a tragic case. He hears voices in his head. He hurts himself all the time. And I think his family sometimes want rid of him.'

What d'you mean, rid of him?'

'Off their hands. I mean, it must be terrible having someone like him in their home especially when they have kids. He's so tormented and I don't think he understands reality a lot of the time. He couldn't be a witness, no magistrate would think him capable.'

'Yet he managed to understand that you were being attacked?' said Alf.

'His brother told me he saw bad things when he was growing up. Believe me, Aaron went berserk at Mickey. I think he acted on instinct. I'm sure I wasn't the first woman he cared about he saw being attacked. His brother hinted that he saw his relatives being hurt by the Cossacks.'

'*The Cossacks*? Blimey, no wonder. They're a ruthless bunch of professional cut- throats.'

'It sounded brutal, even though Mr. Lubnowski didn't say much about it. He's pitiful, Alfie, honestly.'

'How come he was on Dock Street at that time of night?'

'The wife is well on in the family way. I suspect the brother puts him out sometimes when they get sick of him. When that happens, he wanders the streets and comes looking for me to read to him. He gets fixated about me reading to him at times. I read him some Charles Dickens when I looked after him and he really liked it. I think it soothed him and took his mind off the voices in his head. It was gratifying to see the effect it had on him.' She looked at Alf. 'Mickey was set on killing me. Aaron really did save my life.'

'In that case, that's another debt I owe; to this Aaron of yours.'

'Would you mind if I went and read to him sometimes?'

'Course not. It seems a small thing to do for the man.' Alf pushed away his empty plate. 'That was smashing, Polly.' he said. He cut a thick slice of bread and spread it with butter. 'Don't you worry about Mickey Kidney. Sooner or later we'll get him,' he said. 'They always get cocky and that's when they make mistakes.'

When Alf left the house, Polly set to and got on with her duties. She bathed Mrs. Cruikshank. She washed her hair and then she made it into a long plait and curled it around the old lady's head.

'How about you put one of your pretty dresses on today?'

Mrs. Cruikshank scowled in reply.

Polly sighed. 'You have some nice things. You ought not to wear your nightgown all the time.'

'You keep me locked up in here.'

'No, Mrs. Cruikshank, you can go where you like. The park, the library, up the market perhaps? You can't go anywhere in your nightgown, now can you?'

'Am I wearing my nightgown?'

Polly blinked. 'Yes, Mrs. Cruikshank, you are.' She had noticed that the old lady could be a little forgetful, but she had never been confused like this before. That cursed medicine was addling her brain, she was sure of it.

'Mrs. Cruikshank? Do you know where you are?' Polly asked.

'Yes I do, silly goose, I'm in my bedroom.'

'That's right.' Polly smiled, feeling reassured.

'I have to get up. I need to get Daniel off to school,' she said. 'He's never been late and he's never missed a day,' she said with a proud beaming smile. 'He's such a good boy.'

Polly stopped and looked at the old lady. There it was, the pain the poor woman was unable to cope with. That loss was the cause of her addiction and the root of the intolerable grief that made her like this. Polly couldn't help it, she pulled the older lady into an embrace and held on to her. To her surprise, Mrs. Cruikshank did not resist. Perhaps comforting hugs had been missing up to now.

'Tell you what… You have a little rest today and I'll see to Daniel,' she whispered.

'Will you? You're so good to me, Ivy.' She gave a big contented sigh and lay back against her plumped pillows.

'I'm Polly, remember? I look after you now. Your sister, Ivy's at home in Bournemouth.'

Mrs. Cruikshank smiled contentedly. 'Thank you, Ivy dear,' she said.

Polly looked at her. 'We've got to get you off that laudanum.'

# CHAPTER TWENTY FIVE

Alf Cruikshank could feel the tension as he walked into the station and knew something must have happened. Inspector Reid was at the counter which was unusual in itself and he looked up as Alf came through the door. 'There's been another one, Sergeant.'

'Sir?'

'Commercial Street officers are in attendance and have asked us to inform Scotland Yard.'

Alf watched a young officer encode the telegraph message that was to be sent by Morse code over the wire to Scotland Yard.

'Is it definitely him?' Alf asked. 'It's been over five weeks.'

'Yes,' Reid replied. 'Just when we were all beginning to hope the murders had stopped.'

'God above…' Alf murmured. 'Where this time, sir?'

'Dorset Street,' said Reid. 'Or more accurately, one of the grubby little alleys that is an offshoot of that terrible place.' He looked at the lad. 'Come on, Harris, get on with it.' He turned to Alf. 'We must get the situation under control. There'll be rioting in the streets if we don't - George Lusk and his vigilantes will make sure of it. Thank goodness it's the Lord Mayor's parade today, the left-wing groups and the rest of the anarchists will be distracted by it. We have a chance to get the scene cleaned up and the body removed before they start turning up and stirring trouble.'

Alf paced the floor as they waited for a response from The Yard. He watched the young officer decode a telegraph message that had just been received.

'Inspector Abberline has requested you meet him at the scene, sir,' young Harris said to Alf.

Alf looked at Reid who nodded, indicating he should get on his way.

Alf made his way directly to Dorset Street. He knew why Abberline had summoned him. He had seen each of The Ripper's victims and been at the crime scene of three of them. Abberline knew he would be able to identify any elements in common with the other murders. The thought of having to view another victim made his stomach churn.

The maniac had committed a murder in the very street where Polly had so recently stayed. He put it out of his mind and instead thought about her as he walked, giving silent thanks that he had been able to take her out of that life.

When Alf arrived he saw that a crowd was beginning to gather in Dorset Street. Reid was right, it could turn ugly very quickly - especially if the vigilante groups and socialist workers got wind of it and turned up looking for trouble. It could easily turn into a riot. Alf hoped they would remain occupied stirring up trouble at the Lord Mayor's parade instead. Most of the reporters' intent on the same thing would also be involved with the show, meaning there would be time to deal with the murder scene before word got out to the wider public.

As Alf turned down the alley that opened into Millers Court, he had expected to find the victim lying in the yard. To his surprise, this one was indoors. It was a new development for this devil.

Inspector Abberline had not yet arrived. Alf was directed to look through the grubby window of number thirteen by Inspector Beck. He caught Alf's arm before he did so.

'Brace yourself, Alf,' he warned.

Alf looked through the broken pane as the others had done and reeled away from the terrible sight. No one could brace themselves sufficiently for what was inside that room.

A moment later, Inspector Abberline arrived on the scene by carriage, directly from Scotland Yard. Alf could barely speak as he met Abberline at the end of the alley. He took a breath and composed himself.

'It's… it's beyond description, sir,' he said. 'Inspector Beck, who you will know from Commercial Street is in the courtyard.' Alf followed Abberline along the alley and watched as the two men shook hands.

The reinforcements from Commercial Street arrived and Beck set about organising his men to control the crowd.

'Dew? Any trouble must be nipped in the bud.' He gave instructions to the officer to close off both ends of Dorset Street as more men from Leman Street arrived. For once they could completely shield the murder scene from sightseers.

Alf Cruikshank took a good look at Thomas Bowyer. He was an army pensioner who worked as a rent collector for McCarthy and had been the first to raise the alarm. To have witnessed such a thing would probably scar his mind for the rest of his life. Alf moved to Bowyer's side and put a hand on his shoulder. 'Steady on, there. That's the way... Have another swig of brandy and take your time... When you feel ready, tell me what happened.' Bowyer shook his head as if trying to rid his mind of the terrible images he had just seen. He swigged the brandy again, his hands shaking. 'There ain't no hurry.' Alf soothed him, concerned that the older man's heart might give out.

'She was s-s-such a p-pretty girl... w-what he done to her...' Bowyer gave an involuntary howl, then took another minute to collect himself. 'At first, all I saw was two pieces of flesh on the table by the bed.' He blew out his cheeks each time he exhaled, in rapid, forced breaths as if blowing out a candle. His eyes bulged. Alf patted his shoulder but did not interrupt. 'I thought she had come by two large joints of meat and I thought - the cheeky cow, when she owes so much rent. The master would have those in lieu of payment. B-b-but then I saw her lying on the bed.' He screwed up his face and held his breath. 'They weren't loins of beef.' He looked as if he was screaming though no sound came out of his mouth. He shook his head and still, he held his breath. A long time seemed to pass. Alf was about to slap him on the back when he inhaled with a loud rasping sob. 'I shall never be the same again.'

Alf patted him on the shoulder.

'You will,' he said gently, while thinking he was probably right. 'It's just the shock that's got you like this.' Then Alf looked at McCarthy and recognised the tough Irishman. He was a property owner, slum landlord and suspected brothel keeper who was well known in the district. His chandlers shop formed one side of the alleyway into Millers Court. He was a hardened character but even he looked as if he had been clubbed over the head.

'Can you add anything further, sir?'

'My name is John McCarthy and I own numbers 26 and 27 Dorset Street as well as all these here in Millers Court.'

Alf nodded. 'You are the victim's landlord?'

'Yes. She's a young Irish girl named Mary Jane Kelly. She's behind with her rent. I was in the shop as usual when some of the neighbours mentioned that no one had seen her this morning. I thought she might have done a flit, so I sent Thomas 'round. He came back to get me in a bad state. I reached in through the broken window and pulled back the coat that serves as a curtain-' He stopped and took a long inhalation through his nose. His chest swelled like a barrel, he exhaled deeply and took a swig of brandy. 'You have seen for yourself what I found. I sent Thomas for a policeman and he came back with that gentlemen.' He nodded towards Inspector Beck.

'Thank you, Mr. McCarthy.' Alf nodded. 'We'll need to get that down in a statement, later on, sir.'

After an hour, Doctor Bagster-Phillips arrived. He looked through the window and recoiled at the sight.

'I believe this victim is well beyond the help of a medical man,' he said turning away. 'She can be removed.'

'What's the holdup?' Abberline demanded. Beck told him that Commissioner Warren had instructed that bloodhounds were to be brought to the scene.

'In that case, the room should be left as it is, so as not to disturb any scent the dogs might pick up.' Bagster-Phillips decreed.

Alf paced the courtyard. There was nothing to do except hang around awaiting the arrival of the bloodhounds. For another hour and a half, nothing happened. Alf could hear the crowd on Dorset Street getting edgy. The neighbours in Millers Court were getting impatient. There was money to be made from talking to reporters and they knew it.

At half past one, Superintendent Arnold, head of H division arrived in his dress uniform and in a fine carriage which three constables were instantly assigned to guard. Alf assumed that he had been called away from the Lord Mayor's parade.

'We are waiting on the bloodhounds, sir,' said Abberline.

Arnold shook his head. 'There will be no bloodhounds. Commissioner Warren was keen to use the dogs,' he said. 'He resigned last night after some argument or other and his successor, Commissioner Monro, has countermanded the order.'

Abberline's face turned puce. Alf gritted his teeth thinking the top men needed their heads knocking together. There seemed no end to the bickering and backstabbing.

Alf knew that bloodhounds had amazing tracking abilities. They might have been their best chance to pick up the killer's scent, which as far as the dogs were concerned, would be very strong inside that room. The dogs might have led them directly to the killer's door. They had sat around all day and had nothing to show for it.

The Superintendent did not look through the window. He tried to turn the door handle and found it locked. 'Someone procure the means to get this door open,' he ordered. McCarthy said an axe could be found in his shop next door. Constable Dew was sent to get it. Abberline stood aside as Arnold issued the order.

'The whole thing is a farce, Alf,' he murmured. 'I've got a new boss and I wasn't even told. Now Monro is in charge, yet nowhere to be seen and we are left hanging with our arses in the air waiting for instructions that weren't ever going to come.'

'Monro is likely at the Lord Mayor's parade, sir.' Alf murmured in reply.

'Yes, I would imagine that's where all the top brass will be.'

'I wonder if the timing of this is deliberate?' said Alf.

'Perhaps. Who knows what goes through the mind of this devil.'

McCarthy took the axe from constable Dew.

'Wait,' said Alf. He reached in through the broken window and released the door latch.

The first person through the door was Doctor Bagster-Phillips, right behind him was Abberline, who almost walked into him when he stopped in his tracks. The door swung on its rusty hinges and rebounded off the table behind it.

They were faced with a small, dim room. On the wall to their right was an old wooden bedstead which was positioned in the corner next to the table. The victim was lying on the bed. Now they were inside, the true horror and insanity of the crime was apparent.

'Holy Mother of God.' Abberline murmured, stepping past the doctor. 'How can this be the work of a man? Even one who is mad?'

Alf entered the room and his face instantly drained of colour. Again he could smell that foul combination of blood and excrement. He forced himself to look at the victim.

Mary Jane Kelly's body had been appallingly mutilated. The monstrous and grotesque nature of her injuries had almost destroyed her corpse. She was lying in the middle of the bed. Her head and upper torso had been dragged towards the edge. The killer had moved her, Alf surmised, so he could do his filthy work from the side of the bed. She had been wearing a cotton undergarment which was split completely along its length, exposing her naked body to his foul intentions.

'The young woman's thighs have been splayed apart just like the others,' said Alf. 'And he's cut her from genitals to her breastbone like he did with Mrs. Nichols, Mrs. Chapman and Mrs. Eddowes....'

The victim had been disembowelled like the others and the killer had put the innards to one side. It was just like the other murders but so much more brutal.

'That's his signature. It was him alright,' said Abberline. 'What he did after that is beyond any comprehension.'

Alf turned away, needing respite from the hellish scene. 'This is the only victim he was able to have naked and laid out in front of him. Perhaps that's what encouraged him to do these other things. He took his time.'

Abberline agreed. In the privacy of this room, the killer had taken his time and enjoyed himself with the poor girl's body. He had lain her flat on the thin straw-filled mattress. He had taken the long bolster pillow from the bed and placed it out of the way at the back of the bedside table. He had cut her throat from right to left.

'She was on the right side of the bed when he attacked her,' said Abberline. 'The mattress is soaked.'

Alf looked under the bed. 'And there's a pool of blood under here, almost a yard across, it's dripped through the mattress.' He stood up. It was difficult to comprehend what he was seeing.

Despite the horrific mutilation done to her, Alf kept looking at a small cut on her right thumb and the many scratches across the back of her hand and forearm. The poor girl had tried to protect herself from the vicious movements of the knife. It tore at Alf's heart to think of it.

There was blood everywhere. Great lumps of flesh that had been carved from her thighs and placed on the bedside table in front of the bolster. These were the mounds of flesh they had seen through the window. Her nose had been cut off and placed on the same table. The long bone of her right leg had been stripped of all tissue and glistened white in the dimness of the room. There was a long and very deep gash in her left calf that started just below her knee and ran to within a few inches of her left ankle. To Alf, it looked as if the cut had been made for pleasure. Her liver had been placed between her feet. The madman had cut off both her breasts with circular incisions. One of them was beside her right foot next to her liver, the other was behind her head with her kidneys and a red lump of flesh that was probably her womb. It made Alf shudder. Most pitiful was the girl's face. The killer had obliterated it and rendered her unrecognisable. He had cut off not only her nose but also her cheeks, lips, eyelids, forehead, eyebrows and part of her ears. Her lidless eyeballs stared out of their sockets. It was a sight beyond any nightmare.

Bagster-Phillips stepped forward. Like Alf, he had been observing the body. He looked under the bed and then looked again at the body. Alf had never seen him so quiet.  After a moment, the doctor turned to Inspector Abberline.

'The immediate cause of death was the severing of the right carotid artery. Judging by the blood-soaked condition of the mattress, pillow and sheet, as well as the large quantity of blood that has dripped through the straw onto the floor beneath, she was on the right side of the bed when she received the wound. There is blood spray on the wall as with the Chapman case. The mutilations were carried out after death.'

He had a thin film of sweat on his pale face as he looked at Abberline. This was the first time Alf had seen an emotional reaction in Bagster-Phillips. Just like the rest of them, he was struggling with this scene. 'There is no reason why the post-mortem should not be done here,' he said, 'as long as some lighting is brought in and that window completely obscured from onlookers. I fear the corpse would not survive being transported to the mortuary intact and evidence could be lost.'

'Very well, Doctor. I gather Doctor Bond is on his way to assist you,' said Abberline. Bagster-Phillips stared at him for several seconds. Alf wondered what that reaction meant. He and Abberline left Bagster-Phillips making notes and went out into the courtyard. Even the tainted air of Millers Court smelled better than what was in that room. Abberline rolled his eyes back towards the doctor. 'I knew he wouldn't like it. His nose is out of joint because the assistant commissioner asked Thomas Bond from A Division to review all his notes on the other cases; in particular, his assertion that the killer was a medical man. That horror in there doesn't look like the work of a medic, does it?'

'More like the work of a wild animal,' said Alf.

'This one is beyond comprehension.' Abberline shook his head slowly.

Alf looked at him. 'How can such a monster walk this manor, sir and yet fit in so well, that no one suspects who he is?' he asked. 'He has to be a raving lunatic to do *that* in there.'

'I would think the only reason he is able to carry out these crimes is precisely because he seems normal, mild-mannered and harmless. Otherwise, the girls would be on their guard and refuse to go with him.'

'Abberline? I will instruct a photographer to come and photograph the victim's eyes,' said Superintendent Arnold. 'I'm leaving now. Keep me appraised of any developments.' He headed out of the alley to his waiting carriage.

'Photographing the eyes,' said Alf. 'What's that about, sir?'

'There is a school of thought from a German by the name of Wilhelm Kühne, that the retinas at the back of the victim's eyes will show an image of their murderer like a photographic negative. Berlin Police used it a few years ago and got a conviction.'

'Does it work?'

'I'm sceptical, Alf. Berlin police already had their suspect in custody. In my opinion, they used the photograph of the victims' retinas to fit what they wanted and confirm what they had. A bit dodgy if you ask me, especially as the man was executed.'

'We have to try, sir, don't we? Just in case it works.'

'I suppose so.' Abberline sighed. 'We had better make arrangements to get the room sealed off. Some of the residents are hanging about and have managed to get a look at the body. They are bound to talk and we need to keep the lid on this one.'

'Beck is organising that now, sir.'

At about four o'clock the two doctors emerged from the room.

'We have completed a preliminary post-mortem,' said Thomas Bond. 'The cause of death was the severance of the right carotid artery. The cut was so ferocious, its depth extended to the spine, leaving deep marks on the fifth and sixth vertebrae.' He sighed. 'As for everything else… we have tried to piece the body back together, stitching where we could and… it seems the heart is missing.'

'He took her heart?' Abberline said.

'It looks that way; we can't find it and I don't think we have overlooked it somewhere in the room. The pericardium, which is the sack the heart resides in, has been cut open from below and the heart is absent.'

The implications of this were chilling. None of the men present could find the ability to speak for several minutes.

# CHAPTER TWENTY SIX

Polly's smile fell away when she saw Alf's face was grey. She put down the bowl of stew that she had just scooped from the bubbling pan on the stove and went to him.

'Alfie? Whatever has happened?'

Alf dropped into his usual chair at the kitchen table and blew out a long sigh.

'I don't think I can do this job no more, Polly.'

Automatically, she poured him a cup of tea, loaded it with two spoons of sugar and put it in front of him. She placed her hand on his shoulder and waited for him to compose himself.

Alf took a swig of the tea. After a moment, he looked up at her. 'That monster has struck again.' His lips were crinkled with dryness and his eyes were dull. It was clear to Polly that he had been sick to his stomach. 'You can't imagine what he did to her,' he croaked.

A spasm turned Polly's stomach. She dropped into the chair adjacent to him.

'Did to whom? I've been acquainted with all his victims so far, Alfie. Who was it?'

'Her name is Mary Jane Kelly. She's... she *was* a young Irish girl.'

Polly cupped her hand to her mouth. 'I know her,' she said finally. 'She lives in Millers Court just opposite Crossingham's.'

'That's her,' said Alf.

'She's got a lovely singing voice. In Crossingham's kitchen, you could sometimes hear her singing at the top of her voice in her room. She lived with a chap called Joe; I think they parted a few weeks ago-' Polly stopped abruptly. 'She's been killed by The Ripper?'

'*Butchered* by The Ripper.' said Alf. 'What a sight. It's aged me ten years, Pol.' His voice shook. Polly placed her hand over his as Alf shook his head. 'I was hoping he'd gone. There ain't been a murder for more than five weeks.'

'It was him? It was definitely him?'

'Oh yes, it were him alright, only this time...' he paused. 'The men at Commercial Street was sent for by the rent collector this morning. The chap was in a terrible state, but I don't think any of us had any idea what we was about to come across. There weren't a man present who weren't sick to his soul at what we saw.'

'Where was she found?'

'She was in her room in Millers Court. That was the difference you see, he was indoors. He could take his time with her. He had privacy.' Alf bowed his head. 'He can't be human, Polly.' Alf bit out the words. 'No human being could do what he did. Not even a wild animal would do what he did. It looked more like the work of a demon.' He stopped himself and took a deep breath. Polly could see that his whole body was as tight as a coiled spring. 'I don't think I want to be a policeman no more.'

Polly swallowed hard. Her throat had closed up as if there was a stone lodged in it. 'It isn't like you to be fanciful, Alfie. Now you listen to me. He isn't a demon. He doesn't have supernatural powers. He's a *man*, a seriously deranged man.'

'Maybe it's someone who thinks he's got such powers, for why he does what he does, I can't imagine'

'Possibly,' said Polly. 'He can think what he likes, it doesn't mean he's got them, does it?'

Alf covered his face with his hands. Polly stood up, put her arms around him and pulled his head towards her. Her big, unflinching Alfie was shocked to the core and that stunned her. Nothing fazed him, he was imperturbable - until now.

'Mr. Sherlock Holmes would use that delusion against him, wouldn't he?' she said gently.

'We gotta get him, Polly. We just got to get him,' he turned, and wrapping his arms around her waist, he buried his face in her bodice. 'I'm so glad you're here, and safe, my dear,' he said as Polly stroked his hair. 'Each one he does gets worse and worse. Though how much worse than *that* it could get, I dread to think. I ain't never heard of a murderer such as him. It's as though he relishes the killing and who the victim is don't matter.'

'W-what did he do to her?'

'You don't want to know.'

Come on now, you can't come home all distressed and shaken, then tell me half the story. You've got to unburden yourself by talking about it. I'm no shrinking violet, you know that. Drink your tea while it's hot, it'll help you compose yourself.'

He pulled away and sat up. He took a gulp of tea as instructed. He placed his brawny forearms on the table and clasped one hand over the other.

'She was on the bed,' he began. 'I ain't never seen so much blood in my life. It looked like great lumps of red jelly, black and glistening, where it had clotted. It was everywhere, Polly. On the mattress, the walls, the floor. I shouldn't be surprised if it was every drop the poor girl had. The photographer slipped in it when he was setting up his equipment. I shall never forget the look on his face. And the smell in that room. Blood and excrement. For me, that will always be the smell of these murders.'

'The sight of blood wouldn't put you in a state like this. Even if there were a lot of it or a bad smell for that matter. What happened?'

'My word, Polly. I've seen post-mortems and heaven knows they're bad enough, at least there's some dignity to 'em. They do things and they take the organs for a reason. This monster took out all her insides for a reason known only to his insane appetites,' he looked up at her. 'He put them on the table next to her. At her feet... beside her head...' He rubbed his hand across his face.

Polly controlled her rolling stomach by swallowing hard. 'They said he might be a doctor.'

Alf sat back and looked at her. 'This weren't the work of no doctor, not even a crazed one. That room was a vision of hell, Polly. They couldn't find the heart, it turned up in the kettle on the fire. And he filleted her. He sliced the flesh off her every part of her, great chunks of it, down to the bone. I'll never forget the sight of her leg bones gleaming white in the middle of a mess of... of blood and flesh.' His face contorted. 'What he cut off, he arranged around the room. You could see he had placed them, deliberate like, as if he was setting it out like parlour cushions.' He grabbed Polly's hand. 'Her arm was in a little puffed sleeve. It must have been her chemise cos she had only been wearing undergarments. She had a slender arm and wrist and a nice shaped hand just like yours, and I thought about the other night and how the sight of you was a wonder to me.' He closed his eyes, 'and this poor girl's arm was resting on all this... this vile butchery.' He screwed up his face. 'You would hardly have known it was a human being if it weren't for her arm. Even her face, he took all the flesh off. There weren't nothing left.'

'She had a very pretty face, Alfie,' said Polly quietly, putting her other hand on top of his. 'Strikingly so as I recall.'

'Not no more she don't. There's nothing left of her, Polly. He even cut off her… her bosoms.' He pursed his lips like someone about to whistle a tune and instead let out a controlled breath. 'What kind of devil would want to do that? He carved the flesh off her. Much worse than Mrs. Eddowes. What he did to Mrs. Eddowes he did in ten minutes. He spent as much time as he fancied on Miss Kelly and it was so much worse. I can't tell you how much worse, Polly. God help the one that has to identify her because there ain't nothing left. Just the eyes, no lids, no forehead, no cheeks, no nose, just the eyes.'

Polly put her hand on his. 'I suppose it will have to be Joe Barnett who she used to live with. That's a shocking ordeal for the man.'

'You got that right. I don't think the old chap what found her shall ever be the same again. I don't think I shall ever be the same again.'

'Yes you will, Alfie Cruikshank, because you're going to catch this monster and see him hang for this.' She stood up. 'You think of it in those terms. Don't think about what you saw, think on how you're going to catch him and how he's going to pay for it. Isn't that what Mr. Sherlock Holmes would do?'

Alf shook his head. 'It's just my foolishness to think that Sherlock Holmes has the answers. That's a made up yarn, this is real life. Too bloody real.'

Polly blinked. Alf hardly ever cursed. She squeezed his hand. 'Never mind that it's a made up yarn. You think the principle of how he goes about things is right, don't you? He uses his brain - that's what you admire about him. You can do what he does and make it real, Alfie. You're not gonna be put off by what this maniac has done. You're going to use your brain and catch him.'

'Yeah me, a mere sergeant.'

'Didn't Inspector Abberline tell you what they want in a detective? Not too posh, know London like the back of their hand and know how the people think? That sounds like you, Alfie Cruikshank.'

Alf lifted her hand to his lips and kissed it. 'You're such a comfort to me, my love. I bless the day I found you.' Polly leaned into him and kissed him. Alf took her in his arms and turned what had been a mere touch of their lips into a deep, fervent kiss. Eventually, he pulled away and looked at her. With satisfaction, Polly saw that his eyes had their warmth back. 'Not as much as I do, Alfie Cruikshank,' she said softly. She gave him another brief kiss. 'So, what are you going to do about this murderer, Sergeant?'

Alf released her and straightened his spine. 'I got to get back to the station. Every man we have is out looking for him. There are all sorts of people to interview to find out where Miss Kelly was last night and who she was with.'

'Right then. Will you try and put something on your stomach? You can't catch this monster if you're not well nourished.'

Alf ate a small portion of stew and drank another mug of tea. Polly could see that he was restless and had less of an appetite. Nevertheless, she was happy that he had his spark back and was itching to get to Leman Street. He wanted that killer.

Once Alf returned to the station, Polly took Mrs. Cruikshank a bowl of stew and a thick slice of bread.

'Would you like to come downstairs tomorrow and have dinner with Alfred?' Polly asked her. 'I'll make the table all nice and I could do your hair for you. You could put on one of your nice dresses.'

'Phhh...' Mrs. Cruikshank made a sound like someone opening a bottle of ginger beer.

'Very well... That's a "no" then is it?' Polly murmured.

As usual, the old lady ate a hearty meal. Polly had always connected a good appetite with health and well-being. It was not so with Alf's mother. Temperance Cruikshank was in some ways, as unable to function in the world as Aaron. The only difference Polly could see was Aaron was incapacitated by the voices in his head whilst Mrs. Cruikshank was incapacitated by grief.

Polly attended to her personal care and made her comfortable. She measured out ten drops of laudanum onto a teaspoon and stirred it into a small amount of water in a shot glass. Feeling uneasy that she was enabling the older woman to kill herself inch by inch with the vile stuff, she arranged her pillows and settled her down to sleep for the night.

She went down stairs, thinking about how she could broach the subject with both Alf and his mother about weening her off the laudanum.

When she reached the kitchen she gave a gasp. Mickey Kidney was standing there and had already helped himself to the housekeeping money from the jar on the mantelpiece.

'Mickey! I'm not alone.'

'Yes you are. I've been watching the house. There's only you and a barmy old lady here. Your precious lover boy copper is out looking for Jack and I been looking for you.'

Polly moved, putting the table between herself and Mickey.

She fixed her eyes on him. He was well dressed and clean shaven. He looked almost respectable. He couldn't play the part of the grieving husband in his usual condition. His tidy appearance would be George Lusk's doing, Polly assumed. Even Lusk couldn't make a gentleman out of Mickey. He smirked, showing his decayed yellow teeth. He often smirked, Polly noticed. It was if he was imagining how things were going to play out and it gave him some sort of pleasure. He still had some faint bruises from where Aaron had hit him. Polly took some satisfaction that he had been given a taste of his own medicine.

'What Lizzie ever saw in you, I'll never know,' she said.

'I got hidden talents,' he sneered.

'Only for boozing, stealing and murder,' Polly replied. 'I know you killed Lizzie and I already been to the police about you, so put that money back and get out.'

'You ain't in charge of this situation. You see, that's your trouble, Slag. You think you're the boss and you never could keep your nose out of other people's business.'

'Lizzie *was* my business. She was my friend and you lied through your teeth about her at the inquest. Making out you tried to keep her respectable despite her *natural tendencies*. You liar! You pimped her 'round your mates, don't think I don't know that. That's why you wanted her back. You lost your nice little earner didn't you?'

'You still got a big mouth, you filthy whore.'

'I don't know how you've got away with it up to now. You're so stupid you even turned up at the station asking for help to find her murderer before anyone knew she was dead.'

'I read it in *The Times*.'

'Funny how it was the *only* paper that knew her name before she was identified. Even the coroner didn't know it was Lizzie. That alone should have been enough to get you locked up, yet you managed to wriggle out of it somehow.'

'Don't you know? I'm a valuable member of the Vigilance committee. My dear wife was killed by The Ripper and all because of the incompetence of those idiots running the police,' he smirked. 'Mr. Lusk values my services. He's going places and I'm going with him.'

'What did he say when you gave him her name long before she was identified? He must know the only way you could have known it was her, was if you were the one who killed her. Yet, he hasn't turned you in - he must be as crooked as you. He's nothing more than a trouble maker and a gang leader. He's using the murders to get himself elected.'

'Mr. Lusk will help me to better my conditions. Though I admit, you are my one little problem. You're the irritating little tick in my ear, Slag. You're the thing that could spoil it for me - Mr. Lusk is very careful to avoid scandal.'

'After the inquest, Alfie told Inspector Reid. If anything happens to me they will know it's you. My Alfie won't rest until you're swinging on the end of a rope.'

He blinked, weighing her words as if it had just dawned on him that this was the flaw in his plan. He twisted his mouth as his slow brain tried to work things out.

'I know you did it,' Polly grated, as she watched him tussle with the facts. She was not afraid. Her contempt for him and her fury blurring out her other emotions.

'Did I?' he said with an air of innocence.

'Yes, you did and I'll tell you how.' Her face contorted. 'You heard from your mates that Lizzie was out with a new man in *The Bricklayers*. She probably knew it would get back to you. Perhaps she wanted it to, so you would finally get the message that she wasn't coming back. You went storming down there and found her on Berner Street.'

'Now how could I do that? I can prove I was working on the docks.'

'Because you nipped out, like you all do, every night. It's usually to slake your thirst with some ale; this time you went looking for Lizzie. You hadn't been able to find her since that time in Flower and Dean Street. Did someone tip you off where she was?'

'Just one of your fantastical stories, Slag.'

'You were seen, Mickey. Did you know there was a witness? Someone saw you going down Berner Street like you were looking for a fight.'

'How d'you know it weren't Jack he saw?'

'You found her outside Dutfield's Yard.' Polly continued. 'She asked her gentleman friend to wait while she talked to you. She tried to take you inside the gateway for a private talk. You wouldn't have it, you tried to pull her into the street - she resisted. You tried to make her come back to you. You got even angrier because this time she wouldn't budge.'

'Everyone says it was Jack what did her in. Miss High-and-Mighty knows different.'

'Yeah, because the witness said you pulled her into the street - not into the yard like that stupid paper *The Star* said. It's on the police statement clear as day. Jack wouldn't have pulled her into the street. There were people all over that street. There was a meeting going on in the club next door and people were in and out that gate all night. Jack likes dark, quiet places. That's how I know it weren't Jack.' Polly blazed. He smirked at her as she went on. 'She refused to come back to you. You lost your temper, as usual, only this time she stood up to you. You were furious, you pushed her and she fell backward into the yard. She cried out. She didn't make much fuss because she wanted to keep your argument private. If it was Jack who had hold of her, she would have screamed her head off, knowing there were half a dozen people around who would come running. When she got up, she told you straight that it was over. It finally sunk into that thick skull that she meant it. She started to walk away. You grabbed her by her scarf and pulled her into the yard. When her gentleman saw it was getting nasty, he legged it. He was probably married and didn't want to have to explain why he was with Lizzie if the police turned up. You had the knife you use to cut open the pallets on the docks, in your pocket. You took it out, you cut her throat and you left her there.' Polly looked at him with pure hatred. 'You left her there and went back to work. You couldn't even do that right you stupid great arse of a man.'

Her throat had tightened and she could hardly breathe. She took wheezing gasps of air.

'She wasn't dead, Mickey. She lay there bleeding for nearly twenty minutes before they found her and when they did, she wasn't quite gone. They said her blood was flowing. She was still bleeding at ten past one. You even botched that, you stupid, brainless, arrogant, arsehole.' She spat out the words through clenched teeth. 'And, yet again Mickey manages to wriggle out of it,' she said with a wave of her hand. 'Botching it worked for you because when the doctor came he thought it had happened just before Mr. Diemshultz found her. They thought they had missed Jack by seconds. They hadn't. You attacked her when Mr. Schwartz saw you at around twenty to one but she didn't die until around ten past one. You were back at the docks by then and you had an alibi for the time they *thought* she was murdered. They blamed it on Jack. They thought Diemshultz coming along at one o'clock had disturbed him in his jollies. Jack wasn't there, Jack was over Mitre Square looking for a victim.'

'Why didn't she cry out for help all that time?'

'Because you cut her windpipe. She couldn't cry out. She couldn't even whisper. You cut her windpipe but not the big blood vessels that would have killed her quickly. People passed by, inches away from her, with no idea she was lying there in the dark. They wouldn't hear any faint sounds she might have made because there was a sing-song going on in the club. Diemshultz's little pony smelled the blood and shied up. That's why Diemshultz lit a match and found her. She would have lain there until morning otherwise.'

'Still full of yourself ain't you, Slag?' He gave an unpleasant laugh.

Polly was undaunted. 'I bet you couldn't believe your luck when the papers were calling it a double murder by The Ripper. You thought you could make something out of it and went straight round to see George Lusk. You're so stupid it didn't occur to you that nobody knew who she was. You gave Lusk Lizzie's name before anyone knew it was her. I bet it was him who gave the story to his pet monkey on *The Times*. Funny how it was the only paper that named her on Monday morning when even the coroner didn't know who she was on account of her being positively identified as someone else. It never entered that thick head of yours that she hadn't been identified properly. Was it Lusk's idea to go down the station? Did he want you to stir up trouble for the police about your poor dead wife? I saw you at Leman Street and I saw George Lusk waiting outside in a carriage. When it became obvious that you had messed up again did he help you come up with an excuse? You concocted a story about having been to the mortuary cos you read it in the paper. If that was true why didn't you tell them who she was? They were still calling her Elizabeth Stokes the next day. I'll tell you why you didn't... Because you killed her, you absolute, black tongued, lying, bastard.'

'A fairy tale, all that.' said Mickey.

'No it isn't,' said Polly. 'Lusk has been protecting you. It's the only reason you're not in the cells. That and the fact that *The Star* and the rest of the papers love the idea of Jack doing two within the space of an hour on different sides of the east end - that's why they twisted the witness statement. You killed her Mickey. I know you did.'

'You ain't never gonna prove any of it are you?'

'I won't rest until I do!'

Suddenly, Kidney lunged towards her. 'There's no Jew boy to save you now is there?'

Polly ran towards the back door. Her fingertips made contact with the handle. He caught her before she could get a grip on it. He grabbed her by the shoulders and yanked her backwards. She was pulled off her feet and saw stars as her head banged against the stone floor. Kidney leaped on top of her.

'Get off me!' She lashed out with her arms, her knees, and any part of her that she could move. It was no good, he was making sure he was out of reach. She thrashed and struggled. No way was she going to give in without a fight. She screamed. She kicked out. She writhed and struggled. She clawed at him. She pushed against him and tried to roll over. She raised both knees and aimed kicks at any soft target she could find.

She was no match for Mickey and she knew she was fighting for her life. She managed to scramble away from him. He grabbed her ankle. She fell face down, sprawling on the floor. He wrenched her arm and flipped her onto her back. She kept fighting. She lashed out in all directions. She knew if he got his hands on her throat it was over. She fought and struggled for all she was worth. He had her pinned down with his body.

She felt his strong hands around her neck. She tried to scream, but she could make no noise because he had started to squeeze. She could feel the blood thumping in her head. Her windpipe felt as if it was going to collapse. Her vision was going dark. Then he banged her head off the stone floor and there was nothing.

Polly felt herself tumbling over and over as she came back to consciousness. A coarse wooden deck scraped her cheek. This was definitely not the kitchen in Alf's house. She was outdoors. Her vision was blurry. As it cleared, she could see through the gaps in the deck. Cold terror took hold of her as she saw the brown churning waters of the Thames beneath her. Her mind cleared, she looked around and saw that she was at the site of the new bridge next to The Tower of London.

It was a freezing cold night. A bone chilling, pea soup of a fog had descended on London. It twirled itself into long tendrils that snaked along the entire river, cloaking the riverbank in a thick mist that permeated every street. The gas lanterns that lit the building site made only small pools of light in the murk. Their light bounced off the fog as if it was a solid thing that could not be penetrated. The rug from Alf's kitchen was beside her.

She gave a groan as a terrible pain shot through her head. She rolled over and tried to get onto her knees. Mickey Kidney's shape swirled in front of her.

'That's right, wakey, wakey,' he said. He pushed her back down with the hefty shove from his foot. He was sitting on a large tool chest right beside her.

'I been studying on what you said.' He sounded almost casual. 'If they find your body they'll chalk it up to me. Thanks for the tip off by the way. So, I decided that you need to vanish. That way they can't prove anything. I had to think of a place to put you where you would never be found. Then I remembered this bridge.' He jerked his head towards the wooden structure that protruded above the deck. 'The lads were talking yesterday about how they had just finished digging one out one of the caissons and they were ready to start pouring the concrete. They've been pouring it all day.'

He stood up and pushed aside a few of the wooden planks that protected a vast wooden shaft that had been sunk into the river bed. Men had worked for months digging out the soft mud while a dozen deep wooden shafts kept out the waters of the Thames. Now it turned out, they had been digging Polly's grave. Mickey hauled her to her feet and dragged her to the edge so she could see over the side of the caisson. It was dimly lit by a gaslight overhead. At the bottom of its dizzying depth, there was an enormous pool of grey concrete. It made her head spin.

'They say it goes down thirty feet; tons and tons of concrete that the bridge will stand on, and you, Slag, are going in.'

Polly whimpered and started to struggle, it was useless, Kidney had her in an iron grip. He began to push her head first into the caisson. There would be no escape; the cement would suck her down like quicksand. Terrified, she thought of the horror of suffocating in the thick wet concrete as it filled her nose and throat and burned her eyes. It would solidify around her. She would stay there for as long as the bridge stood and Alfie would never know what happened to her.

'Rot in hell!' she grated, her bruised windpipe making her voice crack.

'You'll be there first,' he sneered. 'You're nothing but trouble, Slag. You got a big mouth and I'm going to shut it for you, permanently. If you behave, I'll be kind, I'll cut your throat before you go in. Call it a small gesture of mercy.'

'You didn't show Lizzie any mercy did you?' she hissed through clenched teeth.

'It was so convenient that they blamed it on Jack,' he said. 'Almost like it was meant to be. Fate, you might say.'

'Don't be so stupid. You're just a filthy murderer.'

'You ain't in no position to be calling anybody names, Slag.'

'You're an evil, murdering pig, Mickey Kidney.'

'She had it coming' he snarled.

Polly gave a roar and he tightened his grip on her. Her eyes scanned the building site, looking for any chance to save her own life. Two enormous islands of stone had gradually appeared in the river. As each caisson was filled with cement, a little more of a huge pier was built on top of the solid concrete. A beautiful curved stone structure of Cornish granite and Portland stone had started to emerge, shielding them from view on all sides.

The sides of the caisson were four feet taller than the surrounding deck. If Mickey was to throw her in as he planned, he would have to hoist her bodily over it. Polly knew he was strong enough to do it and she knew she had to fight for her life. She struggled, she kicked out with every bit of strength she had left.

A warning sign in big letters had been written in chalk on the side of the wooden structure. It had a chilling message; '*DANGER. 30 feet of wet concrete. If you fall in, you will die. You cannot be rescued.*'

In terror, she hit out at him. She dug her nails into his foul flesh. She tried to use her elbows to smash him in the ribs. Nothing worked, he was too strong. She tried to grab onto the wooden planking to prevent him from lifting her over the side. He loosened his grip and threw her forwards against the side of the caisson. He forced her head down so that she was bent over the huge wooden box. Her feet were off the ground. She kicked out with everything she had. It filled her with horror to see the dark grey pool, which would swallow her up with hardly a splash.

All Mickey had to do was lift up her legs and she would be pitched in, head first. This spurred her on to fight. She struggled with all her might. She would never give in. She would fight him to her last breath. She managed to briefly break his hold on her, she rolled away and sprawled across the planks that covered the shaft.

She saw a short length of two by four lying on the planks. Frantically she made a grab for it, her muscles red hot with pain as she tried to reach it. She managed to pull it towards her by the very tips of her fingers. She grasped it and, almost at the same second, swung it round with the last of her strength. Kidney ducked and it missed his head. She fell backward onto the deck as she lost her grip on it. It barrelled into the scaffolding of the bridge with a loud crash. She whimpered, seeing her last chance to save herself fade away. Kidney hauled her to her feet. Her strength was failing, with nothing to lose she kept on struggling.  Then, Kidney stiffened. He released his grip on her and Polly scrambled away from him. She turned around gasping and sobbing just in time to see him fall face down on the decking. By some miracle, he was unconscious. Polly stared at him, she was dazed. She couldn't imagine how it had happened.  Maybe she had dislodged something on the scaffolding above. She did not wait to figure it out. She scrambled to her feet and fled from the building site.

She tore along St Katharine Street and turned onto Little Tower Hill. She was out of breath and the smog was choking. The dark street was deserted. She hardly knew where she was going. She turned right and ran along what she hoped was Royal Mint Street which she knew would lead her to Leman Street. She had one thought in her head that she needed to find Alf and he would be at the station. She could hardly see further than two yards in front of her. The fog was disorientating, it was hard to tell if she was going in the right direction.

She came to the junction with Dock Street and the railway bridge loomed out of the murk. She sobbed with relief, beyond the bridge was Leman Street. A figure appeared out of the fog.

'Polly?'

'Alfie,' she croaked.

'Where you been? You left the house without your cloak and bonnet. I was worried- What in the name of-' he began. 'What's the matter?'

'Alfie.' she sobbed. 'Oh, Alfie.' She collapsed against him. She stammered out the story. 'Mickey… Quick,' she rasped. 'At the bridge… He could wake up… He'll get away.'

They hurried through the choking fog to the bridge. The scaffolding was hardly visible in the murk.

Polly led Alf to the spot where Mickey had tried to pitch her into the caisson before falling face down on the deck. The smog was thickest over the river and Alf's bullseye lantern could hardly penetrate it. The whole site had almost vanished into the murk.

'He's over there-' she let out a scream and clamped her hand over her mouth.

'Oh my Lord,' she heard Alf murmur. There was a thick ribbon of scarlet at their feet. He traced it to its origin with his lantern. At its source was Mickey Kidney.

His hands had been tied together and he had been strung up against the caisson, like a side of pork in a slaughter house. His head lolled backward to show a gaping wound across his neck. Scarlet foam filled the gash. It looked as if he had fought to breathe as blood bubbled up and gushed from his severed carotid artery into his lungs. She could see the ghastly, glistening stump of his windpipe sticking through the gash. His eyes were open and his face registered horror and surprise. Perhaps it had been the agony of drowning in his own blood that created this hideous death mask. The red foam had started to congeal and made popping noises in the severed end of the carotid artery which was as thick as a hosepipe. Blood dripped from the corpse making rivulets that joined a thicker stream. It flowed along the decking and fell between the planks into the cement below.

Alf took out his police whistle and gave three long blasts. He took his bullseye lantern and used it to signal towards St. Katharine docks.

They heard a noise in the darkness - out of range of the dim gas light that lit the site.

'Who's there?' Alf demanded. He turned his lantern to the source of the sound. He held out an arm from his side. 'Get behind me, Polly.'

Alf began to cast the beam about so that it made yellow rays that reflected off the dense fog. He strode across to a pile of stacked timber. Polly, ignoring his instruction, was at his side.

The beam illuminated the figure of a man crouched beneath a feeble gaslight between the piles of timber. They could see that his whole body was shaking. He seemed unaware of the light that Alf was shining on him. He had found a fragment of chalk and was completely focused on scrawling something on the layers of wood. Over and over again he had scrawled the same words. They looked like the lines of pointless sentences given to children to copy over and over again as a punishment in board school.

'This is the police! Show yourself.' Alf commanded.

Either he could not hear Alf, or he was ignoring him. As they watched, the figure paused in his task and rocked himself back and forth. He wailed pitifully. He held a bloody knife in his hand. He whimpered as he kept on writing the same sentence.

'Drop the knife.' Alf commanded. 'Now!'

'He's terrified, Alfie. He might have been hiding here all along and seen what happened,' said Polly. 'What's he writing?'

'I dunno… Keep back, Polly.'

Alf turned the beam on the crouching figure. 'Drop the knife and come out, now!' The figure stood up shakily and turned to face them.

'Aaron?' Polly gasped, stepping forward. 'Oh God. It's Aaron.' She turned to Alf. 'He's harmless, Alfie.'

'He's holding a knife, Polly!'

'This is the poor Jewish lad that likes me to read to him. He comes looking for me all the time. He probably followed Mickey here and saw the whole thing. No wonder he's distressed.'

'Polly-' Alf began.

'It's all right, Alfie. Aaron? It's me, Polly. It's all right. Drop the knife. This is my friend, Alfie. Drop the knife. What you doing there? What you writing? Drop the knife.' Aaron looked up at the sound of Polly's voice. 'It's all right.' Polly continued. 'Drop the knife, Aaron. Come over here. Drop the knife. Let me look at you. Oh God, he's shaking.'

He took two steps towards her. He stopped short when he saw Alf was watching him intently. Polly gasped as Aaron came into the circle of light from the gas lamp above the caisson. He was covered in blood. 'What've you done?' she repeated. 'Oh, Aaron. What have you done? Please, drop the knife.'

Aaron looked down at his blood stained clothes an expression of mild curiosity on his face. He noticed the knife in his hand and finally dropped it.

'Stay right where you are.' ordered Alf. 'You're under arrest.'

'Alfie, please no. He's just a poor troubled man. He's saved my life. You can't arrest him. Mickey would have killed me. That must be the reason why he did it.'

'I have to arrest him, Polly. Look at that.' He gestured towards the corpse of Mickey Kidney. 'He's strung him up and ripped his throat out. Did he do that before you ran away?'

'No. Mickey practically had me in that concrete then he got knocked out and I ran away. I thought something had fallen down and hit him on the head. I didn't even know Aaron was here.'

Alf jerked his head towards the corpse. 'That's excessive. Even though I am forever grateful to him for saving your life, I've got to take him in.'

'You didn't see what Aaron saw. Mickey was intent on putting me in there.' She stabbed her finger at the deep shaft. 'I was fighting back, but he would have succeeded if he hadn't got hit on the head. Look at him he's shaking like a leaf.'

Alf picked up the knife. He held it between his finger and thumb since it was covered in blood, tiny flecks of sawdust and flesh.

At that moment, the rope that held Mickey gave way and the body dropped into the shaft. It hit the concrete with a splat, like a hand slapping wet sand. Then, the body was sucked under with hardly a sound.

'If he was defending you, we can straighten it all out at the station. I got no choice, I have to take him, Polly.'

'It's alright, Aaron,' she said trying to soothe the distraught man. 'He can't make a statement, Alfie. Look at him.' Polly took hold Aaron's blood soaked arm. 'It's alright.'

'Damn it, Polly. Get away from him. He's dangerous.'

'No he isn't. He doesn't even know what day it is half the time. And his family doesn't give him much attention. All they do is give him orders. Do this, go there, do that. I'm sure they put him out on the street when they get sick of him. Then he comes looking for me.' Tears had started in her eyes. 'I know it must be hard for them to cope with but-'

'I'm sorry for all that but he's just ripped a man's throat out.'

'It's all right, Aaron,' said Polly. 'I told you about the sergeant I work for, didn't I? Well, this is him.'

Alf took out a notebook from his pocket and copied the words Aaron had written on the timber.

'This ain't English,' he said.

'Well, no. It will be his own language, won't it? He understands English but I don't think he can't write it or read it.'

'Hmm.' Alf put his notebook back in his breast pocket. They heard footsteps on the deck and a constable appeared in response to the three blasts on the police whistle Alf had given moments before.

'Mullins. Get to the station and tell them to get the Black Maria back here at once. Quick as you can.'

Mullins took off at a sprint.

Polly turned to Aaron. She kept hold of his arm. He was still trembling. His eyes were cast downward. She looked at the blank expression on his face and knew his mind would be teeming with the voices that plagued him.

'It'll be all right, Aaron. Don't worry. I'll be with you.'

Aaron finally looked at her. 'You read to me, Polly?'

# CHAPTER TWENTY SEVEN

'Hey! Don't be so rough with him. That man saved my life,' Polly shouted at the two young policemen who were manhandling Aaron from the Black Maria into the back of Leman Street station. 'You don't have to do that. He won't fight back. Just tell him what to do and he'll do it.'

'Polly...' Alf murmured. 'Let me handle things will you?'

They dragged Aaron up a set of stone steps to the main floor.

'They're hurting him. They can't shove him around like that. He saved my life.' She watched as the two officers led Aaron away towards the cells. 'It'll be alright, Aaron,' she called to him. 'Go with the officers. I'll get this sorted out, you'll see.'

'Come in here.' Alf sighed. He steered her into the same interview room they had used when she made the statement about Catherine Eddowes only five weeks ago. 'I'll be back in a minute,' he said.

Polly sat down at the table and suddenly felt bone achingly tired. She placed her elbows on the scratched surface and put her head in her hands, thinking that by now it must be well after midnight. She stayed that way until Alf returned with a tray of tea things.

'Sorry I left you for so long, I had to make it myself,' he explained. 'All our men are out on the beat looking for The Ripper after that terrible business yesterday.'

'How's Aaron?' she asked.

'A bit agitated actually. Don't worry, he'll be alright.'

'Alfie, he doesn't deserve this. He only killed Mickey because he attacked me again. I'm telling you, Mickey would have had me good and proper this time if it weren't for Aaron.'

Alf poured the tea and added two generous spoonfuls of sugar before handing it to Polly.

'Your neck is in a right state.' he said.

'It's not so bad, but he didn't half give the back of my head a bang on the kitchen floor.' She touched it tentatively. 'You've not got a rug anymore, by the way, it's down on the bridge.'

'Never mind the rug. D'you want the doctor to have a look at you?'

'No, I'm all right - it's just a bit of a bump.'

'Damn him to hell.' Alf growled.

'Thanks to Aaron, the Good Lord will be doing that any minute now.' Polly took a sip of tea as Alf shook his head and against his better judgment broke into a smile.

'I'm not sorry he's dead,' said Polly. 'He confessed to me that he killed Lizzie and he gloated that he'd got away with it.'

'You ain't got no proof, Polly.'

'I know, you have to have your evidence,' she replied. 'Listen, I'm not worried about Mickey. I want to know what will happen to Aaron. He's just a pitiful soul, Alfie, and he saved my life.'

'I'm mindful of that. 'Alf replied. 'And I'm indebted to him more than I can express.' He paused and looked at her. 'If anything had happened to you…' He cleared his throat loudly. 'Can you tell me what you know about this man?'

'I already told you he's a very sad case. As I understand it, he's sick in his mind. He's tormented by his own thoughts. He hears voices. He told me they were the voices of evil spirits that haven't be able to leave this earthly plane. They tell him he's evil. Can you imagine what that's like? Voices in your head telling you every minute of the day and night that you're evil and all the horrible things in the world are your fault? He does things to himself to try and distract the voices.'

'What sort of things?'

Polly hesitated. 'He hurts himself… and he does that thing you think makes you go blind.'

'Oh,' said Alf, his cheeks turning pink. Polly tutted.

'Honestly Alfie, you and me are on intimate terms. Are you still-?'

'Hush.' Alf replied in a very low whisper. 'You don't want to go saying things like that in here.'

Polly rolled her eyes at her buttoned up policeman.

Alf cleared his throat and tried to move on in a business-like manner. 'What else d'you know about him? What's his full name?'

'Can't he tell you that?'

'Not at present.'

'Why not?'

'He's curled up in a ball on the floor of the cell.'

'What? Alfie. Let me go to him. See if he has his book with him. He calms down when I read to him.'

'Let's get a few details first,' he said. 'Do you know his full name?'

'The family is called Lubnowski. They live at 16 Greenfield Street.'

'Hmm… that ain't far from here. I'll get someone to go 'round there and get a family member in here.'

'Can I go and talk to Aaron?' she asked. 'If he's curled up like that he must be in a really bad way.'

'Not at the minute, Polly. I've had to arrest him on suspicion of murder. You saw what happened to Kidney. '

'He was only protecting me. I can help to calm him down. You're not going to be able to question him if he's in one of his states are you?'

Alf weighed this up. 'All right, I'll see what I can do. Inspector Reid will be back from The Yard soon.'

'Yard?'

'Scotland Yard. He's been in a meeting all day about The Ripper murders.'

'Ripper murders. Ripper murders. That all I hear these days. Leave Aaron alone and go and catch a real murderer will you?'

Alf stood up. 'Listen, you have some more tea and I'll be back in a while. Use our washroom if you want to - you like doing that.'

When Alf left, Polly went in search of the washroom. She took off her clothes, found a clean washcloth and washed herself from head to toe, revelling in the constant supply of hot water and soap. She looked in the mirror and saw that her neck was purple and bruised. She could see the imprint of Kidney's thumbs on her windpipe and parallel lines of his fingers at each side of her neck. She had often seen similar marks on Lizzie's neck and felt a fresh surge of fury. It gave her some comfort to think that Mickey would now be explaining himself to a far greater authority than the Metropolitan Police.

She dampened the end of a towel and dabbed at the smudges of dirt on her skirt. This was her favourite blue one that she had bought at the market the day Alf offered her a job and changed her life - that lucky, lucky day.

She had sworn to make Kidney pay for killing Lizzie and though she had not had the satisfaction of seeing him found guilty in a court of law, nor seen him hang, fate had made sure he paid for his crime with his life.

She put on her blouse and skirt and arranged the collar to cover the bruises. The reflection in the mirror showed her a respectable lady and although this pleased her, she suspected that Alf's workmates knew about her past.

Someone tapped on the door.

'Miss Wilkes?' She heard one of the young constables who had escorted Aaron into the station. Polly opened the door. 'They want you in the office,' he said. He looked her up and down.

Yes, thought Polly, Alf's workmates knew about her past. 'Thank you,' she nodded, with all the dignity she could muster. He directed her down the corridor and she was shown into Inspector Reid's office.

Reid was at his desk. Alf stood next to an armchair that was to the left of the desk. It was close to a tall bookcase filled with red, leather-bound tomes with gold lettering on the spines. Polly wondered if the Inspector had any Charles Dickens in his collection.

'Please have a seat, Miss Wilkes,' said Reid standing up and gesturing to the armchair, indicating that was where she should sit. She sat down, adjusting her skirts and keeping her back straight in the ladylike way she had been taught as part of her expensive education.

'I am so sorry for the ordeal you have just endured.' Reid began, sitting back down at his desk. 'How are you feeling?'

'I'm quite well, sir.' Polly answered.

'Sergeant Cruikshank has just explained the circumstances. Michael Kidney abducted you?'

'Yes, Sir.'

'And he tried to throw you into the foundations of the new bridge?'

'Yes, sir.'

'You managed to get away from him and you found Sergeant Cruikshank?'

'Yes, sir.'

'When you returned with the sergeant, you found Mr. Kidney hamstrung with his throat cut.' Reid leaned forward placing his forearms on his desk and folded his hands together.

'That's right, sir.'

'Then you found the man, whom Sergeant Cruikshank arrested, at the scene?'

'Yes, sir.'

'You were not aware of his presence prior to this?'

'Well, no. I was fighting for my life.'

'How did you get away from Kidney?'

'I didn't exactly. I thought I was done for. Then somehow, he got knocked out. I thought something must have fallen off the scaffolding and hit him on the head. Now I think Aaron might have done it to save me.'

'You didn't see the prisoner at that point?'

Polly stiffened. 'Hang on a minute. *The prisoner*? When did he go from being a suspect to being a prisoner?'

Alf shifted his weight uncomfortably.

'He was found at the scene of a murder covered in blood.' said Reid.

'You don't know how that came about. Anyway, Mickey would have killed me for sure. Anything Aaron did would have been to help me. He was defending me.'

Reid unfolded his hands and placed them on the immaculately white blotter on his desk.

'You said you escaped.'

'Yes, but up until he got knocked out, I was truly done for. So either something hit him by accident, or Aaron threw something that knocked him out and that's how I got away.'

'I see. The point is you were able to escape.'

'Yes, sir.'

'And you ran from the bridge without seeing the prisoner?'

'Yes, sir.'

'Therefore, suspending Mr. Kidney above the caisson and cutting his throat, happened after you left the scene?'

'Yes.' Polly said guardedly.

Reid thought for a moment before continuing. 'You see, Miss Wilkes, the evidence you have provided suggests that there was no need for the excessive force the prisoner used. When you escaped from the scene, Mr. Kidney was unconscious.'

'Aaron must have seen what Mickey did to me. We don't know what occurred. Perhaps Mickey had a go at Aaron too, and this is how things ended up. He was so distressed when we found him - in one of his really bad states. He has a sickness of the mind, Inspector Reid. You can't hold him responsible for murder.'

Reid leaned back in his chair. 'Tell me what you know about him.'

Polly suppressed a sigh and again told everything she knew about Aaron. 'Sir, whatever he did, he did to protect me because he saw what Mickey was doing to me. You don't know the terrible things he saw in his homeland as a child. His brother told me it affected his mind to a terrible degree. He has become attached to me because he likes me to read to him.'

'So this man enjoys having you read to him and comes looking for you on a regular basis?'

'Yes, it seems to settle him down.'

'What do you do when he comes looking for you?'

'Well, I read to him,' she shrugged. The two men waited for her to elaborate. She sighed. 'If it's in daylight I find somewhere to sit down with him and read to him for a while. He always has the book with him. If it was late, as it often is, I take him home. I think he forgets where he lives and has no idea about time, so he ends up wandering the streets. I think he's been beaten up a few times and the family are at their wit's end with him.'

Reid and Alf looked at each other.

'What's going on?' Polly asked. Neither man answered. 'Look, sir, he's a sad individual; he needs someone to help him. He's ill, just the same as if he had the Consumption or... or a broken leg. You wouldn't expect him to walk if he had a broken leg, would you? It isn't fair to expect him to reckon things out like other people when his mind is sick.'

'How many times have you escorted him home?'

'Maybe half a dozen.'

'Over what time period?'

'A couple of months.' Polly shrugged. 'The family will be able to tell you better than me. The first time I looked after him, they were going to a wedding so they will likely remember the date.' Now the two men exchanged a longer look. Polly glanced from one to the other. 'Would you please tell me what's going on?'

Reid straightened his spine. 'Sergeant Cruikshank had the words the prisoner wrote at the scene, translated.'

'What does it mean?'

'It's in the Polish tongue. It means *For the one I did not do*,' said Reid.

Polly's brow creased. 'So, Aaron wasn't the one who killed Mickey?'

'We found him covered in blood with a knife in his hand, Polly,' said Alf.

'All the evidence suggests he killed Mr. Kidney,' said Reid. 'We don't know what he was trying to say when he wrote it.' He lifted his index finger. 'The *one* I did not do.' His eyes scanned the room then once again came to rest on Polly. 'He knew Michael Kidney was trying to kill you because you believe he killed Elizabeth Stride, did he not?''

'Yes.' Polly replied, gazing back at Reid.

'So why write *For the ONE I did not do?*'

'We think he's The Ripper, Polly.' Alf interjected.

'WHAT?' Polly sprang from the chair. 'Are you out of your mind? If this is a yarn to pin those murders on a poor man who can't defend himself, I'm not having it.'

'Polly, listen,' said Alf.

'Miss Wilkes, we are not trying to blame him for the murders out of convenience,' said Reid, his voice calm and reasonable. 'However, the way the throat was cut, the state of mind of the man, and the fact that he wrote what could be a tormented confession at the scene, must be looked into.'

'How are you going to do that? You won't ever get a coherent story out of him. He can hardly hold a sentence in his head never mind a whole statement, and the voices in his head tell him he's responsible for everything bad in the world. He could confess to anything.'

'We want to find the truth, Miss Wilkes. That's all,' said Reid. Again he glanced at Alf, then back at Polly. 'I thought you might be able to help us.'

'I'm not putting a noose around Aaron's neck.'

'I understand your concerns,' said Reid, 'If he is The Ripper, I doubt it would come to that. He is clearly an insane person and you are correct, he cannot be held responsible for his actions.' He looked at Polly. 'I'm sure you understand, it's vital that we know, Miss Wilkes. Has the sergeant brought in The Ripper? Or do we need to keep looking?'

Polly thought about this. 'What would I have to do?'

'You say you have a forged a bond with the prisoner because of the reading.'

'Like I said, it seems to settle him.'

'Once he settles, do you think he would be more willing to answer some questions?'

'I don't know. He always does what I tell him when he's calm.'

'Do you think he would answer some questions if you were the person who asked them?'

'He might,' said Polly. 'Sometimes he doesn't seem able to follow a topic. He might give an answer that makes no sense.'

'You mean he doesn't have a sufficient command of English?'

'He seems to understand English all right, it's more like he understands the meaning of the words but finds it hard to put them in a sentence. Then, when he starts to talk he forgets what he wants to say. He blames evil spirits for snatching them out of his head.'

'Would you be willing to try?'

Polly thought for a moment. 'I won't trick him and lead him to the gallows.'

'No.' said Reid. 'I promise you, all we want are some answers. We need to know what he meant by that sentence.'


A few minutes later, Polly was shown into an interview room with bars on the windows. There was nothing in the room except a table and two chairs which were bolted to the floor.

She found Aaron slumped on one of the chairs, his forearms on the table. He was absorbed in the task of picking at the hairs on the back of his hand. Some of the hairs had been pulled out with such force that he was bleeding and a drop of blood ran across his skin. Aaron watched it curiously as it made a path towards the crease of his thumb.

Polly sat down on the chair opposite him. There was a grille on the wall to her left. Top Scotland Yard officers had been sent for and Polly knew that Inspector Fred Abberline, Chief Inspector Donald Swanson, who was the head of the investigation at Scotland Yard, Inspector Reid and Alf were watching and listening through the grille. Two constables were posted outside the door.

As usual, Aaron had the book they were reading. It was Oliver Twist by Dickens and it was on the table.

'Aaron,' said Polly gently. 'You saved my life.' Aaron did not look up. He was plucking the hairs from the back of his hand. 'I'm so sorry you were brought here. I know you only did what you did to help me. I told the police that you're a hero.' Aaron glanced up at her but said nothing. Then he looked down at his hand. He seemed fascinated by the dots of blood that had appeared in the places where he had ripped out the hairs and taken tiny pieces of flesh along with them. 'You're a hero and I'm very grateful that you saved me from Mickey. You watch out for me don't you, Aaron? You're my friend.' Aaron did not respond and his expression remained blank. He was focused totally on pulling the hairs from the back of his hand. 'Listen, don't worry, they sent for your brother,' said Polly. 'Would you like me to read to you? It will pass the time until he gets here.'

He looked up. It always amazed her how those words got through to his broken mind.

'Read, Polly.' he said.

'All right then,' she took hold of the book. 'First, would you answer a question that has got me curious? How did you come to be on that bridge?

She understood she had to be patient and wait for an answer. It took him a while to process questions.

'I follow.' he shrugged.

'Why did you follow?'

Again a long pause. He looked at her. 'Mickey Kidney cannot hurt my Polly.'

Her heart curled at his words. 'Aw, Aaron, you really are my hero aren't you?' She wanted to squeeze his hand but thought better of it; she knew he would never tolerate it. He shunned all physical contact. 'Aaron? Mickey had me rolled up in a carpet. How did you know he had me inside it?'

He looked at her, his eyes intense. 'I know everything that happens on this earth.'

'Oh right, I forgot that.' Polly answered slowly, glancing in the direction of the grille. 'So... How is it you know everything again?' She wanted the eavesdroppers to hear this.

'The spirits of the dead who remain on this earth tell me all things.' His voice was without any expression, as though it was simply a fact upon which he held no opinion.

'Oh yes, now I remember,' said Polly. 'Listen, Aaron, when I ran away, did Mickey see you? Did he know you had seen what he did to me?'

Aaron did not respond.

'Did you see what he did to me, Aaron?'

Aaron seemed to have lost the thread of the discussion.

'Read to me, Polly?'

'I will Aaron, I will,' she replied. 'Can you remember? Look at my neck. Did you see how this happened to me?'

Aaron lifted his eyes to look at her but did not answer.

'You were very upset when I found you there on the bridge,' she tried again.

He was sinking into his private reality. It was as if the subject of their conversation had been instantly erased from his mind. She knew Aaron would believe the spirits had done it because they did not want him to answer.

'You wrote a message on the pile of wood. Was it a message for me, Aaron?' she asked. There was no response. 'Were you writing it down in case the spirits took it out of your head?'

He looked at her and his eyes narrowed as if he was trying to make sense of a bewildering conundrum. Polly's heart ached. It was painful to see how tortured he was by his own mind.

'It was written in your own language. Can you remember?' she said gently. 'Your message said *For the one I did not do.* Can you tell me what you meant by it, Aaron?' He looked up. Polly met his eyes and he looked away immediately. He was struggling to keep his thoughts together.

'Was it a message for me, Aaron? Was it for Polly?'

He closed his eyes tightly.

'I told you about my friend, didn't I? And you know that Mickey Kidney was not my friend, don't you? You saved me from him before didn't you?' She could see how exhausting it was for him, however, he seemed to understand that point and nodded.

He was struggling to concentrate. He covered his ears with his hands. Polly could see that the voices were winning. She reached towards him and gently touched his forearm, which caused him to jerk away from her and lower both arms.

'Listen to *my* voice, Aaron. You pay no mind to those other voices. Concentrate on my voice. What did you mean? Who or what is for the one you did not do, Aaron?'

He was becoming more agitated. He closed his arms across his chest and started to rock back and forth.

'Was it about Lizzie, Aaron? Is that what the message was about? She paused for a moment. 'I told you about Lizzie being killed, didn't I? Other ladies have been killed, too, Aaron, can you remember? The last was only yesterday. They were my friends too.'

He looked up again. She could see that his agitation and confusion were growing. He continued to rock backwards and forwards.

She paused, watching him and once again felt intense pity for him. She knew this was torture for him, and no matter what happened after this, it was not going to end for him. He would spend his whole life in this nightmarish tortured state.

'Aaron? Tell me. You always tell Polly the truth, don't you? If you killed Mickey for *the one you did not do*, did you do the others, Aaron?'

He was incoherent. It would do no good to ask him more questions when he was like this. He continued rocking, unable to answer. Then he gave a howl like a wild animal. He clutched at his hair on each side of his head, pulling some of it out. Alf and the two constables were about to come into the room. Polly waved them away. 'It's all right, Aaron. It's all right,' she soothed him. 'Let's read the book.'

She picked it up, found the place they had left off and began to read. Gradually he calmed down, laid the side of his head on his forearms on the table and became motionless. He listened to every word. As usual, Polly used different voices for the characters and Aaron was totally absorbed. It was difficult to tell if it was the story or the sound of Polly's voice that had a calming effect on him. Either way, it had to be obvious even to the watching dignitaries that her reading made a difference.

Polly felt tears come into her eyes as she read the heart-rending cruelty Oliver Twist endured. She paused and wiped the corners of her eyes with her forget-me-not handkerchief. She glanced at Aaron, who was staring blankly into the middle distance. He never showed any emotion no matter how touching or amusing the scene. Despite this, he appeared to be listening to every word.

Polly exhaled a long breath and then closed the book. Her mouth was dry. She had been reading for a long time.

'I'm going to get something to drink,' she said. 'Shall I get you something to drink, Aaron?'

Aaron did not respond. She recognised that he was in one of the incoherent states that separated him from reality, but this one had been induced by her reading, and seemed to give him some sort of peace.

She stood up and left the room as quietly as possible. Wherever Aaron's mind was, it was a more tranquil place than previously and she wanted him to hold on to that calmness.

She met Alf and Inspector Reid in the corridor and rubbed her hands across her face. 'I had to get out of there.'

'You're certainly right about the calming effect of reading to him,' said Alf.

'I'm very impressed. You are doing very well, Miss Wilkes,' said Reid.

'I didn't get anywhere, did I?'

'Some progress was made,' said Reid. 'It showed us the disturbed condition of the man's thinking.'

'That's the thing with Aaron, no matter what he says you never know if it's something real or just his faulty brain imagining it all.'

Reid pinched his chin with a thumb and forefinger. 'Do you think you could get him to tell you exactly what he means by *The one?*'

'I told you, he hears voices in his head and he thinks they are spirits of dead people telling him what to do.'

'He could be referring to himself as the killer and Mrs. Stride is *the one.*'

'He's so demented you could never know if his answers are just his ravings.'

'I understand that,' Reid said. 'If he is the killer, Miss Wilkes, we need to know. If that could be established it would be of enormous assistance'

'I understand, Inspector.' Polly glanced back towards the closed door. 'He needs a rest and something to drink - if he'll have it. He can be funny about eating and drinking; that's why he's so skinny.'

'In what sense? Does he have strange tastes?' asked Reid.

'Strange ideas more like. His voices tell him his food and drink is poisoned so he eats out of bins and gutters unless you can persuade him otherwise.'

'My goodness, the state of this man's mind is being revealed as worse and worse.'

'As I said Inspector. He's a much-tormented person; to think he's The Ripper is just preposterous. Look at him. How could he be? He doesn't have any forethought and isn't Jack the Ripper a soldier, a doctor, a sailor or a butcher? Aaron isn't any of those things and he can hardly keep two ideas in his head.'

'You would be surprised what even the most imbecilic of people have accomplished with their limited resources,' Reid replied.

He smiled at Polly. 'I can't tell you how much we value what you are doing, Miss Wilkes. You have asked the right questions without leading him towards an answer. That is not easy. You are doing incredibly well.'

'Is his brother here yet?'

'Yes. He is presently being interviewed by Chief Inspector Swanson.' Reid surveyed her face. 'You must be exhausted. Take some refreshment. You can take tea in my office.' He looked at Alf. 'Sergeant - if you would be so kind as to escort Miss Wilkes.'

Polly once again sat down in the leather wing chair in Reid's office. All the accompaniments for making tea had been placed on a tray on the desk. Again, Alf added extra sugar to the tea before handing one of the Inspector's fine china cups and saucers to Polly. She sipped the hot liquid. Never had a cup of tea tasted so good. 'Tea does taste better out of a good china cup.'

Alf sat down on an identical chair opposite to Polly. 'It's cos you're thirsty. You were almost two hours in there, reading to him.'

'Was I? I lost track of time.'

'Have you noticed that he don't seem to react to the story when he listens?' said Alf. 'I mean, there are some very sad bits in Oliver Twist and others that make a person feel angry. Yet he don't react to any of it. It makes me wonder what he gets out of it.'

'I think it takes his mind off the voices,' said Polly. 'He seems to like Dickens but I could likely read anything to him and the result would be the same.'

'These voices of his. They seem a very odd thing to me.'

'They are a very odd thing. That does *not* make him Jack the Ripper.'

'I don't know, Polly. That was a peculiar thing for him to write if it don't mean anything and I have to say, what he wrote sounds like a confession.'

'*For the one I did not do*,' said Polly. 'They sure it's been translated properly?'

'Yes. It was translated directly from my notebook by someone The Yard got in specially.'

Polly frowned. 'It's that phrase; *the one.* That's the conundrum. Knowing what he means by it.'

'I can't envisage any other interpretation than he's saying he didn't kill Mrs. Stride, but he did the others.'

'Alfie, it's quite ridiculous. He's not capable of working that out, or doing the sort of crimes The Ripper's done.'

Alf sat forward and clasped his hands together and placed his elbows on his splayed out knees. 'He is, Polly. Think on how we found Mickey Kidney. Trussed up and his throat cut from ear to ear. Then there was that time he beat him up because he attacked you. You told me he gave him a right good pasting.'

'He did and Mickey was twice his size. But that doesn't mean he's The Ripper. You wanted to give Mickey a good hiding and no one's calling you Jack the Ripper. Anyway, they said that bit of writing where Cathy's piece of apron was found was done by the killer, so how could it be Aaron? He can't write in English.'

*'The Juwes are the men that will not be blamed for nothing.'*
Alf sighed. 'I was never convinced the Ripper wrote that, Polly. And I think he cut away the bit apron to carry the body parts in. Maybe he threw them both down next to that bit of graffito because he could make out the word "Jews" even though it was spelled wrong on the wall, apparently.'

'Or maybe it was just a coincidence - it could have a different meaning, Alfie. Lots of Jewish people live around Goulston Street and they are very conscious of taking the backlash for all the problems in the east end. Immigrants take the blame for all the unemployment and driving wages down. What if a Jewish person wrote it? It could mean; *we won't take the blame for all your troubles cos we aren't responsible.* Maybe it's a protest about that and isn't about Jack at all. Someone foreign might not have got the grammar quite right.'

'There are plenty of native speakers who wouldn't get the grammar right neither,' he said. 'Yes, it's possible, Polly. As you say, Goulston Street has a lot of Jewish residents. It could also have been written to insult them or by a reporter to stir up trouble – which is highly likely in my opinion. Where there's trouble there's a story as far as they are concerned.'

'They didn't find poor Cathy's parts with the piece of apron, did they?'

'A rat, stray cat or a dog would have carried them off in no time, Polly. There are hundreds of them down there, especially around the market. Pieces of fresh meat would have attracted dozens of them.'

Polly screwed up her face.

'Sorry, Polly, but it's a fact. An animal ain't going turn down nourishment. Mrs. Eddowes's parts were missing and there's no doubt about that and that piece of apron is soaked with blood so odds on they were carried away in it.'

'Didn't they say he wiped his knife on it and that's why it was all blood stained?'

'If he wanted to wipe his knife he could have done it there and then and used any bit of the poor lady's clothing in a fraction of the time it took to cut away the apron. And, supposing he had cut it off to wipe his knife, once he'd done it, he would have dropped it straight away closer to where he killed her, not carry it all the way to Goulston Street for no apparent reason. No, he needed it to carry away the organs. Then something made him throw it away.'

'It would be a very unpleasant parcel.'

'Perhaps he heard the police whistle and knew they would be looking for him, so he ditched it. He was probably counting on her not being found so quickly. I reckon he was at Goulston Street when they first sounded the alarm.'

'According to the papers, George Lusk was supposed to have got a piece of Cathy's kidney in the post from the killer.'

Alf gave a splutter of disgust. 'Lusk is full of tripe. That was just a made up yarn cos he likes to place himself at the centre of attention. That piece of kidney was properly preserved. Nothing nastily bloody, smelly or decomposed. How convenient. I think if this maniac was to send someone a bit of kidney, it would have been in its natural decomposing state.' He gave a derisory huff. *'Preserved it for you…* the letter said. As if.'

'Wait until he finds out that a Jewish person killed his prize exhibit, Mickey Kidney,' said Polly.

'Yeah, the top brass is currently exceedingly exercised about that. George Lusk stirs up anti-Jewish feeling as it is. If this gets out, it could be his ticket to a seat on the new council. The place will go up like a blue light if the people find out about it and Lusk will do his best to make sure they do.'

Polly smiled. 'Listen to you. You get a real sparkle in your eyes when you talk like a detective, Alfie Cruikshank and you're good at it. Have you told the brass in there the thoughts you just told me?'

'No. I'm just a humble sergeant, Polly.'

'And you always will be if you stick with me.'

'Don't start all that again-'

307

The door opened and Inspector Reid, Chief Inspector Swanson and Inspector Abberline came into the room.

# CHAPTER TWENTY EIGHT

Alf stood up respectfully. Polly placed her cup on the tea tray. She sat with her back straight and her hands folded demurely in her lap, giving the three men her undivided attention.

'How are you feeling Miss Wilkes?' Reid asked.

'Better thank you, sir.' Polly replied. 'You have excellent tea here.'

'I'm sure you must have been very dry after all that reading.'

'Yes, sir, I was rather.'

'You are an excellent reader, Miss Wilkes,' said Swanson, who had never lost his lilting Scottish accent despite being away from his homeland for many years. 'You seem more highly educated than er...' he paused. 'Than I expected.'

'I had an excellent education, sir.' Polly replied as Alf's expression darkened at the implied judgement. Inspector Abberline sucked on his teeth and avoided eye contact with everyone in the room.

'Did you? Where was that?' Swanson asked.

Polly hesitated. She had not spoken in general conversation about that life for a long time. 'I went to school at *Scolaires pour le Doués Filles.*'

'*Scolaires pour le Doués Filles*? But how-' said Swanson. 'My own daughter was unable to gain admittance to that school. It's a very exclusive establishment.'

'Yes, it is, sir.'

'How did you come to be at such a school?' Swanson asked.

'My parents sent me there.'

Swanson studied her intently. 'And just how did they achieve that?'

Polly could see Alf out of the corner of her eye. His complexion had turned a shade of dark crimson. She spoke up before he said something that would ruin his career forever.

'They were well connected, sir.'

'And they subsequently fell on hard times?'

Polly again hesitated. She could see that Alf had turned from red to purple. She took a deep breath. 'Not at all. Things remain well, I believe.'

'Then how-?' Swanson looked perplexed.

Polly's cheeks turned pink. 'May I ask, how old is your daughter, Chief Inspector?'

'She's eighteen.' Swanson replied with pride.

Polly paused and made sure that she appeared calm and dignified before she spoke. 'I made a stupid mistake at the age of eighteen. I was well educated and very well to do. I was indulged by my parents and consequently, I knew nothing about the world. My head was turned by the worst kind of young man. So here I am - the low woman you take me for. You should take a good look at what's going on in those streets, Chief Inspector. The well-off folks in the west of London have no idea what it's like in the east end. Most of the women here have encountered misfortune and tragedy in some form, or made a mistake when young, like me, and they pay for it for the rest of their lives. Unfortunate women are not good time girls with flawed characters. They do what they have to do to make it through another day. They go hungry most of the time and they're desperate. Without four pence for a bed in a filthy doss house, they have to walk freezing cold streets all night. They can't sleep or the gangs and thieves will get them. There's no wonder that someone like The Ripper could do his worst in all that hardship. I was extremely fortunate when the sergeant gave me employment caring for his poor, sick mother because no one gets out of those slums except in a wooden box.'

At the edge of her vision, she could see what appeared to be an expression of admiration on Inspector Abberline's face. She looked at Alf, who gave her an almost imperceptible nod.

Swanson was staring at her. 'That was a very intelligent reply, Miss Wilkes. Forgive me, I had the impression of lowly origins.'

Polly gave him a dignified nod. 'I was a privileged and fortunate young lady like your daughter, Chief Inspector, perhaps even more so. Unfortunately, I didn't appreciate all the advantages I had, I found life dull and my head was turned.'

'My daughter's character is not so flawed that she would have her head turned by a young man's flattery.' Swanson snapped.

Behind him, Polly saw Alf start to lunge forward ready to defend her. Without looking up, Abberline lifted his arm and placed a restraining hand on Alf's chest.

Polly remained composed. 'I'm sure you are right, Chief Inspector, I meant no offence.' she smiled politely, yet somehow conveyed the message that any young girl was capable of having her head turned if the young man was determined enough.

Swanson turned away, pulled out his tobacco pouch and began to fill his pipe. Reid cleared his throat and shattered the silence that had descended on the room. He sat down at his desk.

'I think we all appreciate the assistance Miss Wilkes is providing,' he said. 'And we are grateful that she is such an accomplished reader, as this enables her to reach a person who's mind is in such turmoil that it may have driven him to murder.'

'You still think he's The Ripper, sir?' Polly asked.

Reid paused. 'As you say, Miss Wilkes, he is in no fit state to be questioned by normal means but his attachment to you might help shed further light on this dreadful business even if we cannot get a direct answer out of him. You see, it has always perplexed us that there were extended and apparently random time periods between the murders. Extensive investigations have revealed nothing that would account for this, such as the arrival of a particular ship, or team of workers or even a known reprobate going in and out of jail.' He leaned forward and laced his fingers together before resting them on the blotter on his desk. 'It would help us if you could recall some specific times when Kosminski found you.'

'KOSMINSKI?' Alf bellowed. 'His name is Kosminski?' He checked himself. 'Sorry, sir.'

'Yes,' said Reid. 'The family at Greenfield Street are called Lubnowski, the other at Sion Square are called Abrahams. The suspect we have in custody is, according to his brother-in-law, is Aaron Kosminski.'

'Flaming buckets of blood.' Alf muttered. 'That ought to have been picked up.' He looked at Abberline. 'Sir, Aaron Kosminski's name has cropped up time and time again in the reports from door to door enquiries. He's been under suspicion.' He looked at Polly. 'Why didn't you tell me he was called Kosminski?'

'Because I thought he was called Lubnowski.' Polly shrugged. 'Oh... Matilda and Betsy must be his sisters.'

'*Oh*? Is that all you've got to say? Don't you know he's a dangerous lunatic?'

'Who saved my life twice,' Polly replied.

Alf began to pace the floor as if he did not know where to put himself. 'Of all the things,' he muttered. 'Of all the things on God's good earth.' He looked up at Abberline in exasperation. 'She's been leading Jack the Ripper by the hand and reading him bedtime stories.' He raked his fingers through his hair and looked as if he was tempted to tear some out.

Polly gave him a sharp look. 'Well if I have, it doesn't say much for your surveillance methods, does it?' She thought Abberline was about to laugh but instead he cleared his throat.

'Is it possible that on the occasions that Kosminski found Miss Wilkes, he was out looking for a victim to kill?'

'Could it really be that simple?' said Reid. 'After all the speculation about the spacing between the murders, all the investigations and thousands of interviews, the strange timeline is due to the fact that a young woman has been leading him home?' said Reid.

'He always had the book with him, he sought me out for that purpose. He wasn't looking for a victim.'

'This is only speculation, Miss Wilkes,' said Abberline. 'However, it is a possibility.'

'Excuse me, sirs? Where is the proof that he's The Ripper? Aaron's never threatened me in any way. The only time he showed any signs of a temper was when he saw Mickey Kidney hurting me.' Polly told them. 'And how was it you got his name? The family would never turn him in.'

'Sergeant?' Reid referred the question to Alf.

'I believe his name was given to us by a neighbour in Sion Square.'

'I think Aaron is a handful, sir. The Abrahams live at Sion Square. They are very kind people.' Polly answered. 'Mr. and Mrs. Abrahams have a young daughter. Mr. and Mrs. Lubnowski have four young children and Mrs. Lubnowski is in the family way.'

'What were the grounds for the neighbour's suspicions?' Abberline asked Alf.

'I believe they heard him screaming and shouting and just thought him strange, sir.' Alf replied.

'So Aaron hasn't actually done anything?' Polly cut in. 'Someone just said they didn't like the look of him? Well, that's not exactly detective work, is it? It could have been done for malice, or fear of him being different. I mean he is odd, there's no doubt about that. It doesn't make him a killer.'

'He ripped a man's throat out,' said Alf.

'To defend me.' Polly retorted.

The three men senior men did not comment.

'Did you learn anything from the brother, sir?' Reid asked Chief Inspector Swanson.

'The informant is a brother-in-law, Mosiek or Morris Lubnowski who as Miss Wilkes said, is married to his sister, Matilda. They live at 16 Greenfield Street. Mr. Lubnowski was proud to tell me that he was granted citizenship on the 2nd of October and is now a British subject. According to Mr. Lubnowski, the family shares the responsibility for Kosminski, who is a considerable burden. As a result, he sometimes resides with the other sister and brother-in-law at 3 Sion Square.'

'That could be why when I took him home to Greenfield Street it was all locked up and I had to get them out of bed.' Polly told them. 'I thought they didn't care a fig that he was out roaming the streets and I was quite brusque with them. It seems it could have been because they didn't have custody of him at the time.'

'Mr. Lubnowski claims that the family has had no reason to suspect that he would hurt anyone,' said Swanson. 'He does not have access to knives-'

'Except the one he cut Kidney's throat with, sir.' Alf muttered.

'They have noticed no blood on him other than from the injuries he often causes himself. He apparently deliberately injures himself on a regular basis. They say he is often out and about. He likes to walk around the locality and seems to gain some recreation from it. They say he always returns within an hour or two and does not seem agitated in any way. I think his relatives are at the end of their tether with him,' said Swanson. 'I think they can only cope with him by sharing the responsibility. And, if he's living between two houses, they might not be seeing the full picture.'

'As I said, they are very nice people and I am sure you are right, sir,' said Polly. 'It must be very hard to cope with someone like Aaron day and night. I was suspicious that they hoped he would be picked up by the police and put away for a while. Looks like they got their wish.'

'Miss Wilkes, are you sufficiently rested? Are you prepared to try again with him?' said Reid.

'I believe so.'

'Good, remember all we want is to get a brief coherent answer to the question of who or what is *the one*.'

'I'll do what I can, sir.'

Polly returned to the interview room accompanied by Alf, who stood by the door. Aaron had been offered some tea and a piece of bread; it was untouched on the table. Polly sat down in the chair opposite him.

'Hello, Aaron,' she said scrutinising his pale, tired face. She could see he was exhausted. His eyes were sunk deep into their sockets and surrounded by the darkest of dark circles. His arms were still folded across his chest as though he was hugging himself. Polly was glad that he was calm and had not started rocking himself back and forth, which for Aaron, indicated extreme distress. How could they think this pitiful soul was the fiend who had murdered those women?

'Oh, Aaron. This is a pickle all right,' she sighed. 'Listen to me, this isn't about Mickey. It's about what you wrote on that pile of wood. Those words in your own language. *For the one I did not do.* The police officers, they just want to know why you wrote those words. Can you remember why you wrote it, Aaron?'

She looked at his shabby, dejected shape slumped in the chair and still soaked in Mickey Kidney's blood. 'If you can remember, please tell Polly, then we can all go home. Your brother-in-law is here.'

There was no response.

'He's exhausted,' she said to Alf. 'This is harder for him than for other people. Can't he at least get cleaned up and put some fresh clothes on?'

Alf stepped forward and looked at Aaron. He looked at the burgundy blood stains that covered the arms and front of his jacket. There was so much blood that the original brown colour of the wool could only be seen on the upper part of the arms. 'The family are claiming that he ain't never come home like this before. In a pig's eye, he ain't.' he growled. Then his expression changed. His eyes widened and his brows lifted. 'Polly, step aside,' he said. His voice was calm but the tone was granite hard.

'What's the matter?'

'I said step aside. Get away from him,' he repeated in the same tone. Alf was like a bloodhound, completely fixated on the trail. He beckoned the two constables who were outside the door to come into the room. They complied instantly as Polly stood up and moved to the side of the room, near the door.

'Remove his jacket.' Alf ordered.

The two young officers snapped to the order, well used to manhandling those in their custody.

Aaron did not react to being hauled to his feet, nor his jacket being pulled from his shoulders. His eyes were blank and gazing into the middle distance as before. Whatever he was looking at was not in this reality, and he was completely distracted by whatever he saw in his mind. They stripped the jacket from him as though he was a mannequin.

'Holy mother of God,' said one of the constables. 'Sarge, look at his shirt.'

As the constable stepped aside Polly could see that Aaron's shirt was covered in blood. She lifted her hands to her mouth. Alf stepped forward and looked at the stains that had soaked into most of the formerly white shirt. The two constables kept hold of Aaron by his arms. He showed no sign of resisting them.

'I think his strides are soaked as well, you just can't see it, them being black,' said the constable.

Polly lifted her hands to her mouth. 'Is he hurt? Has Mickey stabbed him?'

'Some of this blood is dry, it's gone brown,' said Alf. 'And they ain't the sort of stains you get from a stab wound.' He looked at the constable who was holding the jacket. 'Get his trousers off.' He turned towards the door and pressed his hand to Polly's back. 'Come on, Polly. Out.'

'Is he hurt?' Polly demanded.

'No. That blood ain't oozing from a wound. Those stains are completely dry, while Kidney's blood is still wet. That blood ain't his and it ain't Kidney's.'

Polly looked at Alf. He had become the resolute and determined policeman. His face was carved from stone. He looked at the constable who held the jacket. 'Get Inspector Abberline. I would put money on that being Mary Jane Kelly's blood,' he said as he hustled Polly from the room.

# CHAPTER TWENTY NINE

'Alfie, what d'you mean? What's the matter? He hasn't done anything.'

'He's covered in blood, Polly. Blood he got on him at different times.'

Abberline came striding towards them. He had been watching through the grille and seen Alf's reaction. 'Sergeant?'

'He's covered in blood from head to toe, sir. It ain't his, and pound to a penny it ain't Michael Kidney's neither.'

'How did you come to that conclusion?'

'Some of it, the most of it, in fact, is completely dry and gone brown, sir. It's been there a lot longer than Kidney's blood which is still damp and crimson red. He got covered with an awful lot of it, way before he came across Michael Kidney. And we know what happened this time yesterday.'

One of the constables inside the room where Aaron was being held, opened the door.

'Sarge? His under garment is soaked as well. It's got more blood on it than the shirt.'

'Right lad. Strip him off and get him into prisoner's togs. Bring his clothes to Inspector Reid's office and spread them out on the table.'

'Sarge? Is he The Ripper d'you think?'

'Don't try to think Robinson, it'll give you a headache.'

'Right, Sarge,' said Robinson as he closed the door.

Alf turned back to Abberline. 'He's The Ripper alright.' he said on a low growl. 'I can feel it in my bones.'

'Copper's instincts? I have the same feeling about him, Alf.' Abberline murmured. It was the first time Abberline had called him by his first name and it filled Alf with pride. 'These blood stains would be the first piece of concrete evidence but we need to more… What does he do for a living? Is it possible that he's a butcher? There's no way to tell the difference between human and animal blood.'

Alf looked at Polly for an answer.

'No, sir. He doesn't work.' Polly said quietly. 'They are a family of tailors and shoemakers, I can't see how he would be a butcher.' She looked up at Alf. 'Alfie, are you sure it's blood? Could it be ink or something?'

Abberline saw Alf's expression darken. 'Let's continue the discussion in here,' he said, opening the door to Reid's office which was directly opposite the interview room. ''Constable?' he called to the lad at the end of the corridor. 'Give Inspector Reid and Chief Inspector Swanson my compliments and ask them if they would be so kind as to come here at their earliest convenience.'

They moved into Reid's office. As soon as the door closed, Alf turned to Polly.

'How many times are you going to defend him? If you had seen what he done to those women- He's a monster.'

'The killer is a monster,' said Polly. 'You keep talking to me about evidence. Where's the evidence against Aaron?'

'I understand, Miss Wilkes,' Abberline cut in as Alf looked at her in sheer disbelief. 'And you're correct, we must have compelling evidence. However, we can also speculate on the chain of events in order to know where to look for it. Alf's analysis of the blood stains is quite compelling.'

Alf looked at Polly. 'He's soaked in the blood of two people,' he replied. 'There are layers of blood stains on top of other blood stains on his shirt. What more d'you want?'

The conversation paused as the Constable Robinson came into the room and laid out Aaron's clothes on the conference table.

'Chief Inspector Swanson and Inspector Reid will be here directly, sir,' he said, looking at Alf.

'Thank you, Robinson,' Alf replied. A lowly constable never spoke directly to a senior person such as Abberline unless spoken to first.

When the door closed, Polly jumped straight back into the conversation. 'What more do I want?' she glared at Alf. 'I want to see more than someone who's got blood on them before you accuse them of being a monstrous fiend.'

'Very well,' said Abberline in a calm voice as Alf looked on, exasperated at her refusal to accept Aaron's guilt. 'Why don't we ponder on that for a while? How else might he get so much blood on him?'

Polly thought for a moment. 'He's Jewish. Some people are horrible to Jews around here and the newspapers are making everybody think The Ripper is a Jew. There are also a lot of slaughterhouses. Someone might have thrown blood on him because he's Jewish and they knew the blood touching him would be a terrible religious insult to him.'

'A racially motivated crime? Yes, it's possible that the blood could have been thrown on him maliciously. We can test that idea by replicating the circumstances. We can get some blood from a slaughterhouse and see what pattern it makes when thrown at a mannequin wearing the same garments. I suspect the pattern might be different to what we see here as the sergeant has pointed out there are layers of stains. Nevertheless, a good detective always checks the evidence to rule things in, or rule things out. Perhaps you would care to conduct that test at Scotland Yard with me, Sergeant?'

'Yes, sir. I would.' Alf's eyes lit up.

'Excellent. That's what good detection is all about,'

Alf looked as if he would burst. This was the kind of meticulous police work he loved and wanted to learn more about.

'At the same time, we also need to investigate any other clues or pieces of evidence that might link Aaron Kosminski to the murders,' said Abberline. 'The only hard evidence we have is the piece of Catherine Eddowes's apron that was found in Goulston Street. We need to find out if there is anything to connect Kosminski to Goulston Street or its surroundings. It will involve a lot of time, checking house occupancies using the census documents and reports from the door to door enquiries. Then there was the graffito written on the wall where the apron was found. "The *Juwes* are the men that will not be blamed for nothing". Can we make a connection with that?'

'Do you think the murderer wrote that, Inspector?' Polly asked.

'Unfortunately, I don't know. Under the orders of Commissioner Warren, it was erased before it could be photographed.'

'Why would the killer stop and write something on a wall when he is carrying body parts and the police are all over the place looking for him?'

'That's a valid point, Miss Wilkes, and because it was erased without a photographic record, we will never know. We can't compare the handwriting, the spelling, or even the use of language with that of a suspect. Therefore we can't rule it in or rule it out. We will never know whether it was a vital piece of evidence or nothing of significance. It might have helped us close in on the killer or it might not.'

'If you knew it was the killer who wrote it,' said Polly, 'it would rule Aaron out, he can't read or write in English, only speak it.'

'That's exactly my point. Even if an eye witness comes forward and says I saw that man write those words. It's no good because the evidence was destroyed.'

'I see,' said Polly.

'What we really need is an eye witness,' Abberline continued. 'The Sergeant and I attended the inquest of Catherine Eddowes as you know. We discovered that there were three witnesses who saw a man with the victim at the entrance to Church Passage fifteen minutes before she was found dead. Can those men pick Kosminski out in a line and positively identify him? It's like putting the pieces of a puzzle together, Miss Wilkes. All the little pieces add up to make the whole picture. We can't prove he's guilty just because he has blood on him but the blood must be explained. We need to take a good look at him and look for further evidence.'

Swanson and Reid came into the room.

'Share your observations with the gentlemen if you please, Sergeant,' said Abberline taking out his pipe and a tobacco pouch from an inside pocket of his jacket. The request sounded casual but it was a huge compliment to Alf.

The senior officers listened to Alf's description of the blood stains and his opinion on how they got on Aaron's clothing. Swanson and Reid stepped up to the conference table.

'Sergeant Cruikshank is correct.' Abberline pointed with his pipe towards Aaron's one piece undergarment and then his shirt. 'The blood stains here are older than these ones.'

'Could this also be Kidney's blood? Perhaps it dried more quickly because of the heat from his body?' Reid asked.

Abberline shook his head. 'I doubt it. We will check of course, by carrying out tests. There are some fresher stains that have bled through the shirt. You can see how the stains match up. They are beginning to dry… here and here.' He stabbed his index finger towards the waist area of the undergarment. His trousers and lower torso are covered in dried blood as are the legs of his undergarment. If he got all the blood on him at once, one would have expected the stains on the chest to dry before these stains, due to the heat of his body - as you can see, they haven't. The conclusion is, some of the stains on the chest are not as old as the others.'

'Also, sirs,' said Alf. 'Kidney's throat was cut deep. I could see that the vessels on both sides were severed. Blood drained out of him like a pig hung in a slaughterhouse. Most of it went into the cement and some of it made a bit of stream that fell through the gaps in the deck into the river. I don't think Kosminski wouldn't have got all that much on him. And there's another thing, Kidney's throat wound had similarities to Mrs. Nichols and Mrs. Chapman.'

'Though not Mrs. Stride and Mrs. Eddowes?' asked Swanson.

'No, sir, they were different. Mrs. Stride's injuries,' he glanced at Polly, 'weren't nearly so deep and she bled out slowly. Mrs. Eddowes was only cut deep on the left side.'

'It's unfortunate that we can't recover the body so we can compare the wounds,' said Swanson.

'Is there no chance of that, sir?' Alf asked.

'None at all,' said Swanson. 'There are 12 caissons in each pier. Even if you know for certain which caisson he fell into, he's 30 feet down at the bottom of a column of concrete. With the cost of that bridge, there is no possibility that the Home Secretary would order a pier to be destroyed to retrieve a body. The body will be there as long at the bridge stands. You and Miss Wilkes are the only witnesses there will ever be.'

'So, Sergeant, you're not convinced that all the blood on this shirt is from Kidney?' said Reid.

'That's right, sir. I think Kosminski got the blood on his shirt because he weren't wearing his jacket on account of being indoors,' he said. 'The fireplace in Mary Kelly's room had evidence of a blazing fire in the grate. From the amount of ash, it had a week's supply of coal put on it all at once. It must have been blazing away all night - being that the kettle had boiled away until there was a hole in it. I think it must have been stifling hot in that room.'

'It's enough to suspect him of the Kelly murder,' said Reid.

'He might even have stood by the fire and dried himself on purpose before he left her, sir. Otherwise, we might have had a blood trail to follow from Miller's Court. He would have been dripping with it.'

'Looking at how much blood is on this clothing, I agree, Sergeant,' said Abberline, looking at the garments on the table.

'Right gentlemen...*and lady.*' Reid nodded at Polly. 'Do we have The Ripper in custody or not?'

---

'I think we have several leads to investigate,' said Abberline. 'But I'd say he's looking juicy at the moment.'

'I agree,' said Swanson.

'I'm convinced of it,' said Alf.

'Good work, Sergeant,' said Reid. 'You may be the man who caught The Ripper.'

'To be fair, sir, I didn't know that when I brought him in. It weren't until I saw the blood stains that I fitted it together.'

'No need to be modest. That was a good piece of observation and it helped to draw attention to crucial elements. You have a good eye for detail.' He turned to Polly. 'Miss Wilkes. I think your role in this is also crucial. I believe that when Kosminski came looking for you and when you read to him, you calmed the beast within.'

Polly looked at him. 'He's not a monster, sir. He's just a poor, sad man tormented by voices.'

'The fact is, Miss Wilkes. I believe that by reading to him or leading him to his home you probably prevented further murders. This could explain the timing between the murders. Three weeks between the second and third victims and five weeks between the fourth and last victim.'

Polly stared at him, her face pale. 'But Jack the Ripper wrote to the papers, that's how we know his name. Aaron can't write English.'

'That letter was a fake. The fact that it was addressed to the central news office rather than a named newspaper convinced me that it was written by one of their journalists. Scotland Yard has received hundreds of letters supposedly from the killer, Miss Wilkes. The odd timescale of the murders however, has always puzzled us.'

'Are you saying when he didn't find me he went on a rampage and killed someone?'

'I don't know, but it *is* a possibility,' said Abberline gently. 'Can you think of specific dates and instances when you encountered Kosminski? Was it before the murder of Mary Ann Nichols or after?'

'It was definitely after. In fact, it was a day or two after we heard about poor Annie that I looked after him for a whole day and found out he liked to be read to. His family went to a wedding.'

'There were only seven days between the murders of Polly Nichols and Annie Chapman. After that, there were longer periods between the murders. We knew there would be a reason for that and the reason, it seems, could be you.'

Reid sat forward. 'This is truly a strange development. This young woman, by befriending him, reading to him and leading him home at night, may have prevented further murders and even more bizarre, in return, this monstrous killer saved her life.'

'What happens now, Inspector? Do we announce to the press that we have him in custody?' asked Alf.

'That's out of the question.' Swanson answered. 'If one word got out that the Whitechapel killer is a Jew, the place would go up like a fire in a firework factory.'

'The wretch appears to be completely insane. I doubt he could ever be brought before a court,' said Reid.

'Absolutely. He cannot be properly questioned nor defend himself,' said Swanson.

There was a long pause as the assembled company pondered the situation.

'So gentlemen; what do we do?' Abberline asked.

'The most important thing is that we have him. The murders will stop. Eventually, things will settle down,' said Swanson.

Abberline shook his head. 'We don't have him. We can't even charge him for the murder of Michael Kidney. The body is at the bottom the Thames under concrete, therefore we can't produce it. And if word gets out that an Irishman was killed by a Jew…' he left the sentence hanging and sucked in air through his teeth.

'Agreed,' said Reid. 'Then if we also disclose that he's The Ripper but he isn't going to face a trial,' he shook his head gravely, knowing that the others got the picture. There was another pause in the discussion.

'It's an extremely delicate situation,' said Abberline, eventually breaking the silence. '*The Met.* doesn't have the manpower to deal with the anarchy that would be the inevitable result if any of this got out. The east end would be laid waste and it would not stop there. The whole country, let alone the whole of London, feels this case very personally.'

'Therefore none of it must ever get out,' Swanson's voice cut in loud and firm. All turned to look at him.

'I agree. In the meantime, what should be done with Kosminski?' Abberline asked.

'We will obtain an assessment of his mental state in the workhouse infirmary,' said Reid. 'He can be sent directly from here. They can accommodate him securely at Stepney. Since admittance to the workhouse is voluntary, we will put extreme pressure on the family to comply.'

'I want him watched day and night,' said Chief Inspector Swanson, 'and in the meantime, we will carry on gathering evidence. At the Eddowes inquest, there were witnesses who saw the victim with a man in Church Passage, minutes before she was murdered. I want to know if they can pick Kosminski out of a line of men. We must have some definite eye witness accounts that link him to that murder. In fact, I want to know if he has any connection to any of the areas where the victims were found.' The senior officers murmured in agreement and Swanson left the room.

'The early shift is about to come on. I'll brief the men, sir,' said Alf.

'Thank you, Sergeant,' said Reid. 'Please let me know when they are assembled in the briefing room. There are a few matters I want to make very clear to all ranks. I also want to have a word with the detectives on the case and bring them up to date.'

'I need to get back home and check on your mother,' said Polly to Alf. 'She's going to want her breakfast in an hour or so and she'll need attending to.'

'There is no need to for us to detain you here, Miss Wilkes if you must go and attend to your duties,' said Abberline.

'Will you be all right walking back on your own?' Alf asked her.

'Me?' Polly looked at him. 'I'll be fine. The man who wanted to kill me is dead, and according to you, I'm the best pal of Jack the Ripper.'

Abberline chuckled as she left the room. 'You've got your hands full with that one, Alf.'

# CHAPTER THIRTY

Polly moved through the rear door of the station and down the wooden steps into the yard. The Black Maria that had delivered Aaron to Leman Street stood next to the door that led to the cells in the basement of the station. The two horses that pulled the heavy waggon had been unhitched and taken away to the stables on the far side of the yard.

A young boy was hard at work mucking out the stalls. Another was brushing down Jasper, the beautiful black gelding that pulled the Maria with his brother, Flint.

Polly crossed the yard, this time she did not stop to pet the horses. She headed straight for the pedestrian gate to the right of the stable block.

The boy mucking out the stalls looked up and tipped his hat to her. Polly was unaccustomed to receiving this small gesture of respect. Had she still looked like a whore, this lad, without a second thought, would have harangued her and shouted insults. Alf had been right when he said clothes made the difference. Alf was right about most things, she thought as she stepped through the gate into East Tenter Street. The gate faced the back of St. Mark's Church. It was Sunday morning. Lights shone through the stained glass window behind the altar and she could hear a hymn being sung.

This was the church where she and Alf would wed one day. A swarm of butterflies fluttered excitedly in her stomach and her spirit soared. Polly looked at the cross that was fixed to the wall of the church. She read the inscription beneath it: *The Lord moves in mysterious ways. His wonders to perform.*

They got that right, Polly thought. Without all the things that had happened to her over the last few years, she might never have met Alf, whom she knew with complete certainty was the love of her life.

She stood respectfully facing the cross and lifted her eyes skyward. 'I'm grateful that Aaron saved my life - again. But, it's got him in a whole lot of trouble... If you could see your way clear to helping him? I mean, you were one of his kind so I'm hoping it isn't against the rules or anything.' She began to turn away and then stopped. 'And, if he is Jack the Ripper, well, You really *do* move in mysterious ways...' She mulled this over as she walked the few yards that brought her to the corner of Scarborough Street.

Polly was in anguish to think of Aaron locked in that cell. This was the thanks he got for saving her life? She knew the voices would be screaming at him and he would be in terrible distress. He needed a safe place to stay, not a jail cell. He needed to be distracted from the terrible torments that made him the way he was. He needed to be looked after. Half the time he was in his own world, detached and pitiful, clinging to reality by asking her to read to him.

She had to admit the blood on his clothing could not be easily explained. Was it enough to accuse him of being a crazed killer? Aaron got up to all sorts of things looking for scraps of food in bins. Perhaps he happened to open the wrong bin behind a butcher's shop and got covered in blood?

She felt responsible for his predicament. It was his attachment to her that had landed him in this mess. He had killed Mickey in a rage because he was hurting her. He had flown into a passion because he saw what Mickey intended to do to her. It made her heart ache to think of the trouble it had caused him.

Abberline said it would take a long time to sift through all the evidence and rule Aaron out. She knew if Aaron had to stay in the cells all that time, he would become a shattered wreck. Even at Stepney workhouse infirmary he would be under lock and key.

Polly liked Abberline and knew he would be fair. He was down to earth, an ordinary working class copper who had climbed the ranks of the Metropolitan Police. Even Suzette, who was scathing of all policemen, said he was a good man. Even though he would treat Aaron equitably, he couldn't make the investigation go any faster.

Mrs. Cruikshank was still asleep when Polly peeped into her room. A narrow gap in the curtains allowed the weak winter sun to play across the older lady's face and particles of dust danced in the beams of light. She must get down to some damp dusting today. So much had happened in the last 48 hours, she had not yet had the time to do any of the weekly chores.

She watched Mrs. Cruikshank for a moment and could see why she took the laudanum. Under its abominable influence, she could sleep, oblivious to all her cares and grief. Her face was relaxed, her breathing was gentle and steady.

Polly knew they had to convince her not to sleep her life away and that she had something to live for in this world. Alf was not yet thirty and if he was her oldest child, Temperance Cruikshank might not yet be fifty. Her majesty, Queen Victoria, had celebrated fifty years on the throne last year, making her 69 years old and as fit as a fiddle, it was said.

Polly folded her arms as she looked at the sleeping woman.

*Well, M'lady,* she thought, *if you're going to be my mother-in-law, this will be sorted out and you are going to start living again.*

Polly prepared a breakfast of bacon, eggs, sausages and fried bread. Her patient's appetite always surprised her - it was very hearty for one who claimed to be so frail.

She helped Mrs. Cruikshank to wash and put on a clean nightdress then, as usual, she asked for her laudanum. Polly measured out the seductive elixir. This was not the time to begin cutting her free of its foul coils. When the Jack the Ripper excitement had died down, she would have an honest talk with Alf and, perhaps together, they could wean Temperance Cruikshank off the life-robbing brew.

Polly cleared away the breakfast things and then put the dirty laundry in the tub to soak. She sprinkled soda crystals into the cold water and stirred the laundry around with a wooden poss-stick. She swirled the water idly, her mind preoccupied with thoughts of Aaron. It gave her a physical pain to think of him in that cell.

His life was miserable and the prison of his own mind was a terrible place. Now he was locked up, it would be so much worse for him. She thought of the times she had found him wandering the streets and wondered what kind of torture his demons must be inflicting upon him, to drive him to eat out of the gutter and from bins filled with filth. He must be hungry all of the time and driven by desperation to eat in such a way.

She thought about the scratches on Aaron's body and the other injuries he had inflicted on himself. The voices must truly be torture if they drove him to harm himself as a means of relief.

She remembered the bad scratch across his neck and chest she had seen the day she looked after him; it had started to fester. He must have clawed at himself in a very determined way to gouge himself like that.

She thought about Aaron's family. Mrs. Lubnowski's baby must be due soon. A woman about to give birth and Aaron in the house? That was not a good idea.

The Lubnowskis had very young children who would have to be kept well away from their unpredictable uncle. The children were afraid of him, she had seen it in their faces the day she had looked after him. The couple also had a young daughter; they would not want Aaron around her either. Perhaps her instincts were right and both families threw him out of the house when his carryings-on became too much, and yet they seemed very caring people. She wondered what they did with him when he was at his worst.

Being locked in that dungeon of a room at Greenfield Street would make anyone crazy. She thought about the flesh he pulled from the back of his hand and the fingernails he tore from their nail beds. She had seen where he had tried to tear at his own flesh the day she bathed him. It was a gouge - the type of injury caused by fingernails. As a former whore, she knew how to inflict them.

She stopped what she was doing. Aaron's own fingernails were bitten down so badly she had seen them bleed. He couldn't possibly inflict such an injury on himself. Perhaps he had used a knife, a nail or piece of glass? Not likely, it definitely had the gouged appearance of fingernails.

The family insisted he inflicted such injuries on himself. She stood still as she thought about it. Had they lied? Damn right they had. Aaron did not inflict those injuries on himself and the family knew it.

She dropped the stick into the tub. Too many things did not add up and without even thinking to check on Mrs. Cruikshank, Polly put on her bonnet and cloak and headed for sixteen Greenfield Street.

Polly knocked on the door of Aaron's sister Betsy's house.

'Good morning, Mrs. Abrahams' Polly gave the other woman a smile. 'Might I have a word with you, please? It's about your brother, Aaron.'

Betsy Abrahams stood aside. She was shown into the room where all those weeks ago, Betsy Abrahams had given her some coffee and pastries when she was cold and hungry. When she entered the room, Polly saw Matilda Lubnowski sitting on one of the chairs by the fire. She was at least eight months pregnant in Polly's estimation.

'Have you news of Aaron? Our men were summoned to the police station many hours ago,' said Matilda. 'We have had no word since.'

'Aaron is still in custody, I'm afraid,' said Polly, 'I know you must be worried sick and how awful it is for him. I promise you, my employer will make sure he is well treated.'

'Please, sit down.' Betsy Abrahams invited Polly to sit on an attractive scroll armed couch beside the window.

'Thank you.' Polly sat down and looked at the two women. 'Mrs. Abrahams, Mrs. Lubnowski, you should know that Aaron has saved my life twice and I'm forever in his debt. I will do what I can to help him.'

'Why is he at the station? Why have they locked him up?' Betsy Abrahams asked.

Polly heaved a sigh. 'This is very difficult,' she said. 'Remember the last time I brought Aaron home, Mrs. Lubnowski, I told you he had stopped a man from attacking me?'

Matilda nodded. 'Yes, you said it was down by the docks.'

'That's right. The same man attacked me again and meant to drop me into the foundations of the new bridge down by the Tower.'

Betsy Abrahams's brow creased. 'Why is this man after you and all the time trying to kill you?'

'He killed my friend and he knew, that I knew he did it.' said Polly. 'Lucky for me, Aaron came along, saved me and… the man is the one who is dead and in the cement.'

'What a horrible way to die.' Matilda looked horrified.

'Oh, no, he was already dead when he went into the cement. Though make no mistake he would have put me in there alive if Aaron had not intervened.' Polly shuddered. 'I'm afraid that's part of the problem. Aaron…' Polly took a deep breath. 'Aaron cut his throat and strung him up on the bridge. After a while his body fell into the cement,' said Polly. 'Mickey Kidney, that's the man's name, had me good and proper, if it hadn't been for Aaron, I would definitely have been a goner. Aaron knocked him out and that gave me a chance to get away. I thought something had fallen off the bridge and lumped Mickey on the head. I didn't know Aaron was there, if I had I would have made him come away once Mickey was unconscious. When I got back with Alfie - that's my employer, it was quite a shock to see what had happened and we found Aaron in quite a state.'

Besty Abrahams turned pale. 'Aaron saw this many times in our homeland, it was commonplace for a corpse to be displayed in that way. It was used as a warning to others.'

'You ought to tell that to the police. I already made sure they know he saved my life and he's not responsible for his actions on account that he's seen a lot of bad things,' said Polly. 'I don't want to distress you ladies, especially in your delicate condition, Mrs. Lubnowski, but perhaps you could tell me why he would write *For the one I did not do* over and over again?'

Both women looked shocked but offered no explanation.

'You see, the police say he used excessive force and he didn't have to do all that to Mickey for me to escape. I thought, if there was a reason why he said what he said, and did what he did... If there was something that explained his actions, it might help him...'

Polly looked at the two women, neither of whom replied. 'Look, I'm afraid there's no nice way to say this. The day I looked after him, I noticed that Aaron had a lot of scars on his body. He had three parallel scratches on his chest. One was a nasty gouge that had gone septic. He also had some other wounds that had already healed.'

'We have told you, he hurts himself all the time-' said Betsy Abrahams.

'The one I'm referring to, was caused by fingernails,' said Polly. 'Aaron couldn't have done it himself, his are picked and bitten away to nothing. It's like someone clawed at him. I wondered if they could be explained somehow. A dog or cat wouldn't have done them, they were too far apart and too long.'

'I'm sorry, we have not seen the injuries you talk of, though it is possible that someone attacked him,' said Betsy.

'They aren't cuts or bruises that could be easily explained away by an attack. I'm talking about a long gouge. I was wondering... Maybe if someone lost their temper with him or had to defend themselves against him during one of his paroxysms...?' she shrugged, looking pointedly at the two women.

The two sisters looked at her blankly. Polly pressed her lips together. 'I'm sorry,' she said with a sigh, 'I'm afraid things have got worse. When they took a good look at Aaron at the station, he was covered in all colours of blood, I mean *really* covered in it, so much so that they said it could not all belong to Mickey Kidney,' she paused. 'Look... there's no easy way to say this. They think he's Jack the Ripper.'

Both women gasped and covered their mouths with their cupped hands as they stared at Polly. 'I told them it was ridiculous.' said Polly. 'He's just a poor tortured man... however, the police insist the blood can't easily be explained away. And the injuries on him are hard to explain. When the police see them, you know what they're going to think.' She saw the two woman, exchange glances.

'Miss Wilkes,' said Betsy, 'we really don't want to talk about this. My sister is in a delicate condition, if you wouldn't mind-'

Polly straightened her spine. 'Look, there's no point in telling me to leave, Mrs. Abrahams. This is very serious, and I truly want to help Aaron. You need to understand, all this is going to come down on your heads one way or another.'

'We don't know anything.' Matilda shrugged. 'In Jewish households, the men are in charge. The women are not consulted. Everything is considered men's business.'

'It's the same the world over,' said Polly, 'but you both have eyes in your heads, don't you?' The two sisters did not speak. 'This killer did terrible things to the women he killed. He must have got blood on him, especially his hands and sleeves of his shirt and jacket. You must know if Aaron ever came home like that.'

'Aaron cuts himself, he often has blood on him,' said Matilda.

'Yes, only this would be *a lot* of blood,' Polly emphasised the words. 'And, what about the injuries? I was told he did them to himself, I can tell you, the police are going to look at them and call them wounds of defence.' The two women looked blank. 'It means they'll think they were done by someone trying to fend him off.' Polly explained. 'Unless you can provide a plausible reason for them?'

They did not answer. Polly sighed. 'I care what happens to Aaron just like you. Woman to woman. We all know how…well, how difficult Aaron's behaviour can be and what he gets up to.' They both looked horror struck. 'I'm sorry to be blunt. Aaron is difficult, there's no way of getting away from the fact. I mean, in Aaron's version of reality, touching himself distracts the voices and that's as good a reason as I've ever heard,' she paused. 'The point is, you both have young children and you are in the family way Mrs. Lubnowski. Brother or not, Aaron is not someone either of you would want around the house with your present circumstances, is he?' She looked at each of them; neither of the women met her eyes. 'I brought him back twice to your house, Mrs. Lubnowski, and each time the household was asleep. To be honest, I was rather upset at the time. It looked like you didn't care about him and he was getting neglected. Then I got to thinking about that room you had him in, when I first met him, I couldn't find any clothes there. I had to put him in clothes I found in your clean laundry bundle. At the time I thought they might not be his since they were far too big and hanging off him.' She looked steadily from one woman to the other. 'He doesn't live with you does he, Mrs. Lubnowski? He was there because you had a suitable basement. Was it rigged up temporary for the wedding? If I hadn't come along, did you plan to lock him in there for the day? Your neighbours complained about him didn't they Mrs. Abrahams and the police have been to see you? So, I would be surprised if he lives with you.'

Matilda Lubnowski pressed her lips together as Polly turned to Betsy Abrahams. 'It looks like you're hiding something, to be honest, and if I can work that out so will the police.' The woman did not reply. 'You might as well tell me. You'll do better in the long run. They don't like it if you waste their time finding things out that you could have told them. The police are going to ask, and they will probably search both your homes if you don't co-operate. Are you hiding something because it might inadvertently incriminate Aaron?'

'You don't know how difficult it is, he is so wild and so crazy. If you say one tiny wrong thing to him he can go berserk,' said Matilda.

'You're right, I don't know what it's like, but I can imagine. What I saw him do to Mickey Kidney down Dock Street was… startling. It was like he went into a blood lust. It would be intolerable to have that going on with someone living with you and your children. Like living with a barrel of gunpowder. Never mind his other "bad habits".' Polly fixed them with a stare. 'So, please tell me: How did he hurt himself? We need to have some answers ready when the police ask. Who does Aaron live with and why have you been cagey about it?'

# CHAPTER THIRTY ONE

'Where's Alf Cruikshank?' Polly said breathlessly to the young copper on the desk at Leman Street Station. 'Never mind, I'll find him.'

'Wait a minute, you can't go down there…' he called after her. She was already half way along the passageway that led to the custody rooms and Inspector Reid's office. At that moment, Inspector Abberline stepped onto the corridor.

'Meticulous police work, Alf. That's the ticket,' he said, then turning around, he saw Polly. 'Miss Wilkes,' he smiled. 'What a pleasant surprise.'

'Sir,' Polly skidded to a stop. 'I think I've come by some information about Aaron that you'll find helpful.'

'Really?' His bushy eyebrows lifted. 'Well, your young man is in here, why don't you join us and tell us what you've discovered?' Abberline said opening the door. 'Alf? Your young lady is here.'

Polly moved into the room as Alf looked up from a pile of documents. He was scrutinising the police reports with meticulous care, looking for any scrap of evidence that might rule in or rule out Aaron Kosminski as a suspect.

'Polly? Is everything all right?' he said standing up.

'I've been to see Aaron's sisters,' she said to the two men, then paused to catch her breath. 'Aaron doesn't live at Sion Square nor Greenfield Street. He's been living with his older brother at number 76 Goulston Street since July. Those brothers-in-law of his have been trying to conceal Aaron's connection to them because he's a bit of an embarrassment. They've applied for citizenship and Aaron has been causing havoc, bothering the neighbours, eating out of the gutter and having paroxysms that make him scream and shout. His brother tries to keep him in the house, but he keeps getting out and looking for me to read to him.'

'Goulston Street?' Alf retrieved a large scale map from the drawer.

'We hardly need to look it up, Alf,' said Abberline. 'It has been the thorn in our flesh since the 30th of September. Wentworth Buildings, 108 to 119 Goulston Street. "The *Juwes* are the men that will not be blamed for nothing" and the piece of Catherine Eddowes's blood stained apron.'

'Yes, sir,' he said, 'I'm having a look where number 76 is.'
He looked up. 'It's a bit further down on the other side of the road.
They are all tenement blocks with a dozen or so addresses in 'em.
Number 76 is just a stone's throw from where Mrs. Eddowes's apron
was found. If he lives there, no wonder he vanished so quick. That
block is riddled with back alleys, back yards and shortcuts. There are
half a dozen places where he could have disappeared like a ferret up a
drainpipe.'

Abberline shot to Alf's side and studied the map. 'You're
right. By all the gods of Olympus, Catherine Eddowes was found less
than five minutes after she was killed, yet there was no sign of the
murderer. If he went to that address, he would have been indoors
before the first police whistle blew.'

'Casting aside his foul parcel as he did so,' said Alf.

'My God, Alf,' Abberline exhaled. 'All this time, all the
hours of investigation and he's been right there in the middle of it.'

'Let's get the brother in here and hear what he has to say,'
said Abberline. 'And I think we will have another little chat with the
brothers-in-law.'

'Please don't tell them where the information came from.
Those nice ladies might catch it from their husbands otherwise,' said
Polly.

'D'you think the family knew what he did?' said Alf.

'Wait a minute,' said Polly 'All I'm saying is they hid him
away because the brothers-in-law had both applied for citizenship and
they thought Aaron's shenanigans might spoil their chances.'

Alf turned crimson. 'Spoil their chances? *Spoil their
chances?* Oh, they think so do they? Yeah, being the brother-in-law of
a sadistic, maniacal killer might just make Her Majesty think twice.'

Polly pulled a face. 'Alfie, the sisters said he often had blood
on in him and even I know he hurts himself to keep the voices at bay.
They thought nothing of it and still deny he ever had a lot of blood on
him like he did last night. I thought the brother he lived with might be
able to give you an explanation.'

'Polly, you just told us he lives thirty yards from where the
piece of Mrs. Eddowes's apron was found.'

'If he lived with his brother in Goulston Street, perhaps the
two sisters are unaware of it, Miss Wilkes,' said Abberline. 'The men
probably sorted it out without telling their wives. That's what an

Englishman would do and I would imagine a Jewish man would do the same.'

'That's what the sisters said, Inspector. They said the men didn't tell them much.'

'And don't forget, each medical man who gave evidence said the killer might have been able to avoid getting a lot of blood on him,' said Abberline. 'Except of course for the last one.'

Polly sat down heavily on one of the chairs. She leaned forward on the table and put her head in her hands. 'The men might have known about it, but those two ladies are very kind and I believe them. All they knew was they were covering up Aaron's behaviour because of the citizenship applications.'

'There would certainly be repercussions for a Jewish family if it was known that their relative was Jack the Ripper,' said Abberline, 'and for the Jewish community in general.'

'Thanks to the rubbish written in the papers almost every day, they're scared of the backlash that could erupt at any time. As are we, sir,' said Alf. 'We can hardly contain things as it is.'

'Yes. Think what happened last year when Israel Lipski was put on trial and then executed,' said Abberline, shaking his head.

'You know my opinion on that, sir... That unfortunate young man was innocent. Kosminski, on the other hand, is guilty as sin. Polly glared at him.

'The repercussions of this are beyond belief, Alf.' said Abberline. 'This has implications for the whole of the east end. The whole of London and the whole of the country if it comes to that.' He put his fingertips to his brow as if it gave him a headache to think of it. 'The amount of anti-Semitism this will set off...'

'I don't blame them for being scared.' said Polly. 'Innocent people are getting set upon all the time. Completely unprovoked. Including Aaron, I saw it when I read to him in the pub. Someone could have deliberately put that blood on him.'

'Polly!' Alf clutched his head and paced the floor in exasperation. 'Why do you insist on calling him innocent?'

'Because I know him. That's why. You've got an idea in your head about him and you just won't shift it.'

'Miss Wilkes,' said Abberline, before it could get any more acrimonious. 'We need to see if there are any definite connections to the other murders. Can you remember where you were on those occasions when Kosminski found you and asked you to read?'

Alf faced the opposite wall, put his hands on his hips and heaved a heavy sigh. Polly sat down at the table and folded her hands in front of her and stared at the back of Alf's head. 'You keep going on about evidence. You show me solid evidence against Aaron.'

Alf's chest started to expand and Abberline intervened.

'Miss Wilkes? Tell us about the times you came across Kosminski.'

Alf moved to the table and sat down opposite her. Frowning, he picked up his pen and waited to write down her words. Polly glowered at him.

'The first time was the Commercial Street end of Fashion Street. That would have been about a week after poor Annie was killed and I took him home. The second time was on Osborne Street next to Feldman's post office, maybe… a week later. Then after that, he found me on Church Lane. Both those times I took him to the gardens of St Mary's Church on Whitechapel High Street. It's quiet and there are benches to sit on. He just wanders about anywhere,' she shrugged.

'After that?' Abberline prompted.

'The next time would be Aldgate. He found me outside *The White Swan* on Aldgate the night Lizzie and Cathy were murdered. Then I started looking after Alfie's mum. It was after that, Mickey Kidney attacked me down Dock Street and Aaron saved me, Alfie said it would be all right to read to him but I didn't see him until he turned up  tonight on the bridge.'

'You said you read to him the night of the two murders,' said Abberline. 'Would you tell me what happened?'

'Aaron found me outside *The White Swan* on Aldgate. He said he would pay me to read to him so I took him in *The Bull*. We found a quiet corner in the snug, had a couple of ginger wines and he gave me two shillings. I read to him for a long time, maybe three hours. By then the pub had filled up. Some ruffians started with the *verbals* and said horrible things about him being Jewish, so I got him out of there before it got really nasty. They still had a go at him on the way out. They pushed him around; Aaron just took it. He didn't get violent or anything.'

'Did you take him home?' said Alf, speaking at last.

Polly shook her head. 'No. I was going to, then he turned up Duke Street and I thought he must be going to that big Synagogue half way up on the left-hand side. I could see he was shaken up. He seemed to know where he was, so, I just let him go and started back for my lodgings.'

'What time would this be?' Abberline asked.

'Probably about one o'clock or shortly before. Yeah, that's right. I remember hearing the brewery clock strike hour as I walked along Aldgate.'

Alf looked at her steadily. 'Duke Street is connected to Mitre Square through a narrow alley called Church Passage. You've just placed Kosminski in the immediate vicinity of the Catherine Eddowes murder.'

'You insist on connecting him to The Ripper don't you?'

'Because he ruddy well is The Ripper. How many more times?' Alf replied.

'Hold on a moment. You have also just given him an alibi for the Stride murder, Miss Wilkes,' said Abberline, 'and as we need to place the killer at all the crime scenes, perhaps he isn't The Ripper after all, Alf?'

Alf sat back and folded his arms. 'That don't actually rule him out, sir.'

They explained the entire story of Lizzie's death to Inspector Abberline.

'Mickey did it, Inspector. When he thought he was about to kill me, he boasted about it. Then Aaron came along and saved me,' said Polly.

Abberline nodded slowly. 'That is very interesting because Kosminski has been telling us all along that he didn't kill her. The words *For the one I did not do,* make sense in that context.'

'And Goulston Street isn't far from Duke Street. He could have been heading home after he left me,' said Polly.

'Mitre Square is even closer,' said Alf. 'And he could have been home at number 76 in two minutes; before Watkins found the body, in fact.'

Polly gave a frustrated groan. 'Everything I say makes it worse for him. He's just a poor, pathetic, tortured man and he can't defend himself against all this.'

Alf stood up and walked away from the table. He put his hands in his pockets and looked at the floor. He rubbed the back of his neck, then turned around and looked at Polly.

'Alright, alright. Explain the blood on him.' Alf blazed.

'I-' Polly began.

'And what about the scratches we found on his chest? The message he left on the bridge? The long sharp knife he just *happened* to have with him to carve Kidney up with? The home address almost opposite where the only piece of evidence in the whole case was found? The family hiding his whereabouts? His unstable mind? What if he had that knife on him every time he came looking for you? He could have turned on you just like that!' He clicked his fingers.

Polly stared at him. 'I... I don't know.'

'What did his sisters actually say?' asked Abberline, intervening to prevent an escalation in the argument.

'Not much, sir,' said Polly. 'They admitted he had blood on him often. No matter what I said, they wouldn't budge from saying he hurts himself. They were scared.' She fixed her gaze on Abberline. 'Suppose Aaron turns out to be Jack the Ripper, none of it is his fault, is it? If he *has* done these terrible murders, you got to look at the family. His brother and brothers-in-law are the ones who need to account for it. If they knew he was coming home covered in blood the way he was last night, and they kept quiet, they are the ones who ought to be held responsible.'

'Quite right, Miss Wilkes. And don't forget, one of them left you with him like a sacrificial lamb; knowing that he could turn violent at any moment.'

'And that's something else what puts me in a cold sweat every night,' Alf muttered.

'Aaron would never hurt me-'

'Why not?' Alf asked.

'I'm his pal, I read to him.'

'And if he suddenly for some reason he decided you were not his pal, how d'you think he might have reacted to you?' Abberline asked her gently.

'I don't know.' Polly thought about the question. 'You mean if I hadn't found the one thing that pacifies him the day I looked after him... You really think he might have-?'

'He was stalking you, my dear.' Abberline replied. 'You were his obsession. He protected you only because you were his prized little pet. We know he carried a knife. If his opinion of you had altered - which it might have done on a whim... well...'

Polly's face turned from chalk white to grey. She gave a whimper.

Alf looked at her. 'Hold on, I know that look… Polly? Washroom. Now.' He flew to her side as Polly's stomach began to writhe and her legs turned to rubber. He almost carried her to the door, yanked it open and guided her to the nearest washroom, grabbing a metal waste bin on the way.

Alf came back a few moments later with a newly washed bin.

'She'll be all right in a while,' he explained. 'She gets a dicky stomach mulling over what might have occurred,' he smiled affectionately. 'Show her a corpse with his throat cut from ear to ear and she's fine. Tell her she's had a near miss or something emotional and she loses her breakfast.'

Abberline chuckled. 'So, Miss Wilkes has a weakness after all? I was beginning to think that girl of yours was invincible,' he said. 'She's a clever one, Alf and she brings out the best in you. Don't let this come between you.'

'That wretch is the only thing we've ever argued about, sir.'

'You thought *that* was an argument?' Abberline gave an amused snort. 'My dear boy…' He shook his head. 'I must say she has a highly logical mind for a female.'

'Er… best not let her hear you remark on any inferiorities in the female mind, sir, as I could not guarantee your safety.'

Abberline laughed and put a fatherly hand on Alf's shoulder. 'Go and see how she is. This has been a massive shock, so be gentle with her, Alf. She can sign a statement when she's feeling better. I'll go and put Reid in the picture about the Goulston Street connection and all the rest of this wretched business.'

# CHAPTER THIRTY TWO

The lock on the washroom in sick bay still had the *engaged* sign on it. Alf tapped softly on the door.

'Polly?' There was no answer so he tried again. 'Polly, are you all right? Open the door.'

'No,' came the reply.

'Please? I want to see that all is well.'

'Leave me alone, Alfie.'

He frowned. 'Are you crying?'

'I said leave me alone,' she replied in a muffled voice.

'Not a chance.' Alf muttered to himself. He took a coin out of his pocket, inserted it into the screw at the centre of the locking mechanism and rotated it to *vacant.* He opened the door and slipped inside, locking it again from within.

'Alfie!' she squeaked indignantly, snatching up a towel. 'What do you think you're doing?' She was cleaning her teeth with some dental powder and her finger. She had taken off her skirt and bodice, which were hanging in the steam rising from a towel she had placed over a hot pipe, and her chemise and petticoat, which were drying next to the boiler. She was wearing only her lace trimmed drawers.

Alf's jaw fell open. 'Oh my- I- I'm sorry, I didn't know you were having a wash.'

She cupped some water in her hand and rinsed her mouth.

'Yes, that's the last thing you expect someone to be doing in a washroom.'

Flustered, Alf turned to leave. His hand reached for the lock. Then he paused, squared his shoulders, stretched his spine to his full height and turned around to face her.

She held the towel to her chest and watched him closely as she took a corner of it and dabbed her mouth dry. 'Didn't you say you were leaving?'

'I did, Polly. Now I think… I'm inclined to think I might stay,' he said, taking in the smooth skin of her naked shoulders and bare arms.

'Is that so? You think you're entitled to interrupt a person's ablutions?'

'I was concerned about you. I know this has hit you hard.' He moved towards her mesmerised by the way she held the towel against her breasts since it was too small to cover her modesty entirely. 'When I heard you through the door I thought you were crying.'

'I was trying to clean my teeth.' She dried her index finger, which was covered in mint flavoured dental powder, on the same corner of the towel.

She watched him intently. His eyes were glowing with that familiar warmth she was always delighted to see. It was a look of genuine tenderness that made her insides melt, but she was in no mood to be wooed nor seduced by Alf at present.

He smiled and his eyes moved from her face to the towel. 'You said I might have more of a look if I played my cards right,' he said.

'You didn't play them right,' she frowned.

His shoulders lifted and he gave a loud huff. 'I was worried for you, Polly. Kosminski is definitely in the running for being The Ripper and the thought of you alone with him, oblivious to the danger, and the fact that he followed you about, well it gives me fits.' Then he saw that her eyes were red. 'You *have* been crying.' He looked horror struck. 'Oh my dear, don't take on.' He put his arms around her and pulled her into an embrace. 'Was it because of what I said?'

She gave a heavy sigh, unable to keep up the defiant face any longer. 'No. It's not you. As a matter of fact, I feel stupid, Alfie. There are a lot of unexplained things that could mean that Aaron might be The Ripper.'

'Yes, there are.' He ran his palm across the soft skin of her back and pressed her closer to him. She loved the look of awe on his face as he discovered new intimacies that filled him with joy and heated his blood in equal measure.

She tucked her head beneath his chin and revelled in the warmth of his chest against her cheek. His body was beautifully sculpted with well-honed muscles. She judged him to be in excellent physical shape.

'You're a good policeman. I know you wouldn't accuse him unless you thought it was right. And there's me fussing and treating him like a sick puppy,' she sniffed. 'If he is The Ripper, I don't think he was in his right mind when he killed Annie, Polly, Cathy and Mary-Jane. He didn't know what he was doing but they're no less dead.'

'No.' he said gently. 'This case has turned out tragic on both sides.'

'I'm furious at myself for not knowing I could have been in danger. Me, who's supposed to have a keen sixth sense. So much for that, eh?'

'You're kind hearted, that's the trouble. It's what I love about you, Polly Wilkes.'

'You should take your tunic off.'

'Uh?' He stepped back from her.

'The steam in here will make the dye run onto your shirt and it won't come off.'

'I think I'm the one making most of the heat in here, seeing how the legs of those draws you're wearing come apart so easy.' He took off the tunic, reached out and hung it on the valve of a nearby pipe.

'I can't put my things back on, they're wet.'

'I'm glad to hear that,' he said and pulled her towards him so they could kiss.

As the kiss lingered on, she pulled away the towel that had covered her chest and let it drop to the floor.

Alf lifted her onto the counter top next to the sink in one easy movement, raising her to his height. The breath caught in his throat as he took in the sight of her. The look on his face filled her with delight.

'Polly.' he groaned, gathering her tightly against him. 'My lovely Polly. Look at you.' He kissed the soft skin of her breast, a look of awe on his face.

Polly wrapped her arms around him, dragging him closer to her with her legs. She returned the kiss passionately. She closed her eyes, overjoyed at how the touch of this down to earth, ordinary man sent blissful sensations scorching through her body and turned her blood to fire.

She delighted in the feel and the scent of him. His fingertips explored her breasts creating glorious sensations that took away her breath. She savoured his touch with sensuous, delirious joy at the desire he ignited inside her. It was something she thought she would never experience. Men had paid to touch her breasts and she felt nothing, yet the touch of Alf's lips on her sensitive, tender skin was a mind blowing pleasure.

'Oh Polly,' he moaned 'I'm half mad with desire for you. I can hardly stand it. What lies beneath here, piques me something fierce,' he groaned, running his hand along her thigh to the place where the two halves of the garment separated.

Polly undid the buttons of his shirt with shaking fingers, eager to feel his muscular torso beneath her palms.

'I never felt this way before, Alfie, I swear. It's like you're a drug I crave and I've abandoned all constraint.' She gave a little gasp as Alf seared her skin with hot kisses. 'Thomas always had to coax me, now, I- I'm… Oh Alfie, it's *me* who wants…' she moaned, giving herself up to the passion of the moment.

Alf groaned. 'I got to have you here, right now, Polly. I can't bear it.' His shaking fingers reached for the ribbon that kept the two halves of her drawers together and pulled the bow apart.

'I want you too, Alfie,' she whispered.' It's…' He kissed the valley between her breasts, and she gave a little moan as he trailed his lips to the hardened bud at her nipple, caressing and kissing, worshipping her body. Thomas had taken what he wanted, they had not shared this wonderful, precious intimacy together and it was new and marvellous to her. To Alfie, she knew she was an exquisite treasure that he cherished with tenderness and love. She knew he would give as much as he took. She was being carried away by her own powerful desires and she did not care a jot for the consequences. This breath-taking excitement was something she wanted to explore. It was a revelation. She had never been loved this way by any other man. Alfie was reaching the point of no return. She tried to regain her senses, knowing it was other men who stood between them now.

'Alfie, we can't,' she murmured.
He gave a tortured groan. 'My love, someone as beautiful as you can't be sick.'

'If I knew that were true, Alfie, I would submit to you this second,' she breathed.

He claimed her lips in an adoring, fervent kiss. 'I need you, my sweet girl,' He gave a long low moan. 'I think I'll die if I don't have you.' His overwhelming desire was a potent brew. 'I can't wait no longer, Polly.' With trembling fingers, he released the buttons on his pants. He groaned as the constraints on him were released.

'Alfie…I-' she gulped. The pleasure of him seeking her most intimate place dissolved her willpower like a snowflake in the sun.

'We'll be man and wife soon. Getting wed is a formality. Two weeks and I won't hear different. Don't worry my love, it will be all right.'

'Alfie…' she murmured knowing that neither of them was going find the will to stop. She wanted him so badly, yet the small voice of reason that nagged at the back of her mind would not be silent. 'It's not about being wed, I want you too, this minute, and would be glad not to wait. It's the danger of-' A little more pressure from him and she gave a whimper of pleasure.

'You're not sick my darling girl, I know it in my bones.' He trailed his lips across her shoulder. 'You're no hard-edged whore, you never have been. I love you more than my life, my sweet Polly. I beg you, let me show you. I'm in agonies for you and I must have you'

'I know, my love,' Polly breathed, overwhelmed by the heat of her own desires. There was nothing to prevent that final inevitable step. She gave a shuddering sigh. 'All…All right, b- but… but you mustn't let yourself...' her small voice trailed away. 'I'm not prepared- I threw away my sponge and-'

He froze. Without another word, he moved to the sink, put his whole head under the cold tap and let the water flow over him for a long time. Polly jumped down from the counter top and tied the ribbon that kept the two halves of her drawers together.

'I'm so sorry, Polly,' he grated. 'You must think me no better than a wild animal.' Polly switched off the tap. Alf stayed bent over the sink. She grabbed a towel and draped it across the back of his neck. He pulled it over his head like a hood and dried his face and hair. 'Please forgive me, I'm so sorry. When I saw you like that, a fever gripped me. After all the promises I made to you about the right way at the right time. I was about to treat you like a-' He could not bring himself to say the word. He quickly pulled up his pants and buttoned them but not before Polly stole a glance at his legs which were as well toned and muscular as the rest of him after years of walking the beat.

'Whore?' she said, watching him. 'That word keeps cropping up doesn't it?' She moved towards him, took the towel from him and dried the parts of his shoulders and neck that he had missed. 'Alfie that was *nothing* like how a whore gets used.' She cupped his cheek with her hand. 'Look at me…' she smiled softly. 'That wasn't all you.'

'It was up to me to stay in control,' he said, 'and instead I seduced you.'

'I loved those sweet words you said to me,' she murmured. 'If it hadn't been for the worry over... you know, I wouldn't have cautioned you to stop.'

'Don't set me off again, Polly. I'm already ashamed of myself.'

'You've got nothing to be ashamed of. There's nothing shameful about this.' She looked down at her bare breasts. 'Look at me, bearing all, and I don't feel bit shameful- not with you. Like I said, it wasn't just you, it was me as well.'

He cupped her breast with the palm of his hand and gave a long shuddering groan. 'You make my head spin, Polly Wilkes. I lose my wits over you.'

'We were expressing how we feel about each other and that's a wonderful thing. It's not shameful.' She pulled him into an embrace. 'You stopping like that was the most intense gesture of love I have ever known.' she murmured. 'You're the one, Alfie Cruikshank.' She kissed him. 'I don't know where you found the will power to stop and put your head under the tap.'

'Neither do I.' he said. 'I think when you said that thing about... not to let myself... and you not being prepared. It brought me to my senses. That's not the way our first intimate act should be.'

She kissed him hard. 'Well, Sergeant, I heard a proposal while you had your fever on and there are no take backs.'

He laughed, picked her up and swung her around. 'That's settled. Two weeks.'

'Alfie, the banns have to be read in church for three weeks. Oh and just so you know, I rather liked that wild animal and I would very much like to see him again.'

# CHAPTER THIRTY THREE

'Where are they sending Kosminski?' Inspector Reid leaned forward on his desk and asked the question of Inspector Abberline, who was sitting in the leather chair Polly had used earlier.

'The workhouse infirmary at Stepney. It's a secure facility for them that's a danger to themselves.'

'The workhouse system is voluntary. He can't be kept in there against his will.' said Reid.

'True, except he isn't exactly capable of expressing his wishes.'

'How have the family responded to his incarceration?'

'They're scared,' said Abberline. 'As well they ought to be, so they're co-operating.'

'Yes, I'm sure. They know this could ruin things for the whole family.'

'I swear, Edmund, if they knew what he was up to… if they stood by and did nothing…' Abberline growled.

'I feel the same way, Fred,' said Reid. 'What about the workhouse employees? Won't they suspect something if we try to extend his stay indefinitely? I take it they don't know the details?'

'Heavens no. All they know is that he is an unknown Jewish man the police picked up off the street who is mad as a hatter. He is known by the name David Cohen, which, as you know, is given to any unknown Jewish man that comes in. As far as they are concerned, he is there for an assessment and his family found.'

Reid sat back in his chair and nodded reflectively. 'Have the physicians made a pronouncement on him yet?'

'Yes, it seems they keep an alienist on staff; a Professor Morrison who has confirmed Kosminski's madness and mental incapacity.'

'Which means according to the law, he can't stand trial,' said Reid with a sigh.

'According to Morrison, they can keep him for around five days, which gives us a bit of thinking time,' said Abberline. 'There can be no order for mandatory incarceration without evidence.'

'Since they can't be told he's suspected of being The Ripper. Our evidence is weak, Fred.'

'Yes, however, there is one ray of hope. It seems City Force have found three witnesses who saw a woman fitting Catherine Eddowes description, talking with a man at the entrance to Church Passage between half past one and twenty-five minutes to two the night she was murdered. She was found dead at quarter to two.'

'There are witnesses? And City didn't tell us?'

'Technically they did. It was buried in a pile of reports they sent over. Alf remembered two of them giving evidence at the Eddowes inquest so he followed it up and found it in the documents he was going through yesterday.' He looked at Reid. 'That man is wasted as a desk sergeant you know, Edmund. I'd like to take him and train him up for The Yard.'

'How d'you think Swanston would react to that suggestion? I had to warn Alf that consorting with a prostitute could affect his chances of becoming a detective.'

'I think if you stop calling Miss Wilkes a prostitute, Swanson will forget all about it.'

'You seem taken with her.' Reid picked up the cricket ball he kept on his desk and began tossing it from hand to hand.

'I am. She's a very intelligent young woman who made one mistake – and girls don't get a second chance. Did you know Commissioner Munro is keen to set up a new unit that will have women working closely with The Yard to rescue girls like her from their fate?'

'Really?'

'Too many of them are being pulled out of the Thames. Usually pregnant, having had some foolish entanglement with a man.'

'And no less often, Fred, it's a servant who's been the victim of the men of the household in which they worked. Only to be dismissed when a pregnancy begins to show.' Reid sat forward and put down the cricket ball with precision in its place on his desk.

'Yes, absolutely. The notion is that we pick these girls up before they jump off one of the bridges, get them medical help, a place to stay and so on. It will be very discrete, very hush-hush so as not to incur the outrage of the hypocritical classes... I think Miss Wilkes would be perfect for the job. She would impress Swanson if she was given the chance.'

'I gather Miss Wilkes is soon to be Mrs. Cruikshank,' said Reid.

'Yes, so I understand. Alf is like a puppy with two tails at present,' Abberline smiled. 'That's even better, is it not? A respectable married woman is much more suited to carry out this work.'

'I wonder how the formidable Temperance is taking the news of her son's nuptials?' said Reid.

'Is she a firebrand?'

'Pha!' Reid said in reply. 'An understatement, Fred. She was an excellent midwife in her time, so I understand, but she's terrifying. I think her domineering nature is what makes Alf so buttoned up and precise in everything he does.'

'Oh, I think Miss Wilkes is more than equal to the challenge.'

'She certainly seems to have changed him for the better, and from the spring in his step lately, I'd say there has been a certain amount of unbuttoning.' Reid smiled. 'Anyway, to return to the case, what of these witnesses?'

Abberline shrugged his shoulders. 'We'll shake the tree and see what falls out. An identity line is being organised for tomorrow, you never know, perhaps they will pick out Kosminski. That would strengthen our position considerably.'


The following day, in a featureless interview room, seven men were assembled for an identity line up. Each one, four policemen in civilian clothes and three civilians, who had the same general appearance as the suspect, had been given a fee of one shilling for taking part.

'Gentlemen,' said the duty officer to the line of men. 'The witnesses will be shown in one by one. Please stand up straight, look directly ahead and keep your facial expression blank. Please do not make eye contact with the witness as he passes you by. Please do not change your expression or speak unless you are asked to do so.'

Alf stood beside Abberline, watching the proceedings.

Aaron Kosminski, who did not receive a shilling, was invited to choose his own position in the line of men. Unable to do this for himself, his brother-in-law, Woolf, led him to a position second from the right in the line of men.

'Thank you, Mr. Abrahams. Be kind enough to leave the room now, please,' said the duty officer.

Aaron remained where Woolf Abrahams had placed him. Alf could see that the wretch was preoccupied and abstracted. He fidgeted with his clothing. He scratched himself and swivelled his head to look around the bland room. He had been shaved and was wearing a fresh and expensive looking suit of clothes, though his knotted hair gave him a dishevelled appearance, being lank and in need of a cut.

For the first time, Alf could see what Polly meant. Aaron seemed unaware of the importance of the things going on around him. It was as if he was not seeing his surroundings as they truly were and his own imagined world was more real to him.

Alf felt a fleeting stir of pity as he watched him. Then he remembered the victims and the frenzy of blood lust in which they died while this wretch indulged his insane appetites.

Polly could have been his next victim. Right under his very nose, this madman could have taken her from him. The thought made nausea cramp his gut and sweat break out on his brow. He tried to focus on the fact that this man, whom he was convinced was Jack the Ripper, had saved Polly's life - twice. Knowing this caused Alf extreme consternation, he was torn between wanting to shake his hand and having the urge to beat the living daylights out of him.


The first of the two witnesses, Joseph Levy, was shown into the room. Short, stout, Levy moved down the line of men. He took just over a minute to decide that he did not recognise any of them as the man he had seen in Church Passage that night.

Abberline leaned towards Alf. 'Make sure they're kept apart, Sergeant. I don't want any possibility of communication between them until they have both viewed the line.'

Alf nodded and escorted Joseph Levy out onto the corridor and into a room opposite. He returned just in time to hear Abberline call for the second witness.

Joseph Lawende was shown into the room to view the line of men. Alf watched him carefully. He looked much more uncomfortable than Levy. He spent an extra few seconds scrutinising the line, then in the end, he came to the same conclusion - he did not recognise any of the men. He quickly joined Levy in the adjacent room.

'They knew more than they were telling,' said Abberline as the line dispersed.

Alf nodded. 'I agree, sir.'

'What did you notice, Alf, that led you to that conclusion?' said Abberline taking on the role of teacher.

'Both of 'em were agitated. Mr. Levy made a big play of looking carefully at each man, but only looked at Kosminski for a second or two and a layer of sweat appeared on his brow and top lip. Mr. Lawende turned pale and the pupils of his eyes were dilated. He looked as if someone had said *Boo* he would have hit the ceiling. I think his conscience is troubling him.'

Abberline nodded. 'Exactly.'

'They recognised him all right, sir. They just didn't want to grass him up.' said Alf, frustration making the veins in his neck stand out. 'What do we do, sir? The whole case hinged on these men and we can't prove they know more than they're admitting.'

'Let's go and have a chat,' said Abberline. 'Now remember, Alf. It's important to stay calm. Keep it friendly.'

Alf followed Abberline into the room and found the two friends sitting quietly, both with their eyes cast downward.

'Thank you very much for your time and co-operation Mr. Levy, Mr. Lawende,' Abberline began.

Lawende looked up. 'I am sorry the man I saw could not be identified.' His voice was hesitant as if at any minute it might crack and make him choke on his words.

It was an evasive answer. Alf's eyes narrowed and he shifted his weight from one foot to the other. He stared at Lawende then at Levy. The fuse on his temper was burning away and growing shorter by the minute. He was used to direct action against those he considered to be hiding something.

He reined himself in. He knew Abberline was just as exasperated, yet the experienced detective showed no outward sign of it. Alf watched him, determined to learn.

'Not at all.' Abberline replied to Lawende's remark in a light and amicable tone. 'I know you did your best, gentlemen.' He heaved a theatrical sigh. 'Such a pity. You see, the man you saw with Mrs. Eddowes was almost certainly her murderer. And, the man who killed Mrs. Eddowes, was undoubtedly the monster who butchered the other women.' Abberline's expression was grave and his tone suggested he was imparting a confidence. 'Gentlemen, I can't begin to tell you - they were the most horrific attacks you could imagine. If you saw what was done to those unfortunate ladies, you would understand our anxiety that it should not happen again. This killer is truly a monster. Not ten minutes after you saw her, the lady was found with her throat cut and disembowelled. Organs had been torn from her in a monstrous fashion.' He looked into the eyes of each man. 'This killer is indiscriminate. Any woman might be his victim.' He paused for this to sink into each man's imagination. 'We felt certain that we had our man. Now, you gentlemen have shown us otherwise and our greatest fear that the killer is still at large has been realised.' Abberline made a show of hanging his head to convey his disappointment. He looked up. 'Mr. Levy, I understand you're a butcher?'

'Yes,' said Levy stiffly.

'Then you will appreciate more than most how horrific these murders were,' said Abberline, still in a companionable tone.

'Unfortunately, yes.' Levy replied.

'Shocking, truly shocking. The sort of individual who could carry out such a crime against a defenceless and poverty stricken woman must be a devil,' said Abberline, an expression of concern on his careworn face. His mouth tugged downwards. 'When you slaughter an animal, I assume you do so in the most humane way possible?'

'Of course. The Kosher way of-'

'These poor women were not afforded that mercy.' Abberline interrupted him in a manner that Alf could see was all part of the act. He really was the master, he thought with admiration. Abberline glanced at him, inviting him to join in the discussion.

Alf sighed, sounding as regretful as his mentor. 'You're quite right, Inspector. I have been present at every murder scene.' He followed Abberline's lead and looked them in the eyes; first Levy, then Lawende. 'Whoever did that to Mrs. Eddowes and the other victims is a madman. He's a monster because of his madness and unfortunately, he remains free to kill again. Nobody is safe until we catch him.'

'Yes, Sergeant, he's a monster as you say, but you must remember, it's not of his own doing,' said Abberline. 'He may not be in control of his faculties. After all, we can't blame a beast for his appetites, however, he *must* be stopped from exercising them.'

Abberline's words had the desired effect. Both men looked queasy. Abberline pushed a little more. 'May I go over the facts gentlemen?' he continued without waiting for a response from either of the two witnesses. 'You made statements to my colleagues on the City Force and to the inquest of Mrs. Eddowes that you left your gentleman's club, the Imperial Club, 16 to 17 Duke Street at 1.30a.m. You saw a man and a woman standing at the entrance to Church Passage as you passed by on the opposite side of the road at approximately 1.35a.m.'

The two men agreed and Abberline continued. 'Mrs. Eddowes was found ten minutes later at 1.45a.m., having been butchered.' Both Levy and Lawende now looked grey. 'The man you saw was not in the line-up of men you have just viewed. Is that correct?' Abberline looked at each man in turn. He did not look away until he got an answer from them. He made them face him with their answer. Each man shook his head briefly. Neither one was able to look him in the eyes. Levy appeared to be sweating profusely and Lawende was hollow-cheeked and pale. Abberline paused, letting his words hang in the air for as long as possible. Alf knew that his mentor was weighing every move he made, every look, every gesture, every word was designed to put pressure on the two men.

'Hmm,' Abberline said, curving his mouth into a frown. He took a long exhalation of breath. 'Well gentlemen, thank you for coming here today.' Both men stood up as quickly as if they each had been sitting on a coiled spring. They started for the door. 'Your co-operation is greatly appreciated. Oh, by the way, I understand you both have applied to become British citizens?'

The two men looked as if they had been frozen where they stood. Then, they turned their heads to look at Abberline who kept up the smiling, sugary friendliness.

Levy nodded, Lawende simply stared.

'Good luck with your applications. I'm sure her Majesty would be delighted to have fine upstanding gentlemen like yourselves as her subjects. Good day, gentlemen,' he nodded.

The two men could not get out of the room fast enough. Without a word, they gathered themselves and headed for the door. Abberline was not finished. 'Oh, by the way, Mr. Levy, where is your butchers shop?' he called after them. Levy stopped abruptly, his shoulders hunched as if he was wondering how long this torment was going to last. He turned round and Alf could see that he had to force himself to straighten his spine. He cleared his throat.

'It is on Hutchinson Street,' he said.

'That's just off Middlesex Street?'

'Yes.'

Abberline nodded slowly. 'And you live on the premises?'

'Yes.'

'I see,' he said, without elaborating further on the question. 'Thank you, again, gentlemen. The duty officer will show you out.'

Alf did not speak until he was sure the two men were well out of earshot. 'Weren't you tempted to threaten them with not getting approved for citizenship if we find out they are withholding evidence, sir?'

Abberline shook his head. 'It's not necessary, Alf. I planted the idea in their minds, you see, even though I did nothing more than wish them well. Believe me, the demons I placed in their heads are more likely to make them talk than you or I making threats. You never know, what they claim might be true and if it is, nothing will make them come forward. If they are lying, they will stew on it and put pressure on themselves. Then, one of them might come back and tell us what they know. Fact is, unless they can positively identify Kosminski, we have nothing on him.'

'But, sir, we've got the blood on his clothing and thanks to Polly, we can place him in the vicinity of at least one murder. Then there's that strange message he wrote. *For the one I did not do.* Surely, if we got him for one, we got him for all of 'em.'

'Unfortunately that isn't enough for a judge, Alf.' Abberline sighed and looked at his pocket watch. 'Swanson wants us all round the table to discuss progress and I would like you to be part of it. You have a good head for noticing detail and you've seen all the victims.'

Alf Cruikshank followed Inspector Abberline into Inspector Reid's office as Reid placed a neat, handwritten statement on the table in front of him at the head of the conference table. He laid it down carefully, as if it contained an explosive device. He looked up as the two men entered the room.

'Anything further, Edmund? Abberline asked.

'Isaac Kosminski is Aaron Kosminski's older brother. He was the first of the siblings to come here. He is listed on the 1881 census as living at 76 Goulston Street and he resides there to this day. I think he was being evasive. He did not volunteer much information, but when I asked him directly, he admitted that Aaron has lived with him since July.'

'Joseph Levy's butchers shop is on Hutchinson Street,' said Abberline. 'That's around the corner from Goulston Street. A Jewish butcher slaughters his animals according to their religious rules. Jewish people will buy their meat from him rather than another local butcher. This means it is quite likely that Levy and Isaac Kosminski know each other.'

'They probably attend the same Synagogue, sir; the big one on Duke Street or perhaps the one on Heneage Lane. There ain't no others close by.' Alf added.

'And if Aaron is living with Isaac, Levy probably knows him too,' said Reid. He thought for a moment. 'So we can establish a likely connection between at least one of the witnesses and the family, though without witness confirmation we cannot establish that Kosminski was the man in Church Passage.'

'Unfortunately, that is the situation,' said Abberline. 'That connection, in my opinion, increases the likelihood that they are protecting a fellow Jew and in Levy's case, the relative of a customer and neighbour.'

'There is nothing we can do, Fred,' said Reid. 'Unless something else comes to light, this line of inquiry can go no further. Where does that leave us?'

'We think Lawende and Levy are withholding information; that's also the general opinion of the officers working on the case. However, we must also consider the possibility they are telling the truth,' said Abberline. 'Supposing they are? They saw a man and a woman standing at the entrance to Church Passage. They said the woman was wearing similar attire to the clothing worn by the Catherine Eddowes. They did *not* positively identify that person as the victim. It is possible the couple they saw was not the victim and her assailant. Though no one has come forward to be ruled out.'

'This was a man looking for the services of a prostitute - that isn't surprising,' said Reid.

'If it was a completely different couple that Lawende and Levy saw, it could mean City has got the times wrong,' said Abberline. 'The amount of mutilation the killer was able to carry out on the body in the time available was astonishing and it doesn't really add up. Look at what he managed to do in nine minutes, gentlemen? He lured her to the murder site, cut her throat and did all those unspeakable things to her in pitch dark, then made his getaway. It has always been difficult to envisage.'

Reid rubbed his temples as if his head was aching. 'I suppose Mrs. Eddowes could have met her murderer at an earlier time. We don't know what she was doing for the thirty minutes between being released from Bishopsgate and encountering her killer.'

'No, we don't, it's possible she could she have met her killer earlier,' said Abberline.

'Sir,' said Alf. 'Eddie Watkins had been through Mitre Square at half past one and was certain nothing was amiss.'

'That's what the report from City says, Alf, but is it to be believed? City would want their officers to appear perfect in our eyes.' Reid sighed. 'Is Watkins telling the truth? The amount of mutilation carried out on the corpse in the time available *is* rather improbable. Could Watkins have missed out his tour of the square at half past one then lied about it? Might he have stopped somewhere for a cup of tea or a rest?'

'We all know being on the beat at night ain't easy. I don't know about City, sir, but we keep close tabs on our lads. I ain't got no reason to doubt that Watkins is conscientious in his work. On the other hand, it's a quiet beat and up until that night, The Ripper weren't City's case. He wouldn't have been expecting trouble and he might have taken a few liberties.' Alf shrugged, 'He might have carried on down Mitre Street and missed out the square now and again. If he did that a couple of times each hour, it would give him a minute or two to rest his aching feet or go and relieve himself.'

'When you have been walking the same route every fifteen minutes for three hours and seen nothing out of the ordinary, it must be tempting,' said Abberline.

'What about the other chap, Constable Harvey?' said Reid checking the notes. 'He was there at… twenty to two.'

'It isn't part of his beat to go into Mitre Square, sir, though it does include Church Passage,' said Alf. 'Being a short distance, it's possible he felt it weren't worth the boot leather to walk up the passage and back down again. He could have just shone his lantern into Church Passage and moved on. And to be honest, sir, there ain't nothing wrong with doing that. He swears he walked to the end of the alley, but he wouldn't dare say otherwise. It's a poorly lit square, and anyhow his lantern would not have cast a light as far as the corner where Mrs. Eddowes was killed.'

'Shame,' said Reid. 'The victim would have been there and probably the killer also'.

'I'm not so sure, Edmund.' Abberline replied. 'Eddowes's movements can't be accounted for after she left Bishopsgate at one o'clock. P.C. Hutt who discharged her, said she turned left towards Aldgate so we know she wasn't heading back to the lodgings at Flower and Dean Street.'

'There weren't no point, sir, she didn't have any money. I think she would have been looking for a customer,' said Alf.

'Yes,' said Abberline, 'and it would have taken her only a few minutes to walk from the station to Church Passage if she went along Bishopsgate, down Houndsditch then along Duke Street. So what happened in those twenty five minutes? Where was she? I think Watkins could be lying. If he is, and the last time he was in the square was one fifteen or even one o'clock, it means she could have met her killer earlier and the timescale would be more believable.'

'Agreed,' said Reid. 'So, do we assume that Lawende and Levy saw Mrs. Eddowes and her killer and are lying by omission that it was Kosminski she was with? Or, do we assume that Watkins was not as vigilant as he might have been and she was murdered at an earlier time; meaning that the couple in church passage was not Mrs. Eddowes and her killer.' said Reid.

'Or Levy and Lawende did see Kosminski with a woman in Church Passage and are withholding that fact, but the woman he was with was not the victim?' said Abberline. He sighed. 'Mrs. Eddowes told Miss Wilkes she needed to get money to get a shirt out of hock. She was probably looking for a customer, as Alf said, which was likely to be the reason she kept asking Constable Hutt to let her out of the cells. There would still be plenty of business for her at that time of night.'

Reid nodded. 'She was arrested for being drunk and disorderly in the same area at half past eight; which is how she came to be in Bishopsgate nick in the first place. It seems she chose to spend what she earned, on alcohol.'

'Pardon me, sir, I don't believe she was drunk.' Alf interjected. 'Miss Wilkes provided some insight into the lady's personality and demeanour. It seems she was a bit of a card and a performer. She had earned a living doing songs and poetry for a time and was good at telling stories. She was arrested for being drunk. Witnesses said she was doing an impression of a fire engine and had drawn a crowd. I suspect she was giving one of her little performances with the idea of getting some money. Before she could cash in, a City constable turned up. She would have got a hefty fine for doing a street performance without a license so I think she pretended to be drunk. That way, she got to have a lie down in the cells and probably a cup of tea into the bargain. It would also account for her being sober and awake by one o'clock.'

'The officer said she smelled of drink,' said Reid.

'She had been in *The Britannia* for a couple of hours and the smell of ale tends to stick. She had also been bought a gin by Miss Suzette Le Fevre an hour earlier. She would have smelled of drink,' said Alf. 'She told Miss Le Fevre that she was stony broke. I don't believe the lady had any money to buy drink. Miss Wilkes saw her at just after seven o'clock and she was sober at that point. If she had subsequently been on the game, she would have put aside tuppence to get the shirt she was so keen on and used the rest to get herself and Mr. Kelly lodgings for the night. It's unlikely she would spend it on drink. They were a solid couple, sir. According to Miss Wilkes, they got on like a house on fire, with hardly a cross word between them. Based on that, I think she would have met up with him like she promised.'

'And being arrested interfered with her plans,' said Abberline. 'She was highly motivated to get a customer in order to get the shirt from the pawn shop and Aldgate was a likely place to find one due to the presence of the bridge workers.'

'It would have taken her less than ten minutes to wander down from Bishopsgate to Mitre Square,' said Reid.

'We have been told that a number of dollymops had gone in *The White Swan* that night, their customers in the main, being itinerant workers off the bridge, who, being the end of the month had just got paid,' said Alf. 'Maybe Mrs. Eddowes knew that and was heading back there to have another try. But the poor woman came across the murderer on route.'

Reid stood up and examined the map on the wall at the head of the conference table. There are so many possible rendezvous points around that area, where she might have met her killer.'

'Once she struck a bargain with him, she took him into Mitre Square to do the business - presumably because it is less occupied and poorly lit.' Abberline added.

'I think she was going to take him into the storage area, sir, on account that she was killed right beside it, but the killer thinks, if he goes in there with her and she happens to make a commotion, there ain't no way out. He would be trapped,' said Alf. 'Being very dark in that corner of the square, he grabbed her and killed her right in front of it, probably as she turned away from him to open the gate. Then the killer had three possible escape routes, via Mitre Street, Church Passage or through St. James's passage.'

Without corroboration from Lawende or Levy, we don't have a case against Kosminski and even if it was Kosminski in Church Passage, it doesn't necessarily make him the killer,' said Abberline.

'A reasonable defence lawyer would demolish the evidence in a trice - even if our suspect was not insane.' Reid shook his head. 'The reports from the terrible business in Millers Court have not yet been written up, we are all aware of what happened and there is no need to air the matter further. So, what do we have? A suspect in custody with a great deal of unexplained blood on him, who is capable of extreme violence, whom we now know resided for at least part of the time in Goulston Street where the fragment of Mrs. Eddowes's apron was found and whom Miss Wilkes placed in the vicinity of Mitre Square at the time of the murder. He is also profoundly mentally impaired. Now for the question we must answer... Is he The Ripper, gentlemen?'

# CHAPTER THIRTY FOUR

It was a cold Monday afternoon on the 12th of November, when Inspector Fred Abberline and Sergeant Alf Cruikshank emerged from Charing Cross Station, and headed along The Strand in the direction of Whitehall. Abberline had asked Alf to wear civilian clothes for this outing.

This request had caused Alf great consternation. Most of the time he wore his uniform, with or without the tunic. His civilian clothes were not at all smart enough for a visit to the great and prestigious Scotland Yard.

'Don't worry, I'll find you something down the market,' Polly had reassured him when he expressed his dismay. 'A good press with a damp cloth and the smoothing iron and you'll look a treat. There's a tape measure in here somewhere...' she opened a drawer in the dresser where the dishes were kept. 'Here we are...' she took the rolled up tape and then knelt down in front of Alf.

'What you doing?'

'If I'm going to find you a pair of trousers that fit, I need to measure your inside leg,' she said patiently. 'We don't want them half-mast, do we? You don't want to look like one of those variety acts for your trip to Scotland Yard.'

She pressed one end of the tape measure to the inside of his groin and unfurled it towards his foot. Alf could feel himself responding to her touch and his ears began to burn as he felt his crotch tighten.

'Right. That's thirty three inches, hang on, thirty one-' she stopped, sat back on her heels, smiled and looked up at him. 'This won't be accurate if Little Alfie wants to come out to play all the time. Let's call it thirty three inches with plenty of room in the crotch.'

'I... I can't help it,' he stammered.

She stood up. 'I know that,' she said softly and kissed him on the lips.

'Not helping, Polly,' he said huskily, his face turning red.

She looked at him. 'Hey. It doesn't matter, Sergeant,' she said gently. 'There's no call for embarrassment between you and me. In fact, I'm rather pleased to see him.'

'What d'you mean?'

'I like to know that you like me,' she smiled.

'*Like you*? My word, Polly Wilkes.' He felt as if his brain was going to explode.

As soon as she was anywhere near him, that part of his anatomy took on a mind of its own and he was powerless to stop it. Most of the time he made sure Polly was unaware of it; this time there was no concealing it.

'Alfie,' she said. 'You ought not to be embarrassed that you have the same urges as other men. It would be a poor show if you didn't.' She slipped her arms around him.

'Oh I got 'em all right,' he said hoarsely.

She studied his face. 'We can't risk the other, but I told you before, there are ways to relieve the-'

'No,' he said curtly. In the part of his mind that controlled basic instincts, the thought of her touching him was making matters worse.

'Alfie. You don't have to put up with it,' she said gently. 'You were driven half mad the other day at the station. Couples do this all the time. Did you know? There is a rumour that Queen Victoria herself wasn't a stranger to-'

'Polly,' he interrupted. 'That ain't an image I want in my head.'

'Then it should help calm the situation down, shouldn't it?' she grinned.

'Not sufficiently it don't.'

She looked at him intently and stroked her fingertips lightly across the straining prisoner. Alf flinched.

'Alfie, it's all right,' she said, continuing to touch him. 'You won't go blind. That's nonsense.' Alf took a sharp intake of breath and looked as if his eyes were about to pop out of their sockets. 'But you might if your eyes keep doing that.' Polly said, raising an eyebrow.

Alf could hardly catch his breath. His mind was filled with the scent and sight of her, all he wanted in the world was to take all the passion he felt for her and make her his own. Cold logic told them they needed to wait out the time until they knew with certainty she was healthy and it was safe to be intimate.

Intense feelings for one another made intimacy difficult to resist but they had set a wedding date for the beginning of January.

'We need to get wed. That's the solution as far as I'm concerned,' said Alf.

'That's not going to happen tonight is it?' She gazed at him for a long moment.

He felt light headed. Blood had surged into his groin so fast it was becoming painful. His breathing was shallow and rapid. He knew that Polly could see exactly what was happening.

'Polly for pity's sake, stop that.'

She did as he asked but continued to look at him 'Alfie,' she said finally. 'I'm not offering to relieve your agitation because I used to be a whore. Is that what you think?'

'Don't call yourself that.'

His pained expression gave her the answer.

'It's not like that, my dearest. It's nothing to do with that. I want to do it because I love you, Alfie Cruikshank, and I can see that a lot of the time, you've got a fever on. This is not the time to have anything interfere with that detective's brain of yours. It's a healthy, private thing for a couple to express their feelings without the associated drawbacks, don't you think?' She was watching him, waiting for his response. She smiled as he met her eyes and nodded almost imperceptibly.

'It's just, I don't want you to think…'

'What?'

'I don't want you to think I'm using you.'

She put her arms around his neck. 'Oh my love, I know that,' she kissed him. 'The girls taught me things, but it's not exclusive to whores. Far from it, I would imagine.' Her cheeks coloured to a deep pink and she placed her palms on his chest. 'Listen, if that's how you feel, there are things they taught me to make it… mutual. There are those who think women shouldn't get pleasure from intimate relations, but there are doctors who say it's vital that they should.'

'Yeah?' said Alf his brows raised. 'Tell me more.'

'Right then. Come here, you big, lovely man.'


'This is where it all happens, Alf,' said Abberline.

'Sir?' Abberline's words snapped Alf out of his daydream and he found they had already reached the entrance to Northumberland Street. His cheeks reddened and he wondered if there had been a vapid smile on his face as he thought about that evening with Polly.

They had taken their time and she had lain with him all night. He relished the freedom of being able to explore her body and caress her in all her nakedness. She was his and his alone to touch and to love. She had given him the most intense pleasure he had ever known and shown him that the act he had feared as self-abuse was another wonderful treasure, and a way of making love that he and Polly could enjoy. She had shown him how to give her pleasure and to his utter fascination, when he brought her to the point of abandoned ecstasy, he found a delight in it beyond words.

He knew without doubt that she was the most precious thing in his life.

The two men turned onto Northumberland Street and walked its length. This was a shortcut to Great Scotland Yard and they emerged at the junction with the bigger and much more grand, Northumberland Avenue.

He caught a glance from Abberline and wondered if he had a lovesick expression on his face. He forced himself focus on the task and stop thinking about Polly. Abberline had invited him to the most important meeting of his career and he must not be distracted. Despite his efforts, his crotch stirred every time he thought about her.

Abberline paused at the junction of Northumberland Avenue and Northumberland Street and turned to Alf. 'All around us are the corridors of power, Alf.'

Alf scanned the street names looking for one that said "Scotland Yard" and looked back at Abberline with a confused expression when he found none.

'I don't mean Scotland Yard,' said Abberline. 'No, no. If only it *was* the centre of things,' he reflected.

He inclined his head towards the adjacent building. 'That, there, is the Constitution Club,' he said. 'The side of it anyway… The entrance is on Northumberland Avenue. Number 28,' he said with emphasis. 'It takes up most of the entire block it shares with the Grand Hotel… and you can take from *that* what you may,' he said with a raised eyebrow. 'It's a club for toffs especially them that's in government… or them that wants to be. That's where all the deals are done, Alf – not in Parliament. Done with a nod and a wink more often than not. That's where the great and the good decide the way things are going to be and the rest of us are obliged to follow.'

Alf did not reply. He watched his mentor. He did not think Abberline was a cynical man, but there was a definite note of cynicism in his tone of voice and facial expression. Abberline turned and nodded towards the other corner. 'Over there is number 25

Northumberland Avenue… the Turkish baths. Don't be fooled by the plain exterior. It's like a Sultan's palace in there - it cost a fortune to fit that place out a few years ago. Most of 'em that's members of this…' he inclined his head back towards the Constitution Club. '…are also members of that.' He inclined his head back in the other direction. 'I'd say even more business is conducted in there than in parliament. And let's just say that much of what goes on in there, we do not look at too closely.'

Abberline turned around and without looking directly at it, drew Alf's attention to the pub that was behind them at the end of Northumberland Street.

'That pub we just passed, *The Northumberland Arms*, is a place where even the walls have ears. We are sometimes invited in there by the great and the good for a friendly tête-à-tête on account of the fact that they won't allow the likes of us inside the Constitution Club or the Turkish baths. Stay away from it unless you're summoned. When us lads want a quiet chat, we go in *The Rising Sun*. The toffs don't go near it since the Irishmen set off a bomb opposite, a few years back. If we need to get right away from The Yard we go to *The Shades* or *The Lord Moon* both of them is just over the other side, on Whitehall,' said Abberline. He looked directly at Alf. 'I'm telling you this because the first thing you got to learn as a detective is to be careful what you say and who you say it to…Above all, it's better to keep your mouth shut.'

'I can't imagine being taken on as a detective, sir,' he said, thinking about Swanson's attitude towards Polly. He was one of the bosses and head of the Ripper investigation. If it came to a choice between Polly and Scotland Yard, Alf knew, it would be no contest.

Abberline studied him. 'Ach, don't listen to Reid. If you're worried about Swanson, don't be; he won't hold a grudge. He's a dour Scot, it's his nature. All he wants is a clean score sheet and no embarrassments. The Ripper murders have been a huge embarrassment and *you* are the man who brought him in. You have a future as a detective if I have anything to do with it.'

'I didn't really bring him in, Inspector, I didn't know he was The Ripper at the time.'

'You worked out that vital clue - the blood on him. That was a good piece of deduction. And a word of advice, lad, don't play down your achievements. You wouldn't catch any of the bastards in there doing that.' He jerked his head towards the Constitution Club.

They crossed Northumberland Avenue diagonally, heading for the entrance to Great Scotland Yard which was approximately a hundred yards to the south. From this side, it looked more like a narrow street than a yard. Alf followed Abberline around the curve of the lane for a short distance before it opened into the well-known yard.

Alf turned his head this way and that, taking in the two and three storey buildings, all of them had something to do with the detective division and all were part of the legendary Scotland Yard.

'That's the criminal investigation department, the C.I.D,' said Abberline, following Alf's line of sight. 'I suppose you could say that's the heart of Scotland Yard, though it shares its space with the public carriage office for some reason.'

They heard the clock on the building opposite strike a quarter to two.

Abberline noted the time. 'Right,' he said. He paused in a doorway of the C.I.D. building. 'Now listen, when we get in there, keep your mouth shut. No matter what you hear, don't offer an opinion, keep it shut. Understand?'

'Yes, sir.' Alf nodded, wondering why Abberline had gone on at so much length about it.

Inside the C.I.D. building, Abberline and Alf were shown into an enormous oak panelled room that was mostly taken up by a large conference table so highly polished that it was like a mirror.

'All the top brass will be at this meeting, Alf.' Abberline murmured 'Just give them a nod as they come in. I'll introduce you when the moment is right. If anything needs an explanation, I will invite you to address the meeting and give you the nod, all right?'

'Yes, sir,' said Alf. He stood to one side as Abberline had instructed.

'Once they're all seated,' said Abberline as a procession of V.I.Ps began to file into the room, 'you take that chair beside the window.'

Two identical windows overlooked the Whitehall side of Great Scotland Yard and on the longer wall, three more looked south and west in the direction of the Thames. Alf could see the familiar covered archway that formed the entrance to the yard and beyond it, all the buildings of Whitehall. No matter where he looked he saw the buildings that housed the seat of government and the power behind the British Empire.

In the surrounding streets, were the grand homes of the men who ran the government and the empire, making vast sums of money for themselves in the process.

Yet, less than three miles to the east, people lived in unspeakable poverty and a madman had been able to move amongst them and commit his vile deeds. He could not imagine such a thing happening on these fine streets. It was the overcrowding and shocking deprivation that had lain Whitechapel out like a playground for a lunatic.

As he watched the powerful men who were drifting into the room, Alf knew it wasn't right. The British Empire whilst making an elite few obscenely, dazzlingly wealthy but had made wage slaves of the nation. They owned property in the east end that was disgracefully neglected and they took unreasonable rents from their tenants. The ordinary people scrambled for crumbs from these rich men's tables and there never seemed to be enough crumbs left to go around. It was an outrage and he wondered if these men actually cared about the murdered women or if it was all about protecting their own reputations and comfortable lives.

Inspector Reid came in, apparently standing in for Superintendent Arnold, head of H Division who had gone off sick the day after Mary Kelly was murdered. Reid saw Alf and gave him a nod. He felt encouraged and swallowed hard, suppressing the feeling that a swarm of bees was buzzing around in his stomach. All these men were, in one way or another, his bosses. It was like a roll call of power within the Metropolitan Police and the nation.

Then Alf's heart almost stopped. The last man to enter the room was Henry Matthews, the Home Secretary himself, accompanied by an apparent minion, whom Alf presumed was the permanent secretary to the Home Office. Alf studied the short, nondescript secretary, but was not fooled. Government ministers came and went but the civil servants remained. If any man in the room had a grasp of the complete picture, it would be the permanent secretary.

Once all the dignitaries were seated around the table, Alf moved to the chair by the window and sat down.

The new Commissioner of the Metropolitan Police, James Monro, opened the meeting.

'Gentlemen, with regard to the recent terrible events in Whitechapel. I am at liberty to inform you that we believe we have the perpetrator in custody.' Murmurs of approval drifted around the room.

'The individual is a Polish Jew named Aaron Kosminski. He is an immigrant though his family is well established in this country. His brother and one of his brothers-in-law have already been granted British citizenship.'

'How was the perpetrator apprehended?' said Sir Henry Smith, the acting Commissioner of the City Force.

Abberline cleared his throat. 'Due to the vigilance and keen observation skills of this man, Sergeant Alfred Cruikshank of H division.' He made a sweep of his arm towards Alf.

Alf's ears turned red as each of the assembled dignitaries looked at him.

'What piece of vigilance and keen observation?' asked Sir Henry Smith.

'Sergeant Cruikshank brought Kosminski in on suspicion of another murder and discovered that he was soaked in blood,' said Abberline. 'By the degree of drying and colour changes in the stains, he deduced that the blood must be from someone other than the person he was under suspicion of killing – an Irishman named Michael Kidney. The vast quantity indicated a blood bath of a murder ergo Miss Mary Jane Kelly.'

Some of the faces around the table looked blank.

'That's the name of the young woman who was killed on the 9th of November in Whitechapel.' Abberline reminded them.

Abberline passed around a very detailed drawing that showed where the blood, down to the last speck, was found on Kosminski's clothing, its colour and the degree of drying that had taken place.

Monro looked at Alf. 'Well done, Sergeant,' he nodded.

Home Secretary, Henry Matthews sat forward. 'Absolutely, very well done indeed, Sergeant.' Alf found that his throat was so dry, he could not have spoken even if asked to do so. Matthews continued. 'It seems there are two issues to settle. Firstly the perpetrator is a Jew, if that gets out there will be rioting in the streets. Secondly, this Jew has murdered an Irishman. The Irish community will not take that calmly and there will be reprisals.'

'I'm afraid there is another issue, sir,' said Abberline. 'Kosminski is insane, he is incapable of standing trial.'

'God above. So in the eyes of the public, not only is The Ripper part of an immigrant community that is the scapegoat for all problems, he is not going to be held accountable for his crimes and will avoid the noose - denying the people the satisfaction of seeing the murderer hang.

'It appears so, sir,' said Monro.

Matthews laced his fingers together and placed his hands on the table. 'You are certain that this man is The Ripper?' he looked from Reid to Monro then back at Abberline.

'The evidence is circumstantial, sir, but we cannot envisage how else he would have got so much blood on him in the way described.' said Abberline.

'You have ruled out other possibilities?'

'Yes, as far as it is possible to do so.'

Matthews sat back in his chair. 'Run the evidence by me, Inspector.'

Abberline began by giving an account of Polly's involvement.

'And that explains the gaps between the timing of the murders?'

'It seems so, sir.'

'What about the family?'

'As the perpetrator is insane, he is looked after by family members - two sisters and a brother,' said Abberline. 'The family concealed the fact that Kosminski was living at 76 Goulston Street. Number 76 is close to the place where the piece of Catherine Eddowes' apron was found and that unfortunate piece of graffito was written.' He looked at Monro across the table. 'The graffito your predecessor ordered to be erased despite overwhelming protests from er... other parties.'

'Close you say?' said Matthews.

'Yes, sir.' Abberline nodded. 'It is a dwelling on the other side of the road. As I am sure Commissioner Smith will confirm, despite the body of Catherine Eddowes being discovered moments after the murder took place, there was no trace of the killer. Goulston Street is a short walk from the Mitre Square murder site. The area has a high Jewish population. Kosminski would know his way around. He would know all the short cuts and which backyard gates and doors were unlocked. He would have been indoors within a couple of minutes, well before the search commenced in fact.'

'I am intrigued by the revelation that he lives so close to the place where the one single piece of tangible evidence was found. I agree, this seems significant.'

'Didn't he take away some of the woman's organs?' asked Matthews.

'Yes, sir. He took the womb and her left kidney,' said Abberline.

'These were not found with the apron,' said Matthews.

'No, sir, the supposition is that he carried them away in the piece of the victim's apron and threw them away before he went indoors, or a second party took them off him and threw them to the other side of the street,' said Abberline.

'And they did this without questioning the origins?' said Matthews.

'It is part of Kosminski's insane behaviour to refuse food - believing it to be poisoned. He will only eat food he has retrieved from the gutter or from waste bins. It's possible the family assumed it was just a bit of offal he'd got out of a butcher's bin. At that point, they would have no reason to suspect it was human flesh, so threw it away in a casual manner. A rat, a dog or a cat would make short work of it.'

'That odious man Lusk claimed to have had the kidney sent to him,' said Chief Inspector Williamson, head of C.I.D. 'The damned fellow unrelentingly gives us a public thrashing for not catching the killer.'

'We think it was either a hoax or Lusk lied, sir. Being that the piece of kidney was properly and conveniently preserved and not as disgusting as it should have been. It was too convenient if you catch my meaning,' said Abberline.

Adolphus Williamson straightened his spine. 'How I would love to confront him with that.'

'Are there any witnesses?' said Matthews. 'I mean, the amount of blood is compelling and the location of his home is a persuasive argument. However, an eyewitness would be best.'

'We have none who will step forward, sir. There were witnesses, but unfortunately, they have suddenly developed amnesia,' said Abberline.

'Reason?

'We think they recognised Kosminski, being that they live in the same area and likely attended the same synagogue on Duke Street. One of them, a Mr. Levy, has a butchers shop around the corner on Hutchison Street, literally a few hundred yards from the Goulston Street address. Being the nearest kosher butcher, it is likely that the

Kosminski's family were customers. Kosminski's brother, Isaac, is a respected member of the community. We can make the case for the witnesses knowing the perpetrator and his family, though it does not prove that it was Aaron Kosminski in Church Passage, nor does it conclusively prove that he's The Ripper.'

'The Chief Rabbi, Rabbi Adler has told all Jews to keep their heads down - that too might have shut them up,' said Matthews.

'You will never get one Jew to rat out another. It just isn't done,' said Melville McNaughton who had not spoken until then. 'There is a strong fraternal fellowship amongst the Jewish population. It would be regarded as unthinkable.'

'The family had no idea that this person was committing these crimes?'

Alf thought Matthews sounded incredulous.

'We are of mixed opinion on that, sir,' said Abberline. 'It's just possible that the family didn't know. They claim the perpetrator hurts himself and often has blood on him… When you weigh up the way he interfered with these women, his hands and arms must have been covered in blood. We suspect the family *did* know what he was doing. They had made applications for citizenship – that of Kosminski's brother-in-law was granted two days after the date of the double murder and we think they kept quiet in case it should interfere with their applications.'

'Having a brother who is murdering and brutalising local women could certainly have delayed it,' said Matthews.

'That was our thinking also, sir.'

'So gentlemen, the wretch cannot stand trial, he has murdered an Irish man, he is Jewish and has relatives who are likely to be culpable in concealing his crimes for their own gain.'

'That sums it up,' said Swanson.

Matthews pursed his lips then blew out a long sigh. 'Where is Kosminski now?'

'He's being held in the workhouse infirmary in Stepney, which is a secure facility.' said Abberline.

'He can't be kept there indefinitely.' said Matthews.

'He isn't complaining, sir.'

'What of the family?'

'They're scared, so they're co-operating.' said Abberline.

'I take it the employees at Stepney don't know the details?'

'No, sir. They know he is a Jewish man the police picked up off the street, that's all. As far as they know, he is there to be assessed, which of course, he is.'

'Hmm…' said Matthews. There was a long silence. He looked up. 'I think we all agree the most important thing is that the murders stop. Then, the newsmen will go away and Whitechapel will return to normal.'

Nobody moved.

'Gentlemen… this means the truth can never come out,' said Matthews.

'Home Secretary, we're a laughing stock, are we to be denied the satisfaction of telling the public we have him?' said Williamson.

'I'm afraid so, Adolphus.' Matthews turned and fixed him with a determined stare. 'This goes beyond individual pride and reputation of the Metropolitan Police.'

'It's not a question of pride, Minister, it's about the confidence of the public in the police service,' said Swanson.

'What is the alternative?' said Matthews. 'Kosminski can't stand trial. Can you imagine what a field day the papers would have with that fact alone? Then if the public finds out that The Ripper is Jewish, no Jewish person will be safe. If it gets out that the family not only let him out on the streets but might have concealed his crimes there will be riots throughout the east end, possibly throughout the country. We don't have the manpower nor the money to deal with wide-scale public disorder and we don't want that sort of publicity, it would be handing the election to George Lusk and his ilk. It's a bad business. As if all that weren't enough, Kosminski killed an Irishman. That in itself has implications for trouble between the two communities. It won't matter to them even if we tell them that it was to save a young woman's life. It could also inflame the Irish troubles further if Kosminski is perceived to have gotten away with it.'

'How can we allow the rest of the world to perceive the capital of the British Empire as unable to deal with crime in its midst,' said Williamson.

'That is precisely what will happen if we allow word of this to get out, the capital will become a battle ground.' said Matthews. 'No gentlemen, we have no choice. I'm afraid you must set aside your pride. Once the murders stop, the public will move onto another issue that excites their interest.'

'That's all very well, Minister, but what are we supposed to do with him? As you said, the workhouse system is voluntary and he cannot be sent to prison,' said Williamson.

'I take it the medics will establish that he is insane? It's not just an act?'

'Yes, and at the most, it will take five days. What happens after that?' said Williamson.

'He must be watched,' said Matthews. 'He must be kept under surveillance day and night. This man has committed abominable crimes and we can't risk another murder.'

'I am inclined to hold the family responsible,' said Williamson.

'Yes, it would give me satisfaction to rescind the recent citizenship award and have them in court to explain themselves, unfortunately, we can't,' said Matthews. 'It would attract attention to Kosminski as well as the relatives. It would also put them in danger. We can, however, hold the threat of it over them to keep them quiet.'

'So that's it?' said Inspector Reid. 'We just forget about it?'

'No. We watch him and keep him under surveillance. That responsibility will rest with H division, of course,' said Matthews.

Abberline stood up. 'What about the man who brought him in? Sergeant Cruikshank? He solved the crime.'

'Normally, a commendation would be in order,' said Williamson. 'Under the circumstances, the details of his heroism cannot be disclosed.'

'Sir? I think Sergeant Cruikshank's talents are being wasted as a uniformed copper. I think he should be here at Scotland Yard, training up as a detective.'

'I have no objection,' Matthews shrugged. He looked at Williamson.

Williamson shrugged his shoulders. 'Nor me, if it's what the Sergeant wants - Donald?' He looked at Swanson. Alf held his breath.

'If Inspector Abberline is impressed by his skills, I am satisfied. He was certainly an asset to the case. I personally have witnessed Sergeant Cruikshank's attention to detail. These are qualities we look for in a detective.'

'Sergeant? What say you?' said the Home Secretary speaking directly to Alf.

Alf sprang to his feet. 'I... I should like that fine, sir. Thank you, sir.'

'Very well, I will leave the matter in your hands, gentlemen.' Matthews stood up. 'Good day.' He left the room, followed by the permanent secretary, whom Alf noticed, had not made any notes.

The rest of the assembly stood up and began to file out of the room. Inspector Edmund Reid hung back until all the others had left. He smiled as Abberline slapped Alf on the back. 'Ha, ha, told you,' he grinned.

'Congratulations, Alf,' said Reid. 'This has been an ambition of yours for a while.'

'Thank you, sir. It has.'

'You will be a miss at Leman Street,' he said, 'but er… just one thing…'

'Sir?'

'Marry the girl, will you? As soon as possible?'

Alf's ears turned red. 'Absolutely, sir. It's all in hand…'

# CHAPTER THIRTY FIVE

Big Ben began to chime twelve o'clock as Polly strolled across
Westminster Bridge wearing her new fashionable outfit in a vivid
shade of blue and carrying a matching parasol. The great bell finished
its last loud *Bong* just as she passed by Palace Green.
Alf had suggested she take a cab, but it was such a beautiful day, she
decided to walk to Scotland Yard from their house in Little Paris
Street, Lambeth.

The sound of Big Ben was very familiar. She heard its
distinctive mellow chimes every day. If it weren't for St. Thomas's
Hospital and the mansions on Lambeth Palace Road, she would be
able to see the clock tower and the Houses of Parliament from her
bedroom window.

Polly loved the home she had made with Alf. He had bought it
when he was promoted to detective inspector three years ago. It was
one of the neat, three storey houses on a well to do street on the south
side of Westminster Bridge. It was a lovely part of London, a world
away from Whitechapel even though, in actual distance, it was only
three or four miles.

At the end of the bridge, Polly turned right onto the
Embankment and headed towards New Scotland Yard - the brand
new, red bricked castle-like headquarters of the Metropolitan Police.
They had moved into their new building next to the river almost four
years ago.

Today, she was meeting Alf for lunch. Normally he was far too
busy - today was different. He insisted on making time today because
it was June 30th, 1894, and the new bridge by the Tower of London,
now named Tower Bridge, was to be opened by the Prince of Wales
and his wife Princess Alexandra.

Polly preferred not to think about Mickey Kidney. Today, no
matter how hard she tried, she was unable to erase him from her mind.
She kept seeing the moment when his lifeless body slipped from the
scaffolding, hearing the noise it made when it hit the wet concrete and
the sight of it being silently sucked under at the bridge site that
smoggy night almost six years ago. It made her shudder to think that
he was still somewhere in the foundations of the north pier. He would
never be freed from his concrete tomb as long as the bridge stood.

Now people and traffic would be passing over his grave without any clue that he was there.

Polly felt no pity for Mickey. It preyed on her mind, that she would be the one entombed there had it not been for Aaron Kosminski. It was one of the greatest ironies that the man accused of being Jack the Ripper had saved her life and yet it would always remain a story she could never tell. As far as history was concerned, Jack had simply vanished.

Mickey Kidney had not been missed. The whole manner and time of his death had been hushed up. A false trail had been laid which led anyone to believe that Mickey had died in the London Hospital a few months later. Only a handful of people knew the true story.

Polly wondered how she would feel when she walked across Tower Bridge for the first time. She had not been near it since that night, the tenth of November 1888. She never ventured into the dismal streets north of Whitechapel Road even though she and Alf had continued to live at the house in Scarborough Street after their marriage in January 1889.

Alf met her by the entrance to the C.I.D. building. He looked smart in his black morning suit, starched white shirt, black waistcoat and silver-grey cravat with a gold pin.
Polly looked at him with pride. He cut an impressive figure, just as a Scotland Yard detective inspector should. Alfie Cruikshank was born to be a detective, Polly thought, smiling as she watched him walk towards her.

'There you are, my dearest. You look beautiful as always.' He took both of her gloved hands in his and gave her a kiss on the cheek that lingered as long as propriety permitted. 'I thought we could go down to the Embankment Gardens,' he said. 'There's usually a chap there selling lemonade and strawberries.'

'That sounds just the ticket,' Polly smiled.

Alf took her hand and placed it in the crook of his arm and they walked along the wide street towards Victoria Embankment Gardens. 'Fred Abberline hoped you were bringing the twins along. He was most put out that he wouldn't be seeing his godchildren,' said Alf as they walked under the arch of Hungerford Bridge which supported the railway tracks of Charing Cross Station and carried half a dozen lines south of the river.

'They're better off with your mother. It's so hot today, they would get tired and uncomfortable in this heat rather too quickly. But be sure to remind him that he and Emma are welcome in our home anytime they want to see them,' Polly smiled, 'and I think Freddie is counting on him for a game of cricket.'

'You can't start them too young according to Fred.' Alf smiled. 'You know, my love, I think Freddie and my little Alice Elizabeth regard him as a grandpa.'

'I hope so, grandparents are a bit thin on the ground for our twins aren't they?'

'I know that still niggles, my dear.' Alf placed his hand on hers sympathetically. 'Anytime you feel you would like to make contact with your family, I would-'

'No.' Polly shook her head, 'Fred and Emma didn't have any children of their own, so this is a convenient arrangement all round, isn't it?'

The arrival of twins three years ago had been a shock. Fortunately, expert midwife Temperance Cruikshank had been on hand. Freddie had been breech as was often the case with twins. Temperance was not fazed in the slightest and thanks to her skill, mother and babies came through the ordeal without a hitch.

It had taken a year to ween Temperance off the laudanum. Once she was free of its seductive, deadly clutches, she gained a new lease on life, just as Polly hoped. Once her grandchildren arrived she had become a doting granny and spent as much time as she could with them. Temperance sold the house in Scarborough Street and used the money to help Alf and Polly buy the three storey house in Little Paris Street. She not only had her own bedroom on the ground floor, but also her own drawing room in which to entertain, though she preferred to be with the children.

Polly and Alf entered the gardens next to the booking office for Charing Cross Station. Alf bought a large punnet of strawberries and they sat on a bench to eat the deliciously sweet, glossy fruit. The gardens were in full bloom and a riot of colour. A gentle breeze came off the river, providing just enough of a cooling effect.

After a while and many strawberries, Alf paused and dabbed his mouth with a handkerchief.

'Have you decided if you want to go along to the opening of the bridge?' he asked. 'It will be a very grand and historic occasion.'

Polly drew in a long breath and then exhaled slowly as she thought about her answer.

'No… I've been thinking about Mickey Kidney down there, under that tower, and I wouldn't feel right, Alfie. Oh I'm not sorry for him,' she added quickly. 'He was going to put me in there and that's what really makes me shiver. He would have put me in alive, to drown in all that concrete, if it hadn't been for Aaron.'

Alf shuddered at the thought. 'You know, Polly, that's the bit of the whole debacle I still can't fathom.' He lowered his voice 'All the terrible things he did to those women and yet he attacked a man twice to save you.'

'I know. I been thinking about Aaron too and I can't fathom it either. Even when he killed Mickey and strung him up in that horrible way, he meant it as a warning for others not to hurt me - the way his sisters said the Cossacks used to do, though what he did to the others, and why, still beggars explanation. All I know is, I wouldn't be here if it weren't for him. I'd be under the north tower of Tower Bridge.'

'It leaves my head in a spin, Polly. I saw first-hand what he did to those women and it was… well, it was sickening and yet I'm forever beholden to him because he saved your life.' Alf shook his head. 'It perplexes me something chronic. I come out in a cold sweat sometimes when I look at you and our beautiful babies, wondering if he could have turned on you at any moment and made you his next victim.'

'It's a curious thing, Alfie. I know who they say he is and everything, and although I know all the vile things they say he did, I never felt in the slightest danger when I was with him. I never felt uneasy.'

'He really took to you, didn't he? That's what's so curious.'

'I beg your pardon? What's curious about that?' Polly demanded in mock indignation. 'You did.'

'I did.' Alf grinned. 'I took to you exceedingly.' His warm brown eyes took on the seductive glow that she loved to see, then he wiggled his eyebrows which always made her laugh.

'You certainly did,' said Polly. 'Over five years and a set of twins later, my head hasn't stopped spinning.'

Alf gave a deep throaty chuckle. 'And it's my intention that it never will,' he said, giving her a kiss on the cheek.

'Alfie, hush, someone might hear you,' said Polly under her breath. 'Even though it pleases me very much to hear it,' she smiled.

Then her expression became serious. 'I wouldn't have you, nor Freddie and Alice if it wasn't for him… I owe him so much, yet I couldn't do anything to help him. It's so sad. He's so tormented.'

'No one can help him, my sweet girl. At least you read to him and helped to settle his demons. We all saw the soothing effect you had on him. I think it was his only relief.'

'I was so sorry when he had to go into the asylum. They're awful places.'

'The poor wretch is beyond help, Polly. He's insane. He couldn't have done the things he did to those women or to Mickey Kidney for that matter if it were otherwise.'

'I suppose you're right.'

'How about a glass of lemonade before we head back?' said Alf.

***

Autumn leaves scattered across the path as Polly passed through the wrought iron gates of Leavesden Asylum and walked up the long straight drive towards the enormous brick building. A central gable gave it a church-like appearance and added a small amount of dignity to a building that was little more than a storehouse for the insane.

Within its walls were endless echoing corridors, and cells that were austere and sparsely furnished. Polly thought it looked more like a prison than a hospital. Aaron had been transferred there five months earlier.

'How is he today, Mr. Cotton?' she asked the brawny, broad-shouldered attendant with bulging arm muscles who was there every time she visited Aaron.

Over the months, Polly and this man had got to be on speaking terms. She had received the impression it was his job to prevent trouble. He looked as if he could sort out a trouble maker with one hand while drinking tea from a china cup with the other. She was sure that crazy or not, none of the inmates messed with Mr. Cotton.

'He's in a tolerable state today, ma'am' he said. 'He never gives us any trouble 'cept that he won't wash nor eat. Sometimes he drinks, but will only do so directly from the tap.'

'He has been that way as long as I have known him. He thinks everything is poisoned, no matter what you tell him to the contrary,' Polly replied.

Mr. Cotton looked at her, a curious expression on his face.

'You seem to know him well, ma'am,' he said as he accompanied Polly down a featureless corridor in the direction of Aaron's room. 'Excuse me asking, ma'am, are you family? I wondered because there ain't no particular resemblance.'

'No, I'm not related.' Polly told him. 'I visit him because he saved my life, Mr. Cotton - on two occasions. I come because I won't ever forget that I owe him a debt I can't repay.'

'Twice?'

'Yes,' Polly nodded. 'He saved me from a man whom I knew murdered his wife, who was my friend.' Polly knew the workers in the asylum had no idea they had in their charge, the man accused of being Jack the Ripper.

'He don't look capable of doing anything in that regard. Much of the time he don't seem to understand what's going on all around him,' said Mr. Cotton.

'He's gone downhill in the last few years, I'm sorry to say. He has always liked me to read to him, so I come here and that's what I do.'

'If you could persuade him to have a wash you would be doing all of us a favour, ma'am.'

'I'll do my best. Has anyone else been to see him?'

'No, ma'am, his family sends him things, like new nightshirts and books in his own language to entertain him. He takes no notice of any of it, I'm afraid. I must say we have noticed that he seems a bit better after you've been here and read to him awhile.'

The attendant took a bunch of keys from his pocket, selected one and unlocked the door of a cell. 'You just call if you need anything, ma'am.'

Inside the cell, a skinny, dishevelled figure was sitting on the bed, knees drawn up, his head resting against the wall, his face expressionless as he gazed into empty space.

'Aaron? It's me, Polly. How are you?' She sat on a chair that was next to a small table on the opposite side of the room.

Aaron did not reply and Polly wasn't sure that he even knew she was there. She saw what the attendant meant, he was filthy, his hair was long and greasy, he had a beard that had sprouted in all directions and he emitted a powerful odour. She sat with him in silence for a while.

'How about I get them to run you a bath? While you have a nice soak, I'll read to you.'

Aaron did not move. His fingernails and the backs of his hands were covered in blood where he had plucked and picked at the skin. His bare feel had ulcers that either bled or oozed a straw coloured fluid. It upset her to see how much he had deteriorated since her last visit a month ago. She watched him, seeing in his eyes, the torment inflicted on him by his own mind. It was pitiful.

'Aaron?' she said gently.

He looked up at her briefly, then turned his attention to the back of his hand. He began plucking at the sores.

Polly sighed. She stood up and moved her chair closer to him. She took a leather-bound book from her basket, opened it, settled herself and began to read.

'David Copperfield by Charles Dickens. Chapter one...'

**Thank you for reading my book.**
**You can find to me on Twitter and  Instagram**

Made in United States
North Haven, CT
15 February 2022

16138759R00207